CAPPADONNA II

JAHQUEL J.

Published by Jahquel J.
www.Jahquel.com

OX

Jahquel J's Catalog ✦

Brookwood Series
Interconnected Standalone Series
- From Come Over To Come Home
- He's My Next Mistake
- From Replied To Wifey
- Welcome To Brookwood

Lennox Hills Series
Interconnected Standalone Series
- I'm Fine...Thanks
- Yeah... Thanks
- Never Better... Thanks

Mathers Family
- Confessions Of A Hustla's Housekeeper 1-4
- Confessions Of A Hustla's Daughter 1-2 *

Davis Family
- Staten Island Love Letter 1-5
- Staten Island Love Affair 1-4*
- A Brownsville, Harlem & Staten Island Holiday Affair *

Vanducci-Cromwell Family
- A Staten Island Love Story 1-3

Harlem King Saga
- In Love With The King Of Harlem 1-5
- In Love With An East Coast Maniac 1-3 *
- Rose In Harlem: Harlem King's Princess *

BAE Series
- BAE: Before Anyone Else 1-3
- He's Still BAE 1-3*
- BAE: Holiday *

Homies, Lovers & Friends
- Homies, Lovers & Friends 1-5
- Homies, Lovers & Wives *

Series:
- Crack Money With Cocaine Dreams 1-2
- Never Wanted To Be Wifey 1-2
- To All The Thugs I Loved That Didn't Love Me Back 1-4
- All The Dope Boys Gon Feel Her 1-2
- Good Girls Love Hustlas 1-3
- I Got Nothing But Love For My Hitta 1-2
- She Ain't Never Met A N*gga Like Me 1-3
- Married To A Brownsville Bully 1-3
- Thugs Need Love 1-3
- What A Wicked Way To Treat The Woman You Love 1-2
- Finessing The Plug 1-2

Standalones:
- My Lover, My Dopeboy
- I Can't Be The One You Love
- I'm Riding With You Forever
- Forever, I'm Ready
- Emotionless
- Blaquehatten
- Ho, Ho, Housewife
- When Can I See You Again?
- What You Know About Love?
- Hearts Won't Break
- Pretty Little Fears
- Save Myself
- Two Occasions
- I Didn't Mean To Fall In Love

* Spinoff

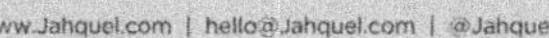

www.Jahquel.com | hello@Jahquel.com | @Jahquel_

SYNOPSIS:

I came home and ended up with two enemies because of the women I choose to love. Kendra was the one I thought I loved, but the feeling I felt when I looked into Alaia's eyes told me that I had never experienced love with Kendra. When I looked into my Joy's eyes, I wanted to give her the stars, moons, and the sky wrapped up with a big fat ass bow. So, for her, I would go to war to make sure Tweety had no parts in touching her ever again.

My son's life was touched because of a man that didn't understand that I'm at the top. Now, I'm about to touch every person he has ever loved until my hands are wrapped around his throat. For my seeds, I will shed blood.

Love wasn't something that I ever felt before. I knew how to love because I loved my Yaya more than life. I knew that I could love, because the baby I had grown within me and now held, I loved her more than I loved myself. As I watched this man sleep peacefully beside me, one arm around me, keeping me close, I knew that I loved him. I knew that I could see forever with him, and I knew that he would kill any and everything moving when it came to protecting me.

HEY THERE,

I so appreciate the support on this series. Getting these books out as quickly as I have, has done some damage to my hands, however, the support you guys have shown makes it all worth it. Love ya'll down!

The Delgato family is just warming up with many branches that connect to the tree.

As always, I write for your entertainment, however, take care of you. This book has sensitive subjects.

Xo, Jah

Here's to every woman finding their joy.

1

CAPPADONNA

I LOOKED at the baby that I had just held a few days prior and then at Jasmine. From the way she was breathing, I could tell that she was close to having a panic attack with the way I was glaring at her. The voice in my head told me to slap the shit out of her and the baby, but Alaia's grip onto my arm told me otherwise.

"Get the fuck outta here... if you think you gonna lie and I won't murk this bitch, Jasmine, you don't know me." Alaia's grip on me became tighter.

I could tell from her little fingers gripping me with all her might that she was praying I wouldn't reach over Jasmine and bust that little bitch in the fucking head.

"Cappadonna, please," Alaia pleaded with me, and I looked down at her.

I could see the fear in her eyes, and I hated that I had been the one to put it there. She was used to seeing me be cool and calm. I didn't bring this energy around her. As much as that voice was begging me to fuck something up, I allowed her to pull me away.

We walked over near the elevators, and she held onto me tightly. "I'm gonna call my brother to come pick you up so you can get home to Promise."

When Jasmine hit me up, I let it roll to voicemail because me and Alaia were about to get into it. We were touring the house in Capone's neighborhood and her ass was being quiet, not wanting to give too much input on shit.

She told me she loved to cook, so I wanted the kitchen to be everything she wanted it to be. If I needed to knock shit out and have a brand new one rebuilt, that was what would happen. Instead, Alaia kept quiet when the realtor was asking her questions on what she wanted.

"If you think I'm leaving you up here alone you got another thing coming. I'm not naive enough to know that I am the only reason you didn't snap that woman's neck." She reached up and grabbed my face. "I need you to calm down so we can find out what's going on with your son."

I looked down into her eyes and then over at Kendra, who was still holding her neck while staring at Aimee like she was an alien. "Yeah... ight."

Alaia took a deep breath. "You can't hurt her or that baby... especially since it's your grandson."

I looked back at her like she had been doing something other than the pain medicine they had given her for her procedures. "The fuck are you talking about, Joy?"

Alaia looked up at me in disbelief. "You go that deaf when you're that mad?"

"Joy, I don't even fucking see straight... what you talking about?" I held onto her waist, as she looked up at me.

If Kendra knew what I knew, she should have been over here kissing Alaia's fucking feet. The only reason I didn't stuff that bitch in the vending machine was because my baby was here. I didn't want to do no shit that could traumatize her, and

I didn't want her to see that side of me. When shit got dark for me, it became pitch black, and I didn't see shit until I saw blood.

"That woman just told you that the baby she's holding is your grandson." Alaia pointed to Jasmine.

I looked over at Jasmine and she quickly came over. Guess she wanted to avoid me crossing that waiting area and busting Kendra's ass. From the way Kendra was standing in shock, I was assuming she didn't know that this baby was our fucking grandchild.

"Cappadonna, you're making security very nervous," Jasmine spoke easy, like she didn't want to further upset me.

"Fuck that bitch," I looked in his direction and his ass quickly looked away, scared I was about to start on his ass next. "Let me see twelve in this bitch and that's yo ass," I pointed to him.

Jasmine looked over at Alaia, and then she looked at me not knowing what to do or say next. I felt for her because she had been cleaning her cousin's shit up. None of this was Jasmine's bullshit, and here she was trying to help her cousin from sitting next to the skittles in the vending machine.

"Aimee is Capella's girlfriend. They were only dating for a few months before she got pregnant," Jasmine explained.

"Why the fuck you know everybody business?"

"Me and my cousin are close, and he tells me almost everything. I knew about her being pregnant, but he wasn't sure the baby was even his because she was messing with some other dude at the same time."

"How the fuck we know Big Head is even his son then?"

Jasmine looked shocked that I referred to the baby as Big Head. After she choked down her surprise, she patted him on the back. "They did a DNA test, Cappadonna. This little boy is you and Kendra's grandson."

"Damn... it's a shame he never going to know his grandmoms." I shrugged, as I looked across the room at Kendra.

Loose pussy had sat on the wrong dick this time and her ass had to go right along with him. "Do yo... you honestly think that she knew anything about this? Kendra is many things, but do you really think she would willingly be with the man who shot her son?"

"Jasmine, get the fuck out my face. This the same bitch that was giving him my money and fucking him while my ass was spreading my cheeks and coughing after every fucking visit. Do you think I put anything past this bitch?"

This wasn't Jasmine's beef, so she needed to allow her cousin to deal with whatever came to her. Kendra could have had the best life, and I would have come home to worship the ground she walked on. If you showed me that you fucked with me, then I was going to show you the same. I understood my sentence was lengthy, but when I gave that bitch an out, she should have taken it. Instead, she wanted to sit there and pretend like she was loyal and could hold it down for me.

I stared at the baby as Jasmine stood there, unsure of what to say. "Do you want to hold him?"

I screwed my face up. "Hell no I don't want to fucking hold him."

"Alright... come on. We need to sit and wait for someone to come talk to us." Alaia pulled me over toward seating that was nowhere near Kendra.

She stood for a minute after I sat until she was sure that I wasn't going to jump back up and snatch Kendra's ass bald. When she sat down, she looped her hands into mine and slowly rubbed the back of my hand. Alaia didn't understand what her touch did to me. It made me calm when I was feeling the complete opposite.

"If that little boy is your grandson, you are going to have to put your feelings aside. He's part of your son, Cappadonna."

I stared at the security who kept stealing peeks at me. "Baby, I ain't worried about that baby right now. My fucking son is in there fighting for his life."

"I know." She kissed the back of my hand and looked up at me.

I watched her eyes, as she looked past me. Soon as I turned my head, Kendra was staring at us. "You got on me for fucking around and you were doing the exact same thing. Fuck that, Cappadonna!" Kendra screamed.

Everybody in the waiting area was tired of our bullshit. They kept looking from her back over to me, as I sat in the chair. Alaia was damn near squeezing my hands as Kendra walked over here.

"Kendra, not the time or place," Jasmine pulled her back over toward them.

I smirked while preparing myself to get up. "Yeah, that bitch asking for it."

Alaia tossed herself across my lap, and held me down. If I wanted to, I could have pushed her onto the floor. This was my baby, so as much as I wanted to shove her onto the floor and grab Kendra by the fucking ears, I remained seated while she held my face, coaching me to look into her eyes.

"Cappadonna, you have to stop or else they are going to kick us out of here. I don't want them to have any excuse to kick us out.... Hey, look at me."

My eyes focused onto hers. Alaia's chocolate brown eyes were my favorite thing to get lost in. "I'ma stuff that fucking security guard in the trash can... I'm not concerned."

"Well, I am. Can you make me a promise?"

I looked at her like she was tripping for asking me to promise her anything right now. My mind had a million things going through it, and I couldn't be sure that I could keep any promises made to her. I never broke my promises to my baby, so I looked away and she turned my face back toward hers.

"I can't make you any promises right now," I said through gritted teeth because I could still hear Kendra carrying on.

She gave me a soft peck on the lips. I was the one that always initiated kisses between us, so that small action did something to me. Alaia didn't even know how much I was in love with her beautiful ass.

"Did you like your breakfast this morning?" I knew she was trying to do anything to keep my mind off the fact that Kendra had grown some balls and had a bunch of mouth.

"Give me another kiss and I'll let you know." She kissed me again, and I smirked as I held her close.

Part of me held her onto my lap because I knew how much I wanted to get up. I knew how much every part of my body was screaming for me to go over there and give Kendra what she was asking for. She wanted a show, and I wanted to give that shit to her.

"Alright... now tell me."

"It was good, Joy... I think you might make eggs better than my mama."

"Don't you dare tell her that, either... Mrs. Jean likes me, and I would like to keep it that way." She smiled, as she rubbed my beard.

We both looked over just as a doctor was coming through the double doors. Everyone, even the people that weren't with us, had stood up hoping to get some news about their loved ones. The doctor stood there like he was trying to see who he needed to tell news to.

"Francie Ross's family?"

Jasmine shoved that baby back into Aimee's arms and rushed over toward the doctor. I remained seated because that wasn't who I was here for. I didn't wish any harm on Kendra's aunt, but I needed to know how my boy was doing.

I couldn't handle losing him because of some little street rat like Ace. The way I wanted to squeeze the life out that man was something serious. The doctor walked over toward the elevators as he spoke to Jasmine and Kendra. Jasmine let out an ear-piercing sob that caused everyone to look their way. She fell onto the floor as she screamed out to the doctor.

Taking a breath, I put my baby onto her feet and walked over to where Jasmine was on the floor clawing at the doctor's legs while accusing him of lying. Kendra stood there stuck, not saying a word. When she saw me walking over toward her, she sobbed with her arms opened as she tried to hug me. I mushed her ass and went to Jasmine, the person who had actually lost their mother.

"Ma'am, I'm sorry. We tried to bring her back four times, and the last time we couldn't," I overheard the doctor as I picked Jasmine up.

She was kicking and screaming as I picked her up and cradled her like a baby. I had a soft spot when it came to Jasmine. It was because of her that I had even gotten the chance to have a relationship with my son.

"Breathe, Jas... come on, you turning red," I whispered as I carried her into the chapel that was next to the waiting area.

It was the only quiet place that I could calm her down in. I knew it wasn't my place to calm her down, and I shouldn't have even cared. However, I couldn't fathom ever losing my mother. In my mind, my mother was going to live forever.

I couldn't even think of the day when I would have to put her in the grave. For some reason, going into the ground before her brought me more comfort. I sat in the front pew with her in my arms as she continued to sob uncomfortably.

Jasmine was like a little sister to me, and I respected her.

Despite me losing my cool with her earlier, I had a lot of respect for her. She was always the reasonable one, and always wanted better for herself.

I didn't know her mother because I barely met Kendra's family. When we met she told me that she and her family wasn't all that close. A part of me wished that I had met her because then I could have thanked her for raising my son and giving him the love that I couldn't give him at the time.

"She...she... g...gone," she choked out, coughing in the process.

I didn't need to say anything because nothing I said would make this better. None of this would ever make it better.

The door to the chapel opened, and I turned to see Kincaid and Capone standing there. When he saw Jasmine, something in his eyes switched as he walked closer to us. He sat down next to me and grabbed Jasmine's hand.

"Jas, I'm sorry."

Usually, I would have punched this nigga into the cross in front of us for even touching her knowing he was with my sister. But I could tell that there was some history there and his touch wasn't disrespectful. He was comforting someone that he knew and mourning along with her.

I slid Jasmine onto the pew and stood up, allowing her to cry into Kincaid's chest. "I got her." He nodded, giving me that look that he wasn't on that type of time.

I walked over and dapped my twin up. "How you holding up?"

"Capo, I know I spoke all that shit about peace and just sitting my ass down... he came at my son. I don't have no cho—"

Capone looked me in the eyes. "Do what you need to do, and I got your follow up. If we on that type of timing, then I'm on it with you."

I held my hand out and pulled my brother into a hug. "I don't need a gun for what I'm about to do to that bitch."

When we came out the chapel, I saw Alaia talking to Kendra. "The only reason you're not back there being brought back to life is because I stopped him from choking your ass out. I've been quiet and remained respectful, but if you think you gonna little girl me you got another thing coming." She stared at Kendra, threatening her to say something else.

It was only after her eyes wandered that she saw me and Capone staring at her that she shoved past Kendra and came over to us. "Damn, Alaia... didn't know you had that in you," Capone chuckled.

She took a deep breath. I could tell Alaia was the type that didn't like confrontation and that was fine with me. I would handle all the confrontation when it came to her. "She came over there talking nonsense about how I ruined her relationship, and that I'm a hoe. I draw the line at her trying to yank my hijab."

"She did fucking what?" Before I could take off over to where Kendra was standing, Capone grabbed my arm.

"Chill yo crazy ass down... Alaia handled her." Capone put his arm around my shoulder and walked me in the opposite direction.

I held my hand out and Alaia came running over and put her hand into mine. Kendra had some fucking nerve to press Alaia like her ass ain't been out here fucking every Tom, Dick, and Harry. Then to touch her hijab had me ready to put her head through a fucking wall.

2

KENDRA

Cappadonna looked at me like he wanted to rip my head off and then take a bite out of me. Part of me felt like I should have left, I didn't belong here. I stuck out like a sore thumb. Jasmine was still in the chapel with Kincaid.

I couldn't face her because I felt guilty about everything that happened. My aunt was the only one that had been there for me after my grandmother died. She took Capella in without any problems and loved him like her own. Cappadonna was confused on how it was so easy for me to leave Capella for her to raise.

It was easy because I knew how much my aunt loved my son. When I came over, I could see the love in her eyes that she had for him. Capella was everything for her and had given her a second chance to be a mother.

Cappadonna was sitting across the room from me and Aimee, and I watched as he continued to kiss the back of Alaia's hand.

Yes, *that* Alaia.

The one he rushed out the door for. The same one that he

avoided talking about, and now he was kissing her hand and showing her love that he hadn't shown me since he been home. How was I the problem when he was out doing his own thing, too?

"Should I call my brother?" Aimee finally spoke as she stood to bounce the fussy baby up and down.

The fussy baby that was my grandson. I was taken back by everything else to even acknowledge the fact that Aimee and Capella even knew each other. When I asked her ass about the father, she brought up how he was locked up because he didn't listen to her. Last I checked, my son wasn't locked up.

"How did you and Capella even meet?"

Aimee smiled as she continued to pat the baby's back. "I was in Brooklyn with my friends. She lived on the block that he was on, and I went into the store to grab some candy because I had a nasty taste in my mouth. He spotted me and asked me to come talk to him and I waved him off."

Capella had always been a Casanova in his own right. I guess he got that from his father, because Cappadonna Delgato could charm the panties off any woman he smiled at. I remember my aunt used to call him a ladies' man because all the little girls used to wait for him to come out and play.

"When I was leaving to head back to campus, I was outside waiting for my Uber, and he came over and started talking to me. By the time my Uber arrived, he convinced me to let him drive me back to my dorm."

"And you just got in some strange man's car?"

Aimee smiled to herself. "It was something about his eyes. They were so kind, and I could tell he was a good person."

"I'm pretty sure the men that went to Dahmer's fucking apartment thought he was a good person." I don't know why I felt the need to lecture her ass, but I did.

"Anyway... I was dealing with somebody at the time. We

kept our relationship on the low and then I found out I was pregnant a couple months later."

"Did he know you had a damn boyfriend?"

Aimee paused and side eyed me as she continued to tell the story. "He knew about my boyfriend. It was the first thing that I told him. We were only hooking up, so he didn't care."

I had too much going on in my head that I couldn't keep it straight. "So, you not his girlfriend? Just some chick that he was messing around and got pregnant."

Her jaw tensed. "He asked me to be his girlfriend when our son was born... Capella has been with me during this entire pregnancy."

"Then why wasn't he at the baby shower?"

"I never told him about the baby shower because my mother assumed the baby's father was my boyfriend."

"Aimee, does your old boyfriend or whatever know that you were even pregnant?"

"I didn't tell him because I didn't want his help when it came to the baby. He wouldn't have stepped up the way Capella wants to be there."

"Is that damn baby my son's?"

"Yes. Rory is his son, and he has the paperwork to prove it." She eyed me down, like she knew something that I didn't know. "It's funny because he always spoke about his mother and how he hated her... never expected it to be you."

"Capella is dramatic. He doesn't hate me."

Aimee snorted. "If you were on fire that man wouldn't waste piss to put it on you."

"Yeah, well, we might as well both be on fire because your brother really fucked up." I sulked, knowing that I was now caught in between my husband and son.

A different doctor came out through the double doors, and I sucked in a bunch of air, nervous about what he was going to say. I couldn't take my son dying like my aunt had just did. Hell, I don't think it even registered that my aunt was gone.

"Capella Ros—"

"Delgato!" he barked. "Capella Delgato," he corrected the doctor, who looked up at him, nervous on what to say or do next.

Cappadonna was going to have to fight me if he thought I was going to sit over here and not know what was going on with my son. I walked over there slowly and stood to the side of him quietly. I didn't want to give this maniac any excuse to go off on me for being too close to him or something.

"He is in recovery right now. Surgery went really well. Your son was very lucky. One of the gun shots went into his chest and came out his underarm. It was meters from his heart, and we could have been having a different conversation. The other two bullets, we were able to remove."

Cappadonna didn't say anything, instead his brother stepped in. "Appreciate you, Doc. When can we see him?"

"They only allow two people in the recovery room. He will stay down there for a bit, and then he will be moved upstairs to CCU to finish his recovery. Your son was very lucky and he's still here with us." The doctor hesitantly reached up and squeezed Capp's shoulder.

Alaia came over and reached up and took my man's face in her hands. "What are you feeling right now, Capp?"

He bent down so that his forehead was resting on hers and I saw tears coming down his face. "I don't know what the fuck I would do if I would have lost him."

She kissed his lips. "You didn't lose him. Capella is still here with us and will continue to be. Stop focusing on what could have happened, and let's focus on what Allah did. He saw that your boy is still here with us."

As he nodded his head, she spoke into his ear, and he

nodded listening to whatever she was saying. As grateful as I was with my son being alive and recovering, I couldn't help but wonder where he met her.

It was clear that she was Muslim because she referred to Allah and her hair was wrapped. She wasn't wearing a scarf like she was in between hair appointments. It was specifically styled like this was what she usually wore on her head.

While I was dressed in a pair of ripped jean shorts, she wore a long-sleeved Skims dress. I knew a Skims dress when I saw one. Cappadonna was the one that probably bought the shit, too. On her feet, she wore a simple pair of sandals.

"Um, are you going back there?"

"Yes. He is... give us a minute. You can go ahead first," Alaia spoke to me while Capp kept his forehead against hers.

Me and Capp had been through some things together and he had never put his damn forehead to mine, or even needed me to talk him down like she was. Bitch was being hella extra right now for no reason.

I rolled my eyes and followed the doctor to the recovery room. "Do you know if your son is taking any medication for his sickle cell?"

My head snapped in the direction of the doctor, and then I stopped. "My son doesn't have sickle cell."

"When we prepped him for surgery, we noticed leg ulcers that are pretty similar to sickle cell leg ulcers. I believe he was in a middle of a pain crisis when he was shot. His legs were pretty swollen as well. I had blood drawn and it confirmed my suspicions. Thankfully we found out before we administered the anesthesia because that would have been another problem."

When Capella was a baby, I took him to one doctor appointment. My grandma used to take him to all his doctor appointments because I was so depressed about losing my man. Even when Francie took over, she never told me that he had sickle cell.

"He never told me," I whispered, feeling like shit because I didn't know my son had sickle cell.

The doctor raised his brow. "They test all newborns for many different diseases when they are born, including sickle cell." His tone had a hint of judgment in it, and I was trying not to take offense to it.

"I had a rough delivery with him. Hell, I don't even remember how much he fucking weighed," I snapped, and he stepped back.

"My apologies. I didn't mean to ofen—"

"Well, you fucking did. Can you take me to see *my* son."

He quickly put a pep in his fucking step and brought me to the recovery room where Capella was. He had oxygen attached to his nose and the machines were attached to him, loud as hell. I slowly walked into the room and around the bed, looking down at my son.

I birthed this boy.

This was my son, and he was laying up in a hospital bed after someone tried to take his life. I touched his hand, the first time I had touched him in years. There used to be a time when he would see me pull into my aunt's driveway and rush to the car to hug me.

He would be so excited to see and spend time with me that he couldn't contain his excitement. As he became older, the excitement had died inside of him, and I went from being 'mom' to being just Kendra.

Those hugs were far and between, and I never paid any attention to them. They never mattered; I chalked it up to him being a moody teenager. As I stood here with tears threatening to fall, I should have hugged him more. Even if he didn't want the hug, I should have forced them. I should have built a bond with my son, even if I knew I wasn't capable of raising him myself.

Everyone was so angry with me for knowing that I would have been a terrible mom. I knew that I couldn't raise Capella, and I chose to give him to someone that could raise him.

My eyes burned with tears the longer I looked at him in that hospital bed. I felt like I was about to pass out because this couldn't be real life. My son couldn't have been in this bed, and it surely couldn't have been my husband who did it.

The sound of the door opening forced me to look up and Capp entered the room. All the air was sucked out the room with him standing across from me. My heart ached seeing this man and knowing how much I loved him. It was a different feeling seeing him outside of those prison walls.

"I don't know why I expected to know my son has sickle cell when I didn't even know about him until last year," he muttered, as he walked to the opposite side of Capella.

He bent over and kissed his son on the forehead. "I didn't know he had sickle cell, either."

The way he looked at me made me feel lower than low. "How the fuck you don't know what disease your son has, Kendra?"

If I thought the doctor was being judgmental, Capp was being full blown judgmental with a side of disgust. The way he was staring at me like I was dog shit on the bottom of a brand new shoe made me want to disappear.

"A lot was going on, Capp... I fucked up, damn!" I screamed, with tears coming out quicker than I could stop them.

That crazy look in Capp's eyes flashed, and I realized that I was cornered in a room with his crazy ass, and Alaia, the Cappadonna whisperer, was nowhere to be found to keep him from tossing me around in here.

"Bitch, you dying, that nigga that you love so much dying

and I'm even killing that fucking fish in the living room at the condo I paid for," he whispered low enough for just me to hear.

Despite his low voice, it was the tone that sent shivers down my spine as I looked into his eyes. "I didn't know, Capp. I swear, I had no idea that Ace would do something like this... he didn't know Capella is my son."

"Yeah, well, now you can get in that fucking grave with his ass."

"We're grandparents... Capella needs both of us to be there for that baby." I tried to use the baby as an excuse.

I had no plans on being no damn grandmother. Hell, I didn't even want to be a mother, so if Capella and Aimee thought I would be that granny that would come pick the baby up, they had another thing coming.

Capp held his son's hand as he stared across the bed right into my eyes. "Kendra, I don't give a fuck... I will tell that fucking baby Mickey Mouse pulled his tool out and killed yo ass... you think I care?"

"Capp, I deserve to be a part of the baby's life, too... I swear I didn't know Ace would do this. I'm loyal to you, Cappadonna. I would have told you if I knew something like this would have happened."

He ignored me which was the worst thing that could happen when it came to this man. I would rather when he was spewing threats. The minute he got silent, that meant that the deal was signed, sealed, and would soon be delivered.

I cautiously bypassed him and left the room with tears streaming down my face. It was one thing having to live without Cappadonna, and another thing when he wanted you dead. There was no talking myself out of any of this because he wanted me to die like he wanted Ace to.

I didn't have any direction as to where I was going. My phone was in pieces in the waiting room, and my baby father wanted to murder me. Tears streamed down my face and my vision became blurred. I was running so fast down the hall that I crashed into something hard and fell on my ass.

Sniffling, I looked up and thought Cappadonna had already boomed my ass. I must have died and gone to heaven. Was this what God looked like? Tall, dark, and handsome with a light fade, thick beard and a tire mark tattoo on the side of his face.

"Um... I'm sorry," I quickly apologized.

He helped me off the floor and I caught a whiff of his cologne. The spicy gourmand tickled my nose while I tried to pretend I wasn't crying moments before crashing into this handsome stranger.

"You good, Mama... everything all good?" He eyed me down, and then looked down the hall.

"I'm alright. Sorry again for running into you." I quickly bypassed him and sped walked down the hallway. "Sorry again," I apologized and turned to head anywhere but this hallway.

When Capella was born, I had just turned nineteen and didn't know what to do. My mother had always been consumed with her own life, so me and my sister were practically raising ourselves. As much as I moved to Florida to get a rise out of Cappadonna, I also moved to familiarity.

My grandmother was home. She had always given me and my sister a sense of normalcy. I learned early on from my mother that the kind of men you went after were those with money. They were the kind of men that would take care of you.

She set an example with all the hustlers she would bring by the house. They were never the same man and none of them ever stayed around long enough that I learned their names.

They would lace her with jewels, money, and if she landed a big one, a brand new car. So, early on I learned if I wanted to have a good life that I needed to find a nigga that would finance it and have me set for life.

Life didn't turn out that way because I met Cappadonna Delgato, and he was broke. Even though he didn't have money, I could see the potential. Cappadonna had this large presence that made you – forced – you to respect him. With or without money, Cappadonna had remained the same. He walked around with his head held high when there was nothing but lint in his pockets.

My mother's voice was in the back of my head telling me that I should run. I needed to find me one of the other hustlers that he frequented around because Cappadonna couldn't take care of me the way that I needed to be taken care of.

Against better judgment, I fell for that boy. I fell harder than I wanted to, and was in love with him. It wasn't about the money when I was with Capp, I loved the security he provided. There was once a time when one of his homies tried to step to me. He drove a nice Benz, had the money, and the thought had come across my mind a few times.

Capp pulled up in his busted ass Nissan and shoved that nigga in his trunk. He didn't give a fuck that that man had more than him, he had the better energy. There used to be this look that Capp would give me, and I knew that he loved me. He would do whatever for me, and he would protect me.

Cappadonna was a protector.

A complex man.

Nonetheless, he was a good man with real feelings and emotions and I took him for granted. When he deserved to be held down and shown loyalty, I was too selfish and worried about myself. Too busy worried about the material things he could give me instead of everything he gave me mentally.

There were times when I was struggling mentally, and I would sit on the phone with him while he gave me words of encouragement. Imagine being the one with your freedom revoked, sitting on the phone telling someone to look at the bright side.

As crazy and scary as Capp was, he was also someone that was a good person. His crazy was for the people he cared for, and I used to be one of those people. I had stayed at Jasmine's house last night and came back up to the hospital to sit beside my son. He was still out of it from the surgery, and I regretted having to be the one to tell him about Francie.

Jasmine didn't move out the bed since she came in last night. When I left this morning, I peeked into her room, and she was lying across the bed with her same clothes on from yesterday. Kincaid had driven her home because she was too distraught to drive herself. He told me he would bring her car to her today. When I tried to talk to Jasmine last night, she looked past me. Like she couldn't see me or didn't know what the hell I was saying. It was like I was speaking a different language to her.

As much as I was hurt about my aunt, it probably didn't compare to the way Jasmine felt, or the way Capella would when he finally woke up and could understand what was going on. My heart ached because this was a loss he would never be able to come back from.

My head snapped up from my book when the door opened. Cappadonna came into the room. I could smell his cologne before his foot fully crossed the threshold of the room. He looked at me blankly before turning his attention to his son. He came around the bed, kissed Capella on the head and fixed his blanket.

"Ken, I'm starting to believe you really want to die."

I gulped.

It was risky coming here knowing that Cappadonna would be here. I wanted to run with the way he was looking at me. "Um, Capp. Can we talk?"

He looked at me like he smelled something foul. For a second, I considered that maybe I did since I hadn't taken a bath or changed clothes either. I hadn't gone back to Ace's house because I was scared.

"You gonna let me choke you until you can't breathe?" he asked, seriously, with his eyebrow raised.

"P...please. I need to talk to you."

He looked at his son and then back to me. "Go out first because I might slap you in the back of your big ass head."

I quickly abandoned my chair and went out into the hall. If I had any chance of survival, I needed to talk to Cappadonna and force him to see that I had nothing to do with my husband's actions.

3
ALAIA

I ROCKED in the rocker that Cappadonna had bought for the nursery. It was beautiful with soft hues of lavender and tiny little ballet dancer decor pieces everywhere. How Jean and Erin put this together in a short amount of time was beyond me. I appreciated them so much for going all out for my baby girl.

At times I struggled with feeling worthy of any of this. When I opened my eyes and looked around the massive bedroom that I slept in, and the arms that were wrapped around me, I felt like I was living someone else's life.

Promise finished her bottle, and I picked her up and put her over my shoulder to burp her. My baby meant the world to me, and I couldn't picture life without her. Whenever she looked up into my eyes with those kind eyes, I melted into a puddle.

After I finished burping her and changing her diaper, I carried her back downstairs to lay her in the bassinet. Cappadonna hadn't left that hospital since Capella had woken up, and I didn't blame him. He almost lost his son and wanted to be with him. I was glad that he was awake, and that we didn't end up losing him.

I've witnessed a piece of Cappadonna's wrath, and I could say that I never wanted to see the entire thing. He turned into a different person when he was beyond upset. His body even became warm, and I was certain he didn't retain information while in that mode. I worried about him because I didn't want him to end up back in prison. There were people that didn't like the Delgato twins and would try to put him back in that place.

The security system beeped, letting me know that the garage door had opened. I felt so safe in the lake house and Capp made sure that I was. At first, I used to be scared to stay by myself. Now, I moved around freely knowing that I was safe behind this gated community.

"Come 'ere, Alaia," I heard his deep husky voice soon as the door cracked opened. Capp filled the doorway, taking up every inch of the doorway.

My eyes always did a happy dance whenever they landed on him. I rinsed the last bottle out before drying my hands on the dish towel. Walking over toward the door, I stood in front of him, and he grabbed my face, placing kisses on my nose before he made his way down to my lips.

"Good morning... you just missed Promise going down."

He continued to kiss my lips. "I missed you last night, Joy."

Mrs. Jean stayed the night with me and went back to her house this morning. I had to convince her that I was fine to be in the house alone. I was moving around a lot better now and didn't need as much help with everything. There was a part of me that felt bad for her having to run over here to help me with everything.

"I missed you, too, even slept on your side, too."

"Probably drooled and sweated all on my pillows, too," he snuck another kiss while holding me around the waist. I was wondering why he was still standing in the doorway and not coming fully in the house.

"Listen, I can't control these postpartum sweats... and I don't drool," I protested, knowing that once I was asleep, I drooled everywhere.

He kissed me on the nose, then neck while holding onto my hips. "Quasim is outside... go ahead and go cover yourself up... okay?"

I smiled up at him. "Okay."

I was wearing a pair of short pajamas shorts from Target and a loose T-shirt so I could easily lift up to pump whenever I tried. At this point, it was useless to keep trying, but Erin told me not to give up. My hair was pulled up in a big messy bun, and it desperately needed to be washed because it was oily.

Everybody, aside from the women, knew not to show up unannounced at the house. Cappadonna took preserving my modesty seriously and had a conversation with all the men in the family.

I tried to walk away, and he pulled me back, staring down at me through sleepy eyes. "Give me another kiss."

Standing on my toes, I placed a kiss on his lips and then went upstairs to change into something else and put my hair up. I felt better knowing that I could finally climb the stairs and sleep upstairs instead of downstairs.

When I came back downstairs, Quasim was sitting at the counter. This was my first time meeting him, but Cappadonna had told me about everybody he ran with. I didn't need any introductions when it came to his brother because I had already met him at the prison.

"Qua, this my baby," Capp put his arms around me and dropped a kiss on top of my head. "Baby, this some sucka I know."

We all laughed as Quasim stuck his middle finger at Capp.

"Fuck you... what's up, Alaia? I'm finally meeting the woman responsible for giving this nigga twinkle toes."

"Fuck up." Capp laughed.

"Hey Quasim!" I greeted him.

I continued to clean the rest of the dishes while Capp showed Quasim the baby. He was so proud with the way he picked her up and showed her off. Promise was his entire world, and from that smile on his face, I knew she was going to be spoiled.

That little girl would never hear the word 'no' from him ever. He showed Quasim the backyard while still holding Promise. She looked like a little bun in his arms. Every time I looked at them together, it brought me so much joy. Knowing that my baby would have a different start in life than I did always made me tear up. Having a father that would do anything for her was something I never experienced, and I couldn't wait to witness her become a daddy's girl.

"Did you eat anything yet?" I asked when they came back into the house.

Cappadonna never complained and he would go without because he never wanted to inconvenience anyone. It was something that I noticed about him, and I was determined to break him out of it.

"Didn't get a chance to because I was about to put my foot in that doctor's ass."

I looked at Quasim as he shook his head. "Reason why I drove his ass home. He need to go to sleep."

"I'm going to make some breakfast... Quasim, any allergies?"

"Nah. I'm good with whatever you make," he rubbed his stomach, and I laughed because I knew both these men were about to eat every last piece of food.

Cappadonna kissed Promise a few times before he placed

her back down into her bouncer. He came around the counter and kissed me on the lips. "We're gonna be in the backyard."

"K," I replied, pulling out the beef bacon, eggs, and cheese.

"Thank you, Baby."

"Anything for you. I need you to stop threatening the staff up there," I reminded him, and he shrugged, knowing he wasn't going to stop giving those people hell.

Capp leaned on the counter. "You mind if he comes and stays with us at the lake house?"

I looked at him like he was crazy. "You're asking me? This is your home, Capp, and that's your son... you take care of family always."

"Why do you insist on pissing me off this early, Joy?"

I stared at him because it was a serious question, and he was waiting for me to answer the question. "What do you mean?"

"This is your home. Wherever I am, is your home. I'm your home... you hear me?"

I blushed and went to grab a mixing bowl. I felt Capp behind me as he reached the top shelf to grab the bowls. "I feel like it's not my place to have an opinion on what you do with your son. Of course, I would love for him to come here... he can recover, and I can make sure he's alright while you're gone."

"Even though I'm the head of this household, and I'm gonna lead, this is an equal partnership. I'm always going to ask what you think about something because I value your opinion."

"Then why didn't you listen to me about Aimee and the baby?"

He tried to walk away, and I grabbed his arm. "Don't try and walk away. He's your grandson, and I know it probably taste like poison admitting, but Aimee is innocent in all of this."

I felt for Aimee because she didn't ask for any of this and was tossed in the middle of her brother's beef. As much as Cappadonna didn't agree with her being around, his son loved her. They shared a child together.

"What you expect me to do, Alaia? Forgive that nigga for trying to kill my son?" He leaned against the counter and started messing with his beard.

Something he did when he was in deep thought. It was funny because I sat and witnessed both brothers do the same exact thing at the same time. I found it funny how their mannerisms matched, and they were also two completely different people.

"I can't tell you what to do when it comes to her brother. However, you can't just get rid of her because your son must love her. I overheard her talking and they're in a relationship."

"Then why the fuck did he keep her away? Hide her ass like a secret. The shit got me ready to go wake his ass up so I can get my answers."

Even though Chubs was awake, he was also on a bunch of pain medicine, so he was constantly in and out of consciousness.

I walked over toward him and wrapped my arms around his waist. "You are not going back to the hospital until you eat and get some sleep. I can see in your eyes that you haven't slept at all."

He looked down at me and cocked his head to the side. "Since when you bossing me around?"

Whenever Cappadonna looked at me with those eyes, I had no choice but to look away from him. He always looked like he was looking past me and straight into my soul. His stare sent the good kind of chills down my spine.

"I think every once in a while, you need someone to boss you around." I smiled and looked at the text message that popped up on my phone. "Oh yeah. Blair is coming over... I forgot to tell you."

His eyes were closed as I was still hugging him. "What you telling me for? You can do whatever you please, Joy."

"I understand that. Just thought you should know in case she showed up and you were trying to shoot her head off."

He chuckled and then yawned. "I only got three people I wanna pop right now and one of them I'm still debating on if I wanna use my gun or hands."

"Taz?"

"You already know... I don't let anything slide when it comes to you, Baby."

I reached up and touched his face. "I love you, Cappadonna."

He puckered his lips, and I reached up to kiss them. "I gotta ask you something, too... not right now though."

I removed myself from him. "Now it's going to drive me crazy thinking about what you want to talk to me about."

"Don't worry about it right now..." his phone chimed, and then he looked at me. "Blair just passed through the gates."

"Go ahead and relax in the back while I finish breakfast. Then you need to shower and take a nap before going back to the hospital."

Cappadonna kissed me again before he swaggered toward the back door, stopping to peek in at Promise before going. I put the bacon on and then went to get the front door for Blair. She stood at the door with a shocked expression on her face.

"Blair, are you alright?"

She looked behind her, then back at me. "This is where you live?"

I couldn't help but to laugh that she was as shocked as she was. When Capp first brought me here, I had the same reaction. Where I came from, people didn't live like this. The fact that these people didn't live here fulltime was something that surprised me, too. It wasn't about how big Capp's lake house was, it was that every house in this neighborhood screamed opulence.

"For now... yes."

Aside from the few times that Zayne had dropped me off to her studio, Blair didn't know my life. Telling people that I was sold by my brother wasn't a great conversation starter. It was also something that I was embarrassed to admit. Which is why it took a minute for me to tell Capp. I thought he would look at me different if he knew, and he proved me wrong.

I welcomed her into the house and secured the door behind her. Blair walked slowly into the house, looking around in pure awe. Each time she tried to speak; her words were caught in her throat. I sprinted into the kitchen to make sure the bacon wasn't burning while she slowly walked deeper into the house.

"This house is beautiful, Alaia... it smells amazing in here." She had finally made it into the kitchen, where I was pulling the bacon out of the pan.

"Thank you."

Blair and I had been texting ever since I had given birth early. She checked in on me after I had complications with birth, and even sent me flowers up to the hospital. When she asked me if she could come visit me and see the baby, I didn't see it as a problem.

After I finished making breakfast and bringing it out to the guys, me and Blair sat at the kitchen counter. I made her some coffee, and then sat down to drink this nasty herbal tea that was supposed to help with milk supply.

"Is your milk still not coming in?"

"It's coming in... just slow," I sulked.

Blair touched my hand. "A lot has happened to your body.

Don't be so hard on yourself... what's best for the baby is a fed baby, which she is. Alaia, she is so beautiful and your twin."

"You think so?"

Everyone said that Promise looked like me and other than her eyes, I was trying to see it. Maybe it was because I was too busy trying to see Zayne in her. I didn't want any pieces of him coming through her. I wanted him to disappear from my memory completely.

"Girl, yes. She's so beautiful and all that hair... Goodness, I know you complained about heartburn, but shit."

Me and Blair both laughed as she slowly sipped her coffee. I had always had this knack for knowing when something was off with someone. Blair was naturally bubbly every time I was around her. As she sat in front of me, I could tell she was struggling to hold onto her bubbly personality.

"Is everything alright with you, Blair?" I tossed caution into the wind and asked her.

I was the kind of person that loved to pour into others. Blair had taken the time to drive all the way out here just to check in on me, and I wanted to pour back into her. Which is why I was so hard on Capp for wanting to help me. I could never pay him back like the way he has come through for me. He had managed to help me get all my documents that I never had and apply for passports for both me and the baby so the least that I could do was keep the house clean and make sure that he had food cooked when he came home.

"Girl, I came here to check in with you... not the other way around." Blair laughed, and tried to play it off like she was okay.

I knew she wasn't okay.

I've spent the vast majority of my life not being okay, so I knew when someone was pretending. I had to pretend my entire relationship with Zayne, so I recognized when someone wasn't fine.

"While I appreciate that, I can see that something is going on with you." It was my turn to touch her hand, and once my hand touched the back of hers, she broke down in tears.

I quickly grabbed some napkins and pushed them into her hands while moving my chair closer to hers. "What's the matter?"

It was understandable if she didn't want to bare her soul to me. All I was, was her student in one of her classes. It's not like I exactly sat down and bared mine to her. She was probably confused on how I told her my husband passed away, to Cappadonna showing up and paying for all my classes. Even if she was nosey about it, she never acted like it.

"I have breast cancer."

Her words knocked the wind out of my chest. "I'm...I'm sorry, Blair."

Instead of stammering more, I wrapped my arms around her and allowed her to get it out. I could tell she hadn't truly processed it herself because the tears wouldn't stop. No matter how much I rubbed her back and told her to let it out, they continued to flow.

What did I say to someone that found out that they had cancer? She was so young, vibrant, and full of life. Blair had so much life to live, and it was unfair how cancer swept in and ruined good people.

"It's not fair. I'm healthy, work out sometimes, and eat pretty clean... I'm not the smallest person in the world, but shit. Why do I have it?" She continued to sob, and I held her hands.

"What stage are you in?"

"Two." She swiped her tears away when we heard the back door open.

Cappadonna and Quasim entered the kitchen with their plates in their hands. "What up, Blair?" Capp said and sat his dish in the sink.

"Hey Cappadonna... it's great to see you again," she sniffled, desperately trying to pull herself together.

Quasim handed his plate to Capp, and then looked at Blair. "You way too beautiful to be crying."

Blair let out a defeated laugh. "Well, I won't be when all my hair starts to fall out in a few months."

I could tell it registered immediately to Quasim what Blair was referring to. "Yeah... you right. You'll be even more beautiful. Keep your head up." He reached and lifted her chin. "I'm out, Capp. Thanks for the breakfast, Mrs. Capp." He smiled, as he headed toward the door.

Blair sat there stunned, unable to put together words. Like her shock with the house, I could understand her lack of words. These men had this aura about them that left you stuck on stupid. Quasim wasn't exempt from that either.

Capp walked him out, and I sat there holding Blair's hand. "Who...who was that?"

"One of Cappadonna's friends... they're old childhood friends." From the way Capp explained his relationship with Quasim, they were good friends from childhood, and remained even after he went to prison.

"Oh."

I squeezed her hands. "Blair, I'm here for you. If I need to come sit with you during chemo, and bring you food when you're too weak, I'm there."

She smiled at me. "You're too sweet. I can't ask you to do that for me. Not when you have a new baby on your hands."

I looked over at the bouncer where Promise remained sleeping. This little girl loved to sleep through the day, then get up screaming at night. It was like she knew when I was the most tired because that was when she cut up the most.

"I've been very blessed with a ton of help, Blair. I can be there for you like you've been for me during my pregnancy. Do you have any family or anything?"

She shook her head no. "I was raised in foster care. My mother passed away when I was twelve, and my family didn't want to take on another mouth to feed," she shrugged her shoulders.

"Sorry."

"It's alright."

"It's not alright, but you're going to be." I believed that with my whole heart that she was going to be fine.

Blair had accomplished so much for some one that grew up in foster care. She owned a successful Lamaze studio, and she was currently studying to become a doula.

"So, um, I hate to be that person... but I wanted to ask that day in class. This isn't your husband."

I started to laugh. "He's not my husband. My husband wasn't even my husband."

Zayne told me to call him my husband, even though we had never got legally married. How could we when he already had three other wives? The only one he was legally married to was Fatima. Like a good wife, I walked around calling him my husband when he didn't deserve it.

From the confused expression on Blair's face, I could tell she wanted to know more, but didn't want to intrude. I walked around the counter to wash the dishes and gave her the full run down on my life. Just like Erin and Cappadonna, she was horrified. I didn't know if I was still numb, or I had lived with this truth for so long that I could tell it was such a straight face.

When I told Capp the story, I broke down crying because it was him. I was battling with myself because I didn't want him to look at me any different. Even while I cried and got the words out, he reached over and wiped my tears away.

Blair put her hand over her mouth while she swallowed back her words a few times. I watched her face while she tried to put those swallowed words together. When she couldn't figure it out, she leaned back in the chair and took a breath.

"I had no fucking idea that you were going through that. Alaia, if I had known I would have called the police on him the moment he dropped you off to the studio... God, I feel so damn bad."

"Don't feel bad. I didn't tell anyone because I didn't want anybody else mixed in my shit." Capp came back into the house and went over to check in on Promise.

"I'm bringing her upstairs to take a nap with me," he said, never taking his eyes off her.

I watched as he put her receiving blanket on his shoulder and carefully picked her up. "Please don't fall asleep with her on your chest again."

Cappadonna had a bad habit of falling asleep with Promise on his chest. I could admit that she slept the best when she was on him. I was convinced I was going crazy until Jean put one of his shirts in her bassinet and she slept without interruptions last night.

"You telling me what to do with my daughter, Joy?" He smirked, as he headed upstairs, and I continued to watch him, even when he disappeared around the corner.

Blair snapped in my face. "Girl. You down bad for him."

I laughed. "Oh please. Just wanted to make sure they got up the steps fine."

Her phone rang, and she silenced it. "Look, I can see you have your hands full, and you are doing alright. I will get out of your hair... thanks for allowing me to vent."

I rinsed my hand and came around the counter, pulling her

into a hug. I wasn't an overly affectionate person like that, for some reason I felt like she just needed one of those hugs.

The kind of hug where you melted into the other person's arms and released everything you had been carrying. I knew from experience because Cappadonna had given me one of those hugs. A hug where I released years of abuse, not feeling worthy or not wanting to live. I woke up every day excited for the day. Whereas I used to loathe the day before it could even start.

"I'm here, Blair. You have my number. Please don't hesitate to use it... okay?"

She smiled. "I won't."

Even though I wanted to be there for her, I could tell Blair was the type of woman that took care of herself. She had never had anyone to have her back, so she learned to have her own back. She dealt with things on her own and kept on moving on.

After I walked Blair out, I finished cleaning the kitchen from breakfast and then went upstairs. Like I expected, his ass had her on his chest while the TV watched the both of them. When I tried to grab her, his hand reached out and grabbed my ass.

"Thought I was sleep, huh?" he questioned with his eyes still closed.

"Bullshit. You heard me trip over your damn boots." When I came into the room, I tripped over his boots and squealed.

Cappadonna started to laugh. "Come take a nap with us... I know you tired, too."

"Actually, I have a lot of energy today."

Today was one of those days when I felt like I could take over the world. "Let's keep it that way... come lay down with us." I hesitated before snatching my pajamas up. "Where you going?"

"To change back into my house clothes... unless you have more company."

He was laid back against the headboard, with his eyes opened, but they were low as he watched me from across the room. "I know what you're doing... why are you going to the bathroom to do it?"

I stood there awkwardly holding my pajamas in my hand. Shrugging my shoulders, I stared at him. "I don't know... just out of habit."

"I've saw your body before," he reminded me. "Even put a diaper on it."

"Okay, was that necessary?" I giggled.

"Come change right here in front of me... I wanna see." He nodded his head, while our daughter remained asleep on his chest.

I slowly walked over toward his side of the bed and stripped out of the long dress I wore. Thankfully, I didn't have a diaper on and just a pair of regular panties. Cappadonna stared me in the eyes, taking in every part of my body.

"What are you thinking?" I whispered.

"That you're so fucking beautiful. How much I'm lucky to have you in this room with me, while I hold our baby. How I want you to put my baby in that bassinet so you could get in bed with me."

I smiled as I pulled my shorts and shirt back on. Taking Promise from him, I kissed her lips a few times before placing her down into the bassinet, right on top of her daddy's shirt. Before I could turn back around, I yelped because Capp had got out the bed and picked me up.

With ease, this man picked me up with no signs of struggle in his face. "Put me down... I'm too heavy."

"For who?" He proceeded to bench press me like I was a dumb bell while I laughed and held him around the neck, scared he would drop me. "Give me a kiss or I'm gonna go faster."

"Alright...Alright!" I screamed out with tears in my eyes.

I kissed his lips and he stopped, debated then started going faster. "I want one of those nasty kisses, Joy. Don't be modest now," he continued to lift me up and down while I held him around the neck tightly.

I was laughing so hard while I pushed my lips against his, sliding my tongue into his mouth while he gripped my ass. Both our tongues danced in each other's mouth while we hungrily required more of each other.

Breaking away, I looked into his eyes, and he sealed our sloppy make out session with a kiss on my lips. "You know I will kill for you, right?"

I nodded my head. "Yes."

Cappadonna didn't have to tell me that he would kill for me because I knew he would. Every part of me knew that this man would protect me without a second thought.

"I love you, Alaia. I mean that shit, too. I used to think I was in love, but shit, I never felt like this before. I used to think that love was supposed to be filled with struggle. That the whole point of love was that you had to have a bit of struggle. Being with you, I know that's not true."

"We won't always be perfect, Capp." I touched the side of his face.

"I love us because we're not perfect, never been perfect. The shit we've been hit with hasn't been perfect. You know what is? Her." He turned us around until we were both peering down into the bassinet. "She's perfect. I'm not saying that we won't argue, and it won't be times when you wanna choke the fuck out of me. I guess what I'm saying is that I promise not to give up on us."

I kissed his lips. "With my whole heart, I promise not to give up on us."

He kissed me again before placing me on the bed and climbing in behind me. We both got settled in bed, and he held me. "There's a lot of shit going on right now, but I want to take you out on that real date."

"The boat date was a real date."

"A real one... you ever been on a date before?"

"No."

He yawned. "Guess we get to experience another first together."

I smiled as I melted further into his arms. Shortly after, I could hear his soft snores while he kept his arms tightly wrapped around me. Turning in his arms, I inhaled his scent and kissed his chest before closing my eyes.

4
CAPELLA 'CHUBS' DELGATO

BEING SHOT HURT LIKE A BITCH.

The doctor kept telling me how I was so lucky that the bullet had entered and came out from under my arm. Ace couldn't even aim right at close range. I was up within hours after surgery and was in so much pain that they had me on a lot of medicine.

Every time I opened my eyes, my father was right there beside me. When I first woke up, he was in the chair next to me asleep while I struggled to get comfortable. They had a machine that I could press, and it would administer medicine to me. No sooner than I pressed that button, I was back to sleep.

The last few days felt like a blur because I had been in and out. Even when I was awake, I didn't know what the fuck was going on. I felt like a fucking junkie with the way I couldn't keep my eyes opened and kept nodding off like I was on that shit.

When the nurse came around today, I told her ass not to give me no medicine. I needed to be up to know what the hell was going on around this bitch. It hurt like a bitch to be sitting up in this bed without all the medication I had been on, but I was tired of everything feeling like a blur.

The door opened and I watched as my father came into the room. He stopped short when he saw me up and alert. As hard and tough as he was, his eyes told a different story when they landed on me.

"Don't fucking scare me like that again," he said, as he came around the bed.

He pulled my head into his chest and kissed me on the head. "Not like I wanted to get shot." I laughed.

He didn't say anything as he continued to hold me. I could feel his heart beating out its chest as we remained like this, no words being spoken. When he was ready, he allowed me to rest back in the bed.

"You know a lot of people about to be dead, right?"

"I'm already knowing... I want in on it."

He screwed his face up as he settled into the chair. "Nah."

"What you mean nah?"

"I didn't stutter."

"Capp, I'm grown... I want in on the bitch that tried to kill me." I paused.

"Capella," he started.

The look on his face made my stomach sink. Had I been standing; my legs would have weakened. "Why you looking like that?"

"Francie didn't make it. She had a heart attack, and they couldn't bring her back." It was like he pulled the band aid off a bleeding flesh wound.

No preparation or easing into it. He just took hold of it and snatched it off me. "Nah. She's not dead."

I ignored him and tried to climb out the bed. He stood up, coming to my side and held me in place. "Capella, I would never lie to you. You think that brings me satisfaction to tell you something like that?"

The door opened and Kendra walked into the room, her eyes slowly rising to meet mine. Me and my mother had never been in tune with each other. I could never relate to her, or wanted to. In this moment, she didn't need to speak words because the look on her face confirmed everything that Cappadonna had just told her.

"Hey Cappa," she called me by my nickname.

She hadn't used it in years, and until she said it now, I had forgotten all about it. "Breathe, Capella."

My eyes watered as she walked closer to me. "She's not gone... right, Kendra? You've lied to me all my life... tell me the truth! Francie is alive, right? I'll believe you... I promise!" I yelled, my voice hoarse and arms weak.

Cappadonna remained at my side. Kendra touched my hand, and I snatched it away from her. "She's gone, Cappa. I wouldn't lie to you about something like that. I hate that she didn't make it... I'm sorry."

An unrecognizable wail released from my chest and out my mouth as I screamed. My father sat on the edge of the bed and held me in his arms. Me, a grown ass man was damn near in my father's lap screaming while he held me.

"I love you so much, boy. I promise I'm going to bring you their fucking heads... you don't need to be strong right now... I got you." He kissed my head as I screamed, holding him tighter than I ever held anyone.

My head throbbed, chest felt like it was on fire and my body ached being in my father's arms as he consoled me. The door opened and the nurse came into the room with the medicine cart.

"Not right now," he sternly told her, and she quickly exited the room.

I felt Kendra's small hands on my back, as I screamed into his chest. Francie was my mother, my entire world. She had given up so much to raise me, and never complained about it.

"I gotta go... I have to pay for the new boiler... she wanted that shit." My mind was mush because it was telling me that I needed to pay for a boiler.

That I needed to make sure that I delivered on my promise to her. "I'll make sure it's done," Capp told me and continued to hold me. My eyes were probably swollen with how hard I was crying.

"I love you, Cappa," Kendra whispered. My eyes started to feel heavy, and slowly closed as I stayed in my father's arms.

THE NEXT FEW days were a blur as I stared into thin air and didn't eat much. Cappadonna and Kendra tried to force me to eat, and I couldn't eat anything. Not when my aunt was dead, and I would never see her again.

I blamed myself.

Had I not picked her up to take her food shopping she would have been here. She wouldn't have been dead, and Jasmine wouldn't have been having to plan a funeral for her. My chest hurt just thinking about it, so I stayed on medicine, so I didn't have to think about it. I was complaining about fake pain just so they could administer the pain medicine and I didn't have to deal with the thoughts running through my head.

The fact that Kendra was with a nigga that killed her aunt made me sick to my stomach. I never paid attention to what the fuck Kendra did. She lived her life, and I lived mine, so I wasn't pressed on her shit. She came up to the hospital everyday looking pitiful and hoping that I would give her some conversation.

What the fuck did she want me to say to her?

I sat up in the bed watching the news as the mayor spoke at a press conference. I turned the volume up. "We have to stop the violence. Just when we thought the city settled down and we were finally getting the city back, we're met with more violence than we have ever seen. Our neighborhoods aren't safe anymore... we have to stop the violence."

I laughed because I already knew my father was responsible. He came up here, and sometimes he thought I was asleep when he sat back and just processed the chaos he had caused. I knew he was turning over every rock to look for Ace. If Ace was smart, his ass would be halfway to fucking Mars because once Capp got his hands on him, it was a wrap.

The door opened and Aimee peeked her head in. "Why you peeking in?"

She blushed. "I didn't know if you wanted to see me after everything."

I waved for her to come into the room, and she walked slowly into the room. Aimee meant a lot to me, and I was in love with her. I guess she thought I was upset because I didn't know her brother was Ace. We both were keeping shit from each other, and somehow God made it where our secrets ended up connecting.

"Where's my son?"

"I left him at my cousin's house. She's off from work today and said she would watch him for a few hours."

She sat on the edge of my bed, and I took her hand in mine, outlining her fingers with mine. "Why didn't you tell me that your brother was Ace?"

"Because I wanted to pretend that he wasn't." She quickly looked away, and the look on her face when she spoke about her brother made me feel unsettled. "Every guy I have messed with or dated knew my brother, or he made it hard to date them. I enjoyed you not knowing who he was. I enjoyed being Aimee for once, not Aimee, Ace's little sister." She shrugged.

I looked at her, and she looked away. "Why you looking away?"

"Your stare is so intense, Capella. I see where you get it from because your father's stare could kill someone."

I laughed, choking in the process. "I'm good, I'm good," I assured her before she tried to jump up and help me out. "I'm assuming you met him on bad terms."

Her face told me that she had met him in the worst way. "He wanted to kill me and the baby."

"To know him is to love him."

"Capella, he wanted to kill his own grandson... what do you mean to know him is to love him."

"Give me your phone."

She reached into her purse and pulled her phone out. I took her phone and plugged in Cappadonna's cell number into her phone. "I put his number into your phone. If you need him, call him."

"What? As if I'm ever going to use it."

I stared her in the eyes. "I'm down bad, Aimee. There ain't shit I can do from this hospital bed. Cappadonna is a lot of things, but he's big on family and loyalty. If you call him and need him, he's going to show up."

"This is so much. I haven't heard from my brother at all. Why would he shoot you?" She sighed as she ran her hands through her hair, stressed at the position she found herself in.

"Because he's pussy, Aimee. I can never forgive that nigga for the shit he did... my aunt is dead because of the shit he pulled. I'm putting that nigga in a grave if it's the last thing I do... I'm not asking you to pick sides because that's not how loyalty works. I'm telling you what side my son is on, and that's with or without you."

She didn't need to sit here and pledge her loyalty to me because it would be forced. All she needed to know was that her brother was going to die, and my son wouldn't be attending the funeral.

"I love you, Capella... you know that, right?"

"Yeah."

She moved closer and pressed her lips against mine. "Like really really love you. I've never been in love like this before. I never cared for anyone like I care for you."

I squeezed her ass and she giggled. "Go lock that door."

"I'm going to hurt you... hell no." She laughed while removing herself from my arms. "I won't preach my loyalty to you, but I want you to know that I do love my brother. This isn't my beef, and I refuse to have me, or my son involved in it. Ace is a grown man." I continued to rub her ass, needing to release this stress. "Are you even listening to me, Capella?"

"Not really... I'm trying to fuck."

"I'm not having sex in the hospital, crazy."

I was about to convince her when Kendra knocked on the door and poked her head in. "The fuck she want?" I mumbled.

"Be nice," Aimee whispered, kissing me on the forehead.

5
CAPPADONNA

When I saw my son that way, it broke something inside of me. My worst fear was never being able to solve my children's problems. I always wanted to be their problem solver, the person they came to when shit was too hard, and they knew I could fix things.

I couldn't fix this.

I could take life, but bringing someone back wasn't something that I could do. It didn't matter how much death I caused; I would never be able to bring Capella's aunt back to him. That was a pain that he would always have to live with, something that I couldn't fix.

Ace was gone in the wind like I expected him to be. He could dish it, but he couldn't take the pressure that was about to come his way. I questioned Kendra's ass and she claimed she didn't know where he was.

All her crying was giving me a headache and I was ten minutes from choking her ass out in the damn hospital hallway. She tried to be there for her son, and he didn't want her near him. He held a lot of resentment toward her, as he should have. Kendra thought she could easily fix things that she broke.

That boy had to grow up without both his parents, and then he lost the one parent that he had. I called Kincaid, and told him to relay the message that I was covering Francie's funeral. I had the utmost respect for this woman because she raised my son. She deserved to go home in style, and I was going to make sure that she did.

I knew it was the grief speaking when he asked about the boiler, but I still had a new one bought and delivered to the house. Kendra had went by there so they could install it. I told my son I would handle something, and I handled it.

"Yung Cuz just put the word out that Ace is safe in any hood." Naheim walked into the trap and plopped down on the couch.

"The fuck you talking about, Nah?" I looked up from my phone.

"Yeah. You know Gates Ave throw they block party every year. All them crip niggas over there talking shit."

"I had to calm this nigga down... tried to pull his shit out." Naheim shot a dirty look over at Kincaid.

They were nowhere near close, but they would let they shit bang for each other. Both of them had something in common, they loved Capri, and never wanted her to hurt behind losing either one of them.

I looked down at my phone. "When he said to tell our weak ass twin bosses to step the fuck back, I should have lit his ass up."

"Come again?" I asked while still texting my baby.

She was getting ready for our date tonight and asked what the vibe was. I wanted to tell her that the vibe was whatever she wore. Alaia could wear a paper bag and I would be trying to rip it off her.

"He said that you and Capone need to fall back. He said Ace is straight... guess he running with them loc niggas now," Kincaid snarled.

I looked up with a smirk on my face. "Oh yeah."

Me: Let daddy wrap something up and I'm coming to you.

Alaia: okay. Be safe, please.

Me: Always.

It was date night, and I wasn't in the mood to deal with these bitch ass niggas today. Yung Cuz was some crip nigga that swore he ran shit. The only reason he was good was because his moms used to baby sit me and Capone when we were younger.

Ms. Gladys was good people, and I never wanted to put her son on his fucking neck. Capone had told me that Ms. Gladys passed two years ago from some virus. When she passed, it was Yung Cuz, better known as fucking Harrison, that asked Capone to pay for her funeral because he didn't have it.

Running with those raggedy ass crip niggas didn't pay the fucking bills. If it had, his mama wouldn't have been on social security and living paycheck to paycheck. Naheim and Kincaid were behind me as I headed out the trap.

Kincaid hopped on his bike, speeding off first. Me and Naheim hopped in my truck and followed behind him. When we exited the block, you could hear the motorcycles following behind us. A few members of Inferno Gods pulled up, driving in the front of my truck and the back, while I cruised in the middle.

Whenever it was a block party, you could always count on them fucking up the blocks by blocking the streets off. The buses had to detour because there was always a party on every other block.

"You not going to drive through that shit?"

I laughed. "I'm not an animal... I'm gonna walk up in this bitch." I parked at one of the barricades, nodding at a few of the Inferno Gods, as I walked around the car. Kincaid didn't give a fuck; he drove his motorcycle around the barricade as I walked beside him.

All the bitches was on my dick the minute they peeped me walking through. I wanted a shorty to come over here so I could mush the fuck out of her. I had eyes for one woman, and her ass was in my house in Lennox Hills. That's the only woman I wanted in my bed and riding my dick.

I spotted Harrison's ass and walked over to him. He was barking orders at some chick on the grill while he held a forty in his hand and finished talking shit to his boys. When he spotted me, I could see his chest physically puffing up to talk some shit.

"Ain't shit personal, Cappadonna. You already know that... he paid for protection. It's about the money."

"Aye, Beloved, you put any pork on that grill?" I asked shorty while ignoring his ass, while he slugged his forty back.

Harrison came down the few steps he was on. "Nigga, this my food. I paid for this whole block party. You not about to eat off my shit."

Still ignoring him, I continued to look at shorty. "Yes, the ribs went on here earlier."

"Appreciate you, Sweetheart."

Once again, Harrison inserted himself into a conversation that didn't revolve around him. "Aye, bitch, get the fuck in the house. Smiling in this nigga's face."

I held shorty around the waist and moved her to the left. "Excuse me, beloved."

"You doing a lot of talking for a pussy," Kincaid spit at his feet.

"Oh shit, you couldn't handle me yourself, so you went and got your fath—"

In one swift movement, I grabbed the back of Harrison's head and slammed his head on the grill, next to the burgers. He sizzled like the food that was on the grill. "What was that, Harry? Why the fuck you out here playing like I'm not really like that?"

"Ahhhhhhh! Arghhhhh getttt..." I pulled my gun with my other hand and aimed it at his homies, and they remained seated.

I didn't even have to do much because Naheim and Kincaid already had their shit pulled. "We allowed you to walk around playing bloods and crips because your mama was a good woman. Bitch, don't ever confuse respect for being pussy." I lifted his head, which resembled the burgers on the grill.

His girlfriend's words were caught in her throat, her eyes wide with horror. I still had my hand on the back of his neck when I turned him to the crowd that accumulated to see what all the commotion was. My phone rang, forcing me to put my gun back in my pants and grab it with my free hand.

Alaia was facetiming me. Whenever my baby called, I was going to answer no matter what. "What's up, Baby Girl?"

The camera was on my daughter, and she was smiling with her eyes opened. "Look at her, Capp... she's smiling with her eyes opened."

I applied more pressure to Harrison's neck. "Look at Daddy's girl... tell my fucking daughter she's beautiful."

"Ahh, sh...she's beautiful, Capp," he stuttered, nearly about to pass out from the pain from his face and the pressure I was applying to his neck.

"Baby, let me finish this, alright?"

"Do I even wanna know?"

"Nah. Love you."

"Love you more," she laughed as she ended the call.

That was how I knew she was meant for me. Any other woman would have been horrified, not Alaia. She was laughing and shaking her head while this misconfigured man was in the camera.

I turned my attention to Harrison's ass. "Capone told me the hell you caused when you were a teen, too."

Capone would tell me how Harrison would push his buttons because he knew he was safe. Harrison had been a thorn in my brother's ass since he was a teen. I called my brother, and he answered right away.

"Yo."

I put it on speaker. "Tell him sorry for all the shit you caused."

"C...Capone, my fault."

"You better say that shit like you mean it."

"My fucking face is burning!" Harrison wailed out in pain, wanting to be anywhere but near me.

"The fuck going on, Capp?"

"I got this pussy ass nigga, Harrison... he got a little burn on his face."

"Little?" his girlfriend hollered.

I turned to look at her. "Wanna be next, Beloved?"

She made the zipper motion and fell back into the crowd.

"Fuck that bitch." Capone laughed.

"Yeah... call himself telling me what to do. Nigga, I'm old enough to be your daddy... matter fact. Let me hit you back, Capo."

"Bet."

He laughed and ended the call. I handed my phone to Kincaid and pulled my belt off. "I'm about to do what yo daddy should have done."

Harrison's eyes was wide as his set looked on while I

whipped his ass with my belt all over the stoop he was claiming as his own. “Ahhh, sto...stop!”

“I... bet... not... hear... shit... else... from ... you... bitch. Tell... Ace...when... I catch... him, I’m gonna pop his fucking head off with my hands.” I tossed his ass onto the steps while holding the belt. “Anybody else want they ass beat?”

They all turned away from me. I put my belt on, grabbed my phone and looked at Harrison cowered on the steps. “I went and got my weak ass twin boss, *Yung Cuz*,” Kincaid spit in his face. “Pussy ass.”

Everybody parted as I walked through the nosey ass crowd until I ran into my nigga Khaos, who happened to be blood. Not that I chose sides, I had homies that banged both. Khaos happened to be one of the older ones that I could fuck with.

“Cappa fucking Donna home... Big Capp!” He dapped me up, and I stopped to check my surroundings.

“What up. I need you to keep your ears to the street. Soon as that nigga emerge, I want ‘em.”

“Bet... you only said a word... welcome home, Big Homie. Appreciate you holding big bro down while on the inside.”

“You ain’t said nothing but a word. Goon always good with me.” I walked to my truck. “Appreciate it.” Yasin, one of the Inferno Gods had driven my truck up on the block, saying fuck this block party. He hopped out, nodded and I hopped in, looking at Naheim. “You good?”

“I’m always straight... hit me later.”

“Bet... hold it down.”

I revved my engine so everybody could move the fuck out my way. Yasin had already made it to the other end, removing the barriers from the opposite side. Turning up my music, I let the sunroof back and sped off the block, leaving Harrison a souvenir to remember what happens when you call for me.

CAPPADONNA II

I SAT across from my baby, after just putting a man's head on a grill hours before. She was cutting into her fish, and she looked up at the same time I happened to be admiring her.

"What? Do I have something on my face?"

I smirked. "Other than beauty... nah."

"Capp, that was corny." She took a sip of her mocktail as she looked at me while smiling. "Do you want to talk about what you were up to today?"

I licked my lips. "Not when you sitting across from me looking like that. Might need to buy another one of those dresses, Joy."

"Why?"

"Cause I wanna rip that shit off you when we make it home." I knew Alaia wasn't ready for sex, but damn, it was becoming harder to resist her.

I was stronger mentally, but when it came to physically, I was ready to wear her ass out. Alaia cut her eyes at me. "You aren't going to rip my dress."

"Wanna try me?"

Alaia wore this stone-colored dress, that touched the floor. She reminded me of my own little plus sized Morticia Adams in that shit. Her curves were enough to make you motion sick. I couldn't get enough of her, and I wanted to bring her ass over on my lap to finish dinner.

Then her smell.

That saying *you look good enough to eat,* applied to her because I wanted her to sit on my fucking face so I could feast. She smelled like a mix of cognac and cinnamon and it drove me crazy the entire ride over here.

"Are you not hungry?"

"Not for this."

She blushed, looking away. “Cappadonna Delgato, can you contain yourself.”

As much as I wanted her, I calmed myself down. “Promise did the body good.”

“You think? I can’t tell with all this extra baby weight on me.”

I took her hands into mine and kissed the back of them. “I do. How are you feeling? I need to check in with you.”

“I’m blessed. I feel lucky that Promise has you, and that I have you. Your mom and Erin have been amazing in all of this. It’s hard to complain when all I feel is gratitude.”

“You’ll tell me if something is wrong?”

“Yes. I promise.”

“You what?” I raised my eyebrow.

“I put that on Promise.”

I held my hand out, and we did our secret handshake, sealing it with a kiss on each of our hands. “You ready to get out of here?”

Spending as much time as we did together, we did little corny shit like that. I enjoyed being tucked away with Alaia, because I learned more about her each day.

“Yes.”

I paid the bill and held her hand, pulling her behind me as we left the restaurant. Tonight, I pulled the mustang out for this occasion. While we waited for valet, I stood behind my baby and held her.

“You so fucking beautiful, Alaia.”

“Thank you,” she cheesed.

I wanted to always remind her how beautiful she was inside and out. “Thank you for the slides... I almost sat on them when I got out the shower.”

I had bought Alaia a pair of Hermes slides, and had it sent

to the house with flowers. My mother must have brought it into the house and put it on our bed.

"Anything for you."

I held her hand as we drove back to the house. Capone called me mid-way there, so I headed toward his house. We pulled up where he wanted me to meet him, and I put the car in park.

"Where are we?" Alaia looked out the window.

"My brother needed me.... be right back." I hopped out the car and headed toward the house.

6
Alaia

I had been out in this car for the last twenty minutes waiting on Cappadonna. I was a very patient person, but I was nervous, too. He pulled up in a haste, and I wondered if something was wrong. Tossing caution into the wind, I climbed out the car and quickly scurried across the driveway.

Who's house was this anyway? And why were we here? I lightly tapped on the door before pushing the heavy double doors opened. I poked my head and closed the door behind me.

"Cappadonna?"

"I'm out here!" I heard him reply, and I followed his voice through the house. It was a beautiful house, with modern touches.

I stopped short when I reached the small staircase that led to the sunken living room. There were candles lit on each side of the steps, and rose petals littered the floor. Pink and red roses were all over the living room.

In the distance, you could see the beautiful view of New York with an infinity pool overlooking it. It wasn't the view that had me teary eyed as I took each step one by one. It was the aisle of roses and candles leading to a huge sign with *will you marry me, Joy?*

Cappadonna stood there next to the sign, standing straight, and waiting for me. "You were waiting in here the entire time?" I choked through tears.

"I told you I'm on your time, Joy." he said as I slowly walked further into the living room, toward the backyard.

I almost jumped out of my skin when the man in the corner started playing a saxophone. I had been so focused on Cappadonna that I didn't notice the man and the woman sitting in the living room next to a harp.

On cue, they both started playing and I recognized the tune to "Don't Change" by Musiq Soulchild. That was when I broke, and Cappadonna had to meet me near the doors. This was the song he played when he ran my bath after picking me up from the hell hole I was living in.

I was pregnant and so broken, and that small gesture restored hope in me. It showed me that there were still good people in the world. Tears poured down my face, messing up my makeup as he held my face and kissed me on the lips a few times.

"Why... how... when?" I said a million different things, because I couldn't form my sentences.

He held my hand as he walked me further into the backyard and stood in front of the sign. I could see he was becoming emotional himself, as he stood there with the ring box that was on the table next to the arch.

"I've never been good with words, and I tend to say the wrong shit. I'm used to saying whatever comes to mind because I don't give a fuck about somebody's feelings." He paused. "Not with you, Alaia. I stop to think before I speak because I want to be intentional with every word I speak to you and over you. You've been through so much that I want to make sure you never go through anything else. Baby, I got your back, your front, your sides... I'm here. I believe you were meant for me. We were meant to find each other, and now that I found you, I'm not letting you go. I can sit and talk about honoring you and protecting you, but truly honoring you means making you my wife. My better half, the one I share my name with. The one I continued to build our family with. Since you've been home from the hospital, it hasn't sat right that you don't share the same name as me and Promise."

"Cappadonna," I choked, still processing that this was happening right now.

He got down on one knee. "Joy, will you be my wife?"

I slowly walked closer to him and kneeled down, holding his face. "Nothing would make me happier or prouder than being your wife, Baby."

I kissed his lips as I wrapped my arms around his neck. He stood up, picking me up in the process, allowing our tongues to dance within each other's mouth. He paused, looking over at the musician who was smiling at us.

"Aye, turn the fuck around."

The guy quickly turned around, giving us privacy as he grabbed a handful of my ass and continued to shove his tongue down my throat. I wanted him so bad that I was about to rip my own dress off just to have him.

"Wait...wait... you didn't put the ring on my finger."

He kissed my lips as he placed me back on the floor. When he opened the box, there was a huge marquise cut diamond ring. It was tacky to ask the carat, but I knew it had to have cost him some money.

Cappadonna slid the ring onto my finger and then kissed my hand. "Don't take that shit off either. Or we gonna have a fucking problem, Alaia."

I admired the ring, ignoring him. He was dead serious

about me not taking the ring off, like he was serious about me not taking my C chain off. Since he had put it around my neck, I hadn't taken it off.

"You sure you want to marry me?"

"I knew I wanted to marry you before I even met you."

I looked at him confused. "What?"

"I prayed for a woman like you, Alaia. I asked Allah for what I needed when I got out, and he sent me you." He kissed my temple as I continued to admire this ring.

"I think we both prayed for each other." I smiled up at him, as he wrapped his arms around me, and we took in the beautiful view. "Are you ready to head home? I don't even want to know who you threatened to use this house." I giggled.

"This is our home, Joy."

I turned around in his arms, searching his eyes for the truth. "What?"

There was so many other words I could have used and none of them had come to mind except that four letter word. "My brother is on the other side of the hill from us. I put an offer on it and closed on it last week."

"Are you being serious?"

"I am. How can I ask you to make a home with me without giving you a commitment. Words are just words, but I've always been about showing the action. I know you *need* to see the action. I've never had a home of my own. I need you to make this into our home... a safe haven for our family. Our paradise away from the world."

Misty eyed, I stared up into his eyes and could tell he wanted this. This was something that he needed, we both needed. I wanted to make this home into our home. "I love you, Cappadonna."

He puckered his lips and I stood on my toes, kissing them.

"Love you more, Alaia Delgato." Cappadonna picked me up and carried me through the house.

How did I become so lucky?

I WINCED when I finally opened my eyes, looking at the carpet that my head lay on. I wanted to move, and then I wanted to remain here forever. My body hurt so much that I didn't want to move an inch, although I knew that I had to.

Before I passed out, Zayne had dragged me out the bed and beat the hell out of me because I went to the store. Fatima had needed more flour, and she didn't want to send their son. I offered and she had given me the money to get it. As I stood in front of the store, I debated on if I wanted to take the twenty dollars she had given me and run with it. Twenty dollars couldn't get me very far, but it could get me away from Zayne and Fatima's house. I could stay in shelters and even try to get into foster care or something.

I was still underage, so they had to help me.

I stood out in front of the store holding the wrinkled twenty-dollar bill until I felt a firm hand on the back of my neck. "Get the fuck in the car right now."

When I turned around, Zayne was standing there staring daggers into my eyes. Could he tell that I was contemplating running away? How did he even know to find me here? When I left, he wasn't there, and Fatima had told me that she didn't know where he went.

I climbed into the front seat of his truck and settled back, my heart racing. Even though I was thinking about it, I didn't run away. As far as he knew, I was enjoying the cool breeze in front of the store. From the way he continued to look over at me on the short ride back to Fatima's house, he thought otherwise.

"Where the fuck is the flour?" Fatima barked soon as I appeared

into the kitchen. Zayne appeared behind me and she changed her tone. "Wha...what's going on?"

"I'm gonna deal with you later. Why the fuck you let her out the house... she was about to fucking run away."

"I wasn't," I said barely above a whisper.

He spun me around and slapped the wind out of me. "I know that fucking look. You think I got to where I am now by not recognizing when a bitch is trying to flee? Get the fuck upstairs."

I held the side of my face as I slowly took each stair one by one. Behind me, I could hear him giving Fatima hell for allowing me out the house. When I entered my hell – room – I sat on the edge of the bed knowing that there would be hell to pay.

No sooner than I said a quick prayer, the room door opened with Zayne unbuckling his belt. "You don't fucking listen. I told you not to leave this damn house unless I said so. Turn yo ass over."

"P...please... Fatima needed flo—" My words were cut short because he punched me in the mouth, and the force sent me onto the floor.

My skin burned from falling hard onto the rough carpet. This wasn't even regular carpet, it was commercial carpet, so the difference was severe. I yelped when Zayne grabbed my hijab, pulling my head back as he continued to fumble with his belt.

My body tensed because I knew what was to come. When I felt it threatening my hole, I bit into the back of my hand and felt the thrust.

"I promise to be a good wife. I promise to listen... Please... you are my king, Zayne!" I sobbed violently as I jumped up in my sleep, my hands swinging in every other direction. "Please, it hurts...it h—"

"Alaia, Baby, it's me," I heard Cappadonna's voice and finally opened my eyes.

My vision was blurry as I watched him sitting up in the

bed. "I...I'm." I couldn't finish my sentence because my heart was beating out of control.

"Come 'ere," he pulled me over into his lap and wrapped his arms around me, kissing my shoulder as I sobbed into his arms.

He didn't force me to talk about anything, all he did was hold me and kiss my shoulder. When I finished crying, I looked into his eyes. "I'm fucked up... why would you ever want to marry someone like that?"

He removed my hair that stuck to my forehead with sweat. "You're not fucked up because you want to be, Joy. Shit happened to you that should have never happened to you. The fuck I look like judging you because of it? When I asked you if I was giving you money or a home, I meant that... It ain't beautiful, and I'm cool with that. I told you that I'm here."

Promise broke out into loud wailing, and I looked at him. "I woke her up."

"Got both my girls in here crying tonight. She'll be ight... she need to exercise those lungs. I want to make sure that you are alright."

"I'm fine."

"You're not and that's alright. As much as I'm not a fan of telling people your business, I recognize that I can love you and be there, but I'm not equipped to help you like a therapist can... I can come with you if you want." He kissed my lips.

I've always been in survival mode, so I never considered sitting down with a therapist. Even moving into this house with Cappadonna, I never considered therapy. I thought his love would be able to heal me.

In some ways he was healing me. Cappadonna was showing me a different life, the real way a woman should be loved, respected, and valued. He was showing me how a real Muslim man respected his religion and his family.

"You think so?"

Promise was over there screaming her head off while I sat in her daddy's lap. "I do." He kissed my shoulder. "I want what is best for you and our family. I know it can't be easy reliving the horrible shit that has happened, and since I can't do anything about him since he's dead... know that Daddy gonna handle Tweety ... okay?"

I couldn't help but to start laughing. "His name is Taz, Baby."

"Nah... he a little nigga." He squeezed me and kissed me on the neck. "I love you with everything, Alaia... I meant what I said, I got your back, front, and sides."

"I've never believed anyone as much as I believe you. Capp, I trust you with our lives. Since coming into our lives, you've made us feel safe. I don't know how I could ever repay you. I feel like I'm holding you back at times."

"How the fuck you think that, Joy?"

I messed with his hands while looking away from him. "You can have any woman that would be ready to give you sex. Meanwhile, you want to marry the broken trauma ridden chick that can't even carry kids... It's hard to believe that you want me at times, Capp."

He positioned me until I straddled his lap and held my face while staring me in the eyes. "Alaia, I'm not worried about getting pussy. I don't give a fuck about these bitches and the pussy they could give me. The only pussy I want is sitting right on me... you feel that?"

I could feel his member rise, the only thing separating us was my pajama shorts and his briefs. He kissed me on the lips, and then stroked my face. "Yes."

"When the time is right it will happen. That's only when the time is right... you hear me?" I nodded my head. "Now give me a kiss, and don't say some shit like that again... you got the ring on your finger... fuck these other bitches."

7
ACE

"What the fuck you mean that nigga beat his ass with a belt?" I paced the floor of my condo with my phone to my ear.

When I shot that little nigga that ran with Cappadonna, I didn't know that nigga was his son. That nigga was crazy as is, the fact that I shot his seed meant that he would go even crazier. I thought if I enlisted the protection of some crip niggas that I had met at the club a few months back that I would be straight.

At least good enough to show my face around without having to worry that Cappadonna would touch me. When my new right hand, Monty, called me to tell me what went down on the block I couldn't believe my ears.

"Nigga, he pulled his belt off and whipped his ass like my pops used to beat me," Monty replied, sounding dead serious.

I couldn't sit down to save my life. My legs continued to carry me from one side of my condo to the next side. Soon as I handled Chubs, I jumped into my whip and headed toward Delaware to dip out for a few.

When I put the word out that I needed to holla at Yung Cuz, he hit me right back. Told me for the right price he would assure that nobody touched me. "What the fuck? How did he even allow that shit to happen? I just paid that nigga fifty racks."

"Well, that nigga couldn't even protect himself, so how the fuck he gonna make it where we straight?" Monty replied.

"Fuck it, I gotta pop out and let him know I'm not scared."

"You sure?"

"The fuck do you mean? I'm not hiding from that nigga... I'm just fucking chilling right now until it die down."

"Yeah, ight. You gonna pop out to the Vanducci-Cromwell shit?"

"What shit?"

"It's Karter's birthday so he rented out the whole block. Niggas gonna be in the club and out on the street with they whips... shit bout to be a movie." Monty's ass sounded way too excited for a nigga that should have been putting together some solutions to our problems.

With Zeke dead, I didn't have my right hand that would back me up. If I didn't know better, Monty was moving like this wasn't his problem. Cappadonna's beef with me fucked with all of us, not just me.

A smile appeared on my face. "Yeah. I'm def gonna pop out."

"Bet. Hit me when you back in the city."

Cappadonna, if he even showed, couldn't touch me if we were at a Vanducci-Cromwell event. The only way I knew to fix shit was to show up back on the scene. He was expecting me to sit back and hide like a scared little bitch, and that wasn't what I was. I had to show Cappadonna that I wasn't scared of his ass, so popping out at that event was a sure way to make sure shit was handled.

From what the streets were saying, his son didn't die. He needed to take the warning and allow me to do my thing while he did his. I already married his bitch, so he needed to realize that he lost.

I wanted to look in his face when he saw me, not hiding and sitting with his bitch in his city. Grabbing my phone, I called Kendra's ass. She had been ghost since everything went down and we hadn't spoken.

"What?"

I pulled the phone away from my ear and looked at the screen. "Who the fuck you talking to like that?"

"You fucking shot my son and think I'm supposed to play nice with you."

"Your son? You told me that you didn't have any kids."

"Well, it seems like we both lied about something. You about how big you are and me about my son," she scoffed.

Her attitude was off the radar, and if she was in front of me, I probably would have choked her ass up. "Why the fuck didn't you tell me that you had a son? How the fuck was I supposed to know that he was your son?"

"Not only is he my son, but he's the father to your fucking nephew, Ace!" she screamed into the phone. "My fucking aunt is dead because you wanted to take matters into your own hands."

I had heard the older lady he was with had passed on and didn't feel anything. Kendra hid so much from me that I didn't know who the fuck she was anymore.

"That's cap. Aimee fuck with some crip nigga that's in Riker's Island." Aimee told me that she was so called in love with this nigga, then he got locked up and she found out she was pregnant.

She was so hell bent on holding him down, which disappointed me. I didn't pay for college and to give her a better life for her to be some common hood rat. Aimee was fucking stubborn like my moms, so I continued to deal with her in doses. She was supposed to go to New York for college, not be engrossed in the street life.

I hadn't even met my nephew because I was so disgusted by her shit. "Yeah, well, she lied to you. My son is her baby father, which makes your nephew my fucking grandson."

This twisted ass family tree was giving me a headache. "Kendra, be ready to go out... we hitting up Karter's birthday party."

"I'm not going anywhere with you. Did you not hear that my son was shot, and my aunt is dead?"

"She still going to be dead if you go to the party or not."

Kendra squeaked, surprised by what I had said to her. She was getting all emotional like her aunt wouldn't still be dead when the party was over. I had lost a cousin, and she didn't hear me over here crying and throwing it in her face.

Zeke's mom didn't even allow me to come to the funeral. She called me the fucking devil when I arrived at the church. It took three members of our family to pull her away from me because she tried to claw my eyes out.

Out of respect for Zeke, I left and would pay my respects when he was buried. His moms had every right to be in her feelings about me. It was my fault that he had lost his life, and that was something that I would forever hold in my heart and take to my own grave.

"Fuck you, Ace," she said barely above a whisper.

If I didn't know better, I could hear the emotion in her voice. "Yeah, well, I'm your husband so you need to choose me. Your son is grown and can handle his own shit."

~

Soon as I made it back to the city the first place I went to was to my sister's house. When she opened the door, she tried to slam it in my face. What the fuck was up with all the women in my life?

"Don't make me slap the shit out of you, Aimee," I threatened, and pushed the door opened, closing it behind me.

"You have some nerve to show your face around here, Ace. What the fuck did you do?" She walked to her kitchen, in the condo that I paid for every month.

She had the fucking nerve to try and slam the door in my face when I paid for her entire life. I did it gladly because I took on the responsibility of both she and my mother when my pops went to prison.

"Why the fuck do I have to find out that you had a baby by that nigga? What happened to Kareem?"

"His name is Khalil." She cut her eyes at me, as she washed bottles and avoided looking my way. "I don't have to tell you everything that is going on in my life. I'm twenty-one, and don't need to run everything by you. You've done enough in my life." She whispered.

"When you need fucking money you have no problem running to me. Anytime a bill is due in this bitch, you got no problem calling and telling me. So, why the fuck shouldn't the same thing apply when it comes to your business." I walked out the room and went to look in the bassinet.

"Leave him alone, Ace. I just got him to sleep," she rushed out the kitchen with soap still on her hands.

If I didn't know any better, I could assume that my own baby sister was scared of me. "You not scared I'm going to do something to my own nephew... are you, sis?"

She swallowed and shook her head no. "I just don't want you waking him up."

Her voice was shaky and from her body language, she was scared I would do something to him. She feared that I would take my anger out on her precious baby. I had Cappadonna's grandson right in my face.

I could send his ass a damn picture and see how the fuck he liked knowing I could touch his grandson with little to no effort. "Ca...can you leave?"

I laughed. She had some nerve asking me to leave from a place I furnished and paid for. Anytime Aimee wanted something, I made it my point to do it for her. She couldn't say she hadn't been spoiled, and I had never came through on a promise to her.

"You want me to leave? I only came to check in on my sister and nephew... damn, Aimee. You cold."

"I don't want to be part of whatever you have going on, Ace. I have a child to protect and that is my main focus."

I coolly walked over toward her, then pushed her against the wall, holding my hand around her neck, applying the right amount of pressure. "You're my fucking family. I don't give a fuck about how good the dick is and what bastard you both created. I can't stand Cappadonna's ass, but those Delgatos protect their own family. You think they gonna protect you? You're a piece of me, Bitch."

"A...Ace, please. You're hurting me." She choked back tears.

"That's not all I'm going to fucking do. You better fucking fix your attitude before you end up on the fucking streets." I released her and she gasped like I choked her that hard. "All of this was given to you because of me. I can give and take that shit back while you figure out shelter for that bastard."

She sobbed behind me as I looked at the baby once more before leaving. "Oh yeah. Keep this conversation between us. I'll know if this gets back to that nigga."

I left her to sit there and think about whose side she wanted to be on. Cappadonna wouldn't hesitate to kill her because he knew she was connected to me. He thought I would hurt, and I may for a while, but life goes on and more money needed to be made.

8
AIMEE

IT TOOK me a few minutes to calm myself down before I could even calm my baby down. Ace had always had a wicked spirit to him, and it was something me and my mother dealt with because he was the provider. Well, mostly me. He was the one who said what went and because he paid my mama's bills and made sure I never went without, she always allowed him.

Their relationship always creeped me out because my mother acted like Ace was more her man than her damn son. Even when she met Kendra at the baby shower, the shade was right in our faces. Kendra choked it down and appeared pleasant, however, I could tell she was uncomfortable. She had always been like that with all of Ace's relationships. There was never anybody perfect enough for her baby boy. Her baby boy could never do any wrong. In her eyes, he was perfect, and I was the problem.

I applied for colleges in New York just so I could get the hell away from the both of them. Low and behold, he followed me here to New York under the guise of work. He claimed he wasn't here to watch me, but I knew better. Ace loved control, and he would do anything to keep that control. With me moving away, he didn't have that same control that he used to have over me.

Ever since our father went to prison, Ace called himself being in charge of everything and my mother allowed him to be. She allowed him to do whatever the hell he wanted and made excuses for him. I wanted to get away because he had fucked mostly all my friends and had even got one of them pregnant.

He walked around saying the baby wasn't his when it was clear that it was his damn baby. I told her to leave my brother alone and she never listened. My brother had a name in Delaware, Philly, and Baltimore area. They knew who Ace was, so there wasn't much I could get away with.

I never felt protected when it came to my brother. He didn't give a damn about protecting me, which proves my point. Cappadonna had come into my hospital room and could have fucking killed me.

Meanwhile my brother was on vacation with Kendra enjoying his life, leaving me to fend for myself. Even when I was with my ex-boyfriend, Khalil, I never felt protected. He would put his hands on me whenever he felt like it, and always made me choose between school and him. If I had class and he wanted sex, he would call me to come to his house.

The minute I told him that I couldn't, I would be met with all kinds of bitches and hoes. Khalil was Ace's age and he acted much younger than that. When I met Capella, I instantly felt safe. The man made me switch sides with him on the sidewalk. I've never heard of the man walking on the outside of the sidewalk until I met him.

Even with him being younger than me, he carried himself differently. He acted more mature than my brother and Khalil combined. A girl fell in love fast and the next thing I knew I was spending all my time with him.

I was climbing that dick and riding it more than my ass was going to school. At the time, I was messing with Khalil, too. We were always on and off, so when we finally were off, I put all my energy into Capella.

When it came to Capella, I told him that I had a boyfriend, and our situation was crazy. He understood and was patient with me. When Khalil got locked up, he tried to call me and tell me that he needed me to be there for him.

The nigga acted like he didn't know me when he was out, but the moment he was behind bars he could remember my number and now wanted me to play my role as his girlfriend. Every now and again I would answer the phone to give him some hope.

When I turned up pregnant, I was scared because I didn't know who the father was. I had been with two different men during the time so my baby could be either of theirs. Even without him knowing if he was the father or not, he showed up for me. I could call and ask him for anything, and it was done.

I purposely didn't invite him to the baby shower because of my brother. You know how you could tell two people aren't going to mesh well? I knew right off the bat that Capella and Ace wouldn't get along. Capella was really about that, while my brother did all the talking and called someone to handle his problems.

When I left the baby shower early, Capella took me to a hotel in the city and had set up our own private baby shower. His aunt and cousin was there, and we ordered room service and talked about the baby. I think deep down he already knew the baby was his.

What I didn't know was that the whole time I was talking

to Kendra, that I was talking to my boyfriend's mother and child's grandmother. Capella always mentioned his mother, never saying a name, and he hated her.

Anytime we had a conversation about her, his face always looked like he smelled shit. From what he told me, she didn't raise him and wasn't shit as a mother. I never pushed too deep because I had my own issues with my mother.

My neck still felt like Ace's hands were wrapped around it, and the menacing look in his eyes when he told me that I was on his side because I was blood scared me. He shot my son's father and thought I was supposed to choose him.

My loyalty was to my son's father, the man that would raise him to be a good man. No offense, I didn't want my son being raised by my brother. I picked my baby up and cradled him in my arms as I looked around my condo.

"It's okay, Baby... it's alright," I shushed him as I went into the bedroom to grab my phone. Scrolling through my call log, I hit the name and put my phone to my ear.

"Yo."

"Cappadonna?"

"The fuck is this?"

I sniffled. "Aimee... Capella's girlfriend."

The line went silent, and I thought he had ended the call on me. "How the fuck you got my number?"

"Capella told me to put it in my phone in case I needed it."

"Well, why do you need my number, Aimee?" Cappadonna was scary, and not because he threatened to kill me and my baby multiple times.

Everything from his height, demeanor, and the way he walked was scary. I was terrified for Ace, and I would be a fool if I chose the wrong side. "Capella said that you will be there for me if we called. My brother just choked me out and demanded I take his side... I'm scared for me and my baby, Capp," I admitted.

"Sit tight. I'm on my way."

"You need the address?"

"Nah."

"You know where I live?" I was slightly horrified that this man knew my address, and here I thought I was safe.

"Aimee, you want me to come or fucking not? If my son told you to call me, then I'm not gonna let him down... but let me tell you something, this a set up and I'm slicing your throat."

I gulped. "I...I promise it's not."

"Have my grandson's shit packed, Aimee," he replied and ended the call, and I placed my baby back down and did as he said.

This wasn't my beef, and I would be damned if I died behind my brother's decisions. I had to live for my son, and I refused to leave this earth because his uncle got us mixed in some shit.

I said a quick prayer, then went to pack a few things we may need.

9
KENDRA

Ace was drinking and having a good time like he didn't have a price put on his head. If not being able to read the room was a person, it would have been this man. Everyone in our section was on edge and trying to pretend to turn up.

Being at Karter Cromwell's party meant everybody was good in here. That didn't stop them from being nervous. Meanwhile, Ace was drinking and doing coke like the shit was going out of style.

I sat with my bottle of water watching my surroundings because I knew Cappadonna was going to show up. There was no way in hell nobody hadn't hit him up to tell him that Ace had popped back up on the scene.

"Here... do some," Ace slapped me in the face with coke filled hands, and I dodged him, with his hand landing on my cheek.

Now I had fucking coke on the side of my face, looking like I get down crazy with that sugar booger. "What the fuck is wrong with you?"

I moved away from him when he tried to get more on his

hand and physically put in my nose. "Chill out," Monty tried to calm him down, and Ace looked at him like he spit in his face.

"You fucking my wife now?"

Monty looked at me then back at Ace confused. "What? Nigga, you trying to shove coke up her nose and clearly, she not into that shit."

Other than doing ecstasy, we never did coke together. This was the first time I saw Ace doing coke and I didn't like that shit. Suddenly, I missed what I considered boring with Cappadonna.

He would have never been in here doing coke. Instead, he would have been posted up with a bottle of water enjoying the party, then he would dip out. As I was near the banister wiping the coke residue off my face, I gulped.

"Oh shit," I whispered.

Our section faced the entrance of the club. Like it was in slow motion, Cappadonna, and Capone both swaggered into the club, the crowd parting with every step they took. Capp was dressed down in a pair of gray Essentials sweatpants, wheat timberland boots, white tank top, and his Inferno Gods biker vest on.

Capone was walking beside him with a bullet proof vest on, jeans, and a pair of black timberlands. It was like the room slowed down as both of them, side by side, walked through the club. Shit, I knew they were fine on their own, but together I wanted to be a fucking conductor so I could run the train that they would run on me.

Naheim and Kincaid followed behind them with Quasim and the rest of Inferno Gods. My mouth was probably hanging open while I stared down at them. They stopped to dap a few people up, and then continued on their mission. When they headed toward the stairs, I wanted to hide under the couch.

Meanwhile nobody in this bitch knew what the fuck was

going on. The people in the section below us were staring up here, and I felt all the hair on my arms stand up. Cappadonna was the first in the section and Ace nearly choked on his coke when he saw him.

"The fuck is up, Pussy?" He rubbed his hands together, smirking.

It wasn't a regular smirk. His eyes were red, and he didn't come here to greet Ace. I looked around and decided to sit next to the chicks on the opposite couch. Maybe I would blend in, and he wouldn't notice me here.

"Get the fuck out my face... we having a good time." Ace waved Cappadonna away, dismissing him which was the worst thing that he could have possibly done.

"Nigga doing his own fucking supply... fucking junkie," Capone spat, looking at him with such disgust that it made me feel ashamed.

Ace didn't like that Capone called him a junkie, so he stood up and lifted his shirt. I don't know how he got in with his gun when it was banned.

"Oh shit. I left my piece in the whip... I don't have my gun," Cappadonna faked like he was scared. "Nigga, I'll make you eat your fucking gun."

Quasim laughed while tapping Capp on the arm. He whispered something in his ear, and Capp nodded.

He stood off to the side, and Ace should have been watching him. Instead, he was taking too much pride in gloating that he had a gun and Capp and Capone didn't have one on them. As his wife, I should have told him to watch Quasim, and I didn't.

My ass kept my mouth shut and watched him continue to dig his hole deeper. All I did was blink, and Quasim walked over to Ace, and he pointed the gun to Qua's chest. "Back the fuck up or I'll pull this shit."

Quasim laughed, a creepy ominous laugh, but a laugh, nonetheless. He grabbed Ace's hand and put the gun to his head. "Do it, Bitch... I ain't got shit to lose."

Ace was scared. This nigga was holding the gun to his own head and daring him to pull the trigger. Monty was nearly behind the couch hiding and not saying a damn word. It was like watching a damn movie.

Qua stared down into Ace's eyes, pinpointing the moment where he could snatch the gun, which he did. Ace tried to get it back and Quasim looked at it, before giving it to Capp.

Capp smirked while holding the gun in his hand. Walking forward, he grabbed Ace up by his shirt and shoved that gun in his mouth. Since he wanted to be shoving coke up his nose, his reflexes were slow.

In his mind he probably thought he was moving faster than everyone else, when in reality the nigga was moving like a snail. He shoved that gun in his mouth so far that there were tears in Ace's eyes as Capp held him up.

"You get to live another day because it's Karter's birthday and my respect for that man goes deep ... but next time you show your gun be prepared to use it. I came to tell you that your fucking days are numbered."

I watched in horror while Ace's mouth was full of gun, and my baby daddy was the one shoving it in his mouth.

From the way Cappadonna was holding that gun in his mouth, I could tell he was considering pulling the trigger. He wanted to pull the trigger, everything inside of him was telling him to do it and deal with the consequences later.

I held my breath because I felt the same. Ace tried to take my son away from me, and he had to pay. I knew I hadn't been shit as his mother, but the thought of losing him broke me more than I thought it would have. I've always been selfish and only gave a fuck about myself. Seeing Capella like that, seeing how hurt he was behind our aunt dying.

That broke me.

Capone put his arms on his brother's shoulder. "Not here, Capp... I promise we gonna end this pussy."

When he pulled the gun out of his mouth, we all winced with all the blood and drool that was on the head of his gun. Ace was damn near trying to stabilize his breathing when Capp took his gun and headed back toward the stairs.

His hands shook.

He wanted to end Ace more than he wanted his freedom or his life. "Ye...Yeah, keep fucking moving."

Why? Why? Why? Why?

Why the fuck would he even say anything when this man was leaving. When this man wanted to end him right here, and he walked away because of his brother. "Capp," Quasim said his name.

"Nah... gotta fall back for this one. Nothing we say gonna stop him," Capone warned him, as Cappadonna rushed toward Ace.

He picked his ass up and hung him over the banister while Ace screamed like a bitch. That big energy he had seconds ago had left his body. Cappadonna held him around the neck, as he stared into his eyes.

"I put that on my seeds that I'm going to fucking kill you. I'm going to rid the fucking world of you, and when I do, I promise I'm going to make sure you're so unrecognizable that the casket has to remained closed. Putting your hands on your own sister... fucking weak ass. You came for my son to get a response from me, well, you got me pussy." He tossed Ace off the banister, sending him onto the couch in the section below us. We all went to look, and he hit the couch so hard that he bounced and hit the section table, sending shattered glass everywhere.

Everybody in that section went screaming while Cappadonna leaned over and spit down on the section. "Anybody help him I'm fucking them up!" Karter roared.

Monty went from hiding behind the couch to now on the floor behind the couch. You couldn't even see his ass because he was that far behind it.

Capp looked at me and I held my breath thinking I would be next. He didn't say anything, as he walked out of the section. I was glad our conversation at the hospital spared me this time. I looked over at Ace on the floor and grabbed my purse to dip out and head back to Jasmine's house.

I wanted no parts of this clumsy ass nigga.

10
CAPPADONNA

When I opened my eyes, Alaia was standing there with breakfast in her hands. Fuck, she was so fucking beautiful. I watched as her face lit up once she noticed that I was awake. Alaia looked at me like I was her entire world. The look never became old because I would always give her the world. She never had to ask for anything because I would always give it to her.

"Are you sick or something?"

I sat up with my back against the headboard. "Why I got to be sick?"

"You're up before me and go on your run. It's eleven and you're just now waking up." She clocked me, with her hand on her hip.

"Did you forget when I climbed into bed behind you? It was damn near six in the morning, Joy."

She handed me the plate of food and sat on the edge of the bed. "How do you feel about Chubs coming home?"

I was excited that he was coming home and finally going to be out that hospital. He could use the time away from the city to rest and have those real conversations. We never had a conversation about his son and Aimee.

All I know is one day I want to kill her ass, then the next I'm picking her up and she has marks around her neck from her brother. Tossing Ace off the banister was partly because of her. Who the fuck raised that weasel? He running around doing coke, putting his hands on his sister, and thought I wouldn't have shit to say about it.

He thought because we were at Karter's party that he couldn't be touched. Karter had already heard what happened and told me to do what I needed to do. The only reason his brains wasn't splattered on those white couches was because there were too many witnesses.

As I held that gun in his mouth, I sat and weighed my options, counted the witnesses, and calculated how much a good trial lawyer would be. I wanted to pull that trigger more than I wanted to live in that moment. He tried to take my son away from me and thought I was going to remain quiet.

You touch my kids, you fucking die.

"Happy that he won't be in that hospital anymore."

"It's nice of you to allow Aimee and the baby to stay here." She removed the blanket from my feet and started to rub my feet.

Seeing her little hands working on my feet caused me to laugh. "Get the corns, too, Baby."

She slapped the top of my foot. "I'm being nice and you over here demanding me to rub your corns."

"Pick the toe jam, too," I pointed my fork at my feet and Alaia broke out into laughter. "Why you rubbing my feet, Joy?"

"Eww, Leroy."

I turned my head to the side. "Who the fuck you been talking to, Alaia?"

She was laughing so hard that she had tears coming down

her face as she rubbed my feet. I pulled my feet out her hands and pointed it at her face. "Eww, stop... omg... my stomach." She held her stomach while standing up.

"Baby, you just pissed on the bed?"

Alaia was nearly crawling to the bathroom while laughing so hard. "I can't help itttt!" she shrieked out in laughter.

I couldn't help but to laugh seeing her sitting on the floor with her legs crossed to avoid further peeing. "Yo pissy ass just pissed on our bed."

"Stop...please," she begged as she held her hand up. "Please don't judge me... I may have pissed on the carpet, too."

I put my plate on the bed and stood up, and sure enough she pissed on the carpet while still laughing. "I'm about to tickle the fuck out of you if you don't tell me who told you my middle name."

"Erin told me... I asked her why she called Capone Winnie, and she explained that his middle name was Winston. I may have mentioned wanting to know yours and she happily told me."

Leave it to Erin's big ass mouth to run around telling my business. "We not on that, Joy."

"So, you can call me Joy, which isn't my name at all, but I can't call you, Leroy."

I held my hands over her, threatening to tickle her ass. "I'm about to call you pissy in a minute."

"How about Roy?"

"How about you call me Daddy?" I picked her up and carried her pissy ass into the bathroom.

"I am not about to call you Daddy in public, Cappadonna."

"I'm cool with that... as long as you screaming it in private." I kissed her on the neck and sat her down.

"Donna?"

"Don't piss me off." I took a piss and washed my hands

before cornering her between the sink and the shower. "How about your husband."

"Well, that obviously comes after an engagement."

I kissed her lips. "Smart ass, I'm talking about now. I wanna get married in Barbados."

She held my face with a smile on her face. "Seriously? I am fine with waiting... we don't need to rush."

"In case you didn't notice, I've been locked up for a long time. I told you; I had a plan for when I came home. Did the plan go as planned, nah. It went better than I planned, and I wanna make sure it continues."

"Why Barbados?"

I kissed her neck. "My parents are from Barbados and were married there. Then Capone and Erin got married there. I want to continue that tradition and stamp our vows there, too."

I would sit and listen to my family tell me about the villa we had in Barbados and dream about the day that I would be able to visit. When you had nothing but gray cinderblock walls to look at, you spent the majority of your time looking forward to the future.

"Awe, I love that... you think we will make it?"

I kissed her lips and pulled her closer to me. "Yeah. As long as when I start to go gray, you still love me."

I wasn't naive about our age difference. Alaia was Capri's age, and there were more than a few years between us. "You are an old man."

"Yeah, ight."

She kissed me on the lips. "You excited for your birthday?"

"What the hell are you and Erin planning?"

She wrapped her arms around my neck. "Stop being nosey and allow us to do our thing."

"Joy?"

"Hmm?" she answered while resting her chin on my shoulder.

"Go wash yo pissy ass."

The howl she let out that was supposed to be a laugh damn near made me deaf. "I forgot that quick." She continued to cackle, and I shook my head.

All I wanted was for her to keep this smile and laugh. If there was one goal that I had, it was this. I enjoyed witnessing her become more comfortable with me. She was becoming comfortable enough to show me the real her. Her guard was slowly coming down, and I was a patient man, so I was accepting every chip off that wall as it came down.

"Yeah, go handle that before I have to wash you up."

"Then why don't you," she teased.

I put my forehead to hers. "Fuck... Joy."

"Alright, alright..." She quickly excused herself from me.

If I walked into that shower with her, we wouldn't be finished anytime soon. By the time we were done, I don't think she would be able to walk. "Go wash yo ass, Pissy."

"Whatever," she giggled. "Can you peek in on Promise. She's downstairs with Aimee... and your grandson."

I grumbled. "Yeah."

"Don't be like that, Roy."

"Alaia!" I warned.

"Alright, fine," she laughed while I left out the room.

Was it risky that I brought Aimee to the lake house? No, because if she pulled the wrong move she was going to be waiting for her brother in hell. As much as I wanted to kill her brother, something told me that she wasn't like him. I could see she was scared when I picked her up, and I had to be there for her.

My son loved this woman.

It didn't matter how I felt about the situation. Her child

was my grandson, an extension of me. He was family, and I had to be there for her. I knew if she proved me wrong, her ass would be face down in the pool at my new house.

When I walked downstairs, Aimee was in the kitchen. She looked up from the dishes and offered me a smile. "Good morning!"

"Morning."

I went over toward where the bassinets were sitting next to each other. Who would have thought I would get out of prison and have a grown ass son. If that wasn't enough, I would meet my soul mate and have a daughter together, then end up with a damn grandson.

I was too young to be a damn grandfather, and here I was someone's grandfather. Capella couldn't just come in and sit down, he had to kick the door in. "Do you want to hol—"

"Sorry, sorry... I need to borrow some mayo for the macaroni salad." My mother came in through the front door.

Fuck.

I hadn't explained any of this shit to her and now she was about to get a crash course on the new branches on the family tree. She was so busy on her mission to get the mayo from the fridge that she didn't notice Aimee standing there like a deer in headlights.

"Ma," I spoke.

"I understand that you need your privacy. I called Alaia's phone, and she didn't answer so I figured I could run over and grab it." She grabbed the mayo and closed the door with a smile. "See, now I am on my way."

"Forget about the mayo right now. I have to tell you something important." Her smile dropped and she sat the mayo down.

"Cappadonna, please tell me everything is alright with you." I watched as she walked over toward me, then she stopped when she noticed two bassinets instead of one. "Wh... who baby is that?"

"He's my grandson." I let out a huge sigh, and looked over at Aimee who was still frozen, unsure of what to say or do. "Chubs is my son."

My mother looked up into my eyes, with hers just as misty. "I...I told your father. I told Desmond that boy looked like you. I told him that he had your eyes and he called me crazy."

I pulled her into my arms as she sobbed into my chest. I understood why she was emotional. Seeing Chubs all this time, and never knowing he was your family probably hurt. Especially when you had a feeling.

My mother's intuition was always strong and on point. It was probably why I trusted it so heavily after losing fifteen years of my life. The night I got pulled over she told me not to go out. I had a cold, and she said she had a bad feeling.

When you are younger, you wave everything your parents say off. Now I can admit years older, that I thought I was big shit and knew everything. Had I listened to my mother, I wouldn't have missed out on all those years, and I probably would have had a chance to raise my son.

"Who is his mother?" she looked up at me, and it pained me to even tell her that it was Kendra's ass.

"Kendra."

Her gasped sounded like she swallowed all the air in the room. "She hid your son away from you. What was her reason. Why otha' reason did she have?" My mother's accent was thicker when she was upset.

"Ma, she has a whole bunch of bullshit excuses that don't make any sense to me. All I know is that I was getting used to having a son, and then the lil' nigg... the boy made me a grandfather."

My mother stepped out of my arms and peered over the bassinet. "Who is his mother?"

It was like it was the first time my mother recognized she was in the same room as us. She smiled at her. "How are you? I'm Jean."

"Hi, Mrs. Jean. It's nice to meet you... I'm sorry it has to be under this circumstance." Aimee slowly looked away when I gave her a look.

I purposely didn't tell my mother about Capella being shot. "What circumstance?"

"Chubs got shot two weeks ago."

"And I'm just now finding out about it? Where is he? Is he alive, or did you hide that from me, too?"

"Ma, calm down. He's being released today and then coming here. I'm about to shower and go get him in a little."

I was happy that my son was finally being discharged and could relax around family. We were set to head to Barbados in a few weeks, and I had spoken to his doctor and asked if he was cleared. He assured that if he was still on the up and up, that he should have no problem traveling. My parents didn't know about their anniversary party that we were throwing for them.

When I say *we*, I should have said Erin because she had been putting everything together. She wanted this anniversary trip for my parents to be special. You found a good woman when your family were just as important to them as their own. Capone found that in Erin because she didn't play about my mother and father.

"Lawd have mercy, look at those eyes."

The baby had opened his eyes, and I couldn't even front. It was like looking into my own eyes. The same eyes his father shared with me, and now had passed onto his son. My mother always told me that she could tell me and Capone apart when we were younger because of my eyes.

Even as a baby, she said I had these intense eyes that would just stare at her all day long. My mother never forgot anything, so I believed everything she said. "Damn... he has my eyes."

"That nose and look at his lips... you spit this baby out."

When I first went to hospital and held him, I could front I wasn't seeing him like I was in this moment. Back at the hospital, he was disposable, and I was seeing red in the moment, even with how calm I was. I wanted to harm Aimee, and because I ended up listening to my heart, I had spared her and my own grandson.

"Jasmine said the same thing when she first met him," Aimee walked over to us, and picked up her baby. "Do you want to hold him?" she asked my mother.

My mother was so giddy that she ran to wash her hands, then grabbed one of the receiving blankets before laying it across her. "Yes, please.... Oh goodness." Tears poured from her eyes as she carefully took the baby from Aimee.

"You really came home and decided that you were going to throw curve balls at me?" She clicked her tongue at me as she walked around the living room. She stopped at Promise's bassinet. "Look at your nephew... Lawd Jesus. Does your father know?"

"Yes. I told him about Chubs... didn't tell him about the baby," I replied, as she continued to walk around. "I don't even know what to feel... I need to hug my grandson, so you need to go get him... today is Jaiden's graduation party... he needs to come."

Jaiden graduated today. Since there was a limit on the tickets given, we decided to throw him a graduation party at Capone's lake house. With school being done for both Jaiden and CJ, Capone and Erin were gonna be spending more time at the lake house this summer.

My mother was doing all the cooking, as usual, and we

hired staff to set up tables and everything for his friends. This party was something small for the family and a few of his friends. I already knew Jaiden would want to do another one without the family around.

I was so proud of the kid. He accomplished all that he did even when the odds were stacked against him.

"If he feels up to it, Ma... the boy was shot, he probably wanna rest." I laughed and kissed her forehead.

"Well, if he doesn't come, I want you to come," she looked at Aimee. "I want everyone to meet my great grandbaby. Jesus. I'm a great grandmama... I'm too young."

"Tell me about it."

While my mother forgot about the mayo she came to steal, I went upstairs to shower. When I walked into the room, Alaia was changing the sheets off the bed, and had the carpet cleaner out.

"Cleaning up your mess, Pissy?"

"We're not about to make that a name, Roy." She smirked, and I rushed over toward her. Pushing her onto the bed, leaning on top of her. "Please, I can't afford to pee myself again," she giggled.

I kissed her lips, looking down into her eyes. "Moms knows about the baby."

"Rory is his name," Alaia reminded me.

"Yeah."

She reached up and touched my face. "You cannot blame that baby or Aimee because of who her brother and his uncle is. I know it's hard, Baby. You went to get her because you know it's not her fault."

I tried to push the conversation to the side by giving her kisses and tickles. "Stop messing around, I gotta take a shower and leave." I finally stood up.

Alaia's mouth hung open wide. "No, you not 'bout to act like I'm keeping you from washing your ass."

"Quit playing around and looking at me like I'm some sex doll, Alaia." I continued to mess with her, and she sat on the bed and rolled her eyes.

"Whatever, Roy."

"Alaia," I popped my head back in the room, and she was already laughing while leaving out the room.

If I ever doubted that this boy was my son, this whole attitude he had because the nurse wanted to push him in a wheelchair was proof enough. He kept trying to get up, and she kept a firm hand on his shoulder to make sure he sat still.

By the time we got in the car, he was cursing under his breath while the nurses wished him well. I laughed as I pulled away from the hospital, happy that I was leaving this hospital with him. I don't know what I would have done if I lost my son.

"How you feeling... talk to me." I broke the silence as we merged onto the highway to make the two-hour drive back to the lake house.

"Grateful to be alive."

He was short with his answer, and I knew it was because he had a lot on his mind. "I'm grateful for you to be alive, too. Why didn't you tell me that you had a seed on the way? And by Ace's sister?"

"Didn't know that she was Ace's sister... would have never fucked with her if I knew that." I could tell he was being honest.

"You love her though."

"You asking me or telling me?"

"Telling you, nigga. I can tell that you care about her because you put my number in her phone. If you didn't give a fuck about her, you wouldn't have done that."

"I know you're not a fan of her being kin to Ace, and trust, I'm not either. Aimee isn't like him though. I love her, Pops."

I smiled when I heard him call me pops. That wasn't something he used since we both sat down and got everything out on the table. "I'm on your time, Capella. If you love her, then she's family." I paused and switched lanes. "Lemme tell you something though. If I find out she disloyal, I'll put her in the ground myself."

He nodded, understanding that Aimee had one time to slip, and her ass would be slipping and sliding right in a fucking grave next to her brother. Rory would be good without her ass.

"Heard from Kendra?"

"Not unless she wanna taste the barrel of my gun."

He laughed. "She came and saw me yesterday. Was apologizing for not being there... I had just taken my medicine, so I wasn't listening to shit she was saying."

I looked over at him, as he stared straight ahead. "How you feel about the situation with your moms? Be real with me, too," I pushed him to tell me how he felt about his mother.

It didn't matter how I felt about Kendra, she was his mother. He could act all unbothered all he wanted, but the reason there was hurt was because he cared. I didn't care for the bitch, and maybe the world would be better off without her selfish ass, however, I had to think of my son.

"She swore she didn't know about him coming to shoot me."

"You believe her?"

Capella looked over at me. "Yeah."

Kendra thought that this was going to be some happy family shit like what Capone and Erin had with Ella. I wasn't about to welcome her to family events and have her around, and I didn't give a fuck if we shared a grandchild.

Kendra betrayed me in the worst way and because of her betrayal, I had a little fucking menace walking around thinking he could go toe to toe with me. Ace had more balls than a few for continuing to fuck with me after I warned his ass at the restaurant.

Here I thought our little bonding moment with him over oxtail pasta would mend things and allow him to see that I wasn't to be fucked with. I can see that Ace had to be one of those kids that had a classroom on the bottom floor that was reserved for the special kids, who weren't all that special, they asses were just bad as shit.

"If you want me to spare your moms, just give me the word. I'm on what you on."

My son looked over at me. "I just lost my aunt. Despite how I feel about her, I'm not trying to lose more family. She's my moms, no matter how I feel, and I don't want to put Jas through that."

I held my fist out. "I got you then."

"That easy?"

"How I feel doesn't matter as much as what you feel. I have to walk around and look at you every day. I could never live with myself if I had to look into your eyes knowing I caused the pain there."

"Thanks, Pops."

"Don't worry about it. You need to just chill and rest... don't need to be out there."

He looked at me. "What are you not telling me?"

"I need you to hang this shit up... you could have lost your life, Capella. You got a seed now."

"Nah."

"Nah?"

"You not going to treat me soft because I'm your son. I have every right to run along with you and Capone. I've been doing it, holding it down, don't do this to me now."

I remained quiet because he was hardheaded – like me. He wasn't going to understand that I would lose my shit if I had to bury him. How I would turn this fucking city upside down if someone tried to take him from me again.

"Not treating you soft."

"Then allow me to rest, and then back to business... come on... give me your word."

I bit back the words because I didn't want to give him my word, however, I knew he wasn't going to let that shit go. "You got my word."

"Bet."

Another reason I blamed Kendra. Had she told me about my son, he would have never been involved in this shit. He would have been like CJ and Jaiden, far removed from it. Chubs was different, he had gotten a taste of this life, and now he couldn't leave it alone.

I just knew that meant I had to have his back, front, and his sides when we stepped out the door. I'd lay down and die for my son, and I meant that.

Capo would take care of my family without hesitation.

11
Alaia

Cappadonna had gone on his run earlier than usual. He left when the sun was just coming up, which was rare. I sat at the kitchen counter drinking a cup of tea while waiting for him. I wanted to be the first person to wish him happy birthday.

He had changed my life in the months I've known him, and I wanted to celebrate him today. Erin had gone all out and rented out a night club in New York. It was a surprise party for the Delgato twins, and everybody was coming out to celebrate them. Quasim had already put the word out that there was no beef tolerated tonight.

I prayed everything went perfect because me and Erin had worked hard planning it behind both Capone and Cappadonna's nosey asses. They were so nosey it was crazy. A few nights I saw him trying to fake use his laptop. Cappadonna didn't even know how to use the laptop, and here he was trying to fake like he had to use it for something.

Every day I found myself falling more and more in love with Cappadonna Delgato. My heart jumped in my chest whenever my eyes landed on him. I wanted to be in this man's skin, and that was a foreign feeling for me. It was the way he went out his way to always make sure I felt good every day. It was a priority for him to make sure I was good, and complimented, and happy. When he stared at me, kissing me on the lips, I could feel the love leaving his lips and entering me.

It was a weird way to explain, but Cappadonna oozed love and security. I wanted to keep the home together for him. I enjoyed washing his clothes and rubbing his big ass feet because he deserved it. A man that provided and went the long way to make his woman feel secure, safe, and respected deserved the world.

I could never repay him in the way I wanted, so I did things that I knew made his day go smoother. His running sneakers were always waiting by the side door, and his smoothie or green juices were freshly blended or pressed.

When I heard the garage door chime, I smiled and spun around in the stool. Cappadonna was so busy kicking his sneakers off that he didn't see me sitting in the dark kitchen. He switched the light on, and his eyes fell onto me.

"Happy birthday, Roy!" I whispered, clapping my hands quietly.

Aimee, Rory, and Capella were in the guest room downstairs, and Promise was asleep upstairs in her room. The last thing I wanted was to wake the babies up or disturb Capella and Aimee. He smiled as he walked over toward me, holding my face in his hands, kissing me on the nose and then down to my lips.

"Why are you up? You were up all night with Promise."

I wrapped my arms around his neck and kissed him on the cheek. "I wanted to be the first one to wish you happy birthday... and I made us some bacon to share."

With how expensive beef bacon was, we ran through it like it was going out of style and would never come back.

Cappadonna pulled me to my feet and wrapped his arms around me, kissing me again. "Thank you, Joy... I told you about that Roy."

"It's perfect... Joy and Roy sitting in a tree," I sang quietly, while staring up into his eyes.

I remembered when I despised the word submit. The word made me feel physically sick because the man demanding it didn't deserve it. With Cappadonna, I wanted to submit to this man, and allow him to lead this family.

"Alaia," he warned.

"Aht aht... the name is Joy."

He laughed and then kissed my neck a bunch of times. "I fucking love you... you know that?"

"You may have mentioned it before... I set our prayer mats outside so we can pray together outside and spend a few minutes together before everyone wakes up."

He kissed me once more before pulling me outside where I had set up our prayer mats and had the plate of bacon waiting for us. "This means a lot to me, Joy."

"I don't have money to buy you a birthday gift, so I wanted to do something from the heart." I hugged him from behind as he looked at the beautiful view of the lake, and then the sun coming up over the lake.

"You got the cards."

"Yeah, those are your cards."

He turned around and held my face up. "You're going to be my wife. What's mine is yours, too. I don't want you to ever feel like you got to ask me to spend money or do something... this is ours."

"I feel guilty though," I admitted.

"For what, Baby?"

"Not working or contributing in a way that I should. I've been a burden since we met. I've never worked a job or contributed anything and all I'm doing is continuing the cycle."

He paused, as he often did, and stared down into my eyes. Before he spoke, he licked his lips and rubbed his thumb down my lips. "I don't want my wife to work. It's my job to provide and have I been doing that?"

"Yes."

"Let me tell you what your job is." He got real close to my ear. "Make our house a home, raise our daughter, riding my dick and face, and shopping whenever you feel like it." The goosebumps that popped up all over my arms and back forced me to shiver. "The reason I bought the house close to my brother was so you and Erin could have that support with each other. Capone don't want her working either, so she finds other things to pass her time."

I kissed his cheek again. "I guess being a wife is a job, huh?"

"Damn right." He slapped my ass, and then pulled me over toward the mats so we could pray. I positioned the mats with mine behind Cappadonna's as, that was the way I was taught. The male always prayed in front, and the women in the back.

After we finished praying, we sat on the couch in the back and continued to catch the sunrise. I had my legs across Capp's, as we both shared the bacon and looked out at the view.

"What is one place that you wished you could visit when you were locked up?" I questioned, biting my bacon.

He looked over at me, as I gave him a half smirk. "Honestly?"

"Um, of course I want you to be honest, silly."

He pulled me closer to him as he leaned back and enjoyed the slight breeze we were getting this morning. "The beach. I remember when I first got upstate, all I wanted to do was put my feet in the sand. I never gave a fuck about the beach when I was out, but once my freedom was taken from me, all I wanted to do was go on the beach and put my feet in the sand. Used to have fucking panic attacks because I could envision it, but whenever I opened my eyes, I was faced with my reality."

I kissed the back of his hands. "You get to experience that when we go to Barbados."

"With you. What is one place you wanted to visit."

"Don't laugh at me."

"What?"

"The Met."

"Like the museum?"

I giggled. "Yes. I love art, and I always wanted to go there. It's not as extravagant as the beach, but it was somewhere I wanted to get lost in. I had a whole bucket list of the museums I would visit. The Louvre being one of them... it was wishful thinking."

"Back then it was wishful thinking... not anymore."

I smiled. "Why did you get up and go running so early?"

"Me and Capone went on a run toward the top of the lake and sat there talking. This is the first birthday in a long time that we spent with me being free."

"I love that you both got to spend that time together."

"What's this big surprise you and Erin been chatting about?" he tried to get more information out about he and Capone's surprise party.

"Wouldn't you like to know."

The backdoor opened, and Capella came walking out. He winced slightly and then smiled at us. "Happy birthday, Pops."

Cappadonna smiled, looking at his son. He stood up, walking over to his son and they embraced. He kissed his forehead and hugged him as tight as he could without hurting him. "Appreciate it, son... how you feeling?"

"Rory kept us up half the night screaming."

"Must be in the air because Promise did the same thing," I sighed.

"That's what you get for having a seed so young," he playfully mushed his son, and then returned back to the couch.

Aimee came out the door holding Rory. "Say happy birthday, Grandpa."

"Pop-Pop," Cappadonna corrected. "Bad enough ya'll made me one, you not about to call me one."

"I mean, you a fine ass grandpa," I muttered, but he heard me and winked at me.

The wink was enough for me to melt onto this sofa we were sitting on. I sensed Capella and Cappadonna needed their father and son time. Not only was this his first birthday free with his brother, but this was also his first birthday as a father and now grandfather.

"I'm going to check in on Promise and get dressed. We're supposed to go next door because Erin is making a big birthday breakfast."

He held my arm and pulled me back next to him before kissing me on the nose. "Thank you for this morning, Joy."

"You never have to thank me," I kissed him back, then went into the house with Aimee following behind me.

Erin: You better not be weak and let that man talk you into telling him.

Me: Wow, E. I thought you had better faith in me.

Erin: Girl, I almost slipped. Be stronger than me, plsss.

I shook my head because her ass was worried about me saying something, and she was over there about to slip and tell her husband his own surprise. I couldn't blame her, these Delgato men were convincing.

12
ALAIA

"NAH... fuck that. You not leaving the house with that dress on," Cappadonna said when he walked into the bedroom.

I looked at him confused because the dress was more than modest. Other than how my curves filled the dress out, there wasn't much I could do about it. I wore a black cape stye dress and a pair of gold Jimmy Choo heels that I borrowed from Erin.

My hair wrap matched the dress with black and gold tying in the dress and shoes. My gold clutch sat on the bed while I put the finishing touches of makeup on. I wasn't the best when it came to makeup, but Capri and Erin had showed me how to do a little something, so I wasn't completely hopeless.

"Other than my forearms and toes, nothing is showing?" I turned, giving him my full attention, and now I was the one that didn't want his ass going anywhere.

He wore a navy blue, mauve, and beige tri-color knitted polo shirt. The way his arms filled out the shirt made me drool. His tan trousers fit him perfectly and hit right above the ankle, showing his navy blue Dior loafers. If that wasn't enough, the

Cartier buffs he wore made me take a breath while I was trying to find my words.

"Guess we both gonna sit in the house because how you talking?"

We both stood staring at each other before his smile cracked, and I broke out into laughter. "You look good as fuck. Joy, I'll put a nigga's head through the fucking window if somebody even look at you tonight."

It was funny how even with me dressed modest, and not showing any skin, you would have thought I had a tube top and my ass spilling out with the way Cappadonna was looking at me. I could tell he loved what he saw.

"Is that your way of saying that I look nice?"

He came and stood behind me, kissing me on the neck. "Hmm, and you smell good, too... what color panties you got on?"

"You so nasty." I laughed and put my earrings on.

Cappadonna nearly snatched my damn arm off. "Where that ring?"

"In the safe. I was cleaning earlier and took it off."

He left the room and then returned with the ring barely on the tip of his finger because it couldn't fit on any of his fingers. "Go on and put that on for me."

I stared at him through the mirror while I slipped the ring onto my finger and then showed him my hand. "Are we ready to go? I'm sure Erin and Capone are waiting for us."

Capp spun me around and then placed a kiss on my lips. "You the most beautiful thing walking, Ms. Alaia."

I blushed. "You really think so?"

He screwed his face up. "Think? Baby, I fucking know it... look at you. Done dropped my baby and looking good as fuck."

I loved his compliments because they made me feel secure. Cappadonna bigged me up so much that I didn't have a chance to allow doubt to creep in. He let me know how he felt about me often, and at times I feared that it might be exhausting having to remind someone that they were beautiful and worthy every day.

If it was, he never acted like it was.

We held hands as we came downstairs. Aimee and Capella were sitting on the couch watching movies. "Alaia, girl, you look beautiful," Aimee complimented me.

I smiled. "Thank you! I feel like it, too."

Cappadonna held my hand and spun me around. "My baby cleans up nice."

"Pops, let me borrow those glasses next." Capella laughed.

He was relaxed on the couch with his son asleep on his chest. This felt so perfect. Cappadonna had his son under his roof, and his grandson. "I left some money for pizza, and the number to the sitter on the fridge."

"You think you funny? I'm a grown ass man," Capella and Aimee both started to laugh at his father's joke.

"I don't know... with the way you both were scrambling earlier when Rory had a blowout." I raised my eyebrow and poked fun.

Aimee and Capella were new at this like I was, so it felt refreshing having someone else as clueless as me. If it wasn't for Jean, I probably wouldn't have known what to do, and would be even more lost.

Jean not only helped me learn how to be a mother to my daughter, but she was also teaching me how to be a woman. Teaching me things that I didn't know that I should have known. Erin was super close to her in-laws. My only hope was that I would be close to them too.

"Did you see how much was coming out? It was all over the place," Aimee shivered in disgust, just thinking about how she was covered in shit hours before.

"We won't keep you. Enjoy your night out and be safe." He carefully handed his son over to Aimee and stood up.

"Always. Hit me if you need me." Capp and Capella both embraced each other before we headed out for tonight.

Cappadonna kissed my hand as we walked down the driveway.

"Gotta make sure I keep you at my side all damn night, Joy."

"Oh please...nobody is thinking about me."

He looked me up and down while licking his lips. "Yeah... ight. You keep thinking they're not."

I had never been to a club a day in my life, and I was both excited and nervous. This was all new to me. I've never had a life outside of Zayne, so this was all new territory to me. He stopped walking when I noticed two Rolls Royce Phantom's parked at the end of the driveway.

Capone and Erin walked over toward us. "About time... thought we would be late to whatever these two planned."

Capone and his brother embraced while I took in Erin's outfit. She wore a lime green dress that had a high slit, exposing her thigh. It tied up around her neck, leaving her back exposed, and I was drooling.

Her dress matched the green in Capone's outfit, which was similar to his brother's outfit. Her skin was bronzed, and she was glowing. Her hair was styled in bohemian knotless braids, pulled up into a high pony with pieces hanging out, framing her face.

The Tom Ford heels she wore set the entire outfit off and I just knew Capone barely wanted her to leave the house. "Erin, when we had a conversation about our fits, you didn't tell me you were about to step on all our necks."

She giggled as we hugged. "Oh please... this dress looks

perfect on you. Look at your body, Alaia... I love how you wrapped your hair up; it looks so good... so regal."

I blushed. "You think?"

"Yes. You look amazing. Had a baby where?"

I did a little spin, feeling myself, and she clapped her hands. "Capp, you better keep her close tonight."

Capp pulled me close to him. "Niggas don't want to die tonight."

While we were joking, I could tell that this man was so serious. The drivers stepped out of both the cars, and held the doors opened for us. "See you when we get there." Erin winked.

"Gorgeous, just tell us what the fuck you got planned." Capone tried to get it out of her, his hand touching her ass.

"Be strong... stand on business," I mocked her, as we walked toward our car.

"What you mean stand on business... you ain't been standing on it," Capp blew his cool breath on the back of my neck, and I understood why my girl was having a hard time standing firm.

"Damn, I need something... got a nasty ass taste in my mouth," Capp said when we entered the city. "Yo, pull up at that gas station real quick," he told the driver, who did as Capp told him to do.

If I hadn't been with Cappadonna, with the car that Capone was in following us, I probably would have been scared to stop at a gas station in a Rolls Royce. We were in the hood, and this man just had to stop.

Capp reached over and kissed my lips. "You want something?"

I looked around. "No, but can you hurry."

"You don't want nothing, Joy?"

"Babe, I promise I am fine... just get something to drink so we can go," I continued to look at all the men crowding the front of the store in the gas station.

Capp hopped out, walking like he owned the damn gas station. He stopped and was talking to somebody before he dapped them up while laughing. Another man came out the store, and that quick Capp's eyes switched and before I could blink, he had the man choked up against the door. Capone came coolly walking out of his car like his twin wasn't choking the hell out of this man.

I watched as he checked his pocket and slapped him with the flap of his wallet because there was no money in it. He let him go and signaled for him to follow him into the store. Capp turned his back on this man he just choked up like he knew he wasn't stupid to try him.

They came out a few minutes later and Capp had chips, soda, and other stuff in his hand. The driver was standing outside, waiting to open the door for him. "Yo my man, you good on gas?"

Erin had rented the Rolls Royce's for the night. "Um... I could use some more."

I noticed the man that Capp had choked up was behind him. "Go ahead and slide that card up in there... fill my man up."

He hopped in the back while the man swiped his card. Capp reached over and kissed me again, then opened the bag of chips he had. "What the hell was that about?"

He chuckled.

Chuckled like he didn't just leave to get something to take the nasty taste out his mouth, then ended up choking out a man. Now that same man was filling up the tank of our ride tonight.

"That nigga owed me some money before I got locked up."

He rolled down the window as the man finished putting his information in the machine. "Good looks... we good."

"You good, Capp... good to see you home." He then dapped Capp up like he didn't choke his ass out.

Capone came out the store with candy and chips, too. "Appreciate it, Homie," he nodded at the man, who then swaggered back in front of the store like nothing happened.

"Seriously, Roy."

"Alaia... you gonna get yourself in trouble." He eyed me down. "I mean, you already in fucking trouble with that dress."

I looked away and rolled my eyes while screaming on the inside. "Joy and Roy remember?"

He kissed me again. "Forever."

I kissed him back. "Put that on Promise?"

"I put that on Promise."

I've never wanted forever with someone. That wasn't the case when it came to Cappadonna, I wanted forever and a day with him. Even then, I wanted an extra day after that day was gone.

With the way the drivers drove, we pulled into an alley so both Capone and Cappadonna wouldn't know where we were. Erin knew her husband well and knew that he wouldn't want to enter the club from the front entrance, so we were coming in from the back.

The party planner came out the back door when we stepped out the cars. She and Erin hugged, before she smiled and waved at both Capp and Capo who were staring at us confused. "Gorgeous, the fuck you got going on?"

"Oh, be quiet... come on," she pulled his hand, while I grabbed Capp's and he held me around the waist as he walked closely behind me.

We went through the kitchen, then down the hall where the bathrooms were. When we finally came out, we were at the bottom level of the club. The music started playing and confetti was flying everywhere.

"Surprise!" Everyone screamed out, and Capp and Capone both started laughing because they were both shocked.

With how nosey they both were, it was hard to even have pulled this off without them knowing. Capone and Capp both dapped each other up, hugging in the process before they both turned to us. Capp held my face in his hands and kissed my nose and then lips a few times.

"You real slick, huh?"

I smiled. "You deserve it... it was really all Erin. I just helped with what I could."

I couldn't take as much credit as Erin. She planned this all and brought me in the loop because I wanted to do something for Capp's birthday.

Capri came over and hugged both her brothers. The professional photographer took a picture of her between both of her brothers. They both kissed her cheeks, as the photographer took their pictures.

"Alaia, look at you!" Capri smiled and hugged me.

"You look beautiful." Capri was wearing a long white slip dress that hugged all her curves. Her hair was spiral curl, with curls all over her head.

"Thank you! Come on, we have the section over there." She pointed to the section that was for Capp and Capone.

When we entered the section, Naheim came over and hugged both Capone and Capp. "Happy birthday, fuck niggas."

"Look at who talking... the biggest fuck nigga," Capp cupped the back of his head, and hugged him back.

"Men and the way they talk to each other," Capri rolled her eyes.

"Where's Kincaid?" I asked, looking around the section for him.

She sighed. "He's been acting weird and said that he wanted to stay in... so whatever. I wasn't going to miss my brothers actually coming out to a club together."

Even though she waved it off like it wasn't anything, I could tell that it bothered her. Naheim came over. "What up, Alaia? You good?"

"I am... how have you been?"

"Chilling... How's Promise? I know she's getting big."

"So big... I feel like before I know it, she's going to be a toddler. How is your son?"

"Bad." Capri cut her eyes at Naheim and laughed. "He be hitting now."

I laughed. "Hey, they didn't have the beer you wanted."

While I was looking at the DJ announcing happy birthday to the guys, I turned around to see a light skinned woman with a pixie cut wrapping her arms around Naheim's waist. I choked on the Doritos that me and Capp shared on the ride to the club.

"Alaia, this is my friend, Nellie."

Naheim looked at me like I was having a stroke, and I probably was. "Hi...Hi Nellie."

She smiled. "Hey Alaia... you look so pretty."

"Thanks... excuse us." I pulled Capri over to one of the few vacant corners.

She noticed and looked back at Naheim and Nellie. "I promise I'm not bothered by his new girlfriend." I guess she thought she needed to assure me, and that wasn't even the reason I brought her over there.

"She was married to Zayne," I whispered, still looking back at them, while Nellie looked nervously.

Nellie had a daughter by Zayne, and she was a nurse. All of his wives were free to do whatever they wanted, except for me. Fatima used to roll her eyes when she told me that Nellie used to be the youngest wife before Zayne showed up with me.

Other than a few family events, we never had a relationship or friendship.

It wasn't often that we were all together in the same room, whenever we were, Nellie either never came, or she had an excuse to cut out earlier than everyone else. Our interactions were limited because I hardly ever saw her, and Zayne only brought her up when she called for him to watch their daughter because she was working an overnight shift.

Aside from me, she was the only other wife that lived within the city. I always assumed the reason was because she made her own money and had her own career. She damn sure wasn't kept by Zayne. Hell, neither of us were because I was struggling while living in that little shoe box of an apartment.

"Seriously? I'll pull her ass out of here real quick. Does she make you feel uncomfortable." Capri was ready to grab her and escort her out the club.

I rested my hand on her shoulder and laughed. "No, I'm not uncomfortable, just confused."

"When Naheim was shot, she was one of his nurses that helped him. He claims they're not together, just chilling, but that nigga done told me other shit in the past that was a lie."

"You're not jealous?"

"No. I love Naheim, and I probably will always love him. Our time happened, and now it's gone... we've hurt each other too much to try to make it work again. We'd need Jesus to come down and sit on that therapy couch with us. I can't help but to act like his wife still... he was my first love... I'm trying to have boundaries, you know?"

"What about the baby? You act like you're his mother, so I assumed... you know." Capri took over when it came to Naheim's son.

Before Cappadonna told me, I thought he was her son and not just Naheim's. "I love NJ so much... that's my baby. It's funny because I hate his birth mother. I also recognize that he's innocent in all of this, and even though I told myself I wouldn't be involved, I became too attached."

I looked over her to the man that walked up on us. He was tatted everywhere with locs that hung down his shoulders, gold teeth, and he wore an Inferno Gods leather vest. "Cappin' ass Capri."

"Quameer, leave me alone," she laughed, turning around, and falling into a hug with him.

"We Gonna Make It" by Jada Kiss played, and everybody in the section went crazy. Capp and Capone were rapping to each other. Capone holding a liquor bottle while Capp held his bottle of water.

"Where my baby at?" I heard Cappadonna holler, his loud voice booming over the music and chatter in the section.

"Over here!" Quameer yelled back, pointing down at me.

Capp didn't have to drink to feed off the energy that this party had. Everyone was doing their own thing and enjoying themselves. When he made his way over toward me, he pulled me close and kissed me on the cheek. "You good?"

"Yes.

"Nah. What's wrong?"

I wasn't going to tell him something was wrong at his birthday party. "I'm fine... I was talking to Capri."

When I went to point to her, her ass was over there talking to Quameer. It was the way he was staring down at her, like he would risk it all for her. I made a mental note to ask her about it the next time we were together.

"You sure?" He didn't look too convinced.

Reaching up, I kissed him on the lips. "Promise. Go finish turning up with your boys."

Erin made sure all of Capp and Capone's friends were here to celebrate them. I didn't want to take away from his fun. He had probably waited so long to be able to have this moment with them.

"Give me another kiss."

I gave him another kiss before he stared at me for a bit, then went to finish hanging out with his brother and friends. When I noticed Nellie heading back downstairs to the bar, I followed behind her.

"Why did I have a feeling that you would follow me?" she asked the minute I stood next to her, while she ordered a drink.

"I'm wondering how you're even out at the club and drinking."

"Alaia, I'm not Muslim... I broke up with Zayne before he went to prison. I couldn't deal with the bullshit, and I damn sure wasn't going to quit my job."

"Oh wow. I didn't know."

"Why would you? He kept you under lock and key. It never sat right with me how you were introduced into the folds... you were always so terrified. Didn't know what to say, how to move, or how to just be."

"Yeah."

"I'm happy that you got away and are able to enjoy your life. I heard that Taz is supposed to be taking over Zayne's spot."

I rolled my eyes. "Yeah... he's not too happy with me."

"Fuck him. His little ass always thought he was bigger than what he was. I got away because I refused for my daughter to be wrapped up in that shit like I was. I was young and stupid when I got mixed up with Zayne and didn't know any better. Leyland is my priority. The minute I ended things with Zayne, that man stopped coming around for my baby. We're all better off without him... let me get this back to Naheim."

"I'm happy that you're doing you, Nellie."

"Same, girl. Take my number... maybe we can have lunch or

something." We both exchanged numbers, and I watched as she headed back into the section.

"You might as well leave your phone out and lock mine in... what are you drinking?"

I turned to face a dark skin man with a tapered fade. "No thanks."

The last thing I wanted to do was encourage his ass to continue talking to me. I texted Jean to ask about Promise and she told me to have fun and not worry about her. "Come on, let me get you a drink... you too fine to be sitting here with an empty hand."

"I don't drink."

"Everybody drinks... why you at the bar? No expectations, I just want to buy a beautiful woman a drink."

He was persistent and I was tired of hearing him beg me to buy a drink. If there was no expectations, he would have told the bartender to get me whatever I wanted on his tab, and then left me alone. Instead, he stood too damn close to me, and continued to badger me about a drink. He was so close that I'm sure I would probably smell like his cheap ass cologne.

Was I an expert of expensive cologne?

Not really.

I did know what he was wearing wasn't anything that my man wore, and all his colognes were expensive. "I really don't drink... thank you though."

"I feel like you playing games though... why you at the bar alone if you don't drink?" he continued to ask questions, and I was ready to move now.

When I looked up, I locked eyes with Cappadonna. He was nodding his head to "Crunk Muzik" by Dipset. My eyes widened with the way he was grilling homie, who hadn't realized that he was in the presence of a damn lunatic who didn't play behind me.

"Aye, she said she didn't fucking drink."

"Mind ya bus—"

His words were shortened when Capp punched him in the chest, sending that man flying. I looked at him, as he crashed into another section on the bottom floor. Capp walked around the bar, and went and picked homie up, and then dragged him back over toward the bar, sitting him on the stool.

"Think you were about to tell me to mind my business... she is my fucking business." He rested his elbow on top of this man's head, while this man was trying to catch his breath. Capp carried his ass over here so effortlessly, like it was nothing for him to drag another grown man. "If she said she good, then keep it pushing. You new age weirdos don't know how to accept when a woman isn't interested. You one of those niggas that make women feel like they gotta take a drink or your number because you fucking weird. You lucky I'm in a good mood because for fucking with mine, I should have shot yo ass," he pulled his gun out, sitting it on the bar counter. "Matter fact, I should make you a fucking example for fucking with my wife."

When he had punched the man, everyone scurried away from them, including me. I walked back over and held his arm. "My feet hurt, Baby."

My feet were fine, I just knew that he would leave this man alone and join me back upstairs. I didn't need him to let off shots in this party because this man didn't understand the word no.

He looked down at me and allowed me to pull him. "Drinks for everybody on me... keep yo fucking eyes off this one!"

Nobody cared that he was about to fuck this man up seconds before, they crowded the bar, ready to get their free drink courtesy of Cappadonna Delgato.

"You need me to pick you up?"

"No, I can walk."

He held his gun by his side while he held my hand with his other. "Joy, don't bring yo ass back downstairs again... next time, I'm gonna make the next nigga eat this fucking gun."

"Alright."

We found an empty spot on one of the couches, and I sat on his lap while we enjoyed the music. I was comfortable in his arms while he kissed on my neck and had me ready for anything. Capp just knew that he could get his way with me.

Just like I knew I could get my way with him, it worked both ways with us. "Why you squirming, Joy?"

"My back itches," I lied.

He kissed my ear while laughing. "Tell me why you really squirming?"

"You already know why." I blushed. "Because my back itches." I was too shy to admit that he had me ready for him.

How my heart was beating out of my chest because I had never felt like this before. I've never been turned on by a man before. With Cappadonna, I was turned on by everything that he did. He could be clipping his toenails, and my ass wanted to be the toenail clipper.

"I know that squirm," his cool breath caressed my ear canal, as he held me tighter.

Cappadonna kissed me once more and we sat watching Capone drunkenly go bar for bar with Naheim. Erin was sitting on the back of the couch bigging him up just as drunk as he was. When he was done, he grabbed his wife up and they were having the best time together.

I yawned, and Capp whispered in my ear. "You ready to go?"

"No, this is your party."

He yawned, mimicking mine. "I'm tired, too."

"Why are you lying?" I giggled.

He tapped my butt for me stand, and then grabbed my hand. "Yo, Capo, we out... happy birthday, nigga."

"Wordddd, alreadyyyy," he slurred.

They both hugged, then Capp looked to Quasim and Big Mike. "Make sure both they asses get home."

"You already know," Big Mike confirmed, while Ryai sat on his lap.

Capp held my hand as he maneuvered us through the club. We left out the back of the club, and our car was still parked. The driver started to get out, and Capp held his hand up. "I got it." He cupped my ass, as I climbed into the back of the car.

13
CAPPADONNA

When my baby got to squirming in my lap, I already knew it was time to go. I had my fun, but after that clown wouldn't leave Alaia alone, I wasn't in the mood to party anymore. I sat back and watched, knowing that my baby didn't like all that attention on her. I told myself that I would walk away if he gave up after she told him that she didn't drink.

Each time she was so sweet and nice when he didn't deserve that shit. I could tell the more he stuck around, the more uncomfortable she became. When he continued, I felt my blood boil because what part of no didn't his funny looking ass understand? He continued, so I stepped in while trying to listen to one of my favorite songs, and showed his ass what no meant when it came to mine.

If a woman didn't want to be bothered, you counted your L and moved the fuck on. Not these new age fuckheads. They verbally assaulted women and sometimes physically assaulted them because they didn't want to give their name or number or accept a drink. The world was a crazy place, and every time I watched the news I was reminded of the shit. Let some dusty nigga pull some shit with my daughter, and I could promise there would be a lot of fucking bodies.

I kissed the back of her hand and pressed the button to rise the divider. "Come 'ere real quick," I pulled her arm, so she could come and sit on my lap. She stood, making sure not to sit on the center console that separated our seats until she was in my lap. Before she sat, I made sure to pull that dress up, and admired the black lace thong she had on. "You wore those for me?" I slapped her ass, watching it jiggle.

Alaia nodded her head, biting down on her bottom lip. I pulled her down on my lap, her back to my chest. I allowed her to feel what she was doing to me. She drove me crazy without ever having to do anything. I kissed her neck, lightly biting her in the process.

"Capp," she moaned, tossing her head back on me.

I slipped my hands down into her panties. "Back still itching, Joy?"

She gasped when she felt me slide my hands down into her panties. I patted her leaking pussy a few times before I teased her with my fingers. She was moving around so much you would have thought she had fucking ants in her pants.

"Oh myyy," she whispered, her breath caught into her chest.

I worked my fingers in and out of her while she held onto my forearm. "I want you to know what pleasure is, Joy. Tell me what you feel... open your eyes and look your man in the eyes."

She opened her eyes, her lips curved in 'o' while I continued to play with her clit. Taking my hand out, I sucked my fingers before kissing her on the lips. "It...I feel good... I feel it all over." She could barely get the words out as I moved my hands back down and watched her face.

I understood exactly what she meant. Good pussy would

have you feeling that nut building from your chest down to your toes.

As she sat in my lap with her legs wide open and my hands deep inside of her, I wanted this for her. It wasn't about me getting mine off, it would be a time and place for that. I needed my baby to know and learn what pleasure was.

How it felt for a man, me being that only fucking man, to pleasure her. Please her, have her arching her back so far that she was damn near in half. I bit down on her neck, as my other hand made its way up her dress, pulling her breast out.

"Cappa.... Cappadonna...I...I." she moaned, as I didn't let up, I wanted her juices on my fingers, so I continued going.

"Look at me, Baby... I wanna see you when you cum."

She focused on my eyes as her body squirmed, and she couldn't take it anymore. She held my forearm, her hands slipping until they were on top of mine as I continued to play with her pussy. "I...I..." she couldn't catch her breath.

"You ever played with your pussy, Joy?" I continued to stare her in the eyes while she was trying with everything to concentrate on my eyes.

"No... no."

"No, what? I told you what I wanted you to scream."

She bit down on her bottom lip as she squeezed my arm. "No, Daddy."

"No Daddy, what? Come on... speak in complete sentences for me." I inserted my fingers deeper, and she gasped.

"I can't be loud, Ba...Baby," she panted.

"Fuck him, Joy. He can't hear you unless I press this button." This was my future wife, and I would kill a nigga before I ever allowed him to see her in this way. "Tell me...you hear that? You fucking dripping for me, Baby." I inserted another finger, and she was about to go crazy in my lap. "I'm waiting."

“I never played with myself, Daddy… I…I… Capppp,” she moaned out, sinking her nails into my arms as my fingers became even wetter.

I patted her pussy. “This mine… you hear me?”

“Yes.” She kissed me on the lips, as I pulled my hand out of her.

Sucking my fingers, I kissed her. “Should start calling your ass Sweet Joy.”

“Oh, my goodness… Roy, please don’t.” I kissed her lips and helped her pull her dress back down. She tried to go back over to her seat, and I kept her on my lap. “What about you?”

“I know what pleasure feels like… I needed you to know what it feels like, and from the way your back was itching at the club, I knew you were ready for that.”

“My back *was* itching,” she whined.

“Yeah, you keep telling yourself that… give me kiss.” She kissed my lips before laying her head against me, and we enjoyed the rest of the ride back to the lake house.

14
CAPELLA 'CHUBS'

"She promised that she would come this weekend. I told her we made the championship and she's not coming." I looked over at my aunt, who took a seat next to me.

I was sitting on the steps on her front porch waiting for my mother. She promised that she was going to come, and we would ride to the school in her new car. My team worked hard to make it to the championship, and I wanted to show her how hard I worked.

I wanted to prove to her that the Jordans that she bought me had worked. My coach even said I was playing better, and I wanted to show my mom. Francie rubbed my back and pulled me into her, kissing the side of my head.

"She had something to do out of town and can't make it. She told me to record it and she will watch it later with you."

I brushed my aunt's arms off me as I stood up. "It's not the same thing. She promised that she would be here to watch me play. We pinky promised, Ma."

"I know, Baby. There's nothing that I can do about it. You wanna know something?"

I looked back at my aunt. "I'm going to be there watching and cheering you on. Whenever you turn to look for me, I'm always going to be there cheering you on, Capella. That will never change."

I was in the shower on my knees in full blown tears thinking about my aunt. How the fuck was I supposed to bury her tomorrow? How the fuck could I sit in a church and know she was in the casket in front of us?

That she would never call me or ask me to watch her favorite shows with her. She would never see my own son grow up. How could life go on knowing that she was gone? I tried to be strong because I hated looking weak in front of my father.

When he asked me how I was, I pretended everything was cool when I was dying on the inside. Dying because I was the reason she was dead. Being involved in the streets is what took her away from me. Had I never went to her house and pushed our errands day back, she would be here. I would even take her screaming at me about lying to her about being in the streets. I always knew that she would leave me one day, I just never thought it would have been so soon. I was robbed of more time with her.

"Honey?" I heard Aimee's voice from behind me. "Oh, Hun, I'm sorry." She came into the shower, fully clothed and wrapped her arms around me while I cried.

The water mixed with my tears, but the redness in my eyes and pain in my face told her that I was crying. "She's fucking gone, Aimee... never going to see her again. Because of me... I fucking killed her!" I wailed, as she held me as tight as she could.

Aimee kissed my shoulder, as she held me. "You did not kill your aunt, Capella. Francie knew how much you loved her, and how much you would do anything for her." She paused, taking a large swallow. "We know who killed her, and I can't tell you how much I hurt for you... for us. Francie meant a lot to me, too. I'm sorry, Honey Baby," she started to cry, too, and I took her in my arms.

We sat in the middle of the shower crying and holding each other. I've never felt a pain as great as losing my aunt. I've felt a lot of pain in my heart, but this one was far too painful to bare on my own.

"I love you, Aimee. You know that, right?"

She looked into my eyes while holding my face. "Capella, you have no idea how much I love you. How much I want us. How much I choose you... us. I'm willing to walk away from my family for us... that's how much I love you."

I searched her eyes for any doubt and there was none. Hugging her tightly, she held me like she never wanted to let me go. Aimee had always told me that I was her safety. That she had never felt safe with anybody else like she did with me.

There was a soft knock at the door. "Yeah?"

"Rory is screaming... I'm going to take him with me over to Erin's house," Alaia called from the other side of the door.

"Oh God, she probably think we're in here being nasty." I laughed at her as I held onto her tighter. "Can I come with you?" she called back to Alaia.

"Sure. I'm leaving in like ten minutes so um... you might want to hurry."

"Alaia, I promise we're not having sex!" Aimee just had to scream back, so she knew I was in here crying and wasn't getting any buns.

"Go ahead and change so you can go over there with her."

She kissed my lips. "I can stay if you need me, Capella."

I took a deep breath. "I'm good. Gonna put some clothes on and sit out in the back."

It was her turn to search my eyes and then she hugged me tightly. "Me and your son love you so much, Capella. We're always going to be here."

"Thank you, babe... go ahead." Aimee hesitantly got up from the floor and stripped out of her wet clothes before finding something else to where.

After my shower, I sat on the back patio and looked out at the lake, thinking of everything. The time I broke my aunt's favorite China plate and then blamed Jasmine. She made Jasmine work for the entire summer to buy her a similar one. When I told her that it was me, she pinched my ears and then made me apologize to my cousin, giving her my money that Kendra had given me for a brand new game system.

I dialed my cousin's number and waited for her to pick up. It hadn't been easy on me, so I knew she was going through it. "Hey."

Jasmine's voice was barely above a whisper. I barely recognized her voice, and that sent more pain straight to my heart. "How you doing, Jas?"

"I don't want to be here anymore, Capella," she admitted, something that had also crossed my mind.

While everybody was praying for me to pull through, I was praying and wishing I was the one that didn't make it. I didn't think about my father, son, or Aimee. I just wanted this pain to stop, and that was the only solution.

"I know."

"We argued the last time we spoke. I fucking told her to stop being so nosey and let me live my life... how fucking selfish of me. All she had been trying to do was look out for me." She sniffled. "She knew how hurt I was when me and Kincaid broke up the first time, and she saw that we were talking in front of the house and wanted to look out for me."

"She was always looking out for us. Even when we were too hardheaded to realize it." When I was younger, I don't know how many times I whispered how annoying she was because she was in my business. Always worried about what I had going on, and never allowing me to just do me.

"I'd give anything to hear her laugh."

"Jas, you shouldn't be alone... let me come get you. You can come here."

She sniffled. "I'm not alone. Kendra is with me... she's been staying with me. Kincaid drops by, too, and makes sure I'm eating."

"I love you, Jas."

I could hear her sobbing in the background. "I...I love you, too, Capella. See you tomorrow, okay?"

"Okay."

She ended the call, and I hung my head, my chest feeling tight like I couldn't breathe. The air felt thin, as I tried to get my breath out. I heard the door open and couldn't turn to look even if I tried my hardest.

"Breathe for me, C... come on breathe," I felt my father's arms around me.

"It hurts so fucking much, Pops," I cried, not being able to pretend for him. I couldn't sit here and pretend all of this wasn't killing me every day.

How could I now have my father and lose my aunt, too? It was like God was playing a cruel trick on me and told me that I couldn't have both. "I know. I know... it's gonna hurt for a while." I fell back into his arms as he held me.

"Shit... I knew he wasn't good." I heard Jaiden's voice and felt him come on the opposite side of me. "Told you that holding that shit in wasn't good for you. I'm here for you, Chubs... always."

"I'm supposed to be the ex...example. Can't be cryi...crying and shit...shi...shit weak," I whimpered like a bitch while my father hugged me.

I could feel how crazy his heart was going in his chest, and even I knew that wasn't a good sign. "I'm gonna tell you both something that I want you both to hold close. A man expressing emotions is not fucking weak. When I first got upstate, I cried myself to sleep for a full year. I felt like I was letting my family down, leaving my twin to fend for himself. I'm a better man because of that shit. I'm a better man for my family, a better man for my fiancée, and a better man for my kids. You lost the most important woman in your life, feel that shit, Capella. Grieve, because that's what real men do."

"Thanks for sharing that with the group, Cappadonna," Jaiden's stupid ass joked, and we all started laughing.

"Fucking asshole." Capp laughed. "Seriously though. You won't raise my grandson with that mentality. That suck it up like a man shit is the reason there's so many unhealed men running around here sucking that shit up and it's damn near killing them."

"I feel you, Capp. You more than anybody know how I felt when I lost Joie."

"How he know?"

"When I called him, he would sit on the phone and let that shit out. I listened... that's all you can do sometimes. Someone grieving don't want you to have all the answers... they just want a listening ear and a shoulder. Let them sit in their pain for a bit. Sometimes that's the only thing they have left to hold onto from the person they lost." I hugged my father tighter as the tears fell from my eyes. He kissed the top of my head. "I haven't always been before, but I'm always going to be here... you don't hurt one of mine and live to speak about the shit."

"Unc, you said we would watch Sonic." CJ stood at the door. "Chubs, what's the matter?"

I sniffled. "I'm good, CJ."

CJ didn't look too convinced, so he walked over toward us,

and leaned on his uncle. "Smooth cat, tell me what makes a man."

"Always taking care of his family," CJ recited back.

"What else?"

"Taking accountability for his actions."

"What else... come on lay it on us."

"Showing emotion. You can't be a man without showing emotions... that's what makes you, you. It's what makes you strong." CJ put his hand on mine. "When I fell during football and cried, Daddy pulled me to the side to hug me and then told me what I had to do."

"What's that?" Capp asked, I could hear the smile in his voice.

"Go beast mode."

"My man... go grab the candy and I'm coming."

"Jaiden cried, too, at his championship game."

"Now why you telling my business? I came over here to watch Sonic and you spilling our secrets." CJ laughed then ran into the house.

I broke down crying so hard that my head started to hurt, and Capp never let me go.

My pops never let me go.

15
KENDRA

THIS WAS the first time that I was seeing Cappadonna since he tossed Ace off the balcony at the club. Being at my aunt's funeral wasn't the place I wanted it to be. I watched as he and Alaia walked into the church hand in hand, dark shades hiding his eyes. They looked so good together that it made me physically sick. He held onto Capella's shoulder, as he stared straight ahead. I couldn't see his eyes because he also wore shades, too.

Here I was supposed to be mourning my aunt, and I was mourning the fact that I would never have him like that again. He would never look at me like I was his whole world, and he damn sure wouldn't give a fuck if I burst into flames. Cappadonna wouldn't use the last of his piss to help me if I was on fire.

He was so gentle with her, making sure that she was guided the entire time. When they filed into the pew, he didn't sit until she did. Even then, he leaned forward to whisper something in her ear. His hand never moved from hers, and I wanted that.

The feeling of being protected by a man that loved you was

everything. I felt that feeling many times with Capp, even when he was locked up. Do you know how strong of a presence that you had to have, to have your woman still feel protected even while locked up? For Cappadonna, it was nothing.

Now, I was standing here watching him give that love and protection to another woman. I just knew he was fucking her every way from here to the moon. Capp's dick was so good, and even though it had been a while since I had it, I could still remember that slight curve at the tip.

"Hey, they are about to start," Jasmine whispered, as she took my hand, and we walked past everyone to sit in the front pew. Capella was already seated and stood when he saw me and Jasmine. He hugged Jasmine, giving her a kiss on her head. I expected him to ignore me, but when he pulled me into a hug, I melted.

He sat in the middle of us, and we all held hands as the pastor spoke. My aunt had known the pastor since they were kids, so the stories he shared with us made us cry more and even laugh a bit. He spoke to the kind of woman she was, and everything he said about her was the truth. Francie Ross was a good woman, the best woman.

She didn't agree with how I chose to live my life, but never turned me away. Always made sure my son was good and encouraged our relationship. I could still remember sitting in her kitchen with Capella in my lap, begging her to raise him because I knew I would do a bad job.

When she should have turned me away, her door was always opened for me. Francie and my grandmother showed me exactly what love was like. Kalisa quietly took a seat beside me, reaching across me to squeeze Capella's hand.

"Traffic getting here was crazy. I had to pick your mother up," she whispered.

Anytime we spoke about our mother, she was always *your* mother. "Then where is she?"

Kalisa sighed. "You'll hear her."

No sooner than the words left her mouth we heard a loud wail from behind us. Everybody turned in the church to watch my mother, stumbling down the aisle in a black tweed two-piece skirt set, pill box hat and a dramatic ass black veil covering her face. The Chanel bag sat on her arm as she held the tissue to her face.

The black tissue looked more like a prop than actual tissue. The bitch looked like she was coming to bury Martin Luther King, not her sister. I covered my face and looked away because I knew she would find some way to make this about her.

Everything was always about Frankie.

"My sis...big sis," she croaked as she walked up to the casket, tossing herself and bag across it while the pastor looked on in horror.

I looked at my own sister and she looked away. "I got her ass here... you get her."

I've never been so embarrassed as I was in this moment. Standing up, I walked over toward her and patted her back. "It's alright, Mom... come sit so the pastor can finish."

"Francie, girl, I know we haven't always saw eye to eye."

"Mom," I whispered harshly. "People are staring at us."

She lifted her head and looked me in the eyes. "I don't give a fuck about any of these people. My sister is dead."

I bit the inside of my cheek as I tried to contain my anger. "This is typical for you to make everything about yourself," I whispered before returning back to my seat.

Capone, Erin, Cappadonna, Alaia, and Kincaid were seated behind us. Capp had his hands on his son's shoulders rubbing them. I plopped back down, crossing my legs as we all watched her do her performance.

After clearing his throat three times, she finally got the hint and then sat down next to Kalisa. I rolled my eyes, pissed that she decided to throw a show like the one she had. Frankie was always used to having everything about her.

She couldn't take a fucking funeral not being about her. When the pastor finished talking, he opened the floor for Capella to speak. Jasmine didn't want to speak, and when I looked over at her, Kincaid was whispering something in her ear while she was trying hard not to break down.

Cappadonna's cologne caressed my nose when I felt him shuffle through the pew to stand behind his son. Capella turned to say something to his father, and he whispered in his ear, giving his shoulder a reassuring squeeze.

"I hate that we even have to be here today. If I know my aunt, she would have been pissed we made a big fuss over her death." Everyone laughed because that was Francie. She never wanted anyone to make a big fuss out of anything. "I miss her so much that it hurts when I think about it for too long. Francie, Ma, as I called her, was my entire world. She raised me the same as she raised Jasmine. Jas is my cousin, but we felt like siblings with the way I used to get on her nerves."

I love you, Jas mouthed to Capella.

"It's hard to sit here and pretend that I'm going to be alright when I know I won't. Francie prepared me for everything else, except for how to live with her being gone. I love you, Ma, and I will see you again... keep my side of the couch warm up there." He kissed his hand and then waved it to the coffin sitting in front of him.

I felt a hand rubbing my back as I sobbed and turned to see Erin. She offered me a weakened smile and continued to rub my back while I broke down. Francie was a constant in all of our lives. You knew you could always go to her house because she would be there.

If there was one person I could always depend on, it was my aunt. Capella returned to his seat and hugged Jasmine. The rest of the funeral was a blur, especially when Frankie went up there to give a speech.

I couldn't tell you a word she said because I had tapped out after I heard my son. After I heard how much pain he was in, and it was because of a man that I married. A man that I thought I could love.

"Give me a reason why the fuck I shouldn't snap your fucking neck?" Capp asked soon as we stepped out the hospital room.

I took a large gulp and looked up at him. There used to be a time when I could bat my eyelashes and he would be like putty in my hands. He'd call me spoiled, kiss me on the lips and give me whatever it was that I wanted.

As he stood with his legs shoulder length apart and his hands folded, I was almost certain he wanted to crack my jaw with the way he was staring down at me.

"I had nothing to do with him... I would never."

"You would never ride another dick, but here we fucking are, Kendra."

I ran my hand through my hair, sweat pouring down my damn face. "I swear to God. Do you really think I'm that heartless? I know I've done some shit, but to know about my son being harmed and not say anything... you think that less of me."

"In my eyes you a fucking liar, so yeah. Actually, walk with me up to the roof real quick," he said casually, as if he wasn't trying to get me up there to push me off.

My eyes nearly jumped out of my head, and I backed away from him because the look in his eyes told me that he wasn't joking with me. "Cappadonna, seriously? What do I have to do? I swear I am loyal to you... I love you."

"Nah, you not loyal to me or never loved me. You loved what I did for you... I mean, I get it."

"Capp, you can't possibly believe that I never loved you."

He sighed, like I was boring him with this conversation. "Honestly, I don't care if you did or didn't. Even sitting here discussing it while my woman out in the waiting room is disrespectful. Kendra, stop wasting my fucking time... what the fuck do you want?"

"I love you. I don't care if you believe it or not, I loved you with everything inside of me. What can I do to prove that I loved you and I am loyal. I had nothing to do with that," I pleaded for my life.

Even though he was standing here talking to me, and there were too many witnesses for him to do what he really wanted to do, I knew Capp, and I knew he could get me other ways.

"I don't give a fuck about you proving that you loved me. Bring me that nigga, and I'll consider allowing you to breathe the same air as me."

My hands shook. "O...Okay, I promise, I promise."

"Hey. The service is over," Kalisa gently shook me.

I looked around and everyone was either up talking or filing out the church. Cappadonna was talking with Capella and the pastor. Alaia stood next to him, holding onto him for dear life. It wasn't her hand on him that caught my attention, it was that big ass ring sitting on her ring finger.

I felt lightheaded and held onto the end of the pew. He proposed to her and had her rocking a big ass ring. I've been with this man all of these years and he never proposed to me. Every time I mentioned it to him on a visit, he always told me he wanted to do it when he was out.

When he pulled up on me at the hair salon, that should have been the moment he dropped down on one knee and proposed to me. I deserved to be his wife, not this young bitch that he barely even knew.

Was it because she was Muslim like him? Because she dressed modest, and I refused to do it. If I had known a ring that big would have been in my future, I would have put on a damn Barney outfit if he asked me to.

"Thank you for coming to the service, Cappadonna," the pastor said, and Frankie paused, backtracking to where they were.

"*The* Cappadonna?"

I put my hand over my face and considered diving into the casket next to my aunt. "How you doing, Frankie?"

Capp and my mother never met; however, he knew all about her. I never really spoke about my upbringing because it triggered me. I knew I should have been sitting on someone's couch discussing it.

"Well, it is not every day that I get to meet my daughter's boyfriend. Come give your mother-in-law a hug."

Capp looked like he wanted to throw up. The displeasure was all in his face, and Alaia peeped it because she rubbed his forearm gently. That's when my mother looked at her with a stank face on.

"I promise I'm good," he told Alaia.

"What the hell is going on?" my mom's eyes finally landed one me, then looked to Alaia and then Capp. "Oh, wait. You are Muslim." She snapped her fingers. "So, is this your first wife?" she pointed to Alaia, and I couldn't move.

I wanted to football tackle her like the winning touchdown at the Superbowl, but I couldn't move. Jasmine held my hand, as she looked at me just as horrified as I was. "This is my *only* wife." Capp shook the pastor's hand, hugged his son, and then held the small of Alaia's back as they headed toward the front of the church.

There was something about a tatted nigga in an expensive suit that just did something to me. His hands, neck and face was tatted, and here he was putting even the flashiest businessman to shame with that suit.

"What the fuck was that all about?"

"You minding your fucking business and going to whoever bed you came from," I snorted, shoving past her.

"Little bitch don't get mad because that man is in here with that woman, and not you. I saw the ring, too... nice and big. Where the fuck is yours?"

I couldn't deal with this right now, not at my aunt's funeral. How was she making this about her when she barely came around. I stood at the top of the stairs of the church and paused when I saw all the motorcycles and dirt bikes posted up. Ace would be a fool if he tried to come by here and do something.

Cappadonna and Capone had both of their whips parked in front of the church. I watched as they both put Erin and Alaia into the car. Capp bent down and kissed Alaia a few times, and I wanted to fucking cry.

How much could a girl take today?

He and Capone met up at the back of his car and talked before dapping and walking to their cars.

The walk.

It was a mix between a swagger and bop, especially Cappadonna's. His bow-legged stance made me wet watching him. He took his suit jacket off, and I noticed his gun tucked in the back of his slacks. He nodded to Quasim, who was sitting on his bike waiting for anything to pop off.

Soon as his ass touched the seat, he sped off the block with his twin following right behind him. I stood there trying to keep myself from breaking out in tears because this was karma. The prize for waiting fifteen years was sitting in the front seat with him.

Being loved the way he was loving her. I'm sure he was wearing her ass out and I was sad thinking about it. Imagine being able to walk around and say that your man was

Cappadonna? I used to be envied by bitches, and now I was one of the bitches that I used to call jealous hoes.

'Cause I envied Alaia.

A wave of nausea hit me, and I held onto the banister. If I didn't have enough going on, I had to deal with the fact that I had a positive pregnancy test in my purse.

16
ACE

WHEN THAT SUPER nigga tossed me over the fucking banister, I had suffered another concussion. Thankfully, I was so damn high that I didn't feel anything for the next few days. Monty took me to the hospital after leaving the club, and that's when I found out I had a fucking concussion.

I had been sitting back trying to figure out my next move. When his ass showed up at the club, I didn't expect his ass to do anything. Clearly that bullshit rule of Switzerland with the Cromwell-Vanducci family didn't mean anything because he clearly tossed my ass over the balcony and Karter threatened to put a bullet in whoever's head that tried to help me.

Monty didn't come and help me until he was gone and the damn lights in the club had been turned on. I was tired of this bitch ass nigga fucking around with me, and thinking he was untouchable.

He moved like he was God, and it was time for somebody to humble his ass. I leaned back on the couch and watched *Different World* reruns when I heard the lock in the front door turn. Grabbing my gun, I was ready for whoever walked through that damn door.

"What the fuck, Ace?" Kendra hollered when she noticed me aiming a gun at the front door. If she hadn't screamed, I probably would have shot her thinking she was somebody else.

This coke had my head on a swivel, and I was suspicious about every damn body, including my wife. Her ass been everywhere but over here in the crib that I was paying for.

"Oh, you remember that you live here?" I tucked the gun back in the couch and kicked my feet back up.

"You can't expect me to just leave my cousin high and dry." She put her bags down, and went into the kitchen to wash her hands.

"You coming back home? I can use some pussy." I damn near snapped my neck when it sounded like she made a gagging noise. When I looked at her, she was looking down with hyper focus at her hands filled with suds. "You good back there?"

"Yes. Just have a lot going on right now... and I'm still staying with my cousin. She needs me right now."

"I fucking need you... when the fuck do I start to matter, Kendra?"

I could see how annoyed she was in the face as she dried her hands and grabbed her bags. "I can spend the night, then I need to go back over there. My family needs me right now, and I expected you to understand."

"Since when you give a fuck about your family? All I've ever heard you say is how you don't fuck with them, and now you over here being family of the year."

She went into the bedroom and sat her stuff down on the couch in the room. I could see she was trying not to argue with me, and that pissed me off even more. I wanted the Kendra that wanted to argue and then fuck right after we finished calling each other everything but a child of God.

"My aunt just fucking died because of you. Do you really think I should even be talking to you? You're lucky that you're able to even call me your fucking wife."

"Bitch, you failed to tell me that he was your son. Stop putting that shit on me like I was supposed to know. I thought he was some random ass nigga that ran with your ex."

"That's the difference between you and him... he does his research and would have never made a mistake like that."

This bitch just hurt my fucking feelings and was going on like she didn't say some foul shit to me. I had half the mind to slap the shit out of her, but calmed myself down before I caught a case.

"Yet you were fucking me."

"Because he was in prison. Had he been out, this pussy would have only been reserved for him." She rolled her neck. Something changed in her eyes, and she sighed, plopping down on the bed. "I'm sorry... I didn't mean that. Everything has me tossed and turned everywhere."

I sat down beside her, even though my feelings were still hurt. Despite how fucked up I was, I felt bad for her aunt. I could have easily shot her too and decided not to and focused on Chubs. How the fuck was I supposed to know she was going to grab her chest and die.

It was pretty dramatic if you asked me.

Gpops: I got the drop on him... come by my crib when you get the chance.

My God father used to run these same streets with my father. He was retired and out the way now, so when I had nobody to turn to, I turned to him, and he put me onto shit I was oblivious to.

Me: bet

"You need to stop fighting me and let your husband be there for you." I put my arm around her, and noticed how tense she was when I touched her.

Kendra had never been like that, and I wasn't going to say Cappadonna was the reason either. Even after he came home and we linked, she wasn't as tense as she was now.

"I have so much going on right now."

"Talk to me then, Kendra. Why the fuck you acting like you don't got me."

She took a deep breath. "You're going to die, and I have to look out for me... Cappadonna isn't playing around with either of us, and I need to stay in his good graces."

I mushed her so hard she had slid off the silky ass blanket she insisted we have on the bed. "What the fuck do you mean I'm going to die? Kendra, why the fuck do you keep trying me? Every time I give you a chance, you have some crazy shit to say."

"I'm being realistic. Do you honestly believe you will win going toe to toe with him? Cappadonna is a fucking lunatic, and he goes far to prove a point and erase people. I've heard," she broke out into tears, clearly scared that his ass was going to pop her ass. "He thinks I had something to do with Chubs being shot... I would never."

"Let him believe whatever the fuck he wanna believe. You riding for me, Kendra. It's my job to protect you."

She snatched her hand away from me. "You can't even protect yourself, Ace! He tossed you off the second floor of the fucking club! How the fuck you gonna protect us?"

She slapped her hand onto her mouth when she looked at me. "Us?"

"I'm pregnant," she sighed.

It made a lot of sense why her ass was so damn fucking

crazy and acting out. It was the hormones. “You about to have a nigga’s baby?”

“Unfortunately,” she muttered.

“The fuck you said, Kendra?”

“I don’t want another kid, but I don’t know maybe this will keep me alive.” The fact that she was using our baby as a fucking bullet proof vest pissed me off.

“I’m going to handle everything. Don’t worry.”

She didn’t look convinced as she unpacked her bags and then repacked them with more clothes. I needed to handle Capp if I had any chance of getting my wife back under the same roof as me.

17
CAPPADONNA

"Good morning, Baby. I didn't get to see you before you woke up, you know Daddy love you. Wanted you to hear my voice when you woke up. I'm handling something before vacation... then you got my full attention. This shit could have been a text, but I know you be liking to hear your man's voice in the morning and I'm sorry I wasn't there this morning. Kiss my daughter for me and know that I love the shit out of you. See you later, Sweet Joy."

Everybody in the warehouse stared at me, including Quasim. "Nigga, you pacing and leaving voicemails like we not in the middle of some shit."

I looked down at my phone, pressing the number one to make sure my baby got that message. "You lucky I finished recording before you said all that shit... the fuck you want me to do? I missed my wife, so I was fucking letting her know it."

"Lovesick ass... she got you bad, C. You really going to marry her in Barbados?"

"Is the sky blue?" I couldn't wait to make Alaia my wife, and I didn't give a fuck who had anything to say about it.

When I told her that she was mine, I meant that. I refused to keep her in limbo on where we stood. Delgato men married the women they loved. I didn't need a few years to decide whether I wanted her to be my wife. She was the mother to my daughter, and I would be damned if I didn't honor her by giving her my last name.

Quasim chuckled. "I'm happy for you though. Alaia is good peoples, and I can see she makes you happy. Happier than you know who ever did." He then turned his attention to the little nigga with his mouth wide open while trembling.

"Oh shit... lemme pull that wisdom tooth out."

I took the pliers from homie's shaking hand and pulled his head back. After the whole Sarge bullshit, I came home and wasn't letting shit fly. Forty called me and told me about some little nigga that had gotten caught up, and he decided to use my name as his bargaining chip. I didn't take well to somebody trying to take my fucking freedom away because they didn't move smart.

"Argh...I...Di." He couldn't finish his sentence because he passed out while I held his head back and ripped his back tooth out his fucking mouth, blood filling up in his mouth.

I reached for the ammonia patch and waved it under his nose, and he jumped out his damn skin. "Whatever happened to holding it down. When I got knocked, I didn't even think about turning nobody the fuck in for my freedom."

Forty had worked it where homie got bail and he was back on the streets for me to grab his ass up. I couldn't respect a snitch, not when you asked to be part of this life. It wasn't like Capone was out there with flyers looking for block boys. When I got knocked, all I could do is blame myself because I asked for this life.

Yeah, I could have turned Trilla's big ass in and been out on the streets. However, I didn't operate like that. I ran with him on my own free will, so I wasn't going to fucking turn him in because I had to sit my ass down.

My biggest mistake was going to fucking trial instead of just taking the five years they offered in the plea deal. You live and learn, and I fucking learned a lot in those fifteen years. Like how to nip the problem soon as it rises.

"Niggas not built like that anymore," one of the young heads said, as he and the rest of them watched.

I walked over to him, and cupped his cheek, my hand full of the blood from this whining nigga behind me. "Then get the fuck from around me. You get knocked, you sit down and do your fucking time, and if I like you enough, I may toss some money at a lawyer for you. Mention me or my twin's name, and I can promise that your mama will be floating in that nice ass pond she got in her backyard."

He gulped. "You right... I'm always gonna hold it down."

I got so close to his face that I'm sure he could smell the fucking beet smoothie I had earlier. "You fucking better."

Quasim looked up from his phone. "Yo, got the word."

I went back and finished pulling the rest of this nigga's teeth out the back of his mouth. "I remember when I asked my moms for that Playdoh dentist head shit when I was a kid. She told me no because that meant she had to buy two... I could have been a fucking dentist... nigga, you don't floss?" I slapped his face up and his eyes tried to focus on me. "You need to take care of your fucking teeth... flossing is important. Matter fact, I want all you niggas to buy floss and start using that shit. If you can't floss, I can't fucking trust you."

While everybody, aside from Quasim was covering their mouth and looking away, I was too interested in knowing what was more important in this man's life than picking up some fucking floss. He had passed out a few times, so I put the plastic bag over his head and kicked the chair over.

Quasim followed behind me as I washed my hands in the sink. "I can do this on my own."

He laughed. "I'm fucking there... you already know."

"Bet."

"You heard from Alaia's friend lately?"

"Who Blair?"

My baby didn't have any friends aside from Erin and Capri, and even then, they were family, not friends. Blair was her only friend that she spoke to occasionally.

"Yeah. Just wanted to see if she was good."

I smirked. "You feeling Blair, nigga? I'll link that up for you... look at me... a fucking dentist and matchmaker... I can vouch your pockets is straight... Blair own her own business and shit, can't be with no fucking bum... feel me?"

"Yo chill the fuck out. I'm just asking if she's good." Quasim laughed.

Naheim came swaggering through the door. "I put you on the list... shit wasn't easy, and the warden wasn't a big fan of you gracing his prison as a free man."

"Cause that bitch scared. When I come back from Barbados, I'll handle that situation." I never thought I would be taking a visit back up to that prison, but this visit was important.

"Capp, go up there and don't start no shit... I hate that warden, too, but you see how I was in and out when I visited you."

"You and me aren't the same person. I never start no shit; I always finish it."

Naheim shook his head and leaned on the wall. "You packed yet?"

"Alaia packed for me... came home and she was folding my draws."

Naheim laughed. "I miss when Capri used to do small shit

like that. You don't realize just how much the small shit matters until it's not there anymore."

I dried my hands. "Yeah, well, you the stupid ass that fucked that up... now you gotta fold your own shitty draws."

What the fuck he wanted me to do? Sit here and feel bad for him? He made his bed and now his ass had to lay in that shit. In my opinion, he was lucky that Capri was so involved in NJ's life. She was a good person and knew how distant Naheim was with his own family.

"We heading out?"

"Where the fuck has Kincaid been?"

Naheim sighed. "With Chub's cousin. She hasn't been taking her mother's death too good, so he been there for her."

I was surprised and a little proud of him for not using this as his chance to toss Kincaid under the bus. "That better be all he fucking doing."

"Nah. It's not like that between them... he really just being there for her. Him and Capri been going through their own shit... she came over to the crib yesterday to climb in NJ crib, and said that they broke up or some shit."

"Yo ol happy ass was probably laying across your bed kicking your feet in the air while planning your second wedding." I clowned him because I knew how much he wanted Capri back.

"She been hanging out with Quameer lately," Quasim mentioned his brother, and I looked at him and then Naheim.

"Oh fuck nah."

On the way out the warehouse, I called my sister. "Hey Cappy... what's up?"

I moved away from Naheim and Quasim and put the phone close to my mouth. "Baby Doll, you better not be out there hopping from homie to homie... the fuck you think this is? A soul train line filled with hood niggas for your choosing?"

"What are you even talking about, Cappadonna?"

"It got back to me that you been hanging with Quameer's ol' touched in the head ass. Did we not love you enough, Baby Doll? Did Pops not hug you enough... why the fuck you keep going for these crazier than a muthafucka niggas?"

Capri broke out into laughter. "You ask this as if you're not fucking bat shit crazy yourself. Or like Capone isn't damn near the same, although, I have to admit, Capone isn't as bad as your crazy ass. He can probably take some pills and be good, you need to be locked away in a ward somewhere."

"Ha fucking ha... you a grown woman and I don't get involved in your shit."

"Then don't, Cappadonna. I am grown and last I checked I can do and see whoever I want."

I looked at the phone. "Capri, I'll come shove my foot up yo ass. Don't fucking piss me off!" I roared.

"Capp, me, and Quameer are cool. I'm not fucking him or even in a relationship with him. Me and Kincaid are having growing pains."

"Take some fucking Tylenol and fix the shit!" I yelled, ended the call.

The fuck she meant by saying growing pains? She better had fixed that shit and continued being with her damn man. I wasn't about to have my sister out here fucking all the homies. Quameer was cool people, but Capri needed to get her shit straight.

I understood that Naheim fucked up and she was having trouble figuring out what she wanted, but hopping from one nigga to the next wasn't going to solve that shit. I hopped in my whip and waited for Quasim to get in before we went to make rounds. Quasim didn't have shit to do with the rounds I was making, but he liked to come along as company. His vampire ass needed to get out the house while the sun was still out, anyway.

Later on that night, we pulled up to a nice brick house in Long Island. The flowers were perfect, the yard was trimmed perfectly, and they even had an American flag outside.

How fucking sweet.

I pulled around the block, parking out the way of any of the houses that more than likely had cameras outside to protect their home. Me and Quasim breezed down the block, staying within the shadows. When we came up on the house, I could see a woman washing dishes while laughing on the phone.

Quasim looked at me and I nodded. He kicked the back door opened and the woman dropped her phone into the dish water and screamed. "Shut the fuck up," I said through gritted teeth, knocking her across the face with the gun.

With the force I could have used, she would have been over the kitchen table. I didn't even use that much force and her dramatic ass was all on the floor. "What in the fuc—"

Mel's ass was knocked over the head when he entered the kitchen, not even knowing Quasim was standing by the pantry. I was always a big fan of hustlers getting out the game and living they best life.

Watering their grass, raising they kids, and doing regular law-abiding citizen shit. I was only a fan when they liked to mind they business. They truly left the streets behind and kept the code of minding they business. "Mel, you been running that mouth of yours."

"Who the fuck is you?" he spat, looking up.

I snatched my mask off and kicked his ass in the chest with my boot. "You know who the fuck I am. I'm wondering why the fuck my business is on the tip of your tongue. Why the fuck are you telling that crackhead of a god son my shit?"

"Capp.... Me, you, and Wink go way back... we go back." He spit blood on my boot and coughed.

Mel and Wink were both locked up with me. When I got there, they had already been there. They were considered the old heads that kept to themselves. Always playing cards or shooting the breeze with each other. Eventually Mel had gotten out, and Wink remained. I think that nigga had life or something like that. All I knew is that he was in there when I first got in there, and his ass was still there, and I had gone home.

Wink was the person who introduced me to Islam. I learned everything about it from him, and how to control my anger. I had converted and loved my religion because of what Wink had taught me. It was funny when Naheim put me onto who Ace's father was, and as Allah would have it, it was fucking Wink.

"We don't go back enough for you to be fucking with my family. All you had to do was keep your mouth shut about my business. You over there running your mouth about my shit, and now look at you."

Mel realized there was no other way he was coming out of this alive. "Fuck you!" He spit on my boot again.

This is why I wanted to chill when I came home. I didn't have the fucking patience for the back and forth like I used to. "Do what you gotta do," I told Quasim as I made my way through the house.

He was watching fucking bowling on TV, and his phone was sitting right beside the recliner he had to have been sitting in when we kicked the back door in. Plopping down in the chair, I looked at his choice of snacks and passed on a few of them.

I didn't fuck with gummy bears because that shit had gelatin in it. I scooped some of the popcorn into my hand and popped a piece in my mouth while pulling up Ace's name. Before calling him, I checked the text messages between them, and smiled when I saw the last message Mel's old ass sent his precious crack head.

Imagine having the drop on me and I drop by your fucking crib. I tried to be better, and these niggas always tried me. I pressed the facetime button and reclined in the chair.

"What's happening, Me—"

"Ah, what up, Pussy? His words were caught in his fucking chest, and his face did very little to hide that he wasn't scared shitless. "Being pussy caught your tongue."

"Why the fuck you got my God father's phone?" he paused. "Why the fuck you sitting in his fucking house?" The nigga's voice was on the verge of hysterical.

I laughed. "That's what the fuck you do when you collect souls, Ace-y bear. I can work my way down the list, or you can come to me... your choice... you know where I am."

"Where the fuck is my God mother?"

"Oh wait... one sec... hold on bro," I chuckled and walked back into the kitchen, and peeped Quasim pulling his God mother next to his God father. "Aw man... dammit. One sec." I flipped the camera around and showed him his God parents on the kitchen floor.

"What the fuck? Yo, I'm gonna ki—"

"Let me stop you there... I'm only doing you a favor. I'm showing you how the fuck you finish a fucking job. One thing I'm always going to do is finish the fucking job, pussy."

"F...fuck you."

"This nigga here," Quasim sucked his teeth when Mel choked out the words.

I held my hand up, lifted his head and did what I had to do. He choked for a bit, before he went peacefully. I looked down at my bloodied boots and tossed the phone on top of his sleeping god father. I had to admit, that old bitch still had a lot of heart.

We left as quietly as we came, without anybody seeing us. I made a mental reminder to watch the news in the morning.

By the time I made it back home, it was a little after two in the morning. The house was quiet, so I was careful not to wake everybody in the house up. Alaia was a light sleeper whenever I wasn't in the bed with her. I was still in the garage, leaning against the work bench that I had just stored my gun in. I had guns all over the house but kept the piece I wore out the house in the garage.

I never took taking a life lightly. At the end of the day, I stepped in and played Allah, and that wasn't my place. I was at a crossroads between doing what was right and protecting mine. Mel was from New York, Ace was not.

He knew the ins and outs about everybody and some of the shit Ace knew, he could have only gotten from him. He was a liability that I needed to handle before shit became out of control. Did a piece of me smile because I knew I took someone from Ace?

Fuck yeah.

"Baby?"

My back was to the garage door. "What up, Joy?"

I could hear slippers sliding across the floor. Closing my eyes, I muttered fuck because I didn't want her to see me like this. I had blood on my shirt and on my boots.

I would have usually been stripped and on my way upstairs, but I had gotten in my head. "Are you mad with me?"

Fuck.

I turned around, and she looked up into my eyes, not even paying the blood any attention. "Why would you think that?"

"Your tone."

I quickly took my shirt off so I could pull her into my arms. "I'm not mad with you. I was thinking about something."

"Is everything alright? You know you can talk to me, right?"

I kissed her lips. "You don't need to worry yourself with this." She looked down at my boots, and then at the shirt with blood on it. "You trust me?"

"With everything."

"Whenever you do my laundry… even if you see a small speck of blood, destroy it."

She wrapped her arms around me. "And your shoes?"

"Burn 'em."

"Got it."

"Give me kiss." She stood on her toes and kissed me on the lips. "I love you… I'm always going to do what I have to do to protect this family. I'm never going to apologize about the shit I have to do."

"I would never ask you to… I can and will play my part so that you can protect this family." We kept our eye contact until I kissed her on the nose, and we got rid of the shirt and my boots together.

I CLAPPED MY HANDS, laughing when I saw Aimee sitting at the counter with another shorty. A shorty that was very familiar and almost unrecognizable with clothes on and glasses on.

"What are the fucking odds that you know this chick?"

Aimee looked like she had done something wrong. "I…I asked Alaia if it was alright, and she said it was fine."

I wasn't worried about shorty coming to my house. She was harmless and came from a small family in Michigan. Her father was a preacher, and her mother a schoolteacher. Which is why I found it funny she was fucking in a trap house when her parents had done their best to raise her opposite of the hood.

I did my research on every fucking body, and she was in such a hurry she left her purse in the backroom. After taking her ID, I had Forty run her name for me, so I could keep an eye on her. I was so proud of myself because Capp in the past would have put one in her forehead but look at me growing.

"Aimee, you didn't tell me..." she didn't finish her words because she was hopping off the stool and trying to gather her things.

"Didn't tell you what?" I walked into the kitchen and leaned against the counter.

She gulped, holding her bag. "That this was your house."

"Why would she tell you that?"

"I...I can leave. I promise I'm not here for any problems. I broke up with my ex-boyfriend... I'm in school." She was rambling and I motioned for her to shut the hell up.

"Let me see those grades... 'cause I told you I would see you again." Did I know she was going to be in my kitchen today?

Nah.

She didn't need to know that. I was glad that she broke up with scary ass and valued herself. I watched as she grabbed her phone and scrolled, walking over to show me the phone. I grabbed my reading glasses from the kitchen draw beside me and put them on while scrolling through her grades.

"Dean's list, hmm."

"Yes. I'm actually very proud."

"As you should be." She reached for the phone, and I snatched it back. "Don't be fucking in a trap house... date a man that's gonna value and respect you." As if on cue, my baby walked in from the garage. I moved toward her, dropping a kiss on her nose. "Like my baby. She don't even know what the inside of a trap look like and she would never. I only bring her to places where she can't see the fucking ceiling... feel me?" I looked down at her. "Where my daughter, Joy?"

She shook her head. "With your mother... I didn't know if you had something to do, so I asked her to watch her."

"I can watch my daughter. I'm never too busy for either of you... remember that." She reached up to kiss me on the lips, then headed upstairs.

She was going out with Capri and Erin. I watched as she switched up them steps, knowing she was putting an extra pep in her step on purpose. "Umm."

Shorty brought me back to what I was doing. "What's your name again?"

"Again? I never gave it to you." I stared at her waiting for her to tell me. "Sk...Skyler... me and Aimee used to have classes together."

"Used to?"

"I dropped out," Aimee admitted.

"Hmm."

"I had a lot going on and had to drop classes."

I laughed. "So much going on with my son, huh?"

Rory started crying and I walked over to pick him up. I had only picked him up once before and that was because Aimee had went to shower and thought he was asleep. She watched me as I carefully picked him up.

"I'm thinking about going back though."

"Thinking?"

"Yeah... considering it, I guess."

I bounced him as I walked back to my spot in the kitchen. "My sister graduated from college and then law school. I don't know what the fuck she does these days besides ride motorcycles, but she got those degrees to fall back onto."

"You think I should go back?"

I looked at her. "This why you need to go back... I just said... never mind, you need to enroll back into school."

"What about Rory? I would have to find a sitter, and then—"

"You had a baby by a Delgato... those problems don't exist. It will be figured out. Talk it over with your man though. Not trying to step on his toes, even though you need to be back in school."

Skyler stood there. "You keep out them damn traps, too."

She smiled. "I will... thanks, Mr. Capp."

I bit the inside of my cheek. "Just Capp."

First those two wanted to make me a damn grandpa, and now she had her friend calling me fucking Mr. Capp. What the fuck had my life turned into?

18
Alaia

"You gonna try that on? It's cute, and they have your size, too," Erin encouraged me to try on a long-sleeved maxi dress. "It's cute, and it's modest, too. I know you said Capp was fine with your forearms showing."

I was still trying to find my style when it came to modest dressing. It was hard when you saw all the cute things that women wore with their skin showing, like what Erin was picking up. Then I thought about how that man looked at me when he saw me dressed up. His entire world stopped, and he took every part of me in, so much so that I felt like the sexiest woman on the planet.

We were in TJ Maxx grabbing some last-minute things before we went to Barbados. I was scanning the aisle, unsure of what I wanted to buy. I had gotten mostly everything that me and Promise would need for the trip. Erin had given me some hand me downs that Cee-Cee couldn't fit anymore, so that helped a lot.

It helped that I loved how she dressed her daughter, so I was grateful for the clothes she had given to me. "Is it so hard to find me a good man?" Capri plopped down on the small, cushioned chair in the aisle.

"Don't you have a man, Capri?" Erin asked, still going through the aisles of clothes. I wasn't sure what the hell she was looking for because she said she already had two suitcases.

"Me and Kincaid are on a break right now."

"Who asked for the break?" Erin asked, her eyebrow raised, as she held up a multicolored maxi dress that complimented her well.

"Me. I needed some space... well, he was giving me space, but I thought by asking for it that he would change. Ever since his ex-girlfriend moved back, he's been occupied with her."

"She lost her mom, Capri," I reminded her.

"Which I am sorry about. It's not even her really... Kincaid has never let her go. He still has pictures of them in his living room. A fridge magnet that is peeling from Coney Island from years ago. It never bothered me because she was gone with the wind, now that she's back, I can tell that things with us has changed."

"You know what I think?" Erin leaned against the mirror. "The thrill of sneaking around has died down and now a real relationship is where you both are. You're scared, Capri."

"I am not scared. Just tired of feeling like I'm getting in the way of his happiness with her. Maybe it was meant for them to have this second chance... I'm a sucker for a second chance situation."

"Of course you are. Which is why you spent the night over at Naheim's house the other night," Erin pointed out.

Capri rolled her eyes. "I slept in the baby's room all night... I just didn't want to be alone that night."

"Maybe that's the problem, Capri. You need to learn how to be alone for a while. Love Naheim but running back to him isn't going to solve your problems. I mean, you can do therapy and all of the necessary stuff to make it work, however, the pain you both caused each other is there. It will be there when NJ becomes of age and wants to know who his mother is. What happens if Tasha wins her appeal?"

Capri sucked her teeth. "She has better luck playing in traffic than winning that appeal." She waved off the conversation about her ex-best friend.

"What about Quameer?" I reminded her of their little interaction at Capp and Capone's birthday party.

"Did you snitch to my brother, Alaia?"

I stared at her confused. "Why would I tell him about your personal business?"

"Then who the fuck told him about Quameer. He called himself trying to check me about talking to him...we're not even on speaking terms right now." Capri rolled her eyes.

"What is this thing with Quameer, Capri? Why do you have a thing for dreadheads... Naheim don't even have locs."

"Good!" she snapped. "Me and Quameer are just cool... I swear we're not messing around; I have a huge crush on him... always have," she blushed.

"Quameer is cute... you might need therapy because you keep going for the loc'd and unhinged." Erin laughed.

"We're just friends and it's gonna stay like that. Qua has too many hoes." She rolled her eyes and checked her phone.

"I'll be back... going to the bathroom." I left my purse in the cart and went to go pee. Erin continued to lecture Capri on not pursuing something with Quameer in my absence.

I usually hated to use public bathrooms, but this TJ Maxx was on the fancy side. It was only a couple miles from the lake house. After washing my hands, I left the bathroom and bumped into a hardened chest.

"Sorry," I apologized expecting the other person to move,

and they remained in my way. “Um, excuse me,” I raised my voice, knowing that sometimes my voice was low.

“Alaia, you looking good.” I didn’t recognize the voice.

I finally got the nerve to look up at the light skin man with beard stubble and yellow teeth. He didn’t look familiar, so how did he know my name? “I don’t know you.”

“That may be true... I know you though.”

“Can you move the fuck out my way.” My heart slammed against my chest, and I was becoming nervous.

“Please don’t make me pull this trigger in this store... I promise you will never walk again.” I heard Capri’s voice and looked around him and saw her holding her gun in his back.

He backed up, and she moved to the side with her gun out and ready. Erin stood behind her with hers, too. “This is a misunderstanding... me and Alaia go way back.” Capri came over and pulled me behind her.

“Looks like she don’t fucking know you.” Erin handed me my purse, and I noticed the abandoned cart that I knew was probably killing her soul to leave.

The man held his hands up. “I don’t want no problems ladies... thought I saw an old friend.” He backed away and left the small area where the bathroom was.

“We’re leaving. I peeped him following behind us around the store. Soon as you went to the bathroom, Erin pointed it out,” Capri said as she put her gun away.

Capri led the way while Erin walked behind me with her gun to the side of her. Once we made it outside, we quickly made it to Capri’s car. She stood checking the parking lot and we all saw him waiting across the parking lot. Soon as he saw Capri hop in and speed out the parking spot, he hopped in his car and followed behind us.

Capri whipped around the parking lot with one hand while putting her seatbelt on. “E, you good?”

"You already know... he made me leave behind that good cart of shit." She cocked her gun back, and I sat in the back seat unsure of what I should do.

Capri hit Capp's name on her car's screen. "You calling to apologize, Baby Doll?" When I heard my baby's voice, my heart sped up.

"What the hell am I apologizing to you for? You called cussed me out and then—"

"Focus, Pri," Erin reminded her.

"Oh yeah. Some weird man tried to corner Alaia in the bathroom... me and Erin handled it, and we left. He's following behind me now, trying to act discreet." She spun the wheel around and exited the shopping center.

"Next time lead with that shit, Capri," Cappadonna's voice changed, I knew he was probably going out his mind.

"We leaving the crib now... bring 'em to me, Baby Doll."

"My pleasure." She ended the call, and then sped up, dipping in and out of traffic on the street.

I turned and watched as he followed closely behind her. Capri easily whipped the car like this was nothing. She held her fist out to Erin, who bumped hers while they both got ready. It was like watching the movie *Set It Off.*

How the hell were they so calm while I was over here about to have a panic attack. Cappadonna didn't sound concerned either, it was like he knew his sister and Erin would handle it until he got there.

Pow! Pow!

I ducked, and Capri whipped into the next lane and sped across the yellow light right before it turned red. "Two cars, Pri."

"What the fuck did he think? I was about to let him leave with my sister-in-law?" She rolled her eyes, as she continued pushing it through a small intersection with trees on both sides.

"Exit to the highway is right there," Erin pointed out. She and Capri locked eyes quickly before she merged onto the exit.

One of the cars didn't have enough clearance or time to make the exit, but the other car did and was right on our ass. "He look like... Capri, he's going to shoot!" I screamed when I noticed the other car was in fact following us, too.

She stomped on her brakes, then merged further over on the highway. Capri continued to play with them on this highway. I could tell they were probably pissed because she was in and out of lanes with ease. Capone's name came up on the screen and Erin pressed the button.

"Hey Baby."

"Gorgeous, tell my sister to stay right in the middle lane for me... hit your brake in like three minutes," he directed.

We were in the middle lane, and there was one car on each side of us. At least they stopped shooting, but what the fuck did they want? Who was that man in the store, and how did he know me?

They kept teetering over the line to hit the car and box us in where we would have to stop. It was Capp that called this time. "Hit that brake, Baby Doll."

We all jerked forward and felt the roar of engines. Our car shook as a black challenger sped by on one side, and the Durango, same color, sped on the other side. I quickly saw Capp's face, and he was focused. Like they were in sync, both of them extended their arms out the window and let they gun go.

Capri merged onto the lane all the way away and slowed down.

"Fuck ass nigga!" Capp yelled before spitting out the window onto the car.

We drove for a bit before we exited off the highway. The guys had gotten off back there, and we all split up. "Still a car following behind us, Capri." Erin watched the side mirrors.

Capri called her brother. "Yo."

"One more car following behind us... what you want me to do?"

"Drive like you don't suspect they following you. Bring 'em to the address I'm about to give you."

No sooner than he said it, a text message popped up and rerouted her to the address. "Got you."

"E, keep that shit cocked back just in case," Capp told her.

"Already ahead of you."

"Capone got the cops on him. Nigga gonna gun it past the cop car when he saw he was about to pull me over."

"He what?" Erin screamed.

"Chill... he taking them past Inferno God territory so he gonna lose 'em there. Capo good... he know how to handle shit."

"I'm about twenty minutes out from the address... how far are you?"

"I'm almost there... I got off a few exits before you."

"Okay."

"Pull up regular and get out like everything normal. Aye baby... you straight?"

"Yes."

"That nigga touched you?"

"No."

"See you in a little bit... love you, Sweet Joy." He laughed.

I knew he was doing this to make me feel better. "I told you about that, Roy."

"Yeah, ight." He ended the call, and I blushed in the backseat like we weren't being followed.

"Do I even want to know?" Erin giggled.

"Girl, no."

Twenty minutes later, we were pulling up to a little yellow house on a quiet street. Capri pulled into the driveway, and hopped out acting like everything was normal. She made sure she was behind me, as we walked to the house.

"I don't think we got off the right foot back at the store. We can make this easy, or we can do this the hard way." It was the same man from the store. His car must have been the one that missed the exit when we first merged onto the highway.

"Sir, this is private property... get on away from here," Capri bit back her laugh as she acted concerned with him being here.

"Funny because you got some property that belongs to a friend." He tried to grab my arm, and Capri blocked him.

"We don't refer to women as property around these parts... That one mine, though," Capone came from the back of the house, winking at his wife, who was relieved her husband wasn't in the back of a police cruiser.

The man was so busy looking at Capone that he didn't see Cappadonna come from the opposite side of the house with malice in his eyes. He walked slow and casually across the lawn as he twirled the wooden bat around in his hand. He reached his arm back and swung like he was a major league baseball player.

"I prefer to do shit the hard way, feel me?" he bit his bottom lip and connected that bat to his head.

"Jesus!" Erin jumped when the bat collided with the back of the man's head.

He fell to his knees, and we looked away, but could hear what was going on. I could hear Cappadonna talking and asking him if he lost his mind trying to touch his wife.

Should I have been scared?

Yeah.

Instead, I was blushing when I heard him refer to me as his

wife. Whenever he did it, which was often, it always made me feel so giddy on the inside. My man was bashing another man's head in with a baseball bat, and I was over here swooning because he called me his wife.

"What if someone calls the cops."

The door opened and Quameer was standing there. "Capping ass Capri... we can't keep running into each other like this."

Capri laughed. "Nobody is going to call the cops. We're in IG territory. All these houses are owned by Inferno Gods... move out my way with yo big head." Capri shoved past Quameer into the house.

"Ain't gonna be too much big head until I show you my big head." Quameer licked his lips and followed behind Capri, who went into the kitchen.

I turned to watch as three men dragged the body off the front lawn, and Capp tossed the bloodied bat onto the grass. Capone walked over toward him, touching his shoulder, and telling him to calm down.

Our eyes locked, and I stood there, showing him that I wasn't scared. He didn't scare me one bit, even with blood all over him.

Cappadonna was doing what he promised he would always do – protecting me.

He walked up the steps past me and went into the back. I followed right behind him like a little puppy at his feet, catching the door before he closed it. "I gotta shower, Joy."

"Can I sit on the toilet while you shower?" He pulled me into the bathroom and closed the door, kissing me on the lips.

He stripped out of his clothes and turned the shower on. Maybe I needed to seek therapy sooner than later, because I was turned on by him even more if that was possible.

"I hate I even had to do that shit in front of you." He finally spoke after he had been in the shower for ten minutes. "When it comes to our family, I'm always coming like that."

"I love you, Roy."

"Love you more, Sweet Joy... freaky ass." He chuckled.

"What are you even talking about? How am I freaky?" I started laughing because nothing got past this man.

"Probably wanna fuck me right now... don't you? I see how you looking at me with those eyes. You forgot I saw those same eyes as you came on my fingers."

I crossed my legs and remained quiet. "Who's house is this?"

"Me and Capo's. It's a stash house we keep in IG territory... consider it a safe house, too." He pulled the curtain back and grabbed the towel. "If you're ever in trouble and I'm not around, Inferno Gods will protect you with their life."

I stood up and wrapped my arms around his neck, pushing my lips against his. "When you finish doing stuff like this, do you ask Allah for forgiveness or pray about them?"

He chuckled and kissed me again. "I always pray for you. You were in my prayers before we had our first conversation."

"I pray for you, too."

"You ready to marry me?"

I shook my head yes because I was ready to marry this man. "Of course... Are you sure it won't ruin your parent's anniversary trip?"

"Not even a little bit." He pulled me close and kissed me on my neck.

I looked up at him. "I ran into one of Zayne's other wives at your party."

I had been trying to figure out a way to tell him without adding Nellie into the mix. "Alaia, what the fuck?"

"Listen, she's not with him and hasn't been with him for a while. I believe her, Roy."

He looked down at me. "Why the hell you didn't say something to me that night?"

"It slipped my mind." How could I remember when he was punching the breath out a man, then making me cum in the back of our ride home. So much happened that night that I had forgot all about Nellie.

"Who was she?"

"Naheim's date."

"The fucking nurse?"

I nodded my head. "She's always been a nurse. I don't have a bad feeling like she's up to something. She said she broke up with Zayne before he got locked up."

Capp kissed me on the nose. "Baby, no offense, let me decide if I have a bad feeling about her. You know where she stay?"

"Why, Cappadonna? She has a daughter." I could see that look in his eyes, and Nellie wasn't someone he had to worry about.

"No. We exchanged numbers."

He held his hand out and I found her number before handing him the phone. With the towel wrapped around his waist, he held my hand and we walked into one of the other bedrooms.

"Hello?" Nellie answered.

"Sweetheart, lemme holla at you about something," Cappadonna replied as he closed the door behind us.

19

TAZ

It always amazed me that Raheem still lived in his grandmama's house. The bitch had been dead for years and he still lived here, selling pussy out of it. This house was like a corner store for pussy. If you were walking in here, then everybody knew you wanted to grab some pussy and then go. Raheem had managed to make takeout pussy and it amazed me that he was making decent money.

The money had dwindled when they came and shot up the block, killing customers, girls, and some of his workers in the process. It took Raheem out a bit, too, because this nigga was in a wheelchair for a little while.

Cappadonna was a fucking headache, but then I learned that his fucking twin was the cause for Raheem's block being shot up. Why the fuck were those freakishly large men like roaches? They wouldn't fucking die, and now I had to figure out how the fuck to get Alaia back.

I promised myself when I got Alaia back, I was going to put her head through every wall that I had. If I couldn't find one, then I was going to make one and shove her disobedient ass through it.

I looked down at my phone and slid my finger across the screen, pausing before I went inside of the house. "Who this?"

"What you doing, Tweety?" Cappadonna casually asked like we were fucking friends or something. "Nothing to say... bet. I'm gonna tell you what you gonna be doing. You can start kissing your ass goodbye... what's this? Me two, you zero... another one bit the dust baby boy. Any fucking way, I sent you a booster seat to your crib." He laughed manically into the phone as he ended the call.

I quickly looked around and headed into the house. He had me all kinds of fucked up, and I was tired of him playing with me. Alaia belonged to me, and I wanted her ass back. If I was a smarter man, I would have just left Alaia alone and realize that she wasn't worth the headache. I couldn't sit back and allow this man to take what was rightfully mine.

"What up, Taz?" Raheem nodded, walking into the small kitchen that could use a mop and clean really bad.

What the fuck did he have these bitches doing besides fucking in here? I made all my girls keep up with the house chores. You couldn't sell pussy in a nasty house, and this is exactly what this house was.

"You spoke to your sister lately?" I cut straight to the chase.

As far as I knew Raheem and Alaia didn't have a relationship. Zayne told me that she didn't speak to him, but I couldn't be too damn sure. "Why the fuck would I talk to Alaia? Haven't spoken to her in years... is she good?"

He had some nerve to pretend to be concerned like he didn't sell her when she was a damn minor. Raheem didn't seem to care what happened to her while he was counting out his money from selling her off.

"She got kidnapped by some other nigga."

"Kidnapped?" Raheem looked at me skeptical, like he didn't believe what the fuck I was saying. "Or did she just bounce because Zayne died?"

"Either way, you sold her to us, and she can't choose when she wants to leave."

Raheem had the nerve to fucking sigh. "What do you want me to do about it, Taz? Me and Zayne made that deal over ten years ago, that money has since run out."

"Bitch, she got a warranty."

He looked at me and then laughed. "Alaia is a grown woman now. What the fuck do you want me to do? I'm under water my damn self here trying to keep the bills paid... nobody comes around this way anymore."

"I can give you a new house and allow you to keep all of the profits."

Raheem had been around long enough to know if it sounded too good to be true, it probably was. This time, I was serious. That was how bad I wanted Alaia back with me. Had she ran on her own, I probably wouldn't have cared as much.

The fact that she went and got Cappadonna to fight her battles forced me to prove something to him. I didn't do well when someone tried to act like I wasn't about that. Zayne may have fell back, but I didn't have that in me.

"What's the catch?" He leaned back knowing that he wasn't getting something for nothing.

This hell hole he was currently in wasn't generating any money, so he was already interested. He wanted me to offer him the job and he would do whatever to secure more money. "Bring me your sister."

"That's all?"

I laughed because he really thought it would be just that easy. I'd rather send Raheem into the lion's den than going in myself.

"Yeah... I want my investment back. She probably had the baby by now, do whatever with it... I don't want it."

"She had a baby?"

"You really should reach out to family more often," I patted his shoulder, and headed toward the door. "Bring me her... and I promise you'll be floating in money. The drought will be over." He licked his crusty lips and rubbed his hands together, probably already counting the money before he even smelled it.

I walked to my car, and grabbed my ringing phone, scanning the number. I relaxed when I saw it was Fatima calling me. "Yeah? I'm head—"

"Why the fuck would someone send a fucking head to my house, Taz? My daughter opened it thinking it was from Amazon!" she screamed.

I looked around quickly and damn near jumped in my car through the window. "Pack the kids up, Fatima... I'm on my way."

I don't know why I didn't take more warning to him saying he sent me a booster seat to my house. I was at least an hour away from Fatima's house, so I called my cousin Dale. He took forever before his stupid ass answered the phone.

"Yeah."

"Head over to Fatima's house and make sure the kids get out alright... some shit went down!" I yelled into the phone while I whipped through traffic trying to make it to Fatima's house.

Zayne left me to protect her, and I couldn't handle it if something was to happen to her. I never felt bad about shit, but I would feel bad if something happened to Fatima because of me. How did he even find out where Fatima lived?

I was always careful with how I was moving when it came to going to her house. How the fuck did this bitch even find me? He had been quiet since I sent my cousin after him, and now I had another useless asshole that couldn't complete the job.

At this point, I didn't want the smoke with Cappadonna's ass. I had them watching Alaia, which was hard because he had her under lock and key. She didn't go out without him or one of the members of the family.

Then they lived in a gated community with a fucking armed guard at the front. What kind of fucking cartel members and drug lords lived in the lake front community that they needed armed guards?

I didn't do my homework on Cappadonna Delgato and that was my fault. Trying to touch him was like trying to touch Jesus, and I was Muslim. I merged lanes and then snatched the car back into my lane when a motorcycle sped up beside me.

When I looked in my rearview, there was another one behind me. I looked to the side and noticed a guy with locs and gold teeth. He had this malicious grin on his face while he nodded to the other man to the right of me. Then the one on the right to me resembled the one with locs, but he didn't have any locs on his head.

The one behind me I recognized as Kincaid, one of the Delgatos top generals. My steering wheel vibrated when I saw the hell cat barreling down the far-left lane. This shit was a fucking set up, so I stomped down on my gas and tried to get the fuck out of this box these three put me in.

We had all but took down the damn EZ Pass booth with how fast we came through it. The Durango was ahead of us, and I wondered if maybe I was the one tripping. That was until I looked in the rearview mirror and saw Cappadonna on a bike.

I assumed he was the one in the Durango, and they set me up. He moved out of the lane, while I grabbed my gun, rolling down my window. I cocked my shit back and tried to decide on which person to shoot first.

The one with locs and the devilish grin moved his bike closer to my BMW, held onto the hood of the car, and drove his bike with the other hand. I couldn't even focus on where Cappadonna's ass went because the other nigga did the same thing. It was like they were trying to keep me in fucking place or something. I moved my wheel, and they moved over some, then locked back on. Sparks flew from the bottom of the bike, as his boot was sliding against the pavement.

"What the fuck?" I hollered when I looked straight ahead and saw Cappadonna riding right toward me, the opposite direction he should have been. He steadied his bike leaning low, and then aimed his gun right at me, while the one on the right moved from my side.

I was stuck, not sure what to do. My fucking body was frozen as I watched his lip curl, exposing his gold teeth, and his finger move on the trigger sending bullets into my windshield, hitting me in the chest.

My hands slipped from the wheel, and the Durango was now pushing me into the ditch we were coming up on. My eyes tried to focus as I watched Cappadonna turn his wheel and shoot across three lanes until he was facing the right direction.

Before my eyes grew heavy, I saw his twin pushing me over toward the side into the ditch. He held his hand out the window and sent two more into my window. My car spun out of control on the highway into oncoming traffic, and everything went black.

20
CAPPADONNA

My eyes were closed as I held my hand out the window feeling the warm breeze through my fingertips. Everybody else was sweating they ass off, but I had the windows down enjoying the smell of sea water, the warm breeze and sweat that accumulated when we stepped off the jet.

I was home.

I've spent the past fifteen years dreaming about the day that I could come and visit this island. I would dream about the day that I stepped off the plane and smelled that beautiful scent of the island.

Alaia rubbed my thigh and smiled as I enjoyed the breeze. She was just so excited to be somewhere. She had never gotten on a plane before, and I had to talk her ass down from trying to run off the jet back to the car.

Capella and Aimee were in the back seat. He was quiet, which was normal for him lately. He had a lot of shit going on, and I couldn't push him into wanting to talk. As long as he knew that I was there for him, and that I wasn't going anywhere.

"Pops, we sweating our asses off back here," he complained, sweat pouring down his face. "The babies are even sweating."

"Go ahead and put the air on," I told the driver.

He rolled all the windows up for these whining ass people and put the air on. Capone and everyone else was in the truck behind us.

Kendra: hey.

Alaia handed me my phone. I hated being on my phone, so she held it for me. I looked at the message and pushed it back into her hand. Not even Kendra's ass was going to ruin this trip for me. What the fuck did she have to tell me?

"You don't want to respond?"

"You respond." I closed my eyes back, and she looked at my phone, then back at me. "Joy, you gonna respond?"

"What am I supposed to say?"

"Start with why the fuck she texting your man talking about some hey like I don't wanna pop her top."

Alaia laughed. "I am not responding. It's probably something important she wants to talk to you about."

I watched as she tossed my phone into her purse, and then checked in the car seat Promise was in. She was still sleeping peacefully since we had landed. "How my baby?"

"Still sleeping from that bottle I gave her while we were landing."

"Baby Capp, you good back there?"

"We're not making that shit a thing, Pops," Capella laughed while Aimee snorted. "How long until we're there? My back hurts."

"Twenty minutes," the driver responded in a thick accent.

"Good looks."

It was crazy that I had purchased my parents a cottage here and had never even been. All I knew is that they loved coming back home, and I wanted to give them something for them. All of their lives they had done everything for me and my siblings, and I felt for once I needed to repay them in some way.

When we pulled up to the white villa that reminded me of Uncle Phil's crib, my face was fucking glued to the window like Will Smith. The grass pavers brought you up to the two large doors that separated us from what was behind the door.

The pictures Capone showed me over the years of the renovations didn't do this shit justice. I opened the door before the driver could get out and open it for us. I held Alaia's hand, as I helped her out, and then did the same with Aimee.

Me and Capella grabbed the car seats out and walked toward the entrance. "Welcome home, pussy!" Capone yelled from behind me and I chuckled.

"Who getting the bigger room?"

Capone laughed. "You think I would do all this renovating and not give us both master suites? You paid for this shit just as much as I did." I felt him hit me on the back, as he opened the door.

"Welcome home, Baby," my mother came and kissed me on the cheeks, and then kissed Capone.

Then she pushed us to the side and went in to hug her grandson. "How was the ride over here? Was it too bumpy for you?" she made a fuss over Capella, and he enjoyed the shit.

Since my mother had found out about Capella, she made it her mission to make up for all the time she missed with him. I could see the way she would stare at him from across the room. That shit hurt all of us because we missed out on years with him.

"I'm good, Nana," Capella replied.

When he tried to call her Mrs. Jean, she almost slapped him with her pressure cooker. "Good. Now where is my other favorite boys?"

Jaiden walked over and kissed my mother on the head. "Young O-Jean, I don't like being second to this puss.... punk," he quickly corrected himself and she laughed.

"Nana!" CJ ran and hugged his grandmother, and she kissed him on his head, and pinched Jaiden's cheeks.

"What are me and Jo going to do when you're away at college?"

"CRY like my wife has been doing for the past few months," Capone called Erin out and she shoved past him with Cee-Cee in her arms.

"Hey Ma," Erin ignored her husband and kissed my mother on the cheek. Before she went further into the house, I took my niece from her.

She started slapping the shit out of me as I kissed her curly head. Cee-Cee looked just like her mother, her spitting image.

While CJ was the mirror image of me and my brother, Cee-Cee took all of Erin with her features. It reminded me of how Promise looked exactly like Alaia.

"Hey Mrs. Jean," Alaia came and hugged my mother.

My mother hugged her, then held her back. "I know you heard that one call me Ma... you are not exempt." She smiled.

Alaia smiled. "Hey Ma."

"That's better... we're gonna talk later... we are all well overdue for some girl time." She looked back at Erin, and Capri, who kissed our mother and breezed by.

Having my mother accept Alaia in the way that she did always made me feel good. I already knew I made the right decision picking her up from that apartment that day, but my family accepting her solidified it. Capone wanted Taz's head as bad as I did, so he was ready when I told him the plan.

Killing that nigga gave me a high that I hadn't felt in a long time, and I had been keeping it from my baby. I wanted her to know that I handled the situation, and she didn't need to worry anymore.

Taz got handled and now we could focus on getting married and building our lives. I spent so much time in prison that the smallest shit excited me. I enjoyed coming home and Alaia was in the kitchen. When I climbed those steps to our bedroom, she always had my house clothes folded on the bed waiting for me.

She always served me my food first, and I waited until she sat down before I even put that fork or spoon to my mouth. Alaia didn't mind submitting and being everything that I needed her to be, and that was because I was doing everything that I needed to and being that for her, too.

Men wanted submission from women and didn't earn that shit. I believed submission from a woman was something that you had to earn. Alaia didn't have to ask for anything because it would be done. Half the time, I was up at night thinking of more ways to give her the world.

"I get we all happy and shit, but ya'll could have helped me. His ass is heavy as shit." Naheim busted the car seat against the wall, struggling with the diaper bag and car seat.

My mother laughed. "Hey baby boy." She kissed him on the cheek and helped him with the car seat.

Even with Naheim and Capri being divorced, my mother still loved Naheim like her own. She knew his relationship with his own family wasn't shit. We were his family, and as much as I thought about knocking his head into a wall often, I respected Capri's wishes on how she wanted us all to proceed with him.

"Hey Ma... sorry for cussing," he apologized and kissed her on the head, as he sat NJ's fat ass down in the car seat.

"What the fuck are you feeding him?"

"He mad greedy... always wanting to eat. The nanny don't

make it no better. She be making him these fat ass bottles with baby cereal, baby food, and milk."

"Where is Jo?" my mother called to Erin.

"She's flying in with Walt tomorrow," she called from the kitchen, sounding like her mouth was full.

When Cee-Cee tried to rip my fucking beard out, I handed her back to her father. "Take your child... the hell she want my beard patchy for?"

Capone took his daughter and kissed her. "It's already patchy... she helping you."

"Hating ass." I bumped him, and walked further into the villa, taking in all of its beauty. This shit was so beautiful that my words were caught in my throat.

I stood in the living room that had the doors opened, exposing the backyard. The fucking beach was steps away. All I had to do was go down a few steps and I was right on the beach. The one thing I had been dreaming about for years.

"All that money spent was worth it just to see this face."

I couldn't formulate the words, and my brother knew. He put his arms around my shoulder and took in the view with me. "Shit so fucking beautiful... never thought I would see some shit like this again. Capo, the shit you did for this family don't ever go over my head."

"The shit *we* did for our family. You took that charge for me, Capp... you sat down for years to protect me. I couldn't sit back and not let you come home to something like this. Now, you about to get married and now it's time for you to start that life you always talked about."

I pulled his ass into a hug and kissed his head. "I love you... never forget that shit. If it all goes left, know that you my heart, Capo."

"Nigga, if it all goes left, we bringing that bitch right... fuck you mean."

"My nigga." We dapped each other.

"For real... I love y'all, too." Jaiden roped his arms around us. "Y'all don't have to sit here and get emotional because I'm going away to college... it's alright... I promise."

We both looked at Jaiden. "What the fuck are you talking about?"

Capone broke out into laughter kissing Jaiden's forehead. "I love you though... but everything ain't about you, Kid. We trying to push you out the door. Think I'm turning your room into a studio or some shit... I got a few bars."

"Why you playing? I'm gonna cry if I don't have a room anymore."

Capone ruffled his hair. "You always got a room in your home... go help your sister bring our bags upstairs."

"Why she packed so much?" he muttered, going to grab all Erin's damn bags.

You would have thought we were going to be gone for two years instead of a week. Capone waved for me to follow him out in the backyard and showed me around. He walked around the house and showed me my suite, which had a door that gave me direct access from the suite to the backyard.

"Nobody has stayed in that suite. I wanted you to be the first person to lay in your own bed," Capone informed me.

"You really did this shit, Capo."

"We did this shit, Capp. You hold a lot of guilt for shit, but I would have never been able to do all of this if I didn't have you. You may have not been out here with me, but knowing that you were a phone call away, and always had my back helped me build this shit... we did this shit, Stunna."

We both started laughing because when we were younger, we thought we would be rappers. The first twin rappers out of New York, so I called him Gunna, and he called me Stunna.

"I'm gonna fuck you up. I already owe your wife a push in the pool."

"What she do?"

"She told Alaia my fucking middle name... she running around here calling me fucking Roy."

"Nigga, you not being called Winnie. I'm having a hard time feeling bad for you."

I shook my head. "We really about to both have wives... shit is crazy."

He smirked, walking backward to the house. "Can't picture my life without my wife...I know you can't picture yours without Alaia...that's how you know she's the one."

"I got your back, Gunna," I called to him.

"And I'm always gonna have your front, Stunna." He saluted me, and I sat down on one of the couches. The backyard reminded me of a resort with all the pool furniture, and spaces to just chill out and relax. My mind was tripping being here, feeling the warm breeze on my skin, and smelling the salt water. If you sat still enough, you could hear the waves crashing onto the beach.

I guess everyone felt the need to let me have my space outside. It went from me sitting to take it in, to me sitting out there for two hours. Capri came and told me everybody was going out to eat. I decided to opt out of dinner and went to my room to shower and chill for a little bit until Alaia came back.

Since we had a bunch of fucking babies around, Naheim's nanny and her sister were watching the babies during this trip. When I opened the door, I saw Alaia with the towel wrapped around her, and her curly hair hanging down her back.

"You enjoyed your alone time?"

I closed the door behind me. "I thought you went to dinner... Why didn't you come out there with me?"

She smiled as she folded up my sleep shorts. Knowing

Alaia, she probably had already unpacked all our shit. "Sometimes you just need to be alone with your thoughts, and you seemed so at peace out there, I didn't want to disrupt that."

"How can my peace interrupt my peace?" I raised my eyebrow, and looked at her, as she clutched her towel tightly around her body. "Why you holding your towel so tightly?"

I went to take a piss, and then washed my hands. Alaia was very self-conscious of her body. Whenever she showered, she made sure she had her towel close, so she could quickly cover herself. She always waited until I had to head out before she went to shower.

"I'm not holding it tightly."

"Then drop it."

She nervously laughed. "Noo... I'm not where I want to be with my body. The C-section mark is ugly, and I have this fold..." her words trailed off when I kissed her lips, pulling her over toward the huge mirror in the corner of the room.

The mirror took up the full corner of the room in length and height. Where the fuck did they even find a mirror that big to begin with. "Look at me," I told her, as we stood in the mirror.

Her eyes met mine in the mirror as I pulled the towel from around her. She dropped her gaze when I dropped the towel on the floor. "Capp," she tried to remove herself from my arms.

"What did I say... look at me, Alaia."

With her lip poked out, she looked back up at me. "I wish you saw what I do when I look at you. You're fucking beautiful, Alaia... why the fuck don't you think you're perfect? Because I fucking do." I kissed her neck.

"You work out every morning... your body looks like that, and it's hard to believe sometimes that you want a body like mine."

I rubbed her body and kissed her shoulder. "A body like

yours... the fuck does that even mean? A body that has given life, and still looks good... that's what I want. That's what you have." I gave her chills as I stared at her through the mirror. "I want everything that comes with you... these stretch marks came because you carried my daughter. That scar is because you risked your life to bring her earth side."

"That sounds all good and all, but Kendra looks nothing like me." She tried to walk away, and tripped on the towel, falling into me.

We both fell onto the fuzzy carpet and started laughing. "Now look at you... falling and naked."

"It's your fault," she laughed while trying to snatch the towel from me, and I tossed it behind me.

"Don't be pissing on the carpet, Joy."

"One time and you keep bringing it up."

"Come 'ere, Baby." I pulled her into my lap and kissed her neck. "You forget that you were thick when I first met you? I don't care how much clothes you had on; I saw that ass from across the room."

She blushed. "I was fat then, too."

I kissed her ear, as I turned her face to look at herself in the mirror. "All I saw was a beautiful woman with pain in her eyes. When I look at you, I gotta talk myself down because my dick gets hard for you, Alaia. I don't see no other woman because all I see is you. Your body is mine, and as long as I fucking love it, nothing else matters... As long as you sitting on my face, who gives a fuck what other bitches are saying. They can't compare and you wanna know why?"

"Why?"

I held her hand up with my ring on it. "You got the ring and the man they can never have ... who bed you in every night?"

"Yours."

"Ours," I corrected her.

"Who do you cuddle under every night and wake up to every morning?"

"Not you... you be up early in the morning with the damn birds." She cut her eyes at me, and I kissed her head.

My hands traveled down to her below and she gasped, staring at me through the mirror. "Who pussy is this, Joy?" I asked, biting down on my bottom lip. Her eyes glazed over, as her legs opened wider. I directed her face back toward the mirror. "Can't hear you," I asked, while slipping two fingers inside of her.

"Yours, Cappadonna."

"Say my name for me again, Baby."

"Capp.... a...donna," she moaned out as I increased my speed.

Our eyes locked as she squirmed between my legs. The sight of us in this mirror was fucking beautiful. I would have it oiled painted if I could, but then I would have to break a nigga's jaw for looking at my wife like this.

"Nah... eye contact, Joy. Remember what I told you... in my eyes," I reminded her, as she held onto my legs.

"I...I can't...it feels too good."

"You look away when I tell you to look away, you hear me... look at me." She turned her head up and looked at me, and I shoved my tongue down her throat, never slowing up my pace. Alaia sucked on my tongue and moaned in my mouth, as that back arched.

"Back itching again?" I smirked, as she tossed her head back onto me and held my arms. "Aye, I'm up here."

Her eyes slowly met mine. "Shit look like fucking art... look how fucking beautiful you are." Her hair was slowly drying and was all over her face. "I'm the only nigga that knows what you look like when you cum... cum for me, baby."

Alaia held onto my legs as my fingers moistened. "Capp... can we, please," she whined pulling on my shorts.

I laughed and kissed her parted lips. "You want this?" I placed her hand on my dick. She looked me in the eyes and nodded her head. "I told you I'm gonna give you this after I make you my wife... you trust me, right?"

"You know I do."

"A lot of people can talk and promise shit... Alaia. You've been used to be people talking and never coming through for you. That ain't me. I asked you to be my wife, and I'm not entering you until you are that." I kissed her ear. "When I'm in there... yo' ass gonna be running from me."

"Promise?"

"Freaky ass," I laughed. "I promise." I turned her head so she could see herself naked in my arms. She was so fucking beautiful, and I needed her to know that. "You are beautiful. I appreciate you. I respect you. I know you're worthy of all good things. You—"

"You belong to me in the best way," she completed the affirmations that I was always speaking into her.

"I need you to know and believe all of that." I scooped her ass up, palming her ass, while staring in her eyes.

"I'm getting there."

"Long as we making progress... you the baddest thing walking and you know how I know?" I kissed her lips.

"How do you know?"

"Because you caught my eye without ever having to show me a piece of your skin... you show the fuck out with whatever you wear, Joy. You trust and respect me enough to cover your hair and body and leave that reserved for just me."

She kissed my neck. "Seeing as you have me butt ass naked in the middle of this bedroom, not considered covered right now."

“It ain’t nobody business what goes on under our roof... I only see all of this... you hear?” I slapped her ass, and damn near bit my lip off while I watched the ripples in her ass.

“Yes.”

I raised my eyebrow. “Yes, what?”

“Yes, Daddy,” she kissed me on the lips, and I wrapped my arms around her, kissing her shoulder.

“Remember, you the prize, not a possession, Joy.”

21
Alaia

I REMEMBER when Zayne took the charger to his phone and whipped my ass until I promised I wouldn't mumble under my breath whenever he told me something. As I sat in the tub, I winced every time the water touched one of the bruises from his abuse. I sobbed in that tub, asking Allah why he put me in this situation.

What had I done to deserve to live this way. I would internally scream and plot on ways to kill myself because I didn't want to live anymore. If this was the life I had to live, then I didn't want to be here anymore.

I got the bottle of Advil from Fatima's bathroom, and I took nearly the entire bottle while chugging water from the sink. The thought of death was the only thing that had made me excited. I knew I was that much closer to being able to truly be free, even if it meant in another realm.

When I woke up to bright lights, I thought I had finally made it. I was free from Zayne, and I could rest knowing that I would never have to see him again. That was until Zayne came into view with the meanest, angriest grimace on his face.

Instead of taking me to the hospital, they pumped my stomach on their own, and stuck me in the room. For four days, I laid in that bed while Fatima brought me food. Zayne didn't speak to me, and I considered that a blessing in disguise.

As I thought about that girl that stuffed those pills down her throat just to get away, I couldn't believe that I was the same girl sitting outside on a pool lounge holding my daughter. The same girl that wanted to kill herself, had two reasons to live.

The same girl that felt so alone, now had a family that had accepted her as their own. Tears burned my eyes as I thought about how I've been through hell, and this little girl I was holding was my heaven.

"Mommy loves you so much, Promise...Goodness, I love you so much. Mashallah," I kissed her chubby cheeks and fixed her bathing suit.

It was a size too big on her, but I wanted to see her in it. The baby sunglasses that sat on her face kept falling down, but I kept them up long enough for a picture. When I looked up, Cappadonna came jogging up the steps and I smiled.

How could a man this perfect exist and want me. Now, I knew that this man I was going to marry had a few screws loose. I've become so well versed in him that I could clock when his ass was disassociating and going into that place.

He was sweaty with his shirt hanging from the back of his shorts. I watched as he took his headphones down from his ears, and leaned down to kiss me on the lips, giving me a sloppy one. He then kissed our daughter on her head and sat down on the lounge across from me.

"What the hell you doing up so early?"

I handed him the bottle of water I brought out here for him. "Cause I knew you would need that. Plus, who sleeps when they are on vacation? I've never been on vacation before, so I am going to soak up every moment."

"You ready to spend the day with Daddy?" he fixed Promise's sun hat, then paused and looked at her bathing suit. "The fuck is this, Joy?"

I laughed. "It's cute... look at her little belly... look like a beer gut."

"She can't even fit it... I don't like it."

"Well, you bought it." I shrugged and handed her over.

The women were going into town to look for something for me to wear. We were supposed to get married on this trip and I didn't have anything to wear. I was excited to get away and have some girl time, while Capp took care of Promise.

He kissed Promise and then held her before looking over at me. "I can't ever repay you for her, Alaia."

"You can't ever repay me? Capp, do you—"

"I would have done everything even if you didn't allow me to be her father. You don't understand how much this little girl means to me."

I looked down feeling guilty. Capp never allowed me to look down long before he was pulling my face back up. "The doctor explained you can't physically have babies, Joy. She even said there were other options. I told you that when we're ready to talk about that, we will. Stop feeling guilty and counting yourself out."

I smiled, as he stared at me. Whenever Capp stared at me, I could feel how strongly he felt for me. It was weird that I could feel that from just him looking at me. My heart jumped around in my chest whenever he was near me.

When he asked me to marry him, I never gave it a second thought because I wanted to be everywhere this man was. "Are you sure that you don't need me to tell the nanny to take care of her while I'm gone?"

"You doubting me? We taking the babies to the beach... it was Naheim's idea."

I started laughing. "So, all of the men are taking the babies to the beach? I need a picture or something."

"Yeah, let me move my daughter away from this hating ass attitude." He stood up and headed to door connected to our suite.

"I'm not hating," I called behind him.

"Yeah, ight. Go ahead and make me something to eat... hater."

"Oh please... bring me my baby back."

He stopped walking and turned Promise around. "She said she don't wanna be anywhere that someone is hating on her daddy... sorry, Joy."

"Roy!" I laughed uncontrollable.

Cappadonna always made me laugh from the belly. The laughs that we always shared made me feel so good on the inside. "Joy."

"Forever?"

He winked. "Even though you a hater."

"I am not." I grabbed my phone and went in through the kitchen to make my man his breakfast.

Aimee was smiling and cooking in the kitchen. "Good morning. I made everybody breakfast."

I walked into the kitchen to wash my hands, and Aimee had everyone's plate already made. As I was about to scoop a plate up for Capp, I paused. "Which bacon did you use?"

She went into the trash bag and pulled out the pork bacon. "Aimee, that man will really kill you if you feed him some damn pork bacon."

"What? Is he allergic?"

How she could live in the house with us and not notice that we were Muslim was beyond me. I covered my damn hair for crying out loud, and she had saw Capp pray more than a few times. All the bacon in the house was either beef or turkey, so how the hell didn't she notice we didn't eat pork.

"Be for real, Aimee. Are you messing with me?" I stared at her for a second, waiting for her to tell me that she was joking. "We're Muslim, Aimee... did you really not know?"

I've noticed that Aimee wasn't the brightest crayon in the box. A few things had gone over her head when we were talking, and I brushed it off as it being part of her bubbly personality. This girl was standing there looking more confused than before I explained to her why we didn't eat pork.

"Why nobody told me?"

"What happened?" Capone came downstairs, stretching.

I looked at Aimee, then at him. "She made breakfast for everyone, but used pork bacon... Aimee, this was sweet of you. We don't eat pork."

"Erin don't eat pork either... go ahead and put hers on my plate."

I quickly started on making me and Capp breakfast while Aimee set the table for breakfast. Capone was already seated and eating his food. "You don't want to wait for Erin?" Aimee asked.

"My wife ain't getting up anytime soon." He chuckled to himself. Aimee missed what he meant, but I knew exactly why Erin was still in that bed.

It was the same reason I wanted to rip Capp's shorts off last night when we were in the mirror. I held my chest while I thought about the way that he made me feel. I always had trouble staring in the mirror at myself. When he forced me to look at us in the mirror, even I couldn't deny that we looked beautiful together.

Cappadonna didn't know, or maybe he did, but he was

making me fall in love with being pleasured. It wasn't something that I had any experience in, and the way Capp knew how to make me feel good should have been studied.

He was assertive, yet soft at the same time. The way he bit down on his bottom lip when he felt my legs shake, or the way he always licked his fingers whenever he was done. "You whipping the fuck out those eggs, Alaia," Chubs said, when he came in from the backyard.

"Morning, baby, here's your breakfast... I know you eat pork." Aimee sat down the plate in front of him.

I realized that I was whipping the hell out of these eggs thinking about the way Cappadonna made me feel. I stopped whipping the eggs and smiled. "Hey, Baby Capp," I teased him.

"Bro', we not making that a thing... I keep telling my pops that shit." He took a bite out the bacon.

"Well, you may need to keep him away from your girl. She tried to give his crazy ass pork." Capone snickered.

"It was an accident...sheesh," Aimee plopped down next to Chubs.

"Our little secret." I squeezed her shoulder and grabbed the butter from the kitchen table. "What are you guys doing today?" I switched the subject, even though I already knew their plans.

"We going to the beach with the babies. CJ wanna build a sandcastle, so I figured we would get some cabanas and chill there for the day."

"Don't even explain nothing to her... she already was hating on us." Capp came from the back with the burp cloth over his shoulder, and Promise balled up like a little peanut in his arms.

He always held her in the crook of his arm like a little basketball, and the crazy part is she liked it. "I was not hating...

all I did was laugh at the thought of you all pulling diaper bags and strollers onto the beach."

"Who bringing a diaper bag? I'm putting Cee-Cee's diaper in my pocket, and her bottle in the other... my baby low maintenance."

"Until you running back to the villa with shit in your hands," Cappadonna replied, giving Chub's shoulder a squeeze before taking a seat at the table.

He looked at everyone eating and then looked at me. "You cooked all that already?"

"No. Aimee cooked this morning."

"Good shit... we ran out of food or something." He was confused as to why he didn't have a plate sitting in front of him.

"Mr. Capp, I almost gave you bacon," Aimee blurted, and sighed in relief like she just revealed the biggest secret of the year.

Chubs shook his head, trying to bite back his laugh. "I told you to stop calling him Mr. Capp, Babe."

Me and Capone locked eyes before we both busted out laughing. I had to cross my legs to avoid wetting myself because the moment was just too funny. While we were laughing, Cappadonna sat there trying to figure out what was so funny.

"Aimee, didn't I tell you and Skyler's ass about that?"

I wiped the tears from my eyes. "I'm about to make us some breakfast right now."

"Nah. Let them eat they swine... you know how nasty a pig is—"

"It's too early to hear a speech about pigs, Cappy." Capri yawned, hugging her brother, and then sitting in the seat he had just got up from.

She pulled her feet up to her chest as she looked at all of us sleepily. "We going to get breakfast on the beach, Joy. You already got Promise dressed like she belong on one."

Capri held her hands out for Promise and snuggled her with kisses. "Look at her little suit... it's so cute."

I always felt like I was in a dream whenever I was around Cappadonna's family. They just accepted and respected that I was who he wanted to be with, and they accepted me. His mother and sister both accepted me, and Promise.

After feeling alone and never belonging for the past few years, it felt like a warm hug whenever I was around them.

"Isn't it? Me and Erin both got one for Cee-Cee and Promise."

Capri kissed Promise's chubby cheeks. "Go ahead and have breakfast together... I'll watch her."

"You sure?"

"Girl, I'm a whole aunty and great-aunt out here... Plus, I need to get on my big brother's good side again."

Capp was side eyeing the hell out of his little sister. "Yeah... ight."

"See. Tell your daddy to stop being so mean."

"You heard what I said, Capri... fix that shit."

Whenever Capp held his hand out, without words my hand was locked into his. We walked out to the backyard and then onto the beach. He kissed the back of my hand and looked down at me. "Mr. Capp, thank you for taking me to breakfast."

He stopped walking and picked me up, tossing me over his shoulder. "Oh, you think you funny, huh?"

"Stop... please... don't put me in the water," I giggled as he ran down the beach to the water and walked in. "Cappadonna Leroy Delgato! Don't you get us wet... please!" I screamed while laughing hysterically.

"Apologize."

"Alright. Alright. I'm sorry... I'm sorry, Mr. Capp," I continued to laugh, and that's when he continued into the water, putting me down, and pulling me into him as he sat down in the water.

The waves crashed around us as we sat in the water staring into each other's eyes. "You lucky I didn't toss yo ass in the water."

"You would never...I don't even know how to swim."

"Me either."

I panicked. "Cappadonna, we just floating in this water. What if a wave takes us even further."

He laughed while kissing my lips. "I'm decent in swimming... I used to swim at Betsy Head pool when me and Capone were younger."

"Who?"

"Never mind." I sat across his lap while the waves crashed around us, as we stared into each other's eyes. "You know you amazing, right?"

"You may have told me a time or two. I think you're pretty amazing, too, Mr. Capp."

He softly bit my neck. "Now I'm gonna make you scream that shit."

"Promise?"

We both laughed. "Yeah, you saying that now."

It was my turn to kiss him on the nose. "We are at the one place you wanted to be... the beach."

He smiled. "Wanna know something else I wanna do?"

"What's that?"

"I want to marry you on this beach."

I hugged him tightly around the neck. "Roy, I will marry you anywhere. However, we don't have nothing planned... I mean nothing."

"How you know that?"

"What do you have up your sleeve?" He fixed my kaftan that was threatening to blow up.

"All I need is for you to get a dress and meet me and Promise down the aisle." He kissed my lips, and I smiled.

"You sure you still want to marry me? You don't think this is crazy, right?"

Capp smirked. "Baby, I know crazy... this is far from that."

He in fact knew crazy. After witnessing him bash that man's head in, I knew he and crazy were on a first name basis. It was funny how I could witness him do something like that, and still feel so safe in his arms.

"Yeah. True. You would know."

"And yo freaky ass like it." He squeezed me, kissing my shoulders while we remained in the water, with no plans on ever getting breakfast. "We got an agreement... you gonna meet down the aisle?"

I smiled. "Yes."

"Dap it up then, Joy."

We did our secret handshake, sealing it with a kiss on each of our hands. "Joy and Roy?"

"Forever." He kissed my lips.

"This is the one," Jean sniffled while she swiped away her tears, fixing the train on the dress that I was wearing.

Capri fixed the material for the wrap that Cappadonna's cousin was going to make to match the dress. "Mommy, this is the one... Alaia, you look beautiful."

I looked at myself in the mirror and felt beautiful. I've never felt beautiful looking in the mirror and avoided them. As I stood here in this small bridal shop in Barbados, I felt beautiful. The floor length white mermaid style dressed looked incredible on me. The beading covered the full dress. My head-wrap would have the same beading that the dress had to tie it all together.

"Jean, you know I can do the alterations overnight to get this ready," Telly, Cappadonna's older cousin, told Jean.

Jean slid a knot of money into her hands, and she refused. "Telly, we take care of our own... Cappadonna insisted."

She took the money and hugged Jean before turning back to finish getting my measurements. Jean fixed the dress on me, as she smiled looking at me.

Erin came over and hugged me, putting her face close to mine. "Imagine meeting the love of your life in a prison visitation room."

"Visiting another man."

"We'll leave that part out when we tell our future grandchildren."

Capri started laughing uncontrollably. "Wait... so you about to be a whole grandmama to Rory."

"This some ghetto mess," Jean shook her head. "How is my son a grandfather and he's not even forty."

"Well, both your sons are one year from pushing forty, so he damn near there," Capri snorted, as she plopped on the couch and started texting on her phone. Her eyes widened. "Kincaid just landed."

We all looked at her confused because we assumed he would just be flying in after her. "Why are you shocked?"

She texted, and then looked back. "That damn Leroy don't mind his damn business. He told Kincaid to hop on a flight to come here."

Jean looked confused. "I'm not understanding, Capri. Why wouldn't you want your boyfriend to be here."

"Because he's not my boyfriend anymore... we broke up."

"No. You broke up with him. Tell the whole story, Pri," Erin sat down next to her, taking a sip of her champagne.

"I don't know with you anymore. You don't want to work on your marriage and now you break up with the person you said you wanted to be with." Jean looked at her phone, then back at me. "Go ahead and get changed so we can head to lunch."

I went to change clothes while Jean lectured Capri about her romantic decisions. Erin and Capri said they had some other errands to run, so it was just going to be me and Jean for lunch. I was nervous having lunch with just her.

I mean, we had spent a lot of time alone together since she first arrived at the hospital. It was silly to feel scared to have lunch with the woman that had been a saving grace in my life since I met her.

We took the car to the restaurant and were seated outside overlooking the beach. The cool breeze from the beach made it comfortable enough to sit outside. While Jean finished her phone call, I quickly checked in with Cappadonna.

Roy: You missing daddy already?

Me: How is my daughter?

I waited for him to respond and got nothing.

Me:??

Roy: You mean our daughter, Joy?

I couldn't help but to laugh because he was so dramatic at times.

Me: yes.

Roy: Taking a nap in the cabana. She's good... enjoy yourself.

I put my phone away and accepted the menu the server handed over to me. "Welcome to The Cliff, have you dined with us before?" the woman asked.

"No."

"I have. My husband can't stay away from the rum punch here. This is my daughter's first time being here."

"Well, welcome. The lunch special today is a braised Branzino with cherry tomatoes over a bed of arugula. We also have a shrimp scampi with capers in a delicious brandy sauce."

Both options sounded good, and I didn't know which one to pick. "Give us a moment to look over the menu."

While Jean was more assertive, Desmond was more chilled and laid back. Not too much ruffled his feathers. Long as he had golf and a cold beer, he was pretty much good with everything. Both Capone and Cappadonna got the perfect mix of both of their parents.

Then there was Capri.

She was somewhere in the mix of things. Capri was a forced to be reckoned with, she just needed to figure out what she wanted, or who she wanted. "I wanted lunch to be with just the two of us."

"Thank you for inviting me to lunch. I feel like we've only been around each other when you were taking care of me. It's nice to be out with you without you having to help me to the bathroom."

She smiled and took a sip of her water. "I know all of this has happened so fast... you barely had a chance to catch your breath after having the baby."

"That's the thing with Cappadonna though. It doesn't feel like that at all... I feel like I've known him for years. He makes me feel comforted, like he was always meant for me."

She smiled. "Even though my boys are twins, they have both had their own way about them. While some twins want to dress alike and do everything like the other, they both fell into their roles. Cappadonna always had this leader spirit while Capone preferred to sit back and watch his brother's back. I'm not saying that I wanted my son to be sent to prison, but him being sent away forced his brother to come into his own. No more the observant quiet type, he had to step up into the light and do what needed to be done. Now, it's funny that Capp has always been the leader between the two of them, and now he's following in his brother's footsteps with having his own family."

I smiled. "I love him so much. I've never loved someone the way that I love him, Ma."

She wiped the tear that fell down her face. "He loves you the same. I've never seen my son glow the way he does when you enter a room. I watch when you both are in the room together, and he just has to be touching you. It doesn't matter where you are, when he holds that hand out, yours just falls right into his like it was supposed to always be there."

"I feel that way." It was my turn to wipe my own tear away.

"I know your story, Alaia. I also know that you've never had anyone be there for you. I wanted us to have this lunch together because I want you to know that I am here for you. Erin has always had her aunt, so she doesn't need me as much. You don't have anyone, and I want to be that person for you. You don't just get Capp when you marry him, you get the Delgatos, and baby, we ride for each other hard. We may bicker and not agree with each other, hence my daughter, but we will fight to the death for our own... you're going to be a Delgato, Alaia."

We were both a wreck at the table by the time the server came back. "Thank you. I don't take everything you've done or taught me for granted."

She grabbed my hands. "I've never been a fan of either of my son's first picks when it came to women. I've always kept my mouth shut because they are grown men and that is their right. The second time is a charm, because they got it right with you and Erin."

I smiled while wiping my eyes. "Lawd have mercy, we are two crybabies. We're ready to order," Jean told the lady, as we wiped our faces, and enjoyed the rest of lunch together. I was blessed to have not only Cappadonna, but also Jean Delgato. She was heaven sent, like my Yaya sent her to me through Cappadonna.

22
CAPPADONNA

I woke up in a dark warehouse, and it smelled like piss. I looked around, wondering how the fuck somebody had gotten me restrained and lived to speak about it. Moving the chair as best as I could, I tried to release my hands, and failed horribly. Whoever the fuck tied these damn restraints must have worked for the fucking military.

Ain't no way I couldn't get out of these. I stopped when I heard the door creak and paused to watch who walked through the door. When that bitch Tweety walked through the door, I tried to rip my arms free. How the fuck was he still alive? With the way we had done his ass over, there was no way he could be walking and breathing in front of me. Behind him, another man walked in pulling someone.

When he shoved the figure into the light, it was my Joy. She had her arms tied behind her back, and she had a black eye. My eyes felt like they were about to pop out of my head with how hard I was trying to get out of these restraints.

"Yo pussy... have that big bitch untie me!" I barked.

Tweety laughed. "I give it to him... he still has that same energy even tied up."

He walked over toward Alaia, who was crying and pleading for me to help her. "Touch her and you fucking dead."

"You aren't in the position to be making deals, Cappadonna." He slapped Alaia's ass, and she trembled in fear.

I tried to get my arms free and was cutting into my skin. "I got us, Joy... be brave for me, Baby."

"Bring her to my house... where she always belonged," he told the big ass man, and he snatched Joy up.

"Roy!" she screamed.

I jumped out of my sleep and looked at Joy sleeping peacefully beside me. Reaching over, I pulled the covers over her arms, and kissed her shoulder before climbing out of the bed. Promise was fast asleep in her bassinet, and I kissed her forehead.

My heart was beating out of control as I replayed the dream I had. My girls were my entire world, and the fact that someone tried to take them from me forced me up. I went into the kitchen and grabbed me some water before leaning on the sink, staring into space.

"Shit." I turned to look at Aimee, who had flicked the lights on. "Sorry, Mr. Cap—"

"It's too early for you to be pissing me off, Aimee. Why are you up, anyway?"

She went into the fridge and grabbed a prepared bottle. "Rory was whining in his sleep, so I know he'll be wanting a bottle soon."

I nodded and continued thinking about that dream. It was just a dream, and I shouldn't have been as angry as I was. Even the thought of someone laying their hands on Joy brought my pressure up.

"On a serious note, can I talk to you?"

"You got a mouth, Aimee... no? You're free to talk whenever you want," I replied, looking at her while she tried to sort her thoughts out.

"I know you're not the biggest fan of me because of my brother. You may not even trust me all the way."

"Don't trust you at all... continue."

Even though I didn't trust Aimee, I was smart enough to keep my enemies close to me. If she made one wrong move, then I was going to tell my grandson that his mama went to get milk, and her ass never came back. I would do whatever I had to do to protect my son and grandson.

She took a deep breath. "Do you have to look at me like that?"

"Like what, Aimee."

"So intense... I don't know. Capella looks the same way when he's annoyed about something... am I annoying?"

"Right now? Yeah. Get to the fucking point."

"I love Capella so much," her voice cracked as she checked the temperature for the bottle on her wrist. "Ace is my brother and because of that you don't trust me which is fair. My loyalty is to Capella, and this family. This family is my son's family. I called you and you came without a second thought for us. I've never had that kind of loyalty when it came to my brother. What he did was wrong, and I can't forgive him for what he did. He took Francie from Capella, and almost took his life, too. Trust isn't easily given, and you have shown me that. Give me a chance to prove to you that you can trust me." The girl was in damn near tears standing in the middle of the kitchen with a bottle in her hand.

I abandoned the counter and held my arms out. Aimee ran into my arms and started crying. "I don't give trust easily, but if my son loves you and trust you, I'm always going to come running for you or my grandson. Aimee, I say this with love, I will rip your teeth out your mouth, I'm a dentist, I know my way around teeth. So if you prove me wrong... I'll do it with a smile on my face."

She lifted her head from my chest with wide eyes. "What?"

I patted her back. "Nothing to worry about, right? We won't have those problems."

After she finished her crying, I sent her ass back to bed and took my ass back to bed. Alaia was sitting up in the bed with Promise when I walked into the room. She smiled when she saw me and patted the bed beside her.

"Couldn't sleep?"

I didn't want to tell her that I had a nightmare that fucking scared me. I wasn't a man that was easily scared, but seeing Alaia's face in that fucking nightmare brought me to my knees. I kissed her temple and took Promise from her.

"Went to grab something to drink. She woke up?"

"Yeah. I could have just rocked the bassinet, but something made me want to hold her. She's been staring at me ever since I picked her up."

"She ain't never seen something so beautiful." I kissed Promise and put her between the both of us.

"We cannot sleep in the bed with her. You heard what the pediatrician said about that."

"You know more than anybody that I don't follow nobody fucking rules."

She kissed Promise who was fighting her sleepiness, and then looked over at me. "Are you alright?"

"I'm good, Baby," I fake yawned.

"You would tell me if something is wrong, right? You don't always have to be strong for me, Roy."

"I also don't need to put shit on your plate, Joy. I promise I'm good, and the minute I'm not... I'm gonna tell you."

"Are you having second thoughts about marrying me?"

Alaia was the type that got into her head once she felt something was wrong.

Since she couldn't figure out what was wrong with me, she was now in her head thinking about every worst-case scenario possible. "Joy it is like three in the morning. I can't even process my damn thoughts."

I took Promise and put her back in the bassinet because she was asleep that quick. She rolled over and pulled the cover over her. "Okay. Just making sure."

Climbing into the bed behind her, I pulled her onto my side and kissed her neck. "I had a nightmare where I lost you. Shit scared me so bad that I couldn't sleep. So, if you think I have second thoughts about marrying you, you fucking crazy."

She turned in my arms until she was facing me. "Let me be there for you like you're there for me when I have a nightmare."

Kissing her lips softly, I replied, "I will. You gotta promise me something though."

She laughed. "Another promise, huh? What is it?"

"Stop getting in your head. I'm naturally quiet, and being locked up, I naturally learned to process my shit alone and quietly. I couldn't have niggas seeing me show a sign of weakness in there. It's nothing personal when I'm quiet... I'm just figuring shit out in my head."

"Sorry."

"Don't be sorry. I just can't wait until I can start giving you some dick to get you out your head." I kissed her nose, and she tossed her leg over me. "Nah... you be sweating. We not sleeping like that."

"C'mon, please," she pleaded.

"For a little bit, then you need to move those cold ass toes over there. How the fuck your toes be so cold and your body burning up."

"Ask the little crouch goblin over there."

She yawned, laying her head on me. "Night, Roy. I love you."

"Love you, Joy."

A few minutes later, I heard her snores. I slid out of bed and went to get Promise, climbing back into bed. Alaia put her leg back over me while Promise scrunched her butt up like a ball and continued sleeping on my chest. I stared up at the ceiling until my eyes eventually grew heavy, and I went to sleep with both my girls next to me.

"DAMN, SLOW THE FUCK DOWN," I ducked as they were carrying chairs and tables onto the beach.

I had finished running on the beach, and the villa was in full swing for my parents' anniversary dinner tonight.

Even though we were all in Barbados to celebrate them, we had sent them on a little getaway on one of the surrounding islands for just the both of them. They were supposed to get in this afternoon, and one of my cousins was going to keep them busy until tonight.

"Good morning, Baby," I kissed Alaia, as she handed me a cold bottle of water, and pointed to the table where she had breakfast. "Where's my daughter?"

"Nanny." She was on the phone and moving around the kitchen to clean it. "That quick? Telly, you didn't have to work that quickly. No, tonight is Jean and Desmond's anniversary dinner. I can pick it up tomorrow... are you sure? Okay. I appreciate you."

"What was that about?"

"Telly is finished with the alterations for my dress, and she's bringing it over in a few." She brought me something to drink, and I gently grabbed her wrist, and pulled her on my lap.

"Did you eat this morning?"

"No."

I pulled the plate closer to us. "Eat some of my food, Alaia."

"Oh, he used my full name... he must be serious," she sarcastically replied, and cut into my eggs.

It was an amazing thing to witness someone become comfortable with you. Little by little, Alaia revealed her personality to me. She was sarcastic as shit and always had a dirty joke. She was slowly allowing her walls down so I could see the Alaia that darkness had covered many years ago.

"Keep being a smart ass," I kissed her ear.

She took a bite of eggs and then ate all my bacon, leaving me fucking eggs and a bite of toast. As long as my baby had some food in her, I didn't give a fuck about me. As much as I wanted my wife to handle home, I refuse to have her so overworked with maintaining our home that she didn't have time to take care of her.

My job was to take care of her, and I took that shit seriously.

"Or what?"

I discreetly squeezed her ass. "I can't wait to see how much mouth you got when I got them legs over my shoulders."

"Awe look at the love birds. Alaia, can you tell my brother to pass the pepper sauce." Capri's petty's ass came and sat across from us.

I snatched the pepper sauce and put it on my eggs. "I'm not getting in the middle of whatever beef that you two have."

"That is because you see me as a grown woman, not a little child."

"Then stop acting like a child." I continued to pour the pepper sauce on my eggs until Alaia snatched it from me.

"Says the one purposely pouring the sauce on the eggs so she can't have none." Alaia handed it to Capri, who put it onto her eggs and bacon.

"Thank you, sis'."

"Good morning." Erin yawned, with Capone right behind her.

I noticed his ass was dressed. "We going to eat at the beach club down the beach... come on punk ass."

He stopped to kiss his wife before he headed out the back. "Have fun. I should make you eat the rest of these eggs you wasted."

I kissed Alaia in the mouth and stood her up, then put her back in the chair I was once sitting in. "See you later."

"Later." She smiled, and I walked away, stopping before double backing and holding her face and dropping a few kisses on her lips.

"Capri?"

"Yes?"

"Grow the fuck up."

"Oh, fuck you, Cappadonna!" she yelled at my back until I turned around, jogging backward while teasing her.

Capri needed to learn to grow up and stop running from shit when it became too hard. Kincaid had fucked up in the past with his bad ass judgment but had long fixed it. He gave me his word that nothing was going on between him and Jasmine, and I trusted him until he gave me another reason.

"You love to show off that you run for fun, huh?" Capone laughed when I caught up with him after busting a light sprint.

"Shit, you need to get out there and do it, too. Our birthday run damn near took you out," I teased him.

Naheim, Kincaid, and Capella were already sitting at the table waiting for us. "About time you decided to show up. I mean, we did all of this for you," Naheim snorted.

They had reserved the part of the patio near the beach, and I noticed all the food over near the bar waiting for me to take my seat. Instead of beers, they had ginger beers on the table since I didn't drink.

I raised my eyebrow. "Is this some bachelor party?"

"Nigga, we wanted to celebrate you. Sit yo ass down so we can crack open these non-alcoholic fucking beers and talk shit." Capone plopped down in his chair, and grabbed a bottle, popping the top off and taking a swig.

"You really about to be a married man, Capp," Kincaid laughed. "Usually, men come home and fall into some pussy... you fell into a whole relationship."

Naheim excused himself and went to answer his phone. "And would do it again in a heartbeat. I'm more concerned about you and Capri... the fuck going on?"

He leaned back and popped open his bottle. "She got it in her head that I'm cheating with Jasmine. I spent the night at Jasmine's house and slept on the couch. Capri called me and I told her where I was at. She took it upon herself to break up with me."

"Capri suspected Naheim of cheating and she wasn't wrong... shoot the real with us... I promise I won't slam your head into the bar," I smiled.

Kincaid looked at me before moving his seat back some. "Shit is complicated, Capp... not even going to hold you. Me and Capri got a lot of shit to figure out. Her moms passed and I'm trying to be there for her. Told Capri that I would fucking hurt myself before I ever allowed myself to hurt her." I could see in his eyes that he wasn't telling me everything.

I really couldn't blame my sister for trying to end things before she got hurt again. Her marriage to Naheim really broke her and fucked her trust all the way up.

Naheim plopped back down in the chair. "Was that Nellie?" Capone teased.

"Yeah. She was showing me some shit she saw for NJ at Walmart."

I leaned back and messed with my beard. "I heard something about your girl."

Naheim leaned forward. "How she and Alaia know each other?"

"How?" Capella sat up, confused on what was going on.

"They were married to the same man."

"She wasn't fucking married to that pussy," I blurted, scaring the table behind us. "She just willingly gave you that information?"

"Yeah. She told me on the way back to my crib that night. She told me she was married to some man that had other wives, but I never put it together."

"You gonna cry if I kill her?"

Capone and Kincaid both choked on their drinks while looking at me. "And he dead serious, too."

"Why the fuck would you kill her? She not mixed in that other shit... you don't think I did my own research."

"Yeah, your other research had you fucking Tasha and actually giving a fuck about her."

"I didn't care about no fucking Tasha."

"And Kendra never sucked my dick." I paused. "My fault, son."

Capella put his hands over his ears and leaned back. "Remind me to burn my fucking ears later."

"Nellie ain't even into all of that. She goes to work and raises her daughter. Everything checks out with her, and she told me soon as she saw Alaia at the party. If I find out she up to some weird shit, I'll be the first person to handle her."

"Yeah, you better... because if you don't, I'm handling both of y'all asses." I looked at them. "We may have handled Tweety, but Ace is still a problem that needs to be handled."

"Soon as we touch down, we gonna handle him," Kincaid assured me.

I raised my bottle for a cheer. "This nigga wanna have a cheers after threatening damn near everybody at this table." Capone laughed.

"A hood nigga that finds a wife, finds a good thing." Naheim raised his glass.

"How the fuck would you know?" Chubs laughed, teasing Naheim, who bumped his shoulder.

"Shut the fuck up... this ain't about me. To Cappadonna and Alaia... May someone finally be able to calm this crazy ass nigga."

"Hell yeah," Capone co-signed.

We sat by the beach and continued to chill and bullshit with each other. Capri had come to get Kincaid, while the rest of us continued to chill on the beach, not wanting to be near the chaos that was going on for the anniversary party tonight.

When I walked into the bedroom and saw Alaia standing in the mirror, I stood behind her, putting my hands on her hips. She wore this wide leg jumpsuit that had a cape feature on the back. It reminded me of the dress she wore for my birthday, but this time it was pants.

"You love a cape, huh? Gotta start calling you Batman."

She rolled her eyes and laughed while staring me in the eyes. "Fuck you."

"Shitt... potty mouth, huh?" I spun her around and tried to bite her bottom lip, and she pulled back.

"My makeup... Erin insisted that we all wear makeup tonight." She fixed her hijab, and then looked over her outfit again.

"You look perfect, Joy."

I bent down and rested my chin on her shoulder while she looked at me through the mirror. "Thank you, Baby."

"Oh shit. She's not questioning it? We making strides, Baby." I spun her around and held her around the waist while we did a fake little two step dance.

"I'm trying."

"Doing... you're *doing*." I gently kissed her lips, careful not to get the red on my lips. "I'm about to head out there... see you out there?"

"Yep."

I held my hand out and we did our handshake, kissing each other's hands before I headed toward the door. "Love you."

She smiled at me. "Love you, too."

23
ALAIA

JEAN AND DESMOND were so surprised by their surprise anniversary dinner. All their family from around the island was in attendance. You can tell how much they mean to Erin by the details of the party. The circular tables were decorated with beautiful tall candles, and flowers native to the country. Above us, there had to be at least fifty lanterns, lighting up the tables and the beach at the same time.

Me and Capp sat at the table watching his parents be so in love. They were having the best time, and it made me want the same thing for my own marriage. I wanted to be so happy that no one else or nothing else mattered. Whenever me and Capp were together, we always laughed.

"I never want to stop laughing with you." I smiled at him.

He lifted my chin and kissed me on the lips. "We never will."

We heard someone beat boxing on the mic and looked up at Jaiden holding the microphone. Jo snatched the mic from him. "Boy, move on over. I wanted to say a few words for Jean and Des. Happy anniversary. Seeing love like yours made me reevaluate my own, and I'm so happy that I did. When I lost my twin, I didn't think I could ever have another friend, or should I say sister." She sniffled, and Jaiden roped his arms around her. "You didn't replace my sister, but you damn sure were added into the bunch, Jean. I love you and the family that we have effortlessly blended together. Des, thank you for always being a phone call away to fix something after I mess it up. Always so patient. I love you guys."

Jean blew her kisses from her table. Capone and Capri took the microphone, while Cappadonna remained seated. "Mom and Pops, you know how I'm coming behind you already. If I can have half the marriage that you two have, I'd be grateful. I learned how to be a husband from watching my pops. He's kind, patient, and loves the dirty socks off moms. He showed me that there's no such thing as being soft when it comes to your wife. I watch how you love each other, and it makes me fall even more in love with my own wife. I want to sit on this beach in thirty years having my own kids speak about my own marriage that molded them into the people they are."

Capri took the mic phone her brother. "Mommy and Daddy, I love you both so much. You know how much I admire your relationship, and if I can have just a little piece of what you have... man, I wouldn't be out here like this." Capone snatched the mic from his sister once he realized her ass was slurring.

Capp stood up and kissed me on the cheek before making his way up there with his siblings. Every hair on my body stood up watching how smoothly he made his way through the sea of tables up there with his siblings. Capone handed him the microphone and he looked at his parents.

"My days didn't always look like this. When life was so uncertain for our family, it was your union that helped me keep going. I would sit in my cell and think about how pops always put you and us kids first. It didn't matter what happened, this man would always sure make we always ate first." He paused. "I don't idolize people because they fucking lie and portray this fake life or relationship. The only people I idolize is my family – my parents. I've watched them struggle with three mouths to feed, and still make time to pour into each other. They never stopped being in love, no matter how hard life got for them. I remember my cellie asked how I ended up in prison if I was raised with both my parents in the house. I told him that it was my burden to carry, not my parents. They did what they were supposed to do, and I just wanted to give them more. I would do it again if it meant I could witness you both sitting here surrounded by your kids, grandchildren, great-grandkid, and family."

Erin came and sat where Cappadonna was once sitting. "I'm so emotional."

I dabbed my own eyes. "You're not the only one. It's so beautiful to witness."

"So, on this anniversary, I asked both my parents how they would feel if I got married on their date. With my own family, I could only pray that my union will be blessed like yours."

I choked on my mock-tail. "What?"

Cappadonna turned toward where I was sitting. "I believe you made me a promise, Joy. You said you would marry me anywhere... and you would meet me down the aisle. What you say, Baby?"

Capone handed me the extra microphone. "I...I'm not dressed, Roy."

"Why do you think your dress was brought today?" Erin whispered in my ear. "Let's go and get you ready."

"You're going to have all these people wait for me to put my dress on and fix my make up?"

"I'm on your time, Alaia... you gonna leave me here waiting?"

I pushed the microphone into Capone's hand, and Erin took my hand while we ran back up to the villa. I expected that I would be sweating and nervous, and I didn't feel any of that. I felt at peace and couldn't put this dress on quick enough to make it to marry him.

Erin and Capri both zipped my dress up and allowed me to fix my beaded turban that matched my dress. "I think I'm going to cry, Alaia," Capri gasped, as she took in my entire look.

Jean came and stood behind me, hugging me. "You look absolutely beautiful. You're going to make him cry, Alaia."

"You think so."

"I know my boys." She held both her hands out for Capri and Erin. "Just like I know my girls."

We all hugged while trying to avoid crying to mess up our makeup. "Well, you can't keep him waiting forever. Even though, I think he may wait forever for you." Erin hugged me.

Me and Erin walked out hand in hand, and Capri held my other hand. "Capp asked us to walk you down the aisle, and it would be my greatest honor to give you to one of the greatest men I know." Capri leaned her head on my shoulder.

"It wasn't by chance that you and Cappadonna found each other. You were meant to find each other." Erin kissed me on the cheek.

We walked out the house and back down to the beach, with them holding my dress and helping me with each step. When we made it to the bottom step, I gasped. The beach had been transformed. The tables were all positioned on opposite sides, with an aisle now in its place.

Down at the end of the aisle, I held my hand over my mouth when I saw Cappadonna standing there waiting for me.

He changed his clothes into a traditional thobe that had the same beading that I had on my dress.

What brought tears to my eyes was that he was holding Promise. We took a step and heard the live band that was tucked in the corner. "Promise" by Jagged Edge played as I started to walk. My legs were wobbly because I was so emotional.

Cappadonna used his scarf that was wrapped around his shoulder to wipe his eyes. The closer that we got, I could see that he was crying while holding our daughter.

Our daughter.

The tears wouldn't stop pouring from my eyes. Even when Capri stopped mid walk to blot my face, I couldn't stop crying. When we made it down the aisle, Capone took Erin to the side, while Kincaid took Capri to the other side.

Jean and Desmond stood beside me, looping their arms into mine. We all stepped up onto the stage together. Jean taking Promise, while Des stood on the side of his son.

"Fuck," Cappadonna said, sniffling and wiping his eyes.

I smiled at him through my tears. "Hi."

"Hey, Baby. You look beautiful." He kissed me on the cheek, and then stepped back.

Jean held my hand, and then held her husband's hand. Des held Cappadonna's hand, and then Capp held my hand, making us a circle.

Me and Capp stared into each other's eyes as the officiant spoke. My heart was calm, and I had never felt calmer in my entire life. Jean and Des stepped back, giving us the floor, and Capp took both my hands into his, massaging the back of my hands while staring down at me.

"I knew today I would be marrying my best friend. No offense, Capo." Everybody chuckled. "I woke up, prayed, and went for a run on the beach excited that I would be marrying her today. Alaia knew we would be getting married on this trip, she just didn't know it would be today. I know some of you were confused by me calling her Alaia, then Joy."

He kissed the back of my hands. "Told you that you would make him cry," Jean whispered in my ear.

"Her name means joy, and that's what she has brought to my life since we met. I can't even picture what life was like before you came waddling into my life again. I'd do everything all over again if that means you'll be at the end waiting for me. I told you that I'm on your time, and I mean that always. I got your back, your sides, and your front, baby. I'm here and I'm never going anywhere."

My makeup was ruined so it didn't make sense to try and fix it because I was a mess. "Cappadonna," my voice broke. "*My* Roy."

My hands were shaking as I held his and stared up into his eyes. He kissed the back of my hands, giving me that reassuring glare. "You saved my life. I don't know if you know, but when you ran into me that day I had given up on life. Just existing, no longer living life. Just praying for something good to happen to me, then you appeared. You loved me when I had nothing to give. You loved me even with how broken I am. Loving me isn't easy, and somehow you make it seem so easy. I've never been someone who has ever been someone's priority. Every day, you choose me." I sniffled, looking out at Erin who was holding Promise. "You choose us. You're the most patient person that I know, and so selfless. You are my superman, the man of my dreams, my home. I'm honored to stand before Allah and become your wife. I love you so much that it hurts at times. Thank you for taking the risk and deeming me worthy while healing a broken heart that you didn't break."

I took a deep breath. "I promise to love you until I take my last breath. I promise to always put you first, and honor you. You are my husband today and forever... Roy and Joy?"

Tears fell down his face as he kissed the back of my hands and stared at me. He didn't bother to wipe his tears, as our eyes connected. Nobody mattered around us, it was just me and him up here. I couldn't hear anything, but I saw everything when I looked at him.

"Forever," he completed the sentence, removed his hands from mine, and held it out so we could do our handshake, slowly kissing the other's hand while staring into each other's eyes.

I don't think I heard a word the officiant was saying. We were both caught up in our own world as we stared into each other's eyes. Cappadonna's stare was still intense, but I had learned to love it.

Before, it used to make me nervous. Now, I was just turned on whenever he stared at me like that. With the way he was staring at me, it was like he was trying to undress me with his eyes.

"You can kiss your wife, Baby Boy," Jean whispered.

Cappadonna took his hands and grabbed my face, giving me a kiss. Everyone clapped and cheered while we turned around and made our way down the aisle. He held his hand out and like a magnetic pull, my hands connected with his as he helped me up the steps to the villa.

When we were alone, he spun me around and shoved his tongue down my throat while gripping my ass, and I accepted it, sucking on his tongue while we swapped spit. "I needed to give you that nasty kiss alone... don't need them seeing how I kiss my wife."

"Your wife." I smiled.

He spun me around, and then kissed me again. "My fucking wife."

24
CAPPADONNA

Alaia danced on the dance floor with Erin and Capri while I watched her. My fucking wife was beautiful. She held her dress up as she danced with them and laughed. Alaia had a laugh that you wanted to bottle up and save for later.

I loved hearing her laugh and have a good time. Before joining her on the dance floor, I sat at the table and watched her. "I remember the first time you looked at her that way. You were in a pair of prison greens." Capone squeezed my shoulder and sat down next to me.

"How the fuck did I get here? Good shit doesn't happen to me, Capo... she's all that's good in this world."

"Good shit happens for you, Capp. Look around, nigga. All of this is ours. You have a wife now... something we spoke about when all of this was just talk. Now, you protect her with your life and love her with everything. Follow the example that was shown to us."

"The example I clearly couldn't follow." Capri came plopped down between us, trying to catch her breath from dancing. She took the beer from Capone and polished off the rest. "He's right, Cappy. Alaia is all that is good for you. You have the biggest heart, and you deserve this. All of this. The both of you do." She smiled at both of us. "I want to thank you both for giving me sisters-in-law. You both know I've never been great with having friends, and you both went ahead and got me built in best friends."

I looked back to the dance floor and Alaia was dancing with CJ, who was doing some off the wall Michael Jackson shit. She was trying to do the dances while laughing with Erin, who was dancing with Jaiden.

"Since you bringing it up... stop calling Erin after ten. That's my time and ya'll be cackling and shit."

"Cause you trying to cackle the draws off her... freaky ass nigga." Me and Capri both laughed while looking at Capone.

"Bet. Don't complain when Alaia on the phone talking about *girl yes. I know...girllll,*" Capone mocked Erin.

"When I walked through that door, Alaia ain't never worried about her phone... I'm not concerned." I looked at my sister who stared out at our parents. "Baby Doll, what's good with you?"

"Honestly, I don't know. I feel like I'm failing at this adulting thing. The one I wanted; I can't have because my heart won't allow me to open up to him like I once did." She sighed.

I followed her eyes to Naheim who was sitting at the bar laughing with Chubs. "And Kincaid?"

"I feel like I'm keeping him from Jasmine. He loves her, Capp, and although he still treats me like gold, I can't help but to feel like he should be with her." She shrugged. "Enough about me... go ahead and dance with your wife. I love you, Cappy."

I kissed her on the forehead. "Love you more, Baby Doll."

I stood up and walked onto the dance floor where my wife

was standing. Touching her back, she spun around, and her eyes brightened when she saw me. "There you are. Are you going to dance with me?"

"I'm gonna dance with you forever, Joy." I kissed her cheek.

The DJ spotted that I finally made it onto the dance floor, and he played the song I requested for our first dance. Alaia was so caught in my eyes that she didn't notice everyone exiting the dance floor until it was just the two of us.

"I don't know this song," she giggled.

"Always and Forever" by Heatwave played as we danced under the lanterns that were above us. I kissed her nose. "Just keep reminding me I'm old as shit, Joy."

She laughed up and rubbed my beard. "I mean, you a whole grandpa out here."

I softly bit her neck and whispered into her ear. "You fucking a grandpa, Joy?"

She blushed. "I haven't yet... you don't know where the night will take us."

If you would have asked me if I would be dancing in the middle of the beach with my new wife while singing oldies, I probably would have questioned if you were using the product I sold. I knew what I wanted my life to look like when I got out of prison, but knowing what you want it to look like, and what it actually looks like was two different things.

I remember when Capone came up to visit me and told me about meeting the love of his life. Capone never spoke like that, so I knew he had to be serious. When he spoke about Erin and how she made him feel, I wanted that shit for myself. Even being with Kendra, I knew I never felt like that about her.

Did I love Kendra? I had love for her, but I was probably never truly in love with her. Witnessing the way Erin loved my brother made me want that for myself. Someone that I could break down these walls for and make me feel comfortable enough to trust them. Alaia had her own walls up when we met.

Slowly, we both learned to trust each other. I learned to trust that someone could love a man as complex as me. She learned what love was and what it felt like to be loved and protected.

"Can I have this dance with my daughter-in-law?" my father cut in, and I handed Alaia over to him, while my mother stepped into Alaia's place.

Alaia and my father danced while I spun my mother around. Jean Delgato was my queen, and the reason I was the man that I am today. I remember sitting in my cell thinking about her all the time. I knew how she worried, and not knowing the outcome of her son's freedom bothered me more than sitting and doing the time.

"Oh Cappadonna, I am so proud of you. I admit, I was worried when you were released. I didn't know what life would look like for you. With Capone getting married and having his own family, I worried how you would fit in with his life. Then you met Alaia, and I could see how much you cared for that girl."

"Love her with my whole heart."

"I know you'll be the perfect husband and father. All my prayers throughout the year have come true. Alaia is a good woman... which makes her perfect for you." A tear slid down my face as I looked down at my mother, and she wiped it away. "I know you never think you're deserving of good things, Baby. What you do to protect your family has nothing to do with the person you are, Cappadonna. You've always felt like you had to take care of me and your father since you were younger. We're okay... it's time for you to live your life and make up for all that time you missed." She wiped her hands down my face to wipe the tears away.

I've never been ashamed to cry in front of my mother. There has been times before I was locked up that I fell to my knees and laid on my mother's lap while she prayed over me. This was my queen, the rock to this family.

"I hear you, Ma."

"You do whatever you have to do to handle those horrible men... always remember your family is home waiting for you, and we'll never judge you or your brother for keeping us safe."

I kissed my mother on the cheek, as my father handed me back my wife. Before he did, he pulled me into a hug and kissed my cheek. "Love you, boy."

"Love you, too, Pops."

Me and Alaia danced for a few more songs while everyone joined us. I couldn't stop staring at how beautiful she looked. She was so damn beautiful that it hurt to think of all the shit she had been through.

We took a shit ton of pictures. Me and the photographer were about to have beef until Joy reached up and kissed me. At the end of the night, everyone lined up and made an aisle for us to run through while they held sparklers. We stood at the top of the aisle, and I held my baby's hand. "You ready?"

She smiled and looked up at me. "I'm always ready."

We sprinted past everyone that cheered and held their sparkler out. When we made it to the other side, I held her face and kissed her on the lips. Alaia yelped when I picked her up and carried her back up to the villa.

She was always surprised when I picked her up like I didn't bench 350. She was light work to pick up and carry. "I got one more surprise for you," I revealed.

"As if putting me on the spot wasn't surprise enough." She smirked.

I sat her on the bed, and she looked at our carry on suitcases packed. "You ready to go?"

"Go? Where are we going? What about Promise?"

"Joy, we got nothing but family and nannies here. We got a few more days here, and I want to spend them with you uninterrupted. We're not going far... okay?"

She smiled. "Okay. Should I change out my dress?"

I looked at her and bit my lip. "Nah. I wanna take that off you."

Before we left, I quickly took my thobe off, and wore the tank top I had under it. I carried our bags out to the front where an old school Bronco with the roof off was waiting for us. There were white peonies in the back with a sign 'just married' tied to the back of it. "You are very sneaky, Cappadonna... how did I miss all of this?"

"I couldn't have done it without my sisters and mom... they really came through and helped my vision come together."

Putting the suitcases into the back seat, I lifted my bride into the front seat. She held onto me longer and kissed me on the lips. Everyone filed from the beach to watch us drive off. My mother and father held onto each other as they looked at us through misty eyes.

Capone held onto Erin and saluted me as I pulled away from in front of the villa. Erin blew kisses at us while crying. Jaiden and Capri both faked like they were gonna run behind me, as I sped out the property.

"You going to tell me where we going?"

I took her hand and kissed it. "Nah."

"Cappadonna!" she squealed.

I smirked as I whipped through the island to our destination.

~

It was only a thirty-minute ride to the private villa that I had booked for us. Cragmere villa was a private villa right on the edge of the island. It sat on a cliff with panoramic views of the ocean. No matter what side of the villa you were on, you would see the beach and the turquoise blue water. The huge infinity pool gave you a front seat view to Allah's beautiful creation.

Most importantly, it was private. There was nobody walking on the beach and no people for miles away. Other than the staff, there was nobody there, and my baby could walk around without any clothes on without anybody looking at her.

I had already threatened the staff and told them that they don't come in unless they knock or let me know. I wanted Alaia to wear a bathing suit and lay out in the sun with her hair out, without either of us worrying about someone walking in.

As happy as I was to have married my baby, I knew the minute we were back home we had a lot to do. We needed to move into the new house, and I had other shit that needed to be handled. Ace had been walking around too long for me, and I wanted to handle him.

I beat myself up for not pulling that trigger in the club that night, but now I can say that I'm glad that I didn't. I wouldn't have experienced marrying my baby if I had been reckless like I wanted to be.

"Baby, this is beautiful... look at the view." Alaia was holding her dress while running around the villa pointing out everything.

I put the bags down and went into the backyard where she was standing. Putting my arms around her, we both looked out at the view. "Shit is beautiful."

"So, there's nobody else around?"

"Nah. The villa down the beach is private, too, and I

booked that one, too, so I know for a fact nobody is on this beach."

She gasped. "Seriously?"

"Hell yeah. I take preserving my wife's modesty seriously. I'll kill a nigga out here if he look at you, Alaia."

She giggled and leaned her head back on my chest. "Did we really get married?"

Kissing her forehead, I replied, "Yeah, and before you start, I would do it all again."

She smiled and then yawned, walking back inside the villa. I stood in the doorway watching her mess with the suitcases to unpack. "Alaia," I called, my eyes traveling down her dress as I stared at her from across the room.

She turned and looked at me. "What happened? Since you packed our stuff, did you pack everything we would need? I just feel like you tossed anything in here."

"I don't give a fuck about what's in those suitcases." I crossed the room until I was standing in front of her.

"Why not?" she flirted back, holding the side of my face.

I took her hand, kissing the palm of it and pulling her behind me upstairs to the bedroom. Pulling her in front of me, I allowed her to push the door open. She gasped when she saw what I had set up for her.

The room was on the corner of the house, so the only solid walls in the room were the wall the bed was against, and the wall across it where the TV mounted above the fireplace. The rest of the room was all floor to ceiling windows with views of the ocean.

There were candles inside of glass containers littered all throughout the room. The shades were pulled back, exposing the darkness that would be a beautiful view come morning. She walked into the room and looked at the gift bags filled with gift for her.

"When did you do all of this?" she turned to look at me.

"What did I tell you when we first met?" I held her chin.

Alaia was struggling to figure out what I had told her. "In my defense, you told me a lot of things."

"I told you that a real man can't never do enough for his woman." I kissed her lips, as she wrapped her arms around my neck, moaning into my mouth.

While our tongues danced in and out of each other's mouths, I messed around with the latches on the back of her dresses. Why the fuck did they design dresses with all of these damn buttons and zippers.

Alaia pulled back, biting down on my bottom lip. "I'm about to break this fucking dress, Joy," I warned her.

She pulled on my lip, and that's when I said fuck it and popped that dress open, sending buttons, zippers and whatever the fuck else flying everywhere. The dress became loose on her, and I pulled that shit down until she was standing in front of me in a slip.

"My dress," she laughed.

"I'll buy you three more," I growled into her ear, as I picked her up and carried her across the room to the bed.

Alaia had that look in her eyes, letting me know she was ready for this. The lust and love in her eyes swirled around like a hurricane on the maps the weather people used to predict storms. I kissed her lips, as I placed her on the bed, pulling her slip dress up and tossing it behind me.

I paused as I took in her laying on the edge of this bed with a matching lace bra and panty set. She removed her turban, loosening the hair tie that held her hair into a tight bun. Her hair fell down onto her shoulders as she stared up at me.

I felt like I was in high school again about to experience my first time with how excited seeing my wife had me. "What?" she ran her hand through her hair.

I licked my lips, taking mental snapshots. "Dreams come fucking true, Joy." I bent over, pushing my lips against her, pushing her back onto the bed.

While I kissed her neck, placing soft bites down onto her chest, I slipped her panties off. She opened her legs, and I unlatched her bra, watching her breast escape. I swirled my tongue around her nipple as I looked up into her eyes.

My hand found its way down to my favorite spot and I felt how wet she was. "Tell me what you feeling, Baby," I demanded, as I bit her nipple.

Her eyes were barely open with how she was moaning. "I...I feel good, Roy."

"Who?"

"Daddy... I feel good," she corrected herself, as I traveled down below, opening her legs wider.

Rubbing my nose all through my pussy, I took in my favorite sweet scent before I kissed her second set of lips while she squirmed. Alaia was leaned up on her elbows, as our eyes locked. I flicked my tongue over her pearl, and she almost jumped back.

I knew she had never had her pussy eaten, and it brought me joy that nobody had ever had her like I was about to. Spreading her legs, I went deeper, nipping at her pearl while she screamed out. She flipped and flopped all over the bed while I held her legs in place. Every time she tried to scoot away, I pulled her even closer to me, and then slowly swirled my tongue around inside her.

"What you feeling, Baby?" I asked, my voice sending vibrations through her body. She couldn't speak as she tried to keep her eyes open and stay in place. "Can't hear you." I asked while slurping her nectar.

When her legs started to shake, I knew she was about to cum. "Daddy... I'm...I'm about to—" she couldn't finish her sentence before her body started to shaking, and I tasted more of her nectar.

Sex was a sensitive subject for Alaia. It was something that was always negative for her, and I promised myself I would make her fall in love with it. To see it as a positive experience. Something that would only be shared between me and her. I would only see her like this, and I would be the only one that made her cum like she had just did.

Alaia was like putty as she lay in the middle of the bed. I looked at her, mesmerized that she was my wife. This was my wife, and I got to spend forever with her. After all the shit I had done, Allah saw me fit to have a beautiful wife that loved me just as much as I loved her. I've never been the type to believe in forever with someone. I was the first to admit that everything and everyone had an expiration date.

Not *this.*

Not *us.*

Alaia and Promise were forever. I was meant to hit that illegal ass U-turn that day when I saw her. She was supposed to call me and ask me to buy her food, because it was meant for us to be together. We were supposed to end up here, and I would do whatever it took to keep this look in her eyes.

When Alaia looked into my eyes, there was love, respect, and trust. This woman trusted me after life had failed her so many times. Her own family failed her, and she still found it inside of her heart to trust me and my family.

That was the reason shit wasn't just words for me. I had to show her action, so she knew I was coming different behind her. Her eyes found me as she leaned up on her elbows and waited for what was about to come next.

"What you thinking?" she asked me.

I bit down on my bottom lip as I loosened my belt and allowed my pants to fall to my ankles. Alaia eyes widened when she saw how my briefs were pitching a fucking tent. She climbed toward the end of the bed, and stared me in the eyes, as she kissed me on the lips. I felt her hands in my waist band of my briefs, as she pulled my shit out for me.

"Can I?" she asked, looking into my eyes, her mouth-watering.

"You don't have to."

Those big brown eyes stared up at me. "I want to, Cappadonna."

"You can do whatever you want... this your dick, baby," she pulled me onto the bed, and then moved to the bottom where she held my dick in her hand. I watched as she stared at it, then me unsure of what to do with it.

"I've never done it before," she looked away from me, slightly embarrassed that she had never given head.

"Go slow, Baby... I'll guide you," I directed her. She held the shaft, as she lowered her mouth, adjusting her jaw to accommodate me fully. "Less teeth, Baby." I put my hands behind my head as I watched her go slowly.

She was slow, stiff even, then she loosened up while she looked me in the eyes. Alaia wanted to please me, and in time with more experience she would become a force to reckon with. "Like this?" she asked when she popped my shit out her mouth.

"Uh huh. Spit on it for me." My eyes remained low as I watched her, naked, bent over while pleasing her husband.

Slapping her ass, she squealed but she never lost her step. I grabbed her ass, playing with her from the back while she spit on my dick, and then devoured it. She moaned with my dick still inside her mouth, driving me crazy. "Shit, Joy." I cursed, biting the inside of my cheek. Her grip became tighter, and I leaned up, looking at her ass.

How she went from being so fucking timid to about to suck

the skin off my dick. I didn't know what to hold onto, so I grabbed her ass tighter while I allowed her to continue doing her thing. When I felt that rush at the tip of my dick, I pulled myself out of her mouth and grabbed her ass up and flipped on top of her. Easing my way between her legs, I leaned over her.

I watched that devilish fucking grin on her face. "Did I do something wrong, Mr. Capp?"

I removed her curly tresses from her face as I kissed her lips. "You know damn well you didn't do shit wrong."

She wrapped her legs around me as I continued to kiss her lips, slipping my tongue into her mouth. Her body squirmed, back arched up, letting me know she was ready for me. I teased her opening before I slowly pushed myself into her, holding the top of the wooden headboard.

Alaia never took her eyes from mine as I stared into hers. "I'm okay."

It was like she read my mind. "Let me know if you're not... okay?"

"Okay." I bent my head down and kissed her on the lips, while I continued to push more of myself into her, slowing down while she adjusted herself. "Hmmm."

"I told you the day I slid up inside of you was the day you would be my wife," I took one of her legs, pushing it up.

"Capp," she moaned out.

I bit down on my bottom lip. "Nah. Remember you wanted this the other day," I reminded her of when she was in the mirror begging for this dick.

I pulled out slowly, then slammed my dick back inside of her while she screamed with pleasure. With one hand on the headboard, then the other holding up her thick thigh, I maneuvered my hips giving her powerful strokes that had her ass tongue tied.

"You so fucking wet, Joy... why you so fucking wet?" I grunted, while staring down into her eyes.

Her nails were in my skin while she tried to get her words together. Alaia's pussy was so wet that she was giving the ocean outside the window fucking competition. Each time I pulled out, it sounded like a fucking slip and slide.

"For.... For you, Capp."

"What I told you... what's my name, Joy?"

"Da...Daddy!" she screamed.

Alaia was trying to catch her breath, and I wasn't letting up. I had dreamed of the day I would slide up in some pussy for too many years. It had been so long that I was starting to forget what it felt like to be inside some.

She was scooting back, and I bit down on her lip. "Stop running from it, Joy... Stay still for me, Baby."

I kneeled down until our foreheads were rested against each other. The shit felt so good that I felt like my bitch ass was about to fucking cry. Every time I felt myself about to nut, I pulled out and then pushed myself back inside of her slower hoping to make it last longer.

"You like that, Joy?" I said, as she kissed my nose, holding me tight while I continued to stroke her cat.

"Uh hmm."

"Baby, use your words... Is this what you wanted?" I softly bit her neck, while holding her leg up.

"I'm about to... daddy, I have to..." she could barely finish her words.

"Hold it... Don't let it go until I tell you, okay?"

She stared into my eyes, holding my face with her hands. Our eyes focused on each other while we got lost in the moment. "Please don't stop," she whispered into my ear.

I was the one telling her not to cum, and here I was struggling. "Joy, fuck."

"It's all yours, Capp... I'm yours," she cooed in my ear, biting my ear lobe.

I flipped us over, positioning her on top of me. She slid down slowly, holding onto my chest while I held onto her hips. "Fuck, Alaia!" I roared, holding onto her hips tighter. "Ride this dick, Baby."

She held onto my chest as she slowly rolled her hips, staring at me through lust filled eyes. "Like this?"

I held her hips and moved her faster. "You can take it... you got it, Mama... fuck...go ahead...ride your man...shit, Joy," I coached her, as I reached up and played with her nipples.

The more I talked to her, I watched as she became more confident in taking control.

My wife had me going crazy. I used to think that pussy was just pussy, and if you had it once you've had them all. I ran through my fair share of pussy back in the day before Kendra. Even after having Kendra's, I still felt the same. I felt like I could get what she had from any thirsty bitch waiting to give it.

I stood corrected because pussy was different once love was connected to it. I watched as my wife rode my dick with tears coming down her eyes. "It...It feels so good. You feel so good," she whimpered, while scratching the fuck out of my chest.

I removed my hands from her waist and put them behind my head while taking in how she had taken control. It was so good to her that she had tears coming down her face while she scratched my chest up.

"Right there, Baby... you bout to make me... wet my dick for me, Joy," I grunted.

I couldn't even play it cool with my hands behind my head, my hands found their way to her hips. "I need you, Capp..." she cooed while holding onto my chest.

"Shit... fuck... you got me, Joy. I ain't going anywhere, Baby."

"Promise?"

"I fucking promise," I tightened my grip on her hip, and I felt her body jerk. "Cum for your husband, Joy."

We both released at the same time. She collapsed on top of me, and I wrapped my arms around her while still being inside her. I kissed her on the forehead. "I love you, Baby." She yawned, as I rubbed her ass.

"Love you, too, Joy." I kissed her lips. "You feel that? You ain't tapping out... are you?"

She leaned up and laughed. "No, Roy."

I watched as she tried to climb out of bed. "Nah... I got about fifteen more rounds in me. Told you I was gonna wear yo ass out, right," I growled in her ear, biting on her ear while pulling her back into the bed as she laughed, not knowing what she sighed up for.

Tonight, I was going to wear my wife's ass out.

25
CHUBS

My cousin was on my mind, and I needed to check on her. The minute we got back from Barbados, this was my first stop. Kendra opened the door and smiled when she saw me. With the way she was standing, I guess she thought I was going to give her ass a hug. I may have spared her from Capp, that didn't mean we were about to act like we were cool.

The only reason I told Capp I didn't want her to be done dirty was because I truly believed she didn't know anything about what Ace had did. I stepped around her and entered the house that she was in the middle of cleaning.

There was dishes piled up in the sink, the kitchen table had a bunch of takeout containers, and the coffee table had a thick film of dust on the glass. Jasmine was a neat freak and we had gotten into plenty of arguments because she saw imaginary dust bunnies.

"What the fuck is going on?"

Kendra sighed, plopping down on the couch. "I was out of town with Sassy and came back to it looking like this. She only leaves the room to use the bathroom and nothing else."

"She sleep?"

"Sleep?" Kendra choked. "All she does is lay on the bed and listen to a voicemail that Francie left her a year ago. I don't know what to do, Capella." For the first time, I saw Kendra actually concerned about someone other than herself.

"Fuck."

"She's really taking it bad. I know we both have our own feelings and how we grieve, but this is physically messing with her."

I took a seat on the edge of the couch and looked around the living room. There were pictures of me, Jasmine, and my aunt everywhere. It had always been just the three of us for everything. Picking up the picture frame, I smiled at the picture of us at Dallas BBQs after my eighth-grade graduation.

Kendra was supposed to show up and I had even went above and beyond to get an extra ticket. While everyone else had only two tickets for their family, I had three and it went to waste. She never showed up but came a week later with a bunch of gifts and an apology like that shit mattered.

"You're so tanned. Where were you?" she asked.

"Went on vacation with my father," I muttered.

Kendra nodded slowly. "I love that you and Capp are building a relationship together. Has he come around to the baby?"

It took a minute before Capp came around to accepting that he was a grandfather. He would look at Rory, never picking him up. Then once he picked him up because Aimee had went to shower and he woke up. Now, he picked him up whenever he passed by his bouncer. It helped that Rory looked like him.

I had something to say at the tip of my tongue and decided not to say anything. As much as I wanted to hurt Kendra like she had hurt me through the years, it wasn't worth it anymore.

How much longer could I continued to be upset and continue to punish her.

"How is your father?"

"Married."

You would have thought I stabbed her in the chest with the bottle opener sitting on the coffee table. She couldn't even play cool if she wanted because it was written all over her face. If I didn't know any better, I would say that Kendra's ass was actually hurt.

"Th...That's nice. Congrats to him," she choked out the words.

I did take some pleasure in rubbing the shit in. "You both went ahead and got married... so proud of my parents."

"Capella, our marriage isn't really legal. I never filed the papers when we got back. I'm going to leave him. It was a mistake to even marry him in the first place. I got caught up, and I guess I wanted to make your father jealous."

It bugged me out that Kendra had known Cappadonna longer than I did, and she thought marrying Ace would make him jealous. Why the fuck would he be jealous of someone he constantly slapped around whenever he saw him?

If I was her, I would have taken that marriage to the grave before I admitted that shit out loud. Word on the block was that Ace was using his own fucking supply and was lowkey crashing out.

Capp was playing it like the boogie man. You didn't know when he was coming, you just knew that nigga was going to come, and Ace couldn't take that.

"Why would he be jealous?"

"A question I've been asking myself every day." She sighed, looking down at her nails. "Is he happy."

"The happiest."

"How did he even meet her to get married that fast? And the baby is his daughter, too?"

I stood up, because she wasn't about to get me to talk about my family and tell her how shit was connected or how it came to be. It wasn't my place to sit here and tell my father's business. She didn't know how my little sister was connected into our life, or if she was Capp's biological daughter.

"Ain't my business to tell, Kendra. All you need to know is that there's a new Mrs. Delgato, and Capp coming hard behind that one." I chuckled and headed upstairs to Jasmine's room.

I tapped on the door, and then opened the door. Jasmine was laying with her back toward the door. The room smelled stale, like she hadn't opened a window in a year. The curtains were drawn, leaving it darker than it was outside.

Walking around the bed, I saw that she was awake. Her eyes were dark from her lack of sleep and all the tears I was sure she cried. When Kincaid told me how bad it was, I felt bad being in Barbados when I should have been here. I don't know what difference it would have made though. Jasmine would have just sent me away.

"I thought I heard Kendra talking to somebody." She sighed.

Jasmine was always so bubbly and animated whenever she spoke. She was always so bright, a bright light in all of our lives. If it was one person that was going to be positive, it was my cousin. She didn't believe in being negative. So, seeing how she was laying on this bed and how depleted she sounded hurt my heart.

I leaned on the wall. "Jasmine, come on."

"And do what? It doesn't matter what I do... my mother is still going to be dead." She took a deep sigh.

"Jas, you can't sit in this house and continue living like this. I understand the shit hurts, and I more than anyone knows how this feels. Still, we can't stop living because she's gone. She would fuck us up if she knew that." Jasmine giggled, and I saw a smile. "Look at that... a fucking smile."

"Shut up, Capella."

"You know I'm always here for you. All you have to do is call me and I'm coming, Jas."

"Which is why I don't call you. You have a family and can't be coming to save your big cousin." She sat up in the bed. "My job called me earlier and told me that they no longer need me. Apparently, I used all my time up, and since I didn't show up this morning, they decided that was the final nail. When it rains, it rains fucking hard."

"Don't worry about that. I'll pay your bills... you don't need to go back to work."

"Absolutely not. I used the last bit of savings to make the mortgage payment on Mama's house. Soon I'm going to have to sit down and talk about selling it."

"We're not selling her house," I sternly told her. "Why didn't you tell me you were low on money, Jasmine?"

"It's not your job to take care of me, Capella. I'm not going to have you out there risking your life to pay for my lifestyle. Eventually, we're going to have to sell the house. Mama left us both the house, so we can split the profit from the sale."

"I ain't trying to hear that shit right now." I waved her off, and she shrugged, knowing she would bring the conversation back up again.

She looked over at me. "How are things with your mother? I didn't hear any screaming, so I guess that's a good thing."

"It is what it is when it comes to Kendra. It's not like she's asked to see her grandchild. I deal with her in doses."

"She's family, Capella. I know she has done wrong and I'm not asking you to forgive that. I'm just asking you to try with her... we can't depend on Frankie's ass, it's just us."

I understood what she meant and had Kendra not done something as unforgiveable as hiding my father away from me, I probably would have been able to forgive her. Maybe with time, but as of now, I couldn't find it in my heart to give her what she desperately wanted – forgiveness.

Jasmine opened up more and even let me go grab Chinese food from our favorite spot. We ate and watched TV in her room while talking about my aunt. It gave us both comfort talking about her. Rather than act like she didn't exist, I liked to talk about her as if she would be calling my phone when she heard the infamous *it's ten o clock, do you know where your kids are*. Even after I had moved out, she still made it a point to call me and Jasmine whenever it came on after the news.

Jasmine had fell asleep in the middle of a movie we were watching. I kissed her forehead and then covered her with her blanket. "Love you, Jas," I whispered, slowly closing the door and heading downstairs.

Kendra had cleaned the entire downstairs up and was sitting on the couch scrolling on her phone. She looked so sad, even lonely as she sat there not knowing what to do. There wasn't shit I could do about it.

She had everything. Cappadonna had made sure she never wanted for anything, and all she had to do was stick by her man's side, and she decided that slanging her pussy around was more important than honoring her word.

"I wanted to tell you something before you hear it from somebody else."

Aimee had texted and asked me to pick up more diapers for Rory. "What's that?"

I guess she thought I was going to sit down so she could tell me whatever this news was. When she realized that I hadn't moved from my spot, she leaned up on the couch. "I'm pregnant, Capella. You're going to be a big brother."

I've never been a man that would ever put my hands on a woman. It took me a cool four minutes to convince myself not to slap her over the couch. The way she just announced that I was going to be a big brother like I was fucking five years old pissed me off.

I headed toward the door, looking back at her. "I already have a little sister... I don't need another sibling. If you wanna do what's best for this baby, you might as well abort it."

"Capella Ross... why are you trying to hurt me?"

"Delgato," I corrected her.

"I named you Capella and your last name is Ross."

"Capp wanted it changed to Delgato and submitted the paperwork for it." Since Capri was a lawyer, he had her submit the paperwork so that it could come back quicker than doing it on our own. Capri was always so unserious, but when I watched her with her glasses on and all the documents, I realized that each sibling may have joked and played around, but when it came down to business, they handled it – Capri included. He even told Aimee that she needed to do the same when it came to Rory's name, too.

"Later, Kendra." I headed out the door, leaving her sitting on the couch stunned. Big Mike was leaned on his truck waiting for me.

"He sent you?"

"You already know, Chubs. Your pops not playing with you. All that moving and shaking around the city you were doing is a wrap. You gotta move different when that last name is Delgato."

I hopped in my whip and whipped out, with Big Mike following closely behind me.

~

When I made it back to the lake house, I found Cappadonna sitting in the backyard with Capone. He stood up and hugged me when he saw me. I guess he could see the sorrow in my eyes from being with my cousin.

It was tough when you saw someone become something that you had never known them for. Jasmine was so broken, rightfully so, and I didn't know how to fix it. No amount of money I tossed her way would be able to fix things for her.

"What up, Chubs?" Capone nodded at me.

"Shit... came from seeing Jasmine." My body felt so weak, like I had been running a marathon and then never stopped running.

"You need to take it easy... a pain crisis will sneak up on you if you overwork or stress yourself out." He finished his beer, and then sat the empty bottle on the table.

I've always felt weak and some days I couldn't get out of bed, but I always pushed through. I found out that I had sickle cell as a grown ass man. Aimee told me the pain I had wasn't normal and it shouldn't have been ignored.

I just told her she was chatting, and she was the one that forced me to go to the hospital. She sat with me as they ran all these different types of test. I hated hospitals with a passion and was always the last person that would be caught in one.

Imagine my surprise when the test came back that I had sickle cell. The doctor explained that this wasn't something you could develop with time like asthma. He told me that I had been born with it. How the fuck could every person in my life have glanced over that? Was it not in my files from when I was born?

Now I had medicine that I had to take every day and I barely remembered to take it. I had experienced parts of my body swollen and it was something that I couldn't control. I was used to being able to control me, and with sickle cell the control was out of your hands.

I could see the concern in my father's eyes as he looked over at me. He was trying to allow me to be a man, but I could see that part of him that wanted to take over.

"Yeah, I'm gonna go lay down after I shower... had a stressful day."

Both my uncle and father gave me their full attention. "What you need me to do, Capella?" my father asked.

"Nothing really. I just need to handle my aunt's house and make sure Jasmine's bills are paid. She lost her job, and she's not in the head space to even be working, anyway."

"It's done."

"What you mean?"

"It's handled. Jas gonna be taken care of, she don't need to worry."

I leaned back on the patio couch, and we all turned our heads when Jaiden came outside. "Y'all sister just dusted me on the dirt bikes in the woods."

"The fuck you talking about, Kid?" Capp asked.

"Capri wanted to race with the dirt bikes. Bro', she dusted my ass. I spent nearly all summer perfecting my ride, and all it took was five seconds for her to dust me." We all laughed because he looked hurt that she beat him. "Then Alaia playing flag girl talking about she called the race."

Capp bit his bottom lip. "Oh yeah. She playing flag girl."

Jaiden looked at him. "Anyway, that's not what I came in here for. You know how I had a birthday just pass and a graduation. The kid eighteen now, soooo."

"So what?" Capone asked staring straight ahead.

I had to turn to look, and he was looking directly at Erin in the kitchen. She was laughing with Capri, and they were dancing, I guess celebrating their victory.

"Let me have a birthday and graduation party."

"Alright."

"I want to have it at Van-Cromwell house.... bring the cars out and racing and shit." Jaiden was so excited he could barely sit still.

"I don't know about that," Capone replied, still never taking his eyes from his wife.

"Come on, Capo. I'm grown now... let me live."

"What your sister think?"

"I was hoping to run it past you first, and then you can convince her. I'm not asking for y'all not to be there... you can come and do whatever you need to make sure it's safe. Let me have my fun before I leave by the end of the summer." He sighed.

"Shit coming faster and faster," I admitted, knowing that I was going to miss my best friend. Jaiden was my best friend, and I was going to miss him.

Capone stood up, stretching. "What you think, Capp?"

"Probably the safest place to have a party. Nobody gonna fuck with him knowing it's at Van-Cromwell house... I'm a member, so I can talk to Karter and see what he says."

"You already know he gonna give you the heads up." Jaiden jumped up too excited that his plan he had been sitting on for weeks worked out in his favor.

If I had to hear him running down all the reasons they should allow it one more time, I was going to blow my own brains out. "Fuck it... we can do it," Capone agreed.

"One last request... the Lamborghini... can I take it out?"

"Don't push it, Kid." Capp laughed.

"C'mon... I'll buy you a new one when I make it to the league, and you know I'm gonna make it. What did coach say to you?"

Capp dapped Jaiden up. "We already know our boy going fucking pro."

Capone chuckled. "Lemme think about it."

"I'll drive," I offered.

"Let's fucking go!" Jaiden got too excited, and Erin looked out the door. He hopped over the small gate. "I'm going back to the house... I wasn't here," he breezed through the backyard back to their lake house.

I shook my head because I don't know what I would do without his ass when he went to college.

26
ACE

"THERE HAS to be a reason she moved out of her apartment and told me that she refuses to bring the baby around us. She told me that I needed to talk to you because you know the reason. Ace, why the hell is she keeping my grandbaby hostage?"

I loved my mama, but I wanted to haul off and slap the shit out of her because she was getting on my nerves. When she asked to come over to my new spot, I hesitated because I knew there had to be a reason for her visit.

It wasn't like she popped up on me often. Money was always wired into her account, so she had no reason to come seek me out. As she stood in front of the TV with a new purse on her arm, she continued to just bump her gums hoping that I could give her a reason why her daughter was a disloyal little bitch.

I guess I should have known that Aimee would go running behind Chub's ass. She could never think straight without dick being swung in her face. When I told her that she was going to ride for my side because we were related, I expected her as to suck it up and hold it down for me. She acted like I was telling her to get out there and shoot at them niggas.

"Ace, do you hear me?"

"I'm really trying not to, Ma," I calmly responded, trying to hold onto my high that she was blowing.

It felt like she was speaking a million miles per hour and slow at the same time. As much as I wanted her to shut the fuck up, I wanted her to leave that much more. What the fuck did she want me to do about my sister? If I got my hands on her or that fucking baby, I was going to choke the life out of them because I knew it would hurt Cappadonna.

Big Capp finding out that I killed his grandson was something that kept me up at night smiling. There was nothing that got under that man's skin except his family. While both twins were different, that was something they both shared.

Before anything else, they were family men that would do whatever to protect them. I smiled and looked at my mother and she looked at me horrified. I fixed my face because I probably looked creepy smiling up at her the way that I did.

"Maybe you should set up something to see her. Do lunch or something, on me." I smirked, thinking about how Aimee would show up, and I would be there.

My mother was so concerned about seeing the baby that she didn't know she was part of my plan. Aimee would be so excited that my mother wanted to see her and fix things that she would come. She and my mother's relationship had never been the best, and Aimee always tried. My mom always resented her for whatever reason. No matter how much she pushed Aimee away, she still tried to make things work with our mother.

It wasn't until she moved away that the efforts weren't as great as before. She stopped calling and checking in like she used to, and that was because she was so busy sniffing behind some dick. Out of all the dick in this damn city she had to go sniffing and jumping on a Delgato?

How the fuck were family events going to happen when we both wanted to kill each other? There would never be any peace between me and Cappadonna. One of us had to go, and I would be damned if it was me.

"You just get her to agree to come, and I will set something up for y'all."

My mom kissed my cheek, wiping her lipstick stain from my cheek. "Alright... thank you for always being the problem solver. Love you, Ace." She was heading toward the door, and I was happy.

No sooner than the door closed behind her, I snorted a line and settled into the couch while staring at the TV. I had to figure a way to bring that big bitch to his fucking knees while I was on top.

Kendra's ass was no help because she was so busy claiming she was mourning her aunt. The bitch wasn't even that close with her family, and now she wanted me to believe that she was so torn up over the death of her aunt. Whenever I called her, she told me she was busy and would call me back. I moved out the old spot to a new one because I was paranoid. I couldn't be taking a shit and that nigga kicked in my door.

As far as Kendra knew, I was still staying at that house. Everything was the same, so whenever she came over, I pretended like I had been staying there. Something told me not to trust my damn wife. She was all too happy to get back in that nigga's good graces that she would do anything.

With her being pregnant, I knew I needed to be there for her. It was hard to be there for someone who acted like you couldn't protect them. The only reason she was walking around free was because I put in work. Cappadonna wasn't stupid, he wasn't going to touch her ass because I put that work in.

"Who the fuck are you talking to?" Monty caused me to jump, and my gun was across the damn room.

Damn. I'm slipping.

"Nobody."

"Only reason he ain't touch Kendra is because she's his baby mother. Which means his seed don't want her touched. With the way he looked at her at the club, I'm pretty sure he wanted to toss her ass over with you."

I rubbed my eyes. "Speaking of the club. Where the fuck were you when that nigga shoved that gun in my mouth and tossed me over the balcony?"

Monty put the bag of food I sent him to grab. "I came back when those niggas was leaving. I went to grab us more drinks because the bottle girl was taking too long."

"Oh."

"Yeah. I would have had that nigga handled if I knew that was his plan." Monty continued to big himself up knowing he wouldn't have gone that far.

I plopped down on the couch and motioned for him to bring me my food. Then opened the fried chicken from the Chinese spot.

My mother texted me that she and Aimee were going to grab something to eat at some Italian spot in Jersey. She said that I didn't need to worry about paying because Aimee offered to cover their meal.

She start fucking with the enemy, and now she had money to pay for everybody's meal. My mother sent me the address to the restaurant, excited that we were about to put everything under the table. I hated to break it to her, but I was about to grab Aimee's ass and that baby. She chose her side when she left that apartment and didn't give a fuck how I would feel.

I was her blood fucking brother, and she was acting like I was some stranger for that nigga. When she had nothing, I was the one that risked my life and made sure we had shit. Aimee always fucking complained. If she didn't have new sneakers like her friends, it was always a problem, and I made sure I made it happen for her spoiled ass.

She could never say I didn't fucking come through for her when it mattered the most. For her to turn her back on me when I needed a united front, she had me fucked up and she would learn. I've always handled Aimee with soft kiddie gloves because she was so sensitive. I sat across the street from the restaurant in the parking lot of the auto body shop. I parked so I was far away, yet, close enough to see when she entered the restaurant. I wanted her ass to get comfortable, because Aimee was known for fleeing when shit didn't go her way.

A black Mercedes G Wagon pulled in front of the restaurant. The tints were dark, even the windshield. The passenger door opened, and Aimee stepped out holding a diaper bag. When the driver door opened, I saw a timberland boot hit the street first, and then the rest of the body followed.

Cappadonna stepped out, tossing the keys over to the valet who rushed to hurry up and catch it. He went into the back, and pulled the car seat out, walking with ease like those car seats weren't heavy as fuck.

He looked around and me and Monty both jumped down in our seats, as if he could see us. I didn't know if this nigga had super nigga vision or something. "She brought Cappadonna to lunch with you? Is she crazy?"

"She didn't know I was showing up today. Fuck!" I beat the shit out of my steering wheel, as I leaned back in the chair pissed. "We probably could take his ass, Monty. He don't have nobody else with him... it's just him."

"Which tells us everything that we need to know."

"Bitch, don't be scary."

"Then why you still sitting here and not heading in there?" he challenged me and I had half the mind to slap the shit out of him for questioning me.

"My mama in there. You think I'm gonna bring beef to her front door?"

"Yeah... well, then I guess we just gonna sit here or get on with our day." He shrugged, not wanting to go inside the restaurant.

I had a strong feeling that this nigga watched him pick me up and launch me over the balcony and never did nothing about it. He was showing me that he wasn't as solid as I thought. We both jumped when my phone started ringing.

"Chill the fuck out, it's my moms," I snapped on him, like I hadn't jumped, too.

"Yeah, Ma."

"What's good, pussy? We're waiting to order... what you want? I'll get it for you, my treat." Cappadonna laughed into the phone.

"Where's my mama? Why the fuck you got her phone?"

He chuckled like we were good friends having a simple conversation. "Moms handed it to me, we locked in... what you youngins be saying... that's twin right there."

"You real fucking funny."

"Nah. You the funny one thinking I was gonna send my daughter-in-law and grandson into the pussy's den. Unlike you, I protect mine. I'm here alone... what up, Ace? Using your moms to set up your sister is nasty work, too. Let me tell you this though... I heard you moved spots. I'm closing in on you, bitch, and when I do, I'm doing you in with my bare hands... no guns." I looked at my phone because he had hung up.

"What the fuck?" I screamed, whipping out the parking lot and speeding with no particular destination in mind. Cappadonna Delgato was a fucking thorn in my fucking side that I desperately needed to pull out.

And I will.

27
AIMEE

"MA, I would love to have lunch with you. I'm not keeping you from your grandson… I just need space from Ace." I sighed into the phone, wanting to get into detail, but deciding against it because she would always take Ace's side.

"I miss you a lot, Aimee, and I need to be involved in my grandson's life. I know he is getting big," she continued to guilt trip me.

"Yes, he is. I know a good Italian spot that we can have lunch."

"Great. Text me the details and I'll be there. I bought him a few things that I want to give you." I smiled because this wasn't like my mother.

I guess when babies came into the picture people could change. Ending the call, I continued looking over the college classes and courses I would need to take once I enrolled back into college. "Lunch with your mother?"

I had forgotten that Capp was sitting in the living room reading a magazine. The glasses pushed on the bridge of his nose with his legs crossed at the ankle was almost comical.

I spun around in the stool to face him. "Yes. We don't have the best relationship, but she wants to see the baby... what do you think?"

Capp felt like a father figure for some reason. Ever since our talk in Barbados, we both had a clear understanding. He wasn't going to trust me until I proved that I was worthy of being trusted. He closed the magazine he was reading.

"Sounds like you need to use your brain, Aimee."

"What you mean?"

"Your brother isn't happy about you choosing sides. Now your mama reaches out to have lunch. I'm not saying she's involved, but it sounds like a set up to me. I'm not getting between you and your mom's shit, but I'm gonna come with you to lunch... cool?"

I smiled. "Thank you. I never even thought of it like that."

He opened his magazine up again. "That's what I'm here for."

The lunch with my mother was going good. Cappadonna nearly slapped the color off the waiter when he brought him pork and chicken meatballs. How he knew the difference before even trying them was beyond me.

He then walked to the kitchen and watched them make his food. While he was assisting them on how to make his food, me and my mother caught up. She gave me the tea on our family in Delaware, and then asked when me and my brother would fix things between each other.

I didn't have the heart to tell her that me and Ace may never see eye to eye again. He was angry with me, and he was the last person I wanted to make up with. Ace had done enough shit to me for me to keep putting up with his selfish and conniving ways. In his eyes, I was a traitor, and he wasn't going to accept that from his blood sister. Instead of beating around the bush, I had to tell her that me and him weren't going to be speaking.

"I expect to see you at my fiftieth birthday party. Your

brother will be there, and for my birthday gift, I want you two to make up."

"Mom, me and Ace are in two different places in our lives right now. I'm not worried about fixing things with him. It's always Ace's way and I'm tired of living that way."

"And being escorted to lunch with your mother is any better? I thought it was supposed to be the two of us, and you brought this man."

I rolled my eyes because she didn't have a problem shoving her breast up and smiling in his face. She even handed him her phone when he asked if Ace would be joining us. I could only imagine what conversation he was having on my mother's phone.

"That is Rory's pop-pop. He just wants to make sure that we're safe."

"From who? What could I possibly do to you or my grandson, Aimee?" I could tell she was hurt, and that was her right to feel that way.

I also had to do what I needed to do to protect me. I followed Cappadonna's lead because I trusted him. This man didn't know me from a hole in a wall, and he showed up for me. Just based on the trust he had in his son's word.

Ace choked me last time and threatened me, and she thought I was supposed to come sit down and break bread with him like that was normal. "Mom, you have allowed Ace to get away with a lot because he's the bread winner. I refuse to be around him and his nonsense. I have a child to think about, and I won't include him in this mess."

"Nobody ever taught you how to sit pasta down... you place it neatly, so you don't get sauce on the customer, bozo."

"My apologies," the waiter said, as Capp sat back down, after making this man carry his food out to him.

He shook out the white napkin and looked at the both of us. "Seems tense... what's going on?" he handed my mother back her phone.

"She seems to have turned her back on her brother."

I put my head down and rolled my eyes because she was adamant on it always being my fault. Not that her son was a fucking lunatic that did coke in his spare time.

"Oh yeah. How's that?" Cappadonna nonchalantly cut into his meatballs while waiting for my mother to answer.

"Aimee is a bit of a liar. The girl had us believing the baby's father was some dude locked up, and it turns out to be some other guy we didn't even know. Ace has always tried to protect his sister, and be there for her, and she's always pushed back and lied on him."

Tears slid down my face as I listened to her talk about me like I wasn't even sitting here. "Aye, we can leave whenever you want... give me the word and we out." Capp touched my arm.

I sniffled and looked at my mother. "Ace choked me in front of my son and you want me to make peace and be back cool with him like nothing ever happened."

"Oh God, your brother has a temper, but he's never touched you... stop putting on a show for this man."

I noticed that he had stopped eating the food and was waiting on me to give him the word that I wanted to leave. "Ace also never fucking raped me, right?" I slammed my hands on the table, and Capp stood up. "You've always fucking defended him and made it seem like I was always the fucking problem. Daddy always said that you spoiled him and never wanted to hear nothing bad about him!" I screamed so loud that spit flew across the table at her.

"Wait a fucking minute... he fucking raped you?" Cappadonna roared, the fire dancing in his pupils.

"He has never touched her. I just sat here and told you that Aimee is a damn liar. And there's a lot that your *father* has said."

I sobbed. "I lied about Capella because every boyfriend I have had, he ruins it. I wanted something for myself... I didn't want Capella near the scum that Ace is."

"You little fucking witch." My mother pointed her hands at me. "Ace has been nothing but good to you. Cars, condos, money, and whatever else you wanted."

"Cause he feels fucking guilty for what he did to me!"

He went and grabbed Rory from my mother, and she hesitated on giving the baby to him. "Lady, give me my grandson... I promise you don't want to play these games with me," he warned her before she eventually gave him up.

"Go ahead, Aimee. Be the victim like you always are!" my mother hollered at our backs, and Capp stopped buckling Rory up.

He sat back down, across from my mother and messed with his beard. "Help me understand. Your daughter told you that your son raped her and she's the liar?"

"Aimee has always lied. Tell them when you lied about that sleepover, and you went to that party."

"So, we comparing her lying about going to a party, which is typical teenage shit, to her telling you her brother raped her. Please tell me that's what you're telling me."

"Look, you don't know me or my family and this is a personal family matter."

He chuckled. "It's mothers like you that deserve to be sliced ear to ear. I have the experience, but I don't want to traumatize Aimee, so I'm gonna let you rock. The fact that your daughter is shaking and crying, and you have no remorse is sick. Sick ass bitch."

"Excuse you."

He stood up. "I called you a bitch, ma'am," he repeated himself. Capp tossed money onto the table, picked Rory's car seat up, and grabbed my hand as we headed toward the exit.

I was crying so hard that my vision was blurred. "Bring my shit around," he told valet.

He sat Rory down on the floor and stared down at me. "This shit ain't your fault, Aimee. Fuck her... If you said that is what happened, then that's what happened."

"I've been called a liar by my entire family. Ace is the golden child because he has the money. My mother will never go against him."

Soon as they pulled the car around, he held the door for me and then put Rory in the back. I watched as he checked his surroundings before hopping in and peeling off while putting his seatbelt on.

I didn't know what happened to his Durango. One day it was in the garage, and then the next this was being delivered. "My son knows?"

"No. I don't want him to know that part of me. I feel embarrassed even telling you. I just hate how she pretends like he's perfect and I'm the problem."

"Don't be fucking embarrassed to speak your truth. She's the one that should feel that way, not you. I'm a good listener, so you can tell me if you're comfortable. If not, we can listen to music. Doesn't change if I believe you or not... I believe you."

I took a deep breath and explained everything. I remembered it like it was yesterday and it often cycled itself through my thoughts. My mother went out with her boyfriend at the time, and I was home alone. Ace was always gone and doing his own thing. He was hardly ever home, and whenever he did come home, he always started some shit.

It was always my mother and him against me, so I stayed in my room. You couldn't gang up on me if I was in my room and out the way. My coach dropped me home, and all I wanted to do was take a hot shower and sleep.

By the time I showered, all I did was sit on the edge of the bed and I didn't remember falling asleep. I woke up to someone between my legs and it was Ace. He was grunting and raping me. I screamed, pushing him away from me, shoving him and all he did was hold me around my neck. He held me, and fear kept me still as I laid there allowing him.

I beat myself up for years, even blaming myself because how could I have allowed him? I should have done more, and I should have fought harder. When he was done, he grunted and then walked into the closet before he realized it wasn't the door.

Ace was high, and that wasn't an excuse. When I told him about it, I could see he remembered, and he acted like he didn't know what I was talking about. The guilt was all over his face. I guess I should have been grateful that he felt guilty for doing that to me. When I told my mother, she slapped me across the mouth and told me to stop making up lies on my brother. She then explained how none of this would have been possible without him, and I needed to stop making trouble or I would be the one tossed on my ass.

Ever since, I had been called the liar and everyone in the family called me that. Ace walked around untouchable while I wore the scarlet letter on my chest. There was no one there to protect me, no one there to hold me. I had to live with that alone for years and it just erupted at lunch today. Seeing how hard she was going for him, and not giving a damn how I felt hurt me to my core.

It hurt to know that she had a favorite child, and it wasn't me.

"Fuck. I'm sorry that happened to you, Aimee. It's not my place to speak on it or tell him. That's for you to do whenever you're comfortable. Just know that what you shared with me is safe with me."

"Thank you, Cappadonna," I sighed, looking out the window, as he drove us back to the lake house.

Cappadonna wanted to kill my brother before, and from the looks of how tight he was holding the steering wheel, I think I had made him want to end him ten times more.

I IGNORED my mother's call again and rolled back over to try and sleep some more before Rory woke up hollering again. He woke up almost every hour and I was tired. Rory had a fever, so I felt bad for my baby, but I was also tired, too. It was early evening, and I was in bed with the covers over my head trying to forget about everything that happened last week. When I heard him whining, I groaned and shoved the blankets off my body.

"Go back to sleep, I got him," Capella replied, coming from the bathroom.

He scooped our son up and kissed his chubby cheeks before coming to sit on the bed. "I've followed everything those mommy blog suggested, and the fever still doesn't seem like it's going to break."

Capella laughed. "You listening to a bunch of women that don't know your baby? All babies aren't one size fit all, Aimee." I plopped back down on the pillow and looked up at him lazily. "What's really good with you? You seem different since that lunch with your moms."

"You haven't spoken to your father?"

"Of course, I spoke to him... he said your mother is a bitch with a crooked wig. Other than that, he hasn't said anything. Why? Should he have told me something?"

"No. Me and Mom just got into it, and I'm tired of the back and forth with her." It wasn't a total lie.

I was tired of the back and forth when it came to my mom. I was so excited when she called and wanted to do lunch. Here I thought she was turning over a new leaf for the sake of her grandson, and it was the same bullshit as it had always been. I was done with my mother, which is something I should have been done.

Every chance she got she sat in my face and called me a liar, and I should have washed my hands with her a long time ago. "You know I love you, right?"

I smiled. "Yes. I love you, too."

He reached over and kissed me on the lips. "You can talk to me about anything, Aimee. I know choosing a side has been hard, and I don't take your decision and sacrifice lightly."

It wasn't hard when his family had treated me more like family than my own. Cappadonna heard me blurt out that I was raped and never questioned me. He stood on my side and believed me, despite telling me that he didn't trust me. That spoke to the kind of man he was, and I appreciated him for it.

Ever since I called to tell him that me and Rory needed him, he had showed up and held up his side of the deal. "I'm gonna have some ice cream."

"Go and sit with the ladies out on the back. They got wine and shit out there and just listening to music and talking."

"You sure?"

"I got him... I'm his father, Aim... I know how to take care of him," he assured me, and I quickly left the room.

Like Capella said, Erin, Alaia, and Capri were in the back with bottles of wine, and cranberry juice. I assumed the cranberry juice was for Alaia. When I poked my head out the back door they smiled.

"You want a drink?" Erin smiled, holding the wine bottle up in the air.

"Desperately." I closed the back door and sat on the couch, pulling my legs up to my chest. Erin handed me the wine glass and I took a long sip.

Music played softly in the background as we sat outside. "Shit just got worst after Barbados. I don't know any more with Kincaid."

"Maybe it was a fun for the moment situation. Just call it quits and continue to be friends... there's nothing wrong with that."

"I agree. Maybe you need some time for you right now, Capri. There is nothing wrong with being single and taking time to heal you."

"Yeah. I know. I've witnessed you and Capone get married, then you and Cappadonna get married. I guess I just want that for myself one day."

"You don't believe in spinning the block with Naheim?" I asked, the wine finally making me social.

She laughed. "Absolutely not. I would get back with him tomorrow if my heart didn't feel the way it did. I love Naheim and probably always will, but my heart won't allow me to trust him, and I have to trust who I'm with. There's too many things that I would be worried about when it comes to getting back with him." She took a swig of her wine. "The dick is still good though."

Erin spit her wine across the couch as she looked at Capri. "You're joking, right?"

"Well, me and Kincaid were broken up when we first got to Barbados. He was begging and have you seen Naheim? How the fuck could I stand on business when my pussy wasn't."

Alaia laughed while shaking her head. "Neither of you bitches know how to stand on business."

Erin snapped her neck in Alaia's direction. "That man rented out two private villas so he could have you alone on the beach. Bitch, I know you didn't stand on any kind of business."

As if Cappadonna knew we were talking about him, he poked his head out. "What up, Joy."

Cappadonna was this scary and ruthless man, but with Alaia he was different. He was soft with her, and from the way he ignore all of us and greeted his wife, he was so in love with her. I bawled like a baby watching them get married.

"Hey Roy." She blushed.

"Um, what's popping, Leroy?" Capri added. "Just ignoring the rest of us like we not out here, too."

Capp laughed. "What up, ladies."

"Your dinner is in the microwave. I wasn't sure when you were coming home."

"Appreciate you. I'm about to shower, then I wanna eat." He winked, exposing the gold in his mouth. "Where my daughter?"

"Over your parents' house. She's staying the night over there tonight." Since it was summer, everybody was staying at their lake houses.

I was still trying to get over how they all had their own lake house. "Carry on." He closed the door back, and we turned to look at Alaia, as she watched him walk through the living room until he got to the stairs.

"This bitch didn't stand on any kind of business. You wanna run after him right now... don't you?"

Alaia rolled her eyes while laughing. "Nope. I'm cool kicking it with you girls."

"Go ahead, Alaia... brunch at my house tomorrow," Capri told her, and Alaia was up and out her seat heading into the house.

"His ass wanted her to come behind him... I peeped that

wink," Erin snickered while sipping her wine. "Anyway, you need to stop fucking Naheim. Ain't he supposed to be coming to stay at the lake house with you?"

"We both know it was wrong and we're not doing it again. He has a girlfriend that's not his girlfriend or whatever."

I yawned, realizing that wine didn't turn me up anymore, it made me tired. "Think I'm going to bed... thanks for the wine."

"Now everybody tired... Capri, come on. We going back to my house."

"Bitch, I'm going home. Soon as you walk through that door Capone is gonna snatch you up. He knows you been drinking wine... nigga like a blood hound." She stood and stretched.

I laughed because Erin didn't even try to defend it because she knew it was true. After walking them to the door, I decided to clean up the back patio. I felt hands grab me around the waist, and a kiss on the temple.

"Did he go back down?"

"Out like a light... I do this daddy shit," he boasted, and I laughed because he was a good father.

Capella loved being a father, and I loved witnessing him be one. "Wanna kill the rest of this wine before bed?"

"Hell yeah." We got comfortable on the couch and looked out at the lake. There were a few boats still out on the lake as we swigged from the bottle. "My pops came home yet?"

"Yeah. I don't think he'll be back down tonight." I snickered.

"I'll catch him the morning before his run... you sure you good, Baby?"

"Yeah. I'm perfect." I kissed him on the cheek and took the wine bottle from him. He held me closer to him, as if he knew all wasn't right in my world.

"You can talk to me about anything, Aim... always know

that." He looked down at me, as I snuggled deeper into his arms.

"I know."

He finished the rest of the wine while I laid up under him, falling deeper in love with him. I mean, how much more could I fall in love with this man?

28
CAPPADONNA

"Wanna jerk my shit, too, damn," I snapped on the correction officer that was going way too hard. She was damn near in the waist band of my briefs searching for nothing.

All I had in there was that shit that put Alaia's ass to bed every night. She looked at me and then shamefully looked away. I never thought I would be walking my ass back up in this bitch willingly. I guess stranger things have happened, and now I was the one on the other side of the table.

Since being back, I had been running around handling shit, so I let this slip by the wayside. I made it my business to wake up early and make the six hour drive out here. Driving here made me appreciate my family, and how they made this drive without a second thought. They came to see me and never complained about the drive.

Kendra on the other hand always fucking complained. As if her ass wasn't sitting in whatever brand-new car I had put her ass in. Should have been got rid of her stupid ass, but I wanted to go following my heart, believing she was out here being loyal. I would never forgive myself for not listening to my brother.

Those infamous bells rang, and the gates popped, and it felt surreal sitting out here watching the prisoners walking out like fucking animals. I've always known I felt like an animal locked in the cage, but seeing it from the other side, they had men locked up behind those visitor's gates like pit bulls.

Wink swaggered out the gate, his thick salt and pepper beard, bald head that housed a kufi on it. He smiled when he saw me, which surprised me considering I had killed his best friend, and son's god father.

Wink, Ace's father, sat across from me and held his hand out and we embraced. "Assalamu alaikum, my brother."

"Wa-Alaikum-Salaam."

He looked around the visitation room before settling down. It was a habit that all of us had developed being locked up. A nigga would wait until you were on a visit to strike. You were never truly safe when you were behind this wall. There was so many times I barely listened to what Capri was saying because I was too busy watching our surroundings.

"I should have known this visit was going to come sooner than later."

I leaned back. "Oh yeah, why is that?"

He lowered his head. "Word got back to me about Mel, and I knew it could have only been you. You've never really liked Mel."

"I take the term keep my name out your mouth literally." I shrugged. "He was bad company." I didn't feel bad about sending Mel where he deserved to be. We all had to answer for all the shit that we did in our lives, and his time had come.

"Hard head makes a soft ass. Mel has done a lot of fucked up shit to people, including me."

"Then I take it the news didn't bother you."

He chuckled. "Not at all. Mel and I had a complicated friendship... loving the same woman for many years."

"He was married... no?" The woman running her mouth in that kitchen was proof enough that he was married, or at least had a woman.

"He's been with Brenda for years. She was more in love with him than he had ever been with her. Cheated on her so much, too... poor woman. His first love was Tiana, *my* Tiana. Eventually learned that Aimee wasn't my daughter."

"I had the pleasure of meeting Tiana... wicked bitch." I leaned back. "So, he fucked your bitch, fathered a child you thought was yours, and you embraced him like a brother. We both know that Mel would have been done dirty in here if you hadn't saved him so many times."

"I was thinking about my family. Mel promised when he was out that he would take care of them. You make sacrifices when you don't have much. The fuck could I do from in here?"

"Aimee know?"

"Nah. Tiana kept that secret between us because I never treated her differently. Aimee has always been my baby girl. She was a damn baby when I got sent up top. Tiana has always been tough on her... always babying Ace and treating her like she's the milkman baby."

"Aimee has a baby with my son," I revealed to him. "She don't come and visit you?"

He shook his head no. "Better off that way. I gotta sit down and do my time... doesn't make sense for her to constantly be up here visiting me. She has a kid you said."

"Beautiful little boy. I got you on pictures when I get home." I wished I could show him what his grandson looked like.

Wink chuckled. "Who would have thought the little knuckle head and I would be sharing a grandchild... always knew you were different, Capp... you don't apologize for shit, so what's the real reason you're here. I know it wasn't to tell me about Mel."

"I thought it was only right for me to come tell you man to man. Wink, you are good peoples and I think I would have been doing life in here if it hadn't been for you stepping in to keep me sane."

"You would have done the same." He was right about that. I would have done the same because that was how loyalty worked.

"I gotta end your son," I lowered my voice while keeping eye contact with him. "Felt the least that I could do was come tell you in person."

He took a deep sigh and then looked back at me. "The streets don't offer favors. I've heard about Ace's reign."

I laughed. "Yeah, I wouldn't call it a reign... he tried to kill my son and I can't let something like that slide."

It wasn't my place to tell Wink about the sick shit that I found out about Ace. If I didn't want to kill him before, the feeling had amplified to a million now. How the fuck could you do some shit like that to your sister?

I could tell Aimee had a hard time trying to hold him accountable, because the first thing she said was that he was high. I don't give a fuck if I was drugged, high, and had been shot with a tranquilizer, I would never fucking rape a woman. Not only did he rape a woman, but that woman happened to be his sister, and then Tiana had the nerve to sit in my face and call her daughter a liar. Her daughter was standing there crying for her to believe her, and all she could do was take up for her weak ass son.

"I haven't seen my son in over eight years, Capp. Only know what is going on with him through other people. His mother got inside his head, and he stopped coming up here to see me. Tiana has always been too fucking close with him. Always making excuses for him, never teaching him accountability. It was easier to tell Tiana that I didn't want Aimee visiting because I knew she would have stopped bringing her to see me... She still writes me every month. Can't bring myself to ever respond to her."

This visit had gone differently than I thought. I thought I was going to have to pay someone to do this old nigga in after he went back to his cell. As I sat across the table, I saw a man that was close to tears talking about his daughter.

"Shit fucked up."

"Capp... you gotta do what you gotta do. I know you, so you gonna do what you gonna do anyway. All I ask is that you keep my baby girl protected. Make sure she's not caught in the crossfire. I know you Capp, you can go dark. You also have a heart, and I just pray my daughter has a space inside of it."

I told Aimee I didn't trust her ass in Barbados, but seeing the way she broke down in front of her mother, I knew she wasn't lying. You couldn't pull emotions like that out of the best actress. When we pulled away from that nasty ass restaurant, I had already made it clear that I would protect her as if she was my own. She was my grandson's mother, so I had to protect her.

I reached my fist over the table, and he bumped his into mine. "I got her. You straight on money?"

Wink laughed. "You don't need to make sure I'm straight."

Wink was too proud to ask for anything. He could be down bad and wouldn't open his mouth and say anything. When I first got up here, I didn't have shit, and it was him who made sure I was good. When I decided on something, I never gave a warning and I damn sure didn't explain the shit that I did to anybody. It was different when it came to Wink, which is why I made the trip and gave him the heads up.

After our visit, I stopped by the commissary desk and put a thousand on his books. I got his information so I could send him a picture of his grandson and daughter. I gave him my word that I was going to make sure that Aimee was taken care of, and I was a man of my word.

Soon as I got out the prison, I leaned on the front of my new truck. Capone had our whips trashed and sent to the chop shop, so I was waiting for my new truck to get here. Apparently, it was a shortage in hell cat Durango's, so I was waiting for one to be shipped to me.

"Hey Baby," I heard my wife's soft voice, and got all soft on the inside. My heart still went haywire whenever I heard her voice, or she was near me.

"I just finished up and about to head back home now. What you doing?" I hit the locks and hopped in my whip, pulling out the prison parking lot, not bothering to look in my rearview.

"I know you hear that seatbelt sound, Cappadonna... put your seatbelt on," she scolded, and I grabbed it while whipping this shit on the highway.

"You ain't answer my question."

She yawned. "Just got home from the doctor's appointment. Everything checked out, and the doctor says I'm healing great."

"Hmm."

"I want to talk to you about something when you come home."

"What is it?"

"When you get here, you'll know," she giggled.

I bit the inside of my cheek. "Tell me what you gotta say, Joy. You trying to leave me or some shit?"

"Never."

"That pussy still mine?"

"Jesus... my ears. I'm about sick of you and Capone," Capri blurted in the background, and I started laughing.

"Your sister is here... the phone is on speaker. She took me to my doctor appointment today," Alaia said through her laughter.

"What up, Baby Doll?"

"Eww.... just eww."

I could hear a door closing in the background. "You gonna answer that question, Joy?"

She continued laughing. "You know it is. I see I'm going to have to tell you whenever you're on speaker because I didn't expect you to say that."

"Why am I on speaker anyway?"

"I'm about to start cleaning the kitchen... I will see you when you get here... drive safe. I love you."

"Love you, too, Baby."

When I pulled onto the block, I saw CJ playing outside with his friends. The boy would make friends wherever he was. I respected Capone's decision to keep his son far removed. CJ wasn't made for this lifestyle and that was alright. He wasn't meant to take over and run the streets. I felt the same way about Jaiden.

As much as Jaiden could get down with guns and bust his shit if needed, he wasn't built for the streets. He had lost his love and fake ass friends to the same streets that everyone worshipped. If I had a choice in the matter, I would have done the same shit with my own son. Kendra's water head ass didn't give me that chance.

I wanted Capella to step away from the streets. He didn't need to be out here running them to prove shit to nobody.

Long as I knew my son was pressure, it didn't fucking matter who else knew. He had his own seed, and he needed to be here for him.

Erin was sitting on the lawn with Cee-Cee in a baby chair. She smiled when she saw me stop and roll my window down. "What up, CJ?"

When CJ saw me, he tossed his bike down and ran up to the car. "Ain't nothing but the sky."

"Smooth ass ni... cat." I caught myself before Ella called me complaining that he was repeating the words to his little stuffy ass friends.

His friend called him, so he ran back over to his bike and breezed down the block with him. I remembered when I called when Capone was first teaching him how to ride a bike. He was upset because he fell and cried in front of his friends. I reminded him that it was alright to cry, but after you drop those tears, what the fuck you gonna do?

Watching him ride effortlessly down the block, CJ had that Delgato blood running through him. He just wouldn't be out here taking lives or selling drugs. "You just missed your brother."

"Oh yeah. Where he heading to?"

"Handle business," she mocked.

"Better for you not to know... how you doing though?"

She stood up, making sure that Cee-Cee was good. "I'm good... your brother has been on me for this baby."

"Stop fronting like watching Cee-Cee getting older isn't making you sad."

"So sad. Why can't they stay babies forever. She's cutting teeth, Capp." Erin stared back at Cee-Cee who was messing with one of the toys on her chair. "You must feel the same about Promise... feels like she just had her."

"I'm ready for another one." Every time I picked her up and

noticed the small changes that reminded me that she wouldn't stay my small peanut for much longer, I got sad thinking of her growing up.

Erin's eyes widened. "You talked Alaia about it?"

"It's been mentioned. We just got married and we still need to move into the house, so I'm tabling the conversation until we're more settled… feel me?"

Even though Alaia had a hysterectomy, the doctor left her ovaries. She explained to us before we left the hospital that the option to have more children wasn't out of the cards for us. She explained that we could always do IVF with a surrogate. Alaia was caught up on never being able to carry my babies, and I understood her hurt. As much as I would have loved to witness her carrying more babies, I was grateful that we could have more kids in the future. Right now, Promise was our main focus, and when the time came, I couldn't wait for us to have that conversation. It wasn't about if she could carry my kids, it was about the kind of mother she was, and Alaia was a good mother.

"Yeah, I get it. Well, we were going to have drinks on my back porch tonight… so remind her when you go in."

"What up, Neighbor?" Naheim yelled from the other side of the street, coming out of Capri's house. "Make sure that trash can is at the curb."

"I can't stand him," Erin laughed and returned back to the lawn, and watched as CJ came racing down the street. "A little bit more and then your mama is coming to pick you up."

"Okay!" he hollered as he breezed on by, having the time of his life with his friends.

I waited for them to pass before I pulled into my driveway and got out to meet Naheim in the middle of the street. "How did that visit go."

I leaned on the back of the truck. "I didn't sign up to play fucking Maury, I know that damn much. Wink knows, and he knows ain't shit he can really do. He and Ace don't even have a relationship."

"Still doesn't make it any easier to hear a man tell you that he's about to wipe your son from the earth."

"Yeah, well, his mama should have swallowed him if she didn't want this to happen to him... You good?"

"I'm straight... Nellie ended shit with me."

I leaned my head back on my truck. "When the fuck is this telenovela over? Why the fuck she broke up with you?"

"Claim that I'm stringing her along and not making it official. She got this whole plan of wanting a commitment and not just being someone's maybe... whatever the fuck that means." He waved it off.

"You know exactly what the fuck that means. You stringing her ass along because you think you and Capri have a chance."

"I'm just not trying to rush into something."

"She met your son?"

"Yeah."

"Spent the night at your crib?"

"Yeah."

"Buying shit from Payless for NJ, right?"

Naheim screwed his face up. "Walmart."

"Nigga, you stringing her ass along. You met her daughter?"

"Yeah."

I waved him off and started walking toward the house. "Get the fuck out my face, Naheim. where you going?" I stopped when I saw his ass was following behind me.

There was a million other conversations I would have rather been having than this one.

"We need to finish this conversation, Capp. I'm fucking

confused about what to do." Naheim's ass was born fucking confused.

"We'll finish this shit another day. My wife in there cleaning so I know she not dressed for company."

"Ight." He dapped me up and then took his ass across the street to Erin, who punched him in the arm.

I could only assume he had told her the same bullshit that he had just told me. Naheim needed to be with himself if he couldn't figure out what to do with another woman. I let myself in the house and could smell the bleach and cleaning products.

When I told Alaia that we would have cleaning people, she turned it down. I never wanted her to feel like she was a slave or some shit. Not when we had the fucking money. She never had to pick up a broom or mop. Learning her, as I still was, I learned that she loved to clean, and it brought her peace.

Her head poked from over the railing, and I was right. She had on an oversized t-shirt, her hair was pulled into a big bun, and she had sweat on her forehead. "Joy, what the fuck you cleaning that got you sweating?"

"I changed our sheets. You try changing a California king size bed alone." She leaned on the railing. "Can you check on Promise?"

I washed my hands before checking on my baby girl. She was sleeping peacefully in her little bouncer shit, so I made my way upstairs to our bedroom. When I walked in, Alaia was bent over gathering all the old sheets into a ball to wash.

Slapping her ass, she turned around and smiled, while I put a few kisses on her lips. "What you got to talk to me about?"

"I bet it drove you crazy all day, huh?"

"Hell yeah." I plopped down in the seating area in the room, and watched as she tossed the sheets to the side.

The oversized shirt stopped a little bit before her knee, so every time she turned or bent over, I could see her ass. I peeped the pajama pants kicked to the side that she must have taken off once she started sweating. I was jealous of the fucking panties from the way her ass was eating them. Alaia was thick in all the right places, and that shit turned me on.

While she was always complaining about something, I was thinking of a million and five ways I could give her this dick. "Are you even listening to me?" she stopped, putting her hand onto her hip.

I had been so caught up in watching her, praying that she had to bend over to pick something up that I didn't hear shit that she had said to me. I tossed the remote over her head, and it hit the floor, sending the batteries out the back of the remote. "My bad."

"What the hell?" She looked at me confused, then bent over and picked the remote up, while I bit down on my bottom lip. "The other battery is missing now... never mind," she walked over toward the bathroom door and bent all the way down to grab the missing battery. Had my aim been better, she would have had to get under the bed to get it.

"Baby, come sit on this for me real quick." I started pulling at my sweat shorts while watching her.

She held the remote in one hand and I could see the moment what I did had registered for her. "You tossed this remote so I could bend over? Roy, be so for real right now... I'm over here discussing something serious."

I was now sitting in this chair with my shorts at my ankles, knowing that she wasn't going to give me none. "I heard what you said."

She screwed her face up, exposing her dimples. "What did I say then?"

"Something about a summer house... I got you." She tossed

the remote back at me and went into the closet. I pulled my shorts up and followed her into the closet. "Tell me, Baby. Whatever is important to you, is damn sure important to me."

I watched as she stripped from her cleaning shirt and put on a graphic t-shirt while looking for a pair of bottoms. "I want to learn how to drive. I feel bad having to depend on Capri or Erin to take me places."

"You don't have to depend on them... I can hire a driving service to take you wherever you wanna go."

"No. I want to be able to get in the car and go places. I've never had that independence before, Roy." This was important to her, and I could tell by how worked up she was getting. "I want to have my own independence, too, you know."

I walked over to her, pulling her closer to me. "If my wife wants to know how to drive... then I'm gonna teach her."

She reached up and kissed me on the lips. "Thank you, baby. I just want to be able to go to the grocery store or Marshall's or something."

"Erin done recruited your ass. If I see you with coupons, Joy."

She looked away while laughing. "I got that roast with a coupon the other day."

I started kissing on her neck. "Since I solved your problem... you gonna help solve mine?" She wrapped her arms around my neck, and I picked her up, carrying her back into the bedroom.

"You always seem to have the same problem, Mr. Delgato." She kissed me on the lips.

"And you always seem to handle it, Mrs. Delgato." The door to our room busted open and Aimee ran in with horror in her eyes. "What the fuck, Aimee?"

"Capella is having a seizure or stroke... I don't know... something is wrong!" she cried out.

I put my wife down on the floor, picked my shorts up that

had dropped to the floor, and ran out behind Aimee. When I made it down to the bedroom, Capella was on the floor shaking and his teeth was clenched.

His eyes were open but there was nothing there. No sign that he recognized it was me over him. "Call the fucking ambulance, Aimee."

Alaia came running into the room. "Chubs... can you hear us?" she snapped her fingers in his face, and there was nothing.

Aimee came back into the room on the phone. "She's asking a bunch of questions... they're on the way—"

I picked my son up and carried him out the room, while Alaia was right behind me. She grabbed her purse. "Bring Promise to her grandparents, Aimee."

Alaia got in the back, and I laid him in the back, his head on her lap while whipping out the driveway. Erin was still outside when she saw, and she immediately jumped to action and ran across the street.

"Calling Capone now... what do you need?" she yelled.

"Promise, Rory, and Aimee." I pointed in the house and sped through the neighborhood. The hospital wasn't that far, and by the time I waited for them to come, my son could be fucking gone.

I felt Alaia's hand on my shoulder and put my hand on top of hers. Just her touch alone soothed the fuck out of me as I drove. "Everything is going to be alright," she tried to assure me through a shaky voice.

We arrived at the hospital ten minutes later, and Aimee was calling to tell me she heard them in the neighborhood. Here I thought having a house in a nice neighborhood would mean they would come quicker.

The hospital's valet was walking to collect the keys from me, and I jumped out and grabbed Capella from the back. Alaia scooted out the car and followed behind me as I ran into the emergency room with him.

"I need a fucking doctor!"

The nurse saw me carrying my son, and she rushed to grab a gurney. She asked me what was wrong with him as doctors came running from the back. I explained everything the best I could before they rushed him to the back.

My fucking heart was beating out my chest as I watched them run him to the back. That was my fucking son, and I couldn't take the thought that I could lose him. Alaia's arms wrapped around me, and I dropped a kiss on the top of her head.

She handed me the phone where Aimee was hysterical. Alaia was crying while holding onto me, and I had Aimee doing the same. I couldn't break down because they were both crying. This was my little family, and it was up to me to be strong for them. I was the head of this family, so I needed to hold it down.

"Aimee, breathe for me... he's gonna be good. I'm gonna have somebody bring you to the hospital."

"I...I can dri—"

"I don't need you crashing because you're emotional. I'll have somebody come get you and bring you... okay?"

"Okay." She sniffled.

I ended the call, and then hugged my wife. "He's gonna be good," I tried to convince her, not even knowing if I believed the shit myself.

29
ALAIA

IF HAVING sickle cell wasn't enough, the doctors had diagnosed Capella with epilepsy. Aimee said one minute they were talking and then the next he started to shake and wasn't making sense. She said that she quickly laid him back, so he didn't fall, and then came to get Cappadonna. The doctor said it was a good thing she thought to lay him back, because the last thing we wanted was a head injury. Within hours, Capella was back to normal and talking like nothing had happened. For the first hour, he was disoriented and was trying to process everything slowly.

We were all scared because we felt like we had just gotten out of the red with him getting shot, then this happened. Cappadonna made sure to let the doctor know that he seemed like he lost weight, too.

The sexiest thing was watching my husband in dad mode. How he spoke to the doctors and made sure he understood everything before the doctor left the room. I could tell he didn't want to leave the hospital that night, so he stayed with him while Capri drove me home. I couldn't wait to learn how to drive because I was tired of everyone having to come and pick me up.

"Kincaid, I don't want to argue anymore. You are right, okay? I'm just getting to the hospital, so let me call you back... okay."

Capri ended the call, and then backed into a parking spot in the parking garage. I looked at her, and she sighed. "Everything alright?"

"I'm tired of arguing with him about everything. We argue about the smallest shit, Alaia."

I rubbed her back. "Sorry."

"It's alright. Let's go so you can bring your man his change of clothes." She smiled, switching subjects.

I didn't know what the beef was between her and Kincaid, but I could tell that the relationship had run its course, and they were both just stressing each other out. It wasn't even about Naheim either, the two of them seemed like they were tired, and that calling it quits seemed like the best decision.

When we walked into the room, Cappadonna was laid back in the small chair. His long legs were hanging over the chair. His hat was pulled down over his face.

"He's knocked out." Capri chuckled.

"He's not sleeping... I know his snores... morning, Baby."

He chuckled. "My baby knows me. Morning, Joy." I went over and removed his hat and kissed him on the lips. "Give me one more."

I giggled and sat the bag on top of him. "Brought you some clothes and toothpaste... breath is funky."

He pulled me back down and kissed me on the lips again. "You letting me kiss you with this funky breath."

"Oh brother... between you and Erin. Neither of you bitches stand on business."

I was still leaned over Capp, and he kissed my ear. "Can't stand on something you riding," he whispered into my ear.

I pinched him while giggling like a schoolgirl. That was what he did to me. Made me feel like I was the only girl in the world, and he only saw me. It didn't help that he was turning me every way but loose every night.

The night after we got married, I found myself crab walking to the bathroom because he had knocked me out the ring. It had been fifteen years since he had been inside a woman, so when he bit down on that bottom lip, I already knew what time it was, and I was always ready.

Soon as he walked through that door, I was right behind him, wanting to be in his space. I know people always said the honeymoon stage never lasted, and I was determined to prove them wrong.

I saw how Erin and Capone were, and they were still just as in love as the first time they met. Capone still looked at his wife like it was the first time he was seeing her.

"Why you come up here being all loud?" Capella yawned, and Capri walked over and kissed him on the cheek.

"Auntie had to make sure her sugar plum is alright. Since you wanna be dramatic and be shaking and shit. Getting shot wasn't enough, you had to go and scare us some more?"

"Capri, leave me alone." He laughed at her nutty ass.

"The doctor came around earlier and said that you can go home tomorrow. He wants to make sure they get the right mixture of medicine."

"I can't wait to leave... I miss my son and Aimee."

We all turned our head when we heard someone yell, "Now!" out by the nurse's station. Cappadonna leaned up, pulling me over toward him, while Capri stared at the door. Kendra popped up in the doorway and Capella sucked his teeth.

"You don't think it was important to call his mother and tell me what happened? I had to find out from Jasmine that you were rushed to the hospital again!"

Capp had been staying clear of Kendra because he knew how his son felt about keeping her alive. I also knew that he wasn't her biggest fan, and he was going to snap if she continued to poke. I've been around Kendra enough to know that she loved to poke to get a reaction out of Capp.

"Pops, can you get me something from the cafeteria? This food is cold over here." I knew he wanted his father out the room.

Kendra snapped her neck in his direction. "You can call her pops, but you call me Kendra?"

"Who the fuck you calling her?" Cappadonna stood up, walking in her direction.

Capri slid right in front of Kendra. "Him...him, sorry. I'm upset."

Capp walked out the door, holding his hand out and I ran and put mine inside of his. He was quiet and he told me that sometimes he needed to sit in his thoughts to process them. "Baby... can you slow down some?"

He was damn near dragging me down the hall to the elevator. One step for him was like three for me. Slowing his pace, he kissed my hand, and then pressed the elevator button. "Sorry Baby."

"Since he's going to be in the hospital until tomorrow, and he still has a full day. Let's go grab him some snacks from the grocery store. I saw one that was in the next town... it's closer than the one near the house."

We headed to the grocery store in the next town, while he continued to be silent. I knew Kendra got under his skin in the worst way. "Can't even believe I was with her bird ass."

“Well, we all can’t have perfect taste,” I tried to get him to smile, and he did, looking over at me.

“Nah. I got perfect taste... just needed to find you.”

“Took you long enough.” I smiled.

“Trust, if that wall wasn’t holding me back, I would have been found you.” He kissed my hand.

I grabbed a little bit of everything for Capella, and even a pack of soda. I knew how boring the hospital was, and it was ten times worse when you didn’t have good snacks. Lucky for him, I had experience being in the hospital without snacks. All I got was different variations of soup that Jean had brought up for me.

The samples lady had bacon flavored potatoes chips and tried to offer Cappadonna some. I pushed the cart over toward the seafood counter, figuring I could grab our dinner for tonight to cook.

Aimee was going to stay at the hospital tonight so when he was discharged, she could drive them back to the house. We were going to watch Rory tonight, and I was already mentally preparing how to handle two babies. Rory was much fussier than Promise, and whenever he started crying then Promise was right behind him. As I was debating on the cut of fish I wanted tonight, I heard a familiar laugh that sent chills down my spine.

Cappadonna was still having a conversation with the samples lady and questioning if the chips were made with real bacon or artificial. My hand clutched the cart, and my body became paralyzed when he turned, and noticed me standing near the seafood counter.

“Alaia, long time no see... how you been?”

I had grown so much, and just that quick I was that scared teenage girl again, and he was the man that had stolen my innocence, along with his cousin.

"It's nice seeing you." He winked at me. "You still a quiet one, huh?"

Cappadonna rounded the corner coolly while eating a bag of chips. I guess the lady told him that they were free of pork. He could see my body language and I was almost sure that he had heard this man continued talking to me.

It was crazy how quick he can go from *my* Roy to Cappadonna. It was like there was two of him, not including his actual twin, because the crazy in his eyes was evident, and if Ralph knew anything, he would have kept moving because death was standing behind him.

"What the fuck you said to my wife?"

The look on Ralph's face should have been used for target practice. My baby walked around him until he was standing next to me. "My bad bro'... sorry. Thought I knew her."

"You real familiar..." he snapped his fingers when he recognized where he knew him from. "Tweety little flunky. Didn't I tap your jaw at the barbershop?"

Cappadonna looked down at me. "You know him?"

I had told Capp about what Ralph had done to me. After the whole massage situation, I had another nightmare about Ralph, and I had no choice but to break down and tell him.

"That's Ralph," I whispered.

His crazy eyes grew wider. "Oh word?" He licked his lips, as he stared down at me.

The man behind the seafood counter even looked nervous as he held the fish I had finally decided on in his hands. Capp walked over toward Ralph.

"Aye man, I don't want no smoke. Just thought I knew your wife." He punched him in the face, grabbing him by the back of his head and mushing his head near the lobster tank. He took his hand and shoved his face inside the lobster tank while Ralph's hand tried to grip everything.

Everyone in line at the seafood counter scrambled away screaming while I stood there. "Baby, we need to go before they call the cops."

I didn't want them to call the cops. Capp didn't give a damn if they called the cops on him. He hated Ralph for what he had did to me. I knew he was way past heated because he wasn't even speaking, just holding this man's head under water. First Kendra had got him pissed, and then we ran into Ralph. His anger was toppling over, and I wasn't sure that I would be able to calm him down.

"Please," my voice cracked because I was scared he would kill this man, and then be taken away from me.

The thought of Capp being taken away from me scared me more than what he was doing to Ralph. He heard the desperation in my voice, and he let go of his head while Ralph held onto the edge of the tank trying to catch his breath.

He tossed the open bag of chips at the man behind the seafood counter. "Put that fucking phone down before I beat yo ass with that fish."

The man hung that phone up quickly, moving back from the counter. Capp took my hand, and we left the cart and left the grocery store. I sat in the front seat as we drove back to the hospital trying to catch my breath.

"That nigga's days is numbered. I'm gonna handle his fucking ass in the worst way," he promised me.

"Roy, please be careful... you literally go from one to nine hundred."

"It will always go from one to a million when it comes to my fucking wife. He got to walk away because my main priority is you. Next time I see him he won't be so lucky."

Prison had a way of making even the crazy calm. Every time I saw Cappadonna in the visitation room, he was calm, cool, and collected. It wasn't until he was on the outside that

I saw why the fuck this man was behind bars in the first place.

Even knowing how he got, I still slept peacefully with my leg tossed right across him. I guess that made me just as crazy because he didn't scare me at all. The only thing I feared was how when he lost his shit, he didn't see anything else. He would have gladly drowned Ralph in the lobster tank, picked his chips up and continued shopping until he calmed down.

I held his hand as we headed back to the hospital, and I replayed the fear in Ralph's eyes. That was the same fear I had when he kicked that door down and raped me. It was the same fear I wanted him to continue to have whenever he thought about me.

Capp looked over at me. "Do you want Daddy to take care of him?"

I looked into his eyes. "Please."

"It's handled."

When Capella came home, all he wanted was some barbeque, and Cappadonna was gonna make it happen. Even though he didn't know how to work the expensive grill that was in the built-in outside kitchen, he was determined to make his son some good barbeque food.

Since we were putting things on the grill, I invited Blair over. We kept in contact via text message and called each other whenever one of us had time to stay on the phone. I really wanted her to meet Capri and Erin.

"Hey beautiful... look at you," she complimented me when I opened the door. "Lemme see," she snatched my hand and got excited.

"Come inside, crazy." I giggled, while she still held my

hand, admiring my rings. Cappadonna had gotten me a matching diamond wedding band that matched my engagement ring.

"Look at this fucking ring, Alaia... it's beautiful. Your hand hurt... arm strong." She continued to laugh.

"How have you been?" I hugged her, noticing that she had lost some weight since the last time that I had saw her.

Even though she smiled, I could see the pain in her eyes. "It's hard, Alaia. Some days I don't have the energy to climb out of bed to start my day. I'm pushing through."

I hugged her tightly while tears escaped my eyes. "I want to be there for you."

She held her hand up. "Inviting me over like this is being there for me. I was home unsure if I was even going to make me something to eat because I've been stuck on the couch all day. The drive out here helped, too."

"Did you pack an overnight bag?"

"It's in my trunk."

"Perfect. You can stay the night in the other guest room, so you don't have to drive back later on."

She squeezed my hand, as I pulled her to the backyard where everyone was. "Bro', this shit is propane... why the fuck you got charcoal," Quasim held the bag of charcoal up.

"Just fix the shit... you claim you know how to, right?"

He shook his head and started getting the grill ready. I told Capp that he didn't know what the hell he was doing. A sly smirk came across his face when he saw me and Blair standing there.

"Oh, what up, *Blair*?"

I looked at him weird. Soon as he said her name, Quasim turned around quickly. "Hey Capp. Thank you for inviting me for the BBQ."

Quasim had a slight crush on her. "You still beautiful, I see. What up?"

Blair blushed. "Hey. How are you?"

"I'm good... give me five to ten business days to get the grill going and put food up on here." He cut his eyes at Cappadonna, who wasn't paying either of them attention.

"I told him that he didn't know what he was doing."

"Joy, who your man? Where the fuck is the loyalty?"

I waved him off and brought Blair down to the lower deck where everyone else was sitting. "This is Bl—"

"Blair fucking Underwood... make a nigga give good wood!" Capri jumped out her seat and rushed over toward Blair.

"Capri fucking Delgato... make a nig—"

"Don't even say what you're about to say," Capone said, not wanting to hear that his sister had a life.

"Eww, don't be like that. Pri-Pri gotta have a life, too."

"Don't piss me off, Capri," Cappadonna came and stood behind me, pulling me closer to him.

I was shocked that they even knew each other. "How in the world? Blair, what are you doing here?" Capri squealed.

"How do you know each other?" I finally asked, after taking in that they knew one another, and seemed to have been close.

"My freshman roommate and hers was best friends. Her roommate always spent all her time in my dorm, so I would go to theirs where it was quiet to do homework or sleep because they were always so loud."

"I was so happy when they both dropped out that next year." Blair laughed and then hugged Capri again.

"Then you dropped out that next year and went ghost on me." Capri playfully pinched her, and Blair had a nervous smile.

"Well, then I guess you only need to meet Eri—"

Erin rushed past us with her hand over her mouth. "Hey." She could barely toss over her shoulder, as she picked up speed.

"I shot that club up again," Capone dapped Cappadonna up, and chased behind his wife. He didn't say it loud enough where everyone heard, I was closer to Capp than Capri and Blair, who were chatting away and making up for lost time.

After calling his father, we finally had food on the grill. Des even stayed to cook the food to make sure we knew what we were doing. Capella was in the room with Aimee, he had been resting and didn't feel like coming outside.

Every so often I saw Aimee come out so she could get him more food. We all sat on the lower deck enjoying the cool breeze that we got today. The sun was setting, and the sky reminded me of a pink and orange starburst mixed together.

Capp had me tucked up under him, with his arms around me, while we both nursed our cranberry and Sprite mix that we both had become obsessed with. Blair was sitting in a single seat while Quasim sat on the couch next to her.

"The food was good... I can't remember the last time I had some grilled corn." She rubbed her stomach.

She told me beforehand that chemo basically took her appetite away, so don't be offended if she didn't eat a lot of food. "Appreciate you coming out. I may need to pick your brain about what the fuck Capri was doing in college."

Blair started laughing. "Whatever happens in college stays there. Me and Pri locked in, her secrets are mine." She smiled. "I'm gonna go grab my bag from my car."

"I'll walk with you," Quasim offered.

Me and Capp watched as they walked back up to the house, and I snuggled deeper into my husband's arms. "You alright?"

He looked down at me. "Yeah, why?"

"I heard what Capone said, and I wanted to make sure you were fine." I knew Cappadonna wanted more kids, despite him trying to assure me that he was fine.

"That's my brother's journey, Alaia. I'm happy for him and Erin... I told you when that time comes, we will have that conversation. Are you alright?"

"I get down sometimes because I know that I can't give you another one... physically." I kissed his lips.

"Long as the rest of them come out with those big brown eyes that Promise has, I'm straight. After how hard your delivery was, I don't want you going through that again, even if you could."

He squeezed me and kissed me on the head. "Quasim has a crush on Blair."

"I know... she might be feeling him, too. Look at me being a matchmaker."

"You didn't even do anything, Roy!" I started laughing. He paused, and then looked down at me again. "What's wrong?"

"I'm gonna teach you how to use a gun so you can carry."

I leaned up and looked at him. "Seriously?"

After the way I saw Capri and Erin were, I wanted to learn. I never wanted to be defenseless again. I felt so useless sitting in the back of the car while it was up to them to protect me.

"Damn, Joy. You too damn excited for me."

I giggled. "I just really want to learn to defend myself."

Capp kissed my lips. "I'm always going to protect you, but if there is ever a time that I'm not close by, I need you to let that shit go until I slide through. I didn't like seeing you so scared and defenseless at that grocery store. As your husband, it's my job to protect you, but also make sure that you can protect yourself, too."

"What kind of gun can I have?"

He chuckled. "Chill out, baby... you need to learn how to use one first."

"Can I carry the one like you do?"

He squeezed my ass while kissing my lips. "Nah. You ain't ready for no eagle."

I wanted to learn how to shoot because I knew what I signed up for when I married Cappadonna. Every night, I watched as he put his gun away in the garage. Even with that one being in the garage, he had one up under his night table and a few hidden around the house.

It wasn't lost on me that this was the life that I had chosen to be part of, and the last thing I wanted was my husband worrying about me. If anything, I wanted to be able to hold it down right beside him.

He stood up, pulling me to my feet. "Let's go and get my baby girl from my mama. She trying to spend all her time with her before they head back to Barbados next week."

"I'm gonna miss them."

"That's their happy place, and I sleep better knowing they there. Away from all the shit." He held his hand out, and I slipped mine inside of his as we walked toward his parents' house.

30
KENDRA

THE EVICTION NOTE on the damn door wasn't on my fucking bingo card this week. I snatched the letter off the door and prepared to use my key and noticed a fucking bolt lock on the damn door. I hadn't been back to the house because I wasn't in the mood to deal with him. My life was falling apart, and I didn't know what the fuck to do.

Everything that could go wrong in my life was going wrong, and I couldn't deal. One day you got nothing but money, a condo, and a car, then the next you're getting your nails done when the repo man is towing you fucking car down the block.

Everyone in the shop was talking shit and laughing, not knowing it was my damn car. I was too ashamed to run after the tow truck and try to convince him to let the car down. Instead, I nervously chuckled while joining in on them talking shit.

Then when I called Cappadonna to tell him some information I knew, he doesn't answer my call. He was so busy getting fucking married to that bitch Alaia, and my whole world was falling apart.

What made her perfect and not me? I was much skinnier than her, my hair was actually out and hanging down my back, and I was probably more fun than her. She could never please Capp like I could.

I squealed and then left from the porch before someone saw me. What the fuck was going on with Ace? We spoke last night, and he didn't tell me shit about us getting evicted from the house. I may have been staying with Jasmine, but that would only last for so long.

Me and Jasmine were getting along and using our grief to bond. She had so much going on that it probably felt nice to have a familiar face around. We grieved differently, and I was learning to accept her process. While my solution was to keep it pushing to keep it out of my mind, Jasmine wasn't the same. She didn't get out the bed for days, and when she did, she could barely talk without becoming choked up about her mother.

After taking the train back to Jasmine's house, I was worn the fuck down. Life had beat the fuck out of me and then handed me a pink slip. I climbed the steps and used my key to let myself into the house.

All I needed was a hot shower and then the bed to get some sleep. When I heard that deep voice, my ears perked up and I tried to fix myself up. I quickly looked out the front door and noticed the G wagon parked across the street.

I had been so beat the fuck down that I hadn't paid attention to my surroundings. Fixing my hair and using the shirt I carried in my arm to wipe my sweat; I rounded the corner.

"Hey Jasmine... hey Capp." I tried to play casual like it was no big deal that he was over here, sitting in the living room shooting the breeze with Jasmine.

She was cuddled up in the armchair with a blanket over her. I spotted a bag of soul food from that expensive ass place around the corner. "Hey. I called you and your phone went to voicemail."

"Yeah, um... my phone has been weird."

"Been weird since I stopped paying for it?" Capp chuckled, like the shit was funny. If standing on business was a person, it was him.

He cut me off quicker than a damn landscaper did shrubs. One minute I had it all and then the next I could barely afford to pay for anything. I stacked money, but that shit was going quicker than anything.

"You here for me?" I asked, staring at Cappadonna with hope. Maybe he had finally felt that I learned my lesson, and he wanted to reward me or something.

Stranger shit had happened, like him being fucking married. Even with Ace running around here telling everybody that we were married, legally, we weren't married. When we got back, I was supposed to submit the necessary paperwork, and it was still folded and tucked under the mattress at the house.

I didn't have the time to truly process if I wanted to actually go through with it before I got the call about Capella being shot. Cappadonna didn't half step shit, so I knew he and Alaia were legally married.

What was it about her that made him act this way toward me? That platinum wedding band on his finger sent shots straight to the heart. Cappadonna looked at me, then turned his attention back to Jasmine.

"The deed to the house is in there, Jas. You own your mother's house and can do whatever you want with it. Capella wanted to make sure that you got that and know that you're straight. Don't worry about work or how you gonna afford shit. I'm gonna make sure you straight."

Jasmine wiped away a tear, as she held the green folder, I hadn't noticed she was holding when I walked in. "I don't know how I could ever thank you for this, Capp. I wasn't expecting that and was trying to figure out a way."

"You looked out for me and my boy more than you know. When you look out for me, I'm always going to do the same. I didn't know your mother, and I never got to thank her for raising my son, so this is my thank you. I can imagine she would want to make sure you are taken care of, and I'm gonna make sure of that."

He stood up and Jasmine tossed the folder on the coffee table and threw her arms around him. "I appreciate this so much. It's always been me, Mama, and Capella. I feel like a piece of me is missing with her gone." Jasmine did her usual sobbing.

I discreetly rolled my eyes because I was tired of hearing the sobs. Girl, your mother was dead, we needed to pivot.

"You're free to come over the crib anytime you need to be around family. You got my number, Jas. Use that shit, I'm serious."

She smiled. "I will."

Cappadonna hugged her once more before swaggering toward the kitchen. "Walk with me, Bird Brain."

"Cappadonna, you don't have to call me names." I was hurt that he was treating me like trash he had found on the street.

Hell, I think he might have treated trash better than the way that he had been treating me. I stopped short when he turned around and was so close in my face that I would have gave him a peck on the lips if I knew he wouldn't beat me with the fridge behind him. "Why the fuck you keep blowing my phone up, Kendra?"

"D...don't you want some updates on how I'm doing?"

"Why the fuck would I want updates on nothing? Have you produced your husband to me? Do I know where the fuck he is?"

"Um, no. I've been here helping Jasmine out."

"Nah. You've been here because you homeless. That nigga moved out that house, and you don't know where else to go."

How the fuck did he know that there was an eviction notice on the house? "Well, um... if you allow me to move back into the condo, I can use that as a way to lure him to you."

Cappadonna let out a big hearty laugh. So loud that even Jasmine had to get up and make sure all was good between us. "Bitch you crazier than I thought. I'll turn that whole condo into my wife's closet before I ever give you the fucking keys." He grabbed my shirt up like I was some pipsqueak in high school. "Let me make something clear, you would be pushing up fucking weeds if it was up to me. The one and only reason you even breathing is because my son asked me not to touch you, and my loyalty for him goes beyond this world. I don't need you to bring me Ace, 'cause I'm gonna bring you his fucking head so you can give him a proper funeral." He released me and I stumbled back into Jasmine.

The bitch had the nerve to be scratching her head and looking away like she didn't just see this man lift me by my shirt and then drop me back down like it was nothing. "I...I."

"Stop playing with me, Kendra. You gave that nigga my money and tried to help him take over my city. Bitch, you forgot that we the kings of this shit? You played games for the last nineteen years... I had patience then... Sweetheart, I don't got much patience before I snap or snap your neck... choice is yours." He patted my wig like a fucking dog, walked by me and Jasmine to leave.

Jasmine tried to turn around. "What the fuck, Jas?"

"What do you want me to do, Ken? I don't have anything to do with what you and Cappadonna have going on. I mind my business."

I followed her ass back to her room so she could continue to sulk in her bed about not having a mama. "That sounds really funny... seeing as you're the one who fucking told him about Capella. I told you that in confidence and you used it against me."

Jasmine laughed. The bitch been moody and crying, and she uses this as the time to want to laugh. "I told Capella who his father was. He was running with them, Kendra. How sick is it that he didn't know he was with his own family. He deserved to know, and being honest, he should have been knew. The boy grew up so confused and questioned everything when it came to who his father was. Your selfish spirit is what prevented him for having a good father."

"He was fucking locked up!" I screamed.

"And he could have still been there. That man took care of your selfish ass while being locked up, while all you did was ask for more and barely gave him anything in return. Why do you act like he couldn't take care of a fucking child? Get the fuck out my room Kendra before I put you out. I overheard what Cappadonna said, so you may want to sit this one out." She turned around, slamming her bedroom door in my face.

The only positive that I had going on for me was the fact that Capella wanted his mother alive. If it hadn't been for him, I probably would have been dead. Every other thing was negative, and I didn't know what the fuck to do.

"Yo?"

"What the fuck is going on? I went to the house, and it was a fucking eviction notice on the door. Then my car got repossessed while getting my fucking nails done... Ace, what the fuck is going on?"

"Money is tight right now, Kendra, damn!" he screamed into the phone like a lunatic.

"Is Capp running in your traps?"

"Nah," he replied calmly, as if he hadn't screamed like a lunatic a few seconds ago. "Nobody won't cop from me... all scared of Capone and Capp."

"Shit."

"Baby, you know I wouldn't ask, but I need to borrow some money from you. You said you got some savings from when you was fucking with Capp."

What money did he think I had? I had run through that money shopping and traveling because I knew it was always more. Now that Capp had cut me off like a bad habit, I didn't have shit but $600 in my account.

Automatic message: [Your bill has been successfully paid. $164 has been applied to your account.]

Well, $436 now that my phone bill decided to charge me today.

"I don't have it, Ace."

"What fucking good are you if you don't have no fucking money?"

I looked at the phone. "Nigga, I am the one carrying your fucking baby and you asking me to fucking give you money. I knew fucking with you was a mistake. Cappadonna would fucking never."

"Yeah, you right. He would never fuck you again! Word is he bought that new wife of his a brand-new mansion... what the fuck he got you?" Ace cackled.

"Fuck you, Ace."

"I wish you would though... been missing getting pussy on the regular." Just like that, his tone changed, and the nigga was acting normal.

I was so frustrated that I was tempted to take him up on his offer. "Where you at?"

"Sending you the addy."

He ended the call, and his address came through a couple seconds later. I sighed, knowing that fucking this man was a mistake, but if I could find out where he was, then I could prove to Capp that I was loyal and worth it. Shit, he may even give me my condo and car back after hand delivering Ace to him.

I WOULD BE DAMNED if I took the train to Long Island. I bit the bullet and caught me an Uber to the address that Ace had given me. He was staying in a cute cookie cutter craftsman house in a nice neighborhood.

It was a cute neighborhood.

We passed a woman jogging with her baby in the stroller, and the lawns were damn near perfect. This was the kind of grass you could spread a blanket on and sit down to read a book. I quickly climbed out the back of the Uber, and rang the doorbell, pissed that I was even subjected to this shit.

Monty opened the door for me and stood to the side while I pushed inside. "How the fuck you doing, too," he mumbled.

"Where is Ace?"

"Upstairs." He grabbed my arm. "Ken, he really been on some reckless wild shit... be easy on your words."

"When has he not been on some wild shit. Ace needs to calm his ass down and figure out a way to make some money." I snatched my arm and stomped up the steps.

Ace was in the bed on his phone when I entered the room. "You come running for some dick, huh?"

"Are we really going to beef right now? I want some dick

and you want some pussy." I sighed, knowing that I would have to deal with his bullshit.

"Come here then." He pulled his shit out and was ready to go, and I needed a shower. After trekking on the subway today, I needed a quick shower before I opened these legs.

"Can I take a shower?"

"Do you, Kendra... you staying the night or you gonna run back to your cousin's house?" he asked, secretly wishing that I would stay here with him.

"I guess I can stay the night with you tonight."

He smirked as he rolled his blunt. I noticed it was something white sprinkled in the blunt, and that reminded me not to smoke shit he was smoking on. It was probably why he was tripping the hell out.

I sat my purse on the chair in the corner and kicked my shoes off. "I'll get you another ride by the end of the week. Can't have my wife taking cabs and the train."

"Thanks, Babe. I was so confused about them taking the car."

"Money ain't been what it usually is, but I'm about to link with somebody that's gonna put that all to an end. We gonna be back up again. House, cars, and everything."

My heart took a leap. "Seriously?"

"Yeah. Capp don't stop shit around here. I'm gonna show you that you chose right." He sparked his blunt. "Go shower so I can get some pussy."

I was damn near skipping to the shower because I actually wanted him. Maybe I slept on him and should have had more faith in what he could do. Ace was young, but he was determined and that was something that was needed in this line of work. He could have been down and hiding, but he was out here trying to look at a way for us to make it.

After my shower, I came out the bathroom with the towel

wrapped around me. Ace was stroking his dick in the middle of the bed, and I was so turned on. Maybe it was the pregnancy, or the fact that I was back close to having it all again. Either way, I tossed the towel from my body and walked over to my man.

He leaned up, kissing me on the lips and pulling me onto the bed. His hands were all over me, and I could taste the liquor and smoke on his tongue. "Pussy dripping for me." He kissed me on the lips and then climbed between my legs.

"Just for you," I cooed, and welcomed him inside of me, moaning with how hard his strokes were.

Ace couldn't fuck worth a damn, and today he had smoked the right shit because I was actually into it. "Fuck... shit..." he increased his speed. His hand found its way around my neck, knowing I loved it rough. "Tell me you love me, Kendra."

"I love you, Baby... always will," I moaned, tossing this pussy back.

"Then why the fuck did you betray me, Baby?" he asked, and my eyes widened when I felt his hands wrap tighter around my neck. "Why did you give that nigga my other address? Huh, Ken-Ken? You were setting me up to be lined up, why?" He had tears coming down his face as he continued to fuck me, and I pushed away but his grip around my neck was too strong.

"A...Ace, I can't breathe." He applied more pressure while he stared into my eyes, his tears falling onto my lips.

I tasted his salty tears as I felt my own life slipping away from me. Trying to choke out the words for him to stop. "Shit, Ken... pussy was always so tight and good. I loved you and you did me wrong. Why?"

I clawed at his hands while he kissed me on the lips and applied more pressure to my neck. The room became dark until eventually all I saw was the darkness.

31
RAHEEM

I WAS SO DAMN BROKE that I didn't even have two pennies to rub together. Times was hard like Florida and James Evans. When Taz told me all I had to do was bring my sister to him, I wasn't with it because all this time had passed, and he needed to deal with the shit himself. He walked in my house and saw that shit was falling apart, then had the nerve to come to me with his problems.

There wasn't enough money going around in here, and these bitches were working they pussies ten times harder without any return. I was tired of having to rob Peter to pay Paul fucking Wall. Times were hard, and I needed what Taz had promised to me.

It was dead around here because I had the same girls. I needed new girls, but that cost money. Money that I didn't fucking have and needed. My moms was on my line every damn day to ask when I could put something on her books. A lot of people depended on me, and it was up to me to make sure that I could make shit happen.

As much as I wrote my sister off when Zayne took her off

my hands, I had to bring her back to where she belonged. I didn't think she was going to stick around anyway. I half expected for her to run away within the first month. Alaia was strong willed like that and would do whatever she needed to.

I was shocked that she had stuck around with Zayne for as long as she did. Then again, I knew how they handled women, so I'm sure she didn't have much of a choice. Alaia had been gone out my mind since I sold her ass to Zayne, so I never checked in with her.

What the fuck could she offer me?

After Taz left my house, I did a little research on where my sissy was spending her time. It had to be somewhere that pissed Taz off, because he was desperate enough to offer me a whole house and all the profits.

Imagine my surprise when I learned that she was tied to the fucking Delgatos. The same fuckers who came through my block and lit the shit up. It took a minute before I found out who was responsible. Being that I was in a wheelchair for months, I couldn't do shit.

Everything always came full circle, so it would be fun taking my sister from them. From what I understood she was with the other twin that had been locked up with Zayne's soft ass. Sis had landed on her feet because she was with true money.

Their money was long that way and I knew she was living good, and I had to get a piece of the pie. Whenever we were younger and tried to sell lemonade, Alaia always had a plan. The girl was smart, and it was a shame that she never got a chance to go to college.

The plan was in motion until that nigga Cappadonna pulled a fucking Uno reverse, and lit Taz up on the interstate. Taz was so fucked up that he was in the hospital with tubes and shit coming out his face. Fatima said that he may not make it, and it was touch and go for a while. I was pissed because I could see the money slipping out of my hands before I could even get it.

That little bitch was tough, and he pulled through. Even with him still in the hospital, having to shit in a bag for the rest of his life, he was still alive and held that hate for Cappadonna even more.

My phone pulled me from my thoughts. "Yeah."

"It's me," Taz said, sounding like Levar from *Get Rich Or Die Tryin'*

He didn't naturally have a deep voice to begin with, but I was having a hard time trying to make out what the fuck he was saying. "How you been?"

"I've been fucking better, Raheem," he snapped like I was the reason his ass got done up the way that he did.

"What's going on?"

"I want you to bring Alaia to me... you want the house, produce your sister. While I'm out of commission you and Dale will handle things until I'm back up." I didn't find it fair that I had to get her ass after I sold her to him. Then again, being able to step in and handle shit for Taz sounded like a dream. A nigga ain't never had that kind of power in my life, and I wasn't stupid enough to turn it down.

In my eyes this was considered a him problem. Even then, it wasn't even his problem to have. Zayne was dead, so why the fuck did he want Alaia when my deal wasn't originally with him. If I hadn't been so hard up for money, I would have ignored his ass.

I knew the money that I could make with that new house of bitches, so I was willing to do what needed to be done to bring Alaia back where she belonged.

"I got you," I replied, going out onto the porch, something that I hadn't been able to do months prior.

I was traumatized sitting out here. Every time I tried and heard the smallest noise, I was ready to fucking jump out the wheelchair and duck for cover. "Handle it, Raheem." He ended the call, and I sucked my teeth.

Telling me to handle the shit while he was laid up in a hospital bed looking like mini me was diabolical. It did make me cautious because if Cappadonna had done that to him, what the fuck could he do to me?

"Ain't seen you on this porch in a long while." Ralph came trotting up the steps with a brown bag clutched in his hands.

I winced when I looked in his face. His nose was crooked, and he was black, blue, and green. "What the fuck did you walk into?"

He shuttered just thinking about what he was about to tell me. "Ran into your sister at the market out in Jersey. Couldn't believe my eyes that she was just out and about like Taz don't have a bounty on her head."

"Bounty is a bit extreme."

"That is the second time that muthafucka got me in the face. Doctor said that my nose is gonna remain like this."

"Who? What the fuck are you talking about?" I was confused on who he was talking about because he was so angry that his nose was permanently crooked.

"That big muthafucka Cappadonna. He fucking punched me in the face and tried to drown me in a lobster tank," he spat.

I didn't mean to laugh at him. "You sure you weren't drunk, Ralph? You start drinking before the sun even comes up."

He popped open what I was sure was a Coors Light. "What I do know is that muthafucka ain't wrapped too tight. He did that shit right in the middle of the grocery store... Taz need to leave Alaia where the fuck she at. Little bitch encouraged the shit by telling him my name."

"What she got against you, Ralph."

He took a long swig out of his can and looked away. "Leave that bitch where she at cause the man behind her is a demon. You didn't see that little smirk on her face when she sicced that man on me."

I chuckled because I had always been hardheaded and did things my way. Even with Ralph giving me the warning to back out, I couldn't afford to because I needed the money more. I guess I would have to go toe to toe with Cappadonna over my sister.

32
CAPPADONNA

I SAT WATCHING the news at the kitchen table eating a bowl of stale ass cereal. It wasn't my choice of meal, but I couldn't be picky with the options given to me. I finished the cereal and poured more into the bowl while watching the news covering a gas station shooting. The news truck and everyone was all over the block while the reporter reported false facts.

"The neighbors said the gang activity has been out of control lately. One of our camera men that arrived on the scene first was taken to the hospital." I chuckled because Capone was the one that shot that nigga.

None of these cities were going to sleep until I had Ace in my fucking hands. Until then, there would be a murder every day until someone brought him to me. Kendra's ass texted me telling me that she had his new address and never wrote back. I didn't bother texting her because she was a lost cause. If it didn't have money attached to it, Kendra wasn't no damn help.

"C'mon, man... what the... I'm cool."

I continued to watch the news, then dragged my eyes from the TV and took a look at my work. His crooked nose still had the liquid stitches tape on it. He went to the couch to grab his gun, and I laughed. "Got that." With more urgency this time, he ran over toward the side table. "Grabbed that one too, Ralphy." I scooped more cereal into my mouth while this man was staggering and having a full-on panic attack.

"What the fuck do you want?" I could smell the liquor oozing from his pores. The whole raggedy ass house smelled like alcohol and bad decisions.

The bad decisions came from him raping my wife. There was nothing I hated more than when a man took advantage of a woman. Violating her body because he was a man and stronger than her. I remember I broke a nigga's jaw in prison when I found out he raped a bitch. The whole cell block kept quiet, and his ass wasn't going to say who tapped his jaw. Imagine my hate for a man who fucking raped a child – a teenager – who was defenseless.

Crazy thing about life was that the tables always turned. Ralph raped Alaia when she was a young, scared girl who couldn't defend herself. She had nobody that would protect her. Now those tables had turned, and she had a husband that all she had to say was *get em*, and I was running to handle whatever she wanted.

You don't make my baby cry and give her nightmares and think you wouldn't hear from me. I hated to see my baby fucking cry. The shit make me sick, angry, mad. All I wanted was a smile on her face. So, whenever this Ralph nigga appeared in her nightmares, it killed me to see her so shaken up over this man. When I saw her at the grocery store, stiff as a tree branch, I knew I needed to handle his ass.

I walked over toward the sink and washed out my bowl, sitting it in the drainer. Homie had enough time to sneak me from the back if he wanted, but I guess he was too damn scared that I was not only in his house, but I had also finished two bowls of cereal, watched the news and attempted to take a shit.

Leaning on the counter, I looked at him. "Clean your fucking bathroom... fucking pig." Damn bathroom was so nasty that I would have rather used a gas station bathroom before even attempting to use his.

"G...Got you... we good, Cappadonna? I don't mean no problems... tell Alaia I'm sorry. I was a drunk back then... didn't care 'bout nobody."

"Nigga, you lying to me now?" I flinched at his ass, and he toppled over the stack of fucking overdue bills on the small table.

"No...No...I swear."

I grabbed him around the neck and slammed him into the seat in front of us. "Ralphy, I hate liars. You lying to me because all your fridge is filled with is fucking beer, and you smell like you climbed out a beer keg."

Ralph broke down crying. "I'm sorry! Man, I'm sorry... I didn't know better. It was years ago... I swear. I'll disappear, you won't ever see me again."

Quasim came through the front door I had left unlocked. "Can't do that... the problem is you keep coming up in my wife's nightmares. She can't move on from what you did until she sees you in pain and scared. Kind of like she was scared and in pain... remember?" I slapped him in the back of the head.

"I promise I will leave... I promise I will cut my own dick off... I will do whatever to live, please. You want Taz, I'll give you him on a platter."

"Sounds all nice, but I will deal with the little hobbit that won't die when its time... I'm more concerned with you, my boy."

Quasim opened the door and my wife walked in looking as beautiful as ever. She insisted that she wear a black sweatsuit like mine and matched her hijab to the shit. When Alaia told me she wanted to see his face before I ended him, I was against it. She made a good point that it would help with her nightmares, and I would do anything to stop her from waking up in a panic at night.

"Please just let me live. I have a daughter."

Alaia looked at Ralph with disgust. I could tell she was scared, even with me standing here behind him. He made her nervous, probably making her feel like she was that scared teenager. "Hey, I'm right here... he ain't doing shit to you," I reminded her.

She shook the fear from her face when she looked me in the eyes, then back down at Ralph who had pissed in this chair. "You fucking deserve everything that will happen to you. I hope you never rest peacefully." She spit in his face.

I smirked. "She been around you too much, Capp. Some shit that you would have done." Quasim laughed.

"I'm sorry, Alaia... I swear. I'm so sorry."

"My baby told me she wanted me to handle you. What can I say, Ralph... I'm a sucker for her. Happy wife, happy life... feel me?" I winked at her, and Quasim took her back outside.

"Please," he croaked out, seeing his words were getting nowhere with me.

I snickered to myself as I fished in my pocket for the scalpel. "Count to three and then I'll leave... you better not say shit to nobody either."

That man had saw his whole life flash before him, as he got excited that he was getting a second chance at life. "Thank you so much, man. I promise I'm gonna change my life around."

"Count, nigga."

"One.... Tw—"

He started choking on his blood after I had gave him a permanent smile. Nigga was so busy begging for his life that he didn't notice me slip on the black latex gloves before doing him in, slapping his face. "The boss has spoken... no hard feelings, pussy."

I came out the house and my wife was waiting in the front seat of my new Hell Cat Durango. Shit took long enough to come. Swaggering around the car, I hopped in, and looked at Alaia.

"You good, Baby Girl?"

She smiled. "Yes. Thank you."

I held my hand out and we did our handshake, sealing it with a kiss on each other's hand. "I'll do anything for you, Joy."

"And I'll do anything for you, Roy."

I reached over and kissed her lips before I whipped off the block. Kincaid was ahead of me, and Quasim and Quameer following behind me.

"I'm not even gonna front... Erin did her thing with planning this shit," I was jamming to Method Man, while we sat on the hood of our cars.

All Jaiden little private school friends he made were going crazy over his graduation and birthday party. The small one he had at Capone's lake house wasn't enough, he had to go big or go home. I mean, he deserved it and seeing Jaiden be a teen was what made us all happy. Once Jaiden told Erin what he wanted, she worked with the employees at Van-Cromwell house to pull it together.

It helped that I had a membership, and me and Capone went way back with the Vanducci-Cromwell family. The theme was 90's, so everybody was dressed in their best 90's gear. I wore a simple wife beater with oversized jean shorts and a pair of timbs. I put my Inferno God vest on and that was as much as he was getting out of me.

Alaia on the other hand got with the theme. She had on oversized overalls, matching timbs like mine, and she had her hair wrapped up like India Aire. The street that Van-Cromwell house was on was blocked off, with different vendors and shit.

Rahmeek even sent over his cars to display and use for photos. Jaiden was jumping around, enjoying the party and hype that his vision had come together. I watched my wife as she and Erin worked the party.

The best thing I could have asked for was for my brother's wife and mine to be close. Erin and Alaia were thick as thieves, and both were couponing fools. I allowed it because it made Alaia happy.

She explained the thrill of getting food cheaper than what it cost, and how it felt like she was sticking up the grocery store. The more Alaia came out of her shell, I realized my baby wasn't all the way there either.

It explains why I had to pull the fuck over after I slit Ralph's neck. We pulled over and did the nasty. I mean, I wasn't complaining about that part, but I accepted her shit like she did mine. Naheim came over, and I almost ran the other direction.

"Your sister bout to race Star," Naheim came and leaned next to me.

"Stop frontin."

"Dead serious... Jaiden driving with Star."

I leaned up off my whip and made my way through the crowd where Capri was behind the wheel of her challenger. Star was in the same car, and that's when I realized it was Jaiden's car.

"Chill out, Capp. We didn't bring out the real race cars... gotta take it easy with the minor in the whip."

Capri was talking to Erin and Alaia, and I slipped in the front seat, adjusting the seat. “Mind if I ride with you?”

She had a bright smile on her face. “Seriously?”

“We out... you better win.”

“Yeah, right. Star Cromwell is going to dust me, but I wanna challenge myself.” She shrugged, knowing that Star wasn’t shit to mess with.

“We dusting yo ass!” Jaiden was too damn hype hanging out the window. Star pulled him inside the car. “My bad, my bad.”

“Jaiden, don’t play with me!” Erin scolded.

He was hype and I wasn’t mad at the shit. After all the shit he went through, he needed this. He had his friends all waiting to see the race. Kincaid came riding by on his dirt bike. “We cleared the way... ya’ll straight.”

“Thanks, Baby.”

“Oh, you fixed it?” I muttered.

He winked at her and then took off ahead of them so he could call the race. I put my seatbelt on as Capri got in her head and prepared herself. We drove slowly to the starting line and waited for them to wave the flag.

We pulled up beside Star. “Starting here... take the BQE, then come back here. Can’t take the belt ... cops been thick over there.”

“Bet.” Capri messed with the mirror.

“Breathe... we having fun. Give me a run for my money.” Star laughed, rolled her window up and Capri looked even more nervous.

“You got it, Baby Doll.”

Soon as they waved the flags, Capri took off down the block, and I held onto the side as I watched her do her thing. As her older brother, I had to realize that I had to fall back and allow her to find her own path. I couldn’t make the path for her; she was a grown woman and could do that on her own.

As I watched her driving, and taking the turns like a pro, I felt proud. Star was gaining on us, and Capri switched lanes in front of her, while Star switched into the lane we once were in. Soon as we made it to the bridge, she and Star were neck and neck going through the cameras for the toll. I'm pretty sure we were moving so fast that they didn't register the plates.

Even if they did, we had darkened tints for the plates anyway. Star switched lanes again, as Capri crossed in front of her, and we breezed across the bridge onto the BQE. The car was going so fast that I felt like we were flying.

I closed my eyes and felt the wind whipping across our face. Never did I imagine this would be my life. In the passenger seat while my sister floated a whip in a race. Capri grew confident as she switched in and out of the slow traffic we had been met with. Star was gaining on her in the opposite lane.

I leaned my head back and enjoyed the ride because I knew Capri had it. She didn't need me to tell her where to go or what to do. "I know you having your Carrie Bradshaw moment, Cappy. Um... we got company. Star just flashed her lights."

Leaning forward, I looked behind us and sure enough there was a car tailing the fuck out of Star's whip. Cool as hell, she continued to whip the car in and out of traffic. This was no more about a race. Niggas really was following behind us.

I took Capri's phone and pressed Jaiden's name. "Give me the move," Star answered.

"Baby Doll take this exit." She whipped over three lanes and exited the lane. "Soon as we get off the exit, take the fuck off."

"Bet."

"Jaiden... you straight?"

"Hell yeah... I got my shit." He was all too hype that he had his gun on him.

All of our cars was fitted with the same gun safe. "You know how to handle that?" Star asked him.

"Aye, let me cook... I know what I'm doing," Jaiden replied.

I held the phone to my ear and watched as they got caught up in the traffic behind us, preventing them from exiting the exit as quickly as we did. "I'm on whatever you on... I'll follow your lead, Capp," Star replied.

"Bet." I called Capone and he answered.

"How'd she do."

"Less about that... bring my wife home. We got company and I got a feeling they not only following us."

"They waited for us to leave the island, knowing they would be good," Capri said, as she turned the corner.

"Which means it's that little pissy ass Ace," Capone replied.

"Facts. Get my wife to the crib."

"Bet... Yo Gorgeous... we out!" he yelled.

"Where's Ja—"

My original plan was to gun it, but I wasn't running from this pussy. Star and Capri was parked side by side waiting for the traffic to clear from the exit. Both of them were revving their engines as we watched. Soon as traffic clear, I peeped both cars whip around the slow-moving traffic.

Star was the first one to take off and she hooked a left, while Capri made a right heading down an industrial street. She whipped the car with one hand, as she watched her mirrors, and whipped around all the dumpsters and work trucks. Stepping on her break, she made a sharp left, and both she and Star zoomed across each other in opposite directions.

Me and Jaiden exchanged a head nod, and I watched as he cocked his shit back at the same time as me. "This my shit." Capri danced to the song that came on the radio.

Kincaid: Ten mins out.

"Baby Doll, hit this left, and then stop."

She did as she was told, and I aimed my shit out the window and hit the side of the car when they tried to do the same. Capri backed up, making a quick U-turn. We rounded near a Ikea, and School Bus Depot.

RAT TAT TAT!

We both ducked down. "Need me?"

"Nah. Stop the whip right here."

The car hadn't hit the corner yet, and I hopped out. "What the fuck, Capp?" Capri hollered.

"Stay the fuck in the car!" I yelled back.

Soon as they hit that corner, I let my shit go, walking toward the speeding car. My aim was A-1, so when I squeezed that trigger, I knew I hit the driver because the car sped out of control into the metal gates of the Bus Depot.

Reloading, I continued shooting while walking to the car. In the distance, I heard a dirt bike and knew Kincaid had touched down and was probably with Star. I damn near ripped the door off the car and pulled the nigga in the front seat out.

I didn't need anybody to tell me who sent these niggas. I recognized the driver as Monty, the one that ran with Ace. I saw him hiding the night I tossed Ace off the balcony. Star pulled up with Kincaid behind her.

"Bring him home... good shit, Jaiden," I told him, and he saluted, as Star whipped down the block and was soon gone.

The one in the passenger seat was still breathing, so I helped him get to hell quicker. Kincaid stood behind me. "Other whip had Ace... he got hit, but they dipped down one of those blocks... we gotta dip though...twelve is all over the other way."

"Bet... head out. Baby Doll, passenger seat."

She quickly ran to the other side of the car, I adjusted the seat, hopped in, and burned rubber getting out of there. That crackhead was just adding to the long list of shit that was building. I got to feel his skin under my skin when I was snapping his fucking neck. That was how bad I wanted his ass.

"Good shit, Baby Doll."

"I was raised around a couple gangstas or whatever... I does me." She giggled, and put her seatbelt on while I sped past Red Hook, and onto the BQE and back through Staten Island until we made it to Jersey.

33
ACE

"Fuck! How was I supposed to know that was a Cromwell in the fucking whip?" I paced the floor of my kitchen holding a dish towel on my gun wound, not knowing what to say or think.

Monty wasn't answering his phone and if Cappadonna had anything to do with it, his ass was as good as gone. My heart was fucking beating out of control because I had broken that one rule. You don't bring your shit to a Vanducci or a Cromwell, and now I had touched Karter Cromwell's fucking wife.

I may have been born and raised in Delaware, but even I knew all about Karter Cromwell, and the shit that he was into. The man was lethal, and he came for your ass, nine times out of ten, you wouldn't be speaking about it after.

"You need to be worried about Rahmeek Vanducci... that was his fucking youngest daughter." Rob, one of my little niggas pulled on his blunt. "You got two families gunning for you, fam."

I put my head on the kitchen counter while I tried to get

my thoughts together. All I wanted was for Cappadonna to fucking suffer like I had been. Because of him, I had to fucking kill the love of my life.

That shit had me so fucked up that I had been getting high for the past week trying to put that shit behind me. I still found myself about to call her and then remembered that she was downstairs in the basement.

I wanted to cry just thinking about the shit and it was because of Cappadonna. He forced my baby to be disloyal. She chose me and he couldn't deal with the fact that she had chosen me, and not his ass. Kendra loved me, and just loved the money that he had, and that shit bothered his ass every day.

"NIGGA, what did your fucking uncle say?" I asked Rob, who claimed that his uncle from Virginia could front me some work and help me with my problem.

I may have told him with the Delgatos gone, he could move into their territory and that would be a lot more money for the both of us to split. It sounded all good and shit, but I needed his connection to make shit happen.

"He said he thinking if the problem is worth his time. Told you he's not stupid and not gonna just make moves. You a stranger to him."

"When the fuck is that nurse student bitch gonna get here? She know what the fuck she doing, right?" I barked, starting to feel the pain in my arm more.

Rob checked his phone and looked up at me. "Chill the fuck out, shorty doing you a favor... don't call her no bitch," he checked me.

Usually I would have had some shit to say back, but since I

was at his mercy, I had to shut the fuck up and just deal with that shit.

I need to do something and quick because the city is hot right now. There was so much going on that I didn't know what to do or who to trust. I purposely waited for them to leave Staten Island before I made a move.

I knew the rules.

What I didn't account for was Star Cromwell behind one of the wheels, and now my ass had to look out for more than one enemy. All of my problems started when they let that freakishly large muthafucka out of prison.

He turned my own sister against me, made me have to kill my wife, and now he had the world turned against me. I was going to kill him, even if it was the last thing I fucking did.

34
CHUBS

When they said it rained, that bitch threw buckets of water. I felt like every time I got up, I was knocked back down while trying to swing. I was on so much medicine that I didn't even enjoy waking up in the morning because I knew I had to take a bunch of medicine. Aimee had been there for me, and I loved her for that shit.

She could have dipped, and instead she had been by my side at every doctor's appointment. If anything, she was the one asking the questions and trying to understand things more clearly. I told myself that I was going to marry her. Seeing my father go after what he wanted, and not waste time, I wanted that for me and Aimee.

It took a minute for my body to become used to all the medication, but I was back to feeling a little like myself. Moving around and not feeling like I was living in an old man's body. With my birthday approaching, and Jaiden leaving for college, I didn't know how to feel. One part of me wanted to celebrate, then the next was sad that my homie was leaving.

He was going to start his new life, and I felt some kind of

way because that didn't include me. I knew I would always be family and here when he eventually returned home. A nigga was still sad that he was going off to college, and happy at the same time.

"What you out here doing, Aim?" I found Aimee on the back patio with her laptop, and feet kicked up on the couch. I had passed by my son sleeping in the living room.

"Your father has given me a deadline to enroll back into college, so I'm trying to get all my ducks in a row."

I chuckled. "Stop acting like it's not something you hadn't thought of doing."

"Do you know hard it's going to be going back to school with a baby." She sighed, closing her laptop, and looking over at me.

I knew Aimee, and I knew that something was wrong. Something had been wrong since she went to lunch with her mother. My pops didn't mention anything going on, so I didn't think I had anything to worry about. The more time that passed, I could tell some shit went down that she didn't want to talk about.

"Talk to me, Aim." I sat down beside her, pulling her onto my lap, while she leaned her head on my shoulder.

Aimee always smelled like peaches, and it drove me crazy. Probably the reason I put a seed up in her because she knew I couldn't resist her ass. I kissed her on the cheek and looked in her eyes.

"Tell me what's wrong, Aim."

"I don't want you to look at me differently," her voice cracked.

I moved her so I could stare into her eyes. "Somebody did some shit to you, Aimee." The tears poured down her face as she looked into my eyes.

I could tell she didn't want to tell me, but she knew that

she had to. I wouldn't leave the subject alone until she told me. Knowing she was hiding something from me and was hurting because of it had me upset.

"Remember when I told you that someone close to me had hurt me? It was the reason that I was so closed off to telling you how I felt about you."

When me and Aimee started messing around, I considered her another fly chick that I got to smash. The more we got to know each other, the more my feelings developed for her. I could tell that she was feeling me, too, but she was so closed off and scared to admit the shit to me.

She told me someone she trusted hurt her in the past and it was the reason she was hesitant to tell me how she felt about me. I respected that she had other relationships in the past and knew that some niggas weren't built the same as me, and she experienced her first heartbreak.

"Yeah. Tell me how that person hurt you, Aim."

She held my hand as she stared me in the eyes, tears falling from her eyes. "Ace raped me when I was younger. He had gotten high, and he thought I was his girlfriend or something."

I stared at her without saying anything because I didn't know what I expected her to say. I know damn well that I didn't expect this shit to leave her mouth. How the fuck could your own brother do some shit like that.

"He knows he did it?"

"He denies it, and says he doesn't remember that night, but I know he does. I saw it in his face when I told him."

"Your moms knows?"

"Capella, I don't like when you're this calm." Aimee knew when I became calm that nothing was cool.

My blood was boiling, and I wanted to fuck some shit up. I wasn't even mad with Ace for shooting at me anymore. I wanted his blood for what he did to my fucking baby. "She know?"

"Yes. She's known for years and always calls me a liar. Your father saw how she called me a liar when I screamed it out at lunch."

"My pops knows?"

"Yeah. I didn't mean to blurt it out, and then my mother pissed me off so bad that it came out."

She sobbed into her hands, and I pulled her into my arms. "I don't look at you differently, Aim. I still love you, if not more now that you shared that with me. That nigga is gonna get done so dirty, and I put that on my son."

"Please don't ever leave me, Capella."

"I'm not going anywhere, Aim. I promise... you and my son are my life." I kissed her lips, and then hugged her tightly.

It had been a few days since Aimee told me what her brother had done to her. I had to take a few days to process my thoughts because the shit made me sick. A lot of shit was making sense about Aimee. When we met, I remember how closed off she was, and how it took a lot to break down her walls.

She didn't trust easily, and she always mentioned feeling safe with me. I brushed it off because bitches would tell you anything. Now, I realized that she did feel safe with me because her own brother didn't even protect her. He violated her in the worst way possible, and then walked around like he was the man.

I smiled when I saw Jasmine's name on my screen. "What up, Jas?"

"Hey Capella... um, have you heard from your mother?"

"Me and Kendra don't speak... haven't heard from her since she was being dramatic at the hospital," I explained.

Jasmine sighed. "I haven't seen her in like two weeks. She said she was leaving to go handle something and she hasn't come back."

"That's normal for Kendra, Jas. How many times do she disappear and then pop up with a new car or something."

"Sassy said she didn't hear from her either. I'm worried about her... she always answers her phone for me," Jasmine stressed.

"Let me ask around and see if I can find where she at."

"Thanks, Capella."

"Other than that, you good?"

"Yes. I'm getting there... can't thank you and Capp enough." Jasmine was so grateful, and I would do anything to make sure she was taken care of.

"I'll hit you when I know something."

"Alright."

I found my father on the porch with reading glasses on while reading a car magazine. I think his ass was the only person that still got a magazine subscription. He looked up from the magazine over at me.

"Jas called me and told me she hadn't heard from Kendra and she's worried about her." I sat down on the chair next to his.

"Kendra probably fucking in some hole... she's emerge when she fucked enough," he nonchalantly replied, then went back to reading his magazine.

"Why didn't you tell me about what happened at the lunch with Aimee and her mother?" I questioned.

"Wasn't my business to tell. She told me that in confidence and I wasn't gonna break that by telling you. She told you when she was ready for you to know."

"I feel fucking sick thinking about the shit."

"Join the club... sick bastard." His phone interrupted our conversation. I leaned back in the chair as he answered and held a conversation. "Good looks... we out tonight then. Not sitting on this information. Bet."

"What happened?" I asked when he ended the call.

"Karter told me he got the drop on where Ace been staying."

"I'm out with you then."

"Nah."

I looked at my father, the same look I'm sure I had in my eyes was in his. "You want me to fall back from the streets and I respect that. I'm prepared to do that for you and my family, but you have to let me get this nigga. He tried to kill me, and then he did that shit to my girl. I can't sit back and allow you to handle this without me. I know how to handle myself, been holding it down alongside Capone... I'm not new to this shit, Pops."

Capp closed his magazine and looked at me. "After his ass is done... you're done."

"Deal." I reached my hand out, and he pulled me out the chair and hugged me. "Love you, Pops."

"You don't even know the half." He squeezed my shoulder before heading back into the house. Whenever some shit was about to go down, I noticed that Capp retreated. He remained silent and got his head in the right space. I allowed him space to get his mind right.

Karter was sitting on a generator when we made it onto the block. "I heard this is where he been staying. There's been movement on the inside."

"Good looking on letting me know. I know you could have handled this shit on your own," Capp thanked him.

He smirked. "I know the beef between you two is more real.

Rahmeek told me to fall back and assist if needed. Don't think I really need to assist but I'm here."

"Appreciate you, K," Capone dapped him up.

Capp kneeled down and fixed the tongue on his timbs, and then checked his gun before putting it back into the pocket of his black hoodie.

"The basement is clear... could go in from down there." Big Mike came around from the back.

"Three niggas in the living room, one upstairs. I haven't seen Ace yet. But we gonna assume five." Kincaid came from the other side of the house.

Capp walked around the house, pulling his ski mask down. We entered from the basement, and we all jumped back. "The fuck is that fucking smell?" he whispered.

"I'm about to fucking throw up," I held my hand over my mask, because the smell was so damn bad.

"That's a body. He done stashed somebody down here. Little nigga more twisted than we thought, Capp," Capone said, as he bypassed me and walked further into the basement.

"I know a body when I smell one," Karter agreed.

Capone popped his head from around the furnace. "Bingo... body right here."

Capp walked over and then he paused before turning back toward me. "Yo... go upstairs and round them niggas up."

I knew when he was giving orders and when he was trying to get rid of me. "Why you sending me away... the fuck is up?"

He looked away. "Capella, this is your moms."

"What?"

He kneeled down and picked up the wrist that hung out the sheet. There was a charm bracelet, the same bracelet that Kendra always wore. It had a K and C charm on it. I always thought the C was for me.

"I bought her this charm bracelet for valentine's day a few

years ago... had Capo pick it up for me to give her on valentine's day." He closed his eyes.

I knew Kendra gave him hell, and he couldn't stand her, but I could see that he was hurt too. "Capp, you and Chubs go... I got it down here," Capone said.

Capp stood up, and I watched as he pulled his gun from his pocket and took the steps up two at a time, he kicked the door off the hinges, sending all the niggas chilling to their feet. They tried to get their shit out to bust back, but Capp already was collecting bodies by the time they grabbed theirs.

Me and Kincaid went to the top floor and was searching for Ace. I wanted this nigga bad, I needed him, that's how bad the craving was. Other than one other guy that Kincaid handled, nobody else was here.

"Fuck!" I barked.

"We out... he not here," Kincaid told me, as we bounced, leaving the house.

We left the same way we entered. Capp lingered for a bit before using the sheet to fully cover her. He may have hated her before her death, but I never denied that my father loved her.

We stayed in the shadows as we headed back to our cars, and then sped off the block. I leaned my head back, watching my father. He was quiet as he drove through the city.

"You good?" I finally broke our silence.

"I feel like I've done a lot but nothing at all. This pussy is still running around and keep slipping through my fucking fingers."

"I'm talking about Kendra."

He looked over at me. "I should be asking you that."

"I didn't expect to feel this way... I'm a little fucked up," I hated to admit that I was fucked up over finding my mother dead in a basement.

Capp looked back over at me. "I'm a little fucked up too. Kendra deserved a lot of shit, but she didn't deserve that shit from that nigga."

"I've never wanted somebody so fucking bad."

Capp held his fist out. "Then we know we gotta do his ass in... it's all smoke behind that pussy."

"All smoke." I dapped his fist.

35
CAPPADONNA

I PULLED through the gates as the driver was putting the last of Jaiden's bags into the back of the car. Erin and Capone were flying down with him to get him moved into his dorm. As excited as we all were for him, the shit was sad too. Jaiden was who kept us on our toes with his little jokes and stupid ass humor.

Who was he going to call when he couldn't sleep and just needed to shoot some hoops around? As much as I was going to miss his ass, I knew that this was a good thing. We could have been having a memorial for him, and not sending him off to college with a full scholarship.

Capone dapped me up and then looked back at the car. I could tell this nigga wanted to be emotional, but Erin had already beat him to it. "He really going."

"Means that you accomplished what you wanted for him. You said you wouldn't allow this life to consume him... pat yourself on the back, Capo."

"Shit hard though. Erin all fucked up over it and been crying for weeks knowing this day was coming."

"That's her baby. She raised him... you gonna feel the same way when CJ heads off to college."

He sighed. "Yeah."

Jaiden came out the house and I could tell he was feeling down. Everyone was in their feelings because we would miss him. I looked at him and smirked, as he came and dapped me up. He hugged me and I kissed the top of his head.

Little nigga was catching up in height with me. "It came too fast, Kid."

"Yeah. I know... CJ slept in my room with me last night. Erin been crying all morning, and Jo has been trying to feed me everything."

"We all love you and gonna miss you. It's gonna take a minute for us to get used to you being miles away."

When he sniffled, I knew he was becoming emotional and then I heard him start crying. Pulling him into me, I hugged him, then pulled him back to look in his eyes. Taking both my hands, I wiped the tears from his face.

"Kid, you going to beast out on those fucking college squares. You were made for this shit. While you fucking shit up, we gonna be right here rooting for you and waiting for you to come back home. The goal is the pros, remember? You think Curry was crying when he had to leave home to do what needed to be done?"

"Nah," he toughed up.

"You get on that court and break fucking ankles, feel me?"

He hugged me tightly. "Gonna miss you, Capp. Just got used to you being home and now I'm the one that has to leave."

"Check it, I'm here, Kid. Not going anywhere... you call me and I'm coming. No matter how far you are."

"Bet."

I kissed his forehead. "Love you ol' pickle headed ass."

"Love you, too." He checked his phone. "Elliot is at the airport with her parents."

Jaiden and Elliot weren't together, but he damn sure acted like she was. They were going to the same college, and now she was waiting at the airport with her parents. He could pretend that there wasn't feelings there, but I knew better.

Erin came out the house and her eyes were puffy as hell. "Hey Capp." She smiled, hugging me. "I knew you wouldn't miss coming to see him off."

"Hell nah. Stop crying though... you did what needed to be done. You wanted him to go to college and now he's on his way. Soon we gonna be up in the sky box watching his ass break necks in the pros."

"You right. Thank you." she hugged me again and then got into the truck.

Capone came over and dapped me up. "I'll hit you when we land."

"If you not crying."

"Fuck up. Me and Erin gonna dip off to Miami since it's close by for a few days to reset. I'll be back by the weekend."

"Do you. I'll hold it down."

"Bet. Love you, nigga."

"Love you, too, pussy." We both laughed as he hopped up in the truck and the driver closed the door.

I watched as they pulled out the gates and then went to chill with Jo for a little bit. My mind had been on Kendra, and the shit was keeping me up at night. She had done some foul shit to me, and I hated her for it, but to see how she was done fucking hurt me. He discarded her like she was a fucking piece of trash.

No matter how I felt about Kendra, that was my son's mother, and no matter how shitty of a mother she was, she was still his mother. She was who he knew as his mother, and he took her from him. Kendra and Capella had their own complicated relationship, but I knew this shit hurt. He just lost his aunt and now his mother.

I tried to take a page out of Capone's book, and I realized we were different for many reasons. His book wasn't mine, and that was what made us the best team. Whatever one of us lacked, the other made up for it.

Me: I want his mother.

Qua: Done.

~

ALAIA, again dressed in all black, stood behind the bar with the gun in her hand. She had a steady hand as she took her final shots, and then sat the gun back down on the bar. I stood back with my arms crossed watching my wife shoot a gun.

I remember when Capone was telling me when Erin started her lessons, and how she was always so damn emotional, and upset that she even had to do it. I half expected the same thing from Alaia, but she was proving me wrong with the way that she was shooting the gun like it was nothing. The first few lessons she had, she missed the target entirely and was discouraged.

My wife was hard on herself, and it was something that I was learning about her. "Dammit." She sucked her teeth when she didn't hit the target exactly where she wanted.

I came behind her and kissed her on the neck. "You gotta calm down. Stop working yourself up because then that's when you gonna fuck up." Grabbing the gun, I put it back in her hand and stood behind her with my hand still around the gun. I raised her arms and aimed it at the target while in her ear. "You love me?"

"Very much."

“Aim and shoot like a nigga trying to take your man out. Every time I aim, I think of somebody trying to snatch my family away... snatch you away. And you know daddy won’t let that happen.”

“I don’t even wanna think that way, Roy.”

I removed my hands from the gun and moved them to her hips as she closed one of her eyes, bit down on her lip and then pulled the trigger. She continued until she emptied the clip. I smirked. “That’s my girl.” I patted her ass.

She sat the gun back down, and I walked toward the door, holding my hand out. Like it always belonged, I felt her soft small hand slip into mine and we walked to the front of the gun range. It was a hole in a wall gun range that Capone had told me about. The shit was illegal and could use some air conditioning. Other than that, it was the perfect lowkey spot to teach my baby how to protect herself.

Soon as we got into my truck, Alaia grabbed her big ass water bottle. She had a bunch of these shits. I told her she was better off carrying a gallon of water like I did. “Here take a sip.” She shoved the pink cup into my hand.

I took a few sips and sat it in the cup holder. “You hungry?”

“Yes. Then we need to go pick out furniture for the house. Erin and Capone went back home, and the lake house is lonely now.” She laughed.

Summer was coming to an end, so Capone and Erin had headed back home. Having the summer with my family being right on the same street felt like a good ass dream. Whenever I needed one of them, it was a quick walk to the next house.

Our new crib had been sitting there collecting dust while we were living our best lives at the lake house. Alaia and Erin had gotten used to doing things with the babies together, so I understood why she wanted to be close to her.

“Baby, I’m telling you this right now... I don’t want to offer no opinion on what you pick. Just make sure the bed is big enough so my legs ain't hanging the fuck off."

"Why not? You should have some opinions on our home."

"That's all you, Joy. All I want is to come home and have my wife and daughter there... I'm simple. I lived in a small ass cell for years; anything is good with me."

She giggled as she checked her phone. Alaia was so into her phone that she didn't realize that I pulled into a parking lot and killed the engine. "Hell no, Leroy!"

"Oh, fuck no, Joy. I told you I'm cool with Roy... don't be fucking using the whole shit." I got out and walked around to open the door for her.

"You know the food is nasty here," she whispered as I held her hand and we walked into *our* diner.

I never tasted the food, but I trusted what she said when she spoke about it. It was less about the food and more about this being our spot. It was the first place I had taken her, and really got to know her.

Luckily, our booth was free, and we slipped into it as the server came and sat the laminated menus on the table. "Good morning, let me know when you're ready to order."

Alaia stared across the table at me. "Are you having big feelings, Roy," she teased, and the truth was that I was.

I was sitting across from my fucking wife. The girl I had saw and knew that I wanted. I've spent my life believing good shit didn't happen for me. Now, as I sat across from my wife smiling at me like I was her whole world, I realize that good shit didn't happen to me, good people did.

Alaia was one of the good people that happened for me.

"You know the first time I brought you here, it was when I knew I had to have you. Didn't give a fuck who I had to see, but I knew you were going to be mine."

She grabbed my hands. "When you brought me here, I was

nervous. Nobody has ever been nice or caring to me, and here this big ol' man with a mean scowl comes being the sweetest person to me. I've never trusted, but when I met you, I instantly wanted to trust you. Fear prevented me from doing it."

I kissed the back of her hands. "You trust me now, right?"

"With my whole entire heart, Cappadonna." I continued to kiss her hands while messing with her wedding ring. "I overheard you and Capella's conversation."

"You heard what the fuck nigga did to his own sister?" The shit made me even more disgusted the more I thought about it.

"When someone takes that part of you," Alaia choked on her words. "You lose a piece of yourself. Then having to always be around that person feels like the rape is occurring all over again. It's not something that truly ever leaves you. Her brother doing it makes it that much worse."

I moved to her side of the booth and kissed her lips as the tears fell from her eyes. "Nobody is going to hurt you anymore, you hear me? I can't erase the pain from the past, but I'm gonna make sure you never know what pain is moving forward."

"I know, Baby," she kissed me back and wiped her tears away. I wrapped my arms around her and hugged her as best as I could in the little ass booth. "Can we eat somewhere else, please."

I started laughing because she was serious about not eating here. "Nah. You eating those pancakes... this trip for nostalgia."

"Stop playing with me."

I removed myself from the booth and helped her up as we left. No matter how nasty the food is in that diner, it would always be one of my favorite places. It would forever remind me of when I found my Joy.

36
CAPRI

It was clear that something was bothering Kincaid, and he wouldn't talk about it. We had been in this weird space not knowing what to do with each other. It was like we both wanted to try so we could prove everyone wrong, then we wanted our own space. I loved Kincaid, but I knew that we both needed to stop wasting each other's time.

One minute I was with him and then the next we were broken up. It seemed like since Jasmine had entered back in the picture that things with us had been weird. I could tell he still loved her, however, his loyalty and love for me wouldn't allow him to cross those lines with her. It was the reason I kept breaking up with him.

Like tonight, we were out for Quameer's birthday bash. I shouldn't have come to the party because I was sitting here looking bored while Kincaid was chopping it up with his buddies. I crossed my legs and pulled my phone out to text Alaia and Erin in our group chat. I knew both my brothers were not coming out tonight. You damn near had to pay

Cappadonna to leave the house these days. Unless he had a reason, he wasn't popping out for nobody.

Me: What are ya'll doing?

E-money: Taking a pregnancy test while Capone is sleep.

Me: Results?

E-money: Still waiting.... Wyd?

Alaia: popping a pimple on Capp. Sending baby dust, E!

E-money: oh shit... she answers after her man comes home.

Alaia: haha! Wyd, Pri?

"Why you over here being antisocial and shit?" Quameer came and stood on the couch, sitting on the back of it.

He smelled so good. Like a mixture of a pepper and a sandalwood. Qua's hair was freshly retwisted with a fresh line up to go with it. He was dressed in a pair of Amiri shorts, white tank tee, and wore his Inferno God vest.

His fresh white uptowns were kicked up on the couch, as if I wasn't sitting on it. "Excuse you, rude ass."

"Stop fronting like you don't like when I'm rude to you... capping ass."

I folded my arms. "How do I be capping, Quameer? The only one that be capping is you... and your baby mama."

He smirked, exposing his gold fangs and I quickly looked away. "How am I capping?"

"You with her."

"No the fuck I'm not. That's what you get listening to these hoes. Brandi is fucking married... happily. See, this is why I call you capping."

Blair came back up into our section with our drinks. The bottle girl was so busy smiling up in all the men's face that she hadn't paid attention to us once. Quasim watched Blair, like he had been for most of the night, never taking his eyes off her. I was waiting for him to come over and talk to her, and he never did. It was clear that he was feeling her, and I noticed that at Capp's BBQ.

"The bar downstairs is crazy... had to repeat my order three times." She rolled her eyes and sat down beside me.

Alaia and Erin were married and in their wife era, so I couldn't expect them to come out to the club with me. It was meant for me and Blair to cross paths again, because in college we used to have so much fun.

I was in my fun era now, wanting to chill without being stressed out. Naheim's ass had stressed me enough, and I didn't want that anymore. Despite sleeping with him while me and Kincaid was broken up, I knew it was wrong and I couldn't go back there.

It was hard when someone was so familiar that it felt good for the moment. Soon as the moment was over, you knew it was wrong and regretted it.

"You needed drinks?" Quameer said. He snapped his fingers, and the girl with her uniform shoved up her ass came over. "Get them bottles... don't know why she had to get her own drink anyway. The fuck I'm tipping you for?"

Kincaid came over as the bottle girl rushed to grab bottles that me and Blair wouldn't even drink. "She been smiling in Quasim's face all damn night." He kissed me on the cheek, and I smiled. "I'm ready to get out of here whenever you are."

"I been ready. You were the one running your mouth," I teased, and kissed him on the lips, while he pulled me up from the couch.

"We out, Qua."

Blair looked up at me. "I think I'm going to stay a little bit longer... I'm having fun."

"Okay. Call me when you make it home."

"I'll make sure Quasim's girl gets home," Quameer teased.

"Don't even do that," Blair laughed.

We made our way through the club and made it to the entrance. The club was small, on Inferno God territory, so the cars were all parked in the front with valet. I held onto Kincaid as we waited for the valet to bring his car around.

It was funny because Kincaid barely drove his car these days. He was always on a bike whenever I saw him. "I forgot your bread." Quameer came out the entrance. "You were right... I always honor a bet."

"A bet on what?"

"If Quasim would speak to Blair or not. Other than staring at her, he ain't say shit to her," Kincaid laughed, accepting the money that Quameer put in his hands.

"He spoke to her at Capp's house."

"He ain't speak to her ass tonight, so I'm a couple dollars richer." Kincaid hugged me, slipping the money into the pocket of my jeans. "And so are you."

When things were good with us, they were good. I wanted to live in this moment forever. All the beef that we had been going through didn't matter anymore. I had to stop forcing him to be with Jasmine because I wanted to avoid getting hurt.

I felt if I pushed him to her, I would be less hurt if he decided to be with her. I wouldn't have to deal with him telling me that he cheated with her. Naheim had truly fucked me up, and I couldn't have a healthy relationship to save my life.

Time slowed down when we saw a dirt bike ride down the block, an arm was extended with a gun, and I saw the flashes while being tossed onto the floor. Everything slowed down when I felt Kincaid on top of me.

"Ace said hold this nigga!" the man yelled out.

The entire block erupted in chaos, and the man on the dirt bike didn't make it off the block before one of the Gods got his ass. I nudged Kincaid. "Baby, I'm alright."

He didn't move. "Fuck... he got Kincaid...yo, get my brother!" I heard Quameer bark at someone.

"Bring my fucking whip!" I heard Quasim's voice now. "Bring Capri to Capp now!" he hollered, and I felt the weight being lifted off me.

Quameer picked me up and carried me to his car that was parked behind the club. Everyone was going crazy while I fought for him to put me down. "He's shot, Qua! I need to get to him."

"And do what, Capri? Quasim got him... he's gonna call me. My priority is getting you to your brother's house." He placed me in the front seat of his car, and then ran back around, giving one of the other Gods a nod, and they pulled off in front, with a few more following behind us.

I was sobbing as we drove past where Kincaid had been shot. I've never seen him down before. Kincaid always popped back up and could get shit done even after being shot. My heart was beating out my chest as I continued to cry. Kincaid was tough, nothing got him down. He was always ready to bust his gun and seeing him lying on the pavement like that made my chest crumble.

Quameer squeezed my thigh. "He gonna be good. Kincaid is strong as fuck... don't cry. I never seen you cry before, and I know I don't like it."

I cried even more because my mind was going out of control with my thoughts. His screen on his car lit up and Capp's name popped up. "You got my sister?"

"On my way to your crib now."

Alaia and Capp had moved into their new house, so the drive wasn't going to be as long. I sat my head back. "Baby Doll, you good?"

"I..." I croaked.

"She's shaken up. We'll be there in a minute."

"Bet."

As Quameer drove, I tried to control my breathing because I needed to know what was going on with Kincaid. Quasim had already gotten him into the car and pulled off before we left the block. We were just having a good night and then all of this shit happened. Why the fuck did bad things always happen to me?

Every time that me and Kincaid had gotten into some shit, we held each other down and made it out. I felt like I was letting him down by not being by his side. I couldn't do anything because I didn't have a gun on me. Kincaid told me to leave it home because we would be good.

By the time we pulled through Cappadonna's gates, he came out dressed in sweats and no shirt on. Alaia was behind him holding Promise in her arms as I snatched the seatbelt from around me, and ran straight into my brother's arms. He wrapped his arms around me and kissed the top of my head. "He's gonna be good. Kincaid always comes through," he assured me, and I wasn't sure if I believed it right now.

Capone or Cappadonna could tell me the world was a triangle and I would believe it because I trusted their word. Right now, I couldn't trust that Kincaid was going to be alright. Something in my gut was telling me that something was wrong.

Quameer came around the car with a somber look on his face. He held the phone in his hand and put it on speaker. "He right here."

Quasim took a sigh. "Capp, he didn't make it. When they pulled him out the car, he was gone." I felt the tension in my brother's body as the tears flooded my eyes.

"Noooooooo!"

To Be Continued

Made in the USA
Las Vegas, NV
06 May 2025

21806689R00208